Desire

By Nicole Jordan
Published by Ivy Books:

THE SEDUCTION
THE PASSION
DESIRE

Desire

Nicole Jordan

IVY BOOKS • NEW YORK

An Ivy Book
Published by The Ballantine Publishing Group
Copyright © 2001 by Anne Bushyhead
Excerpt from *Ecstasy* by Nicole Jordan copyright © 2001 by Anne Bushyhead

ISBN 0-7394-1954-4

Manufactured in the United States of America

To all my wonderful cyber pals at The Romance Journal,
RBL Romantica, Romance and Friends,
ALCAP, and GRAN.
My heartfelt thanks for your love and encouragement
and for helping keep me sane (relatively)
these past few years.

And a special thanks to Laura,
aka Webmistress Extraordinaire.
And to dearest Maggie, who started it all.

{{{HUGS!!!}}}

The women of your house will be
forever cursed for their beauty.
Any man they love will die.

Gypsy curse, 1623

Prologue

Cornwall, England, October 1813

Her gown fell to the floor in a whisper of silk, leaving her completely nude. Lucian drew a sharp breath at the alluring sight—her exquisite white body tinged golden in the flickering dance of candlelight, her radiant hair glowing like fire.

Was she bent on seduction . . . or betrayal?

Whatever her scheme, Lucian had to admit it was highly effective. Already he was hard enough to burst. Yet his every instinct remained alert to danger.

He forced a smile, his gaze roaming over the taut nipples, the luscious thighs parted slightly in sensual invitation. "Is this a seduction, my love?"

Her own smile was provocative. "Merely a welcome. I am glad you have come."

A lie, he knew.

For a long moment he met her emerald eyes. Was that guilt he saw there in the jeweled depths?

Time stretched between them as Lucian stared at his beautiful wife, his gaze a veiled search. At length the soft hiss and crackle of the fire in the hearth broke the spell.

With a graceful shrug of her naked shoulders, she went to the mahogany side table, where a tray bearing a crystal wine decanter and goblets rested. When she had poured two glasses, she crossed the bedchamber to him and offered him one.

The wine was bloodred. Was it poisoned, or merely drugged? She'd had time to prepare either, even though he had startled her by unexpectedly following her here to the Cornish coast from London.

He took a sip, pretending to drink, and noted that she looked relieved.

She was too transparent, Lucian thought grimly, fighting the lure of her nude body and the heat rising in him. Her nervousness gave her away. She was an amateur at intrigue—unlike him. He had matched wits against the best spies France had to offer. Against Britain's worst traitors as well.

Even as he stared at her, she averted her gaze, unable to meet his eyes any longer. His mouth thinned. Would Brynn betray him? Was his beautiful bride in league with his enemies? Had she committed treason with her damned brother, aiding the Frogs and their bloody Corsican leader, Napoleon Bonaparte?

The thought caused such an ache in his heart that he suddenly found it hard to breathe.

"Is the wine to your taste?" she murmured, sipping from her own glass.

"Yes. But then the French do make the finest wines."

She shivered at his mention of the French.

"Are you cold?" he asked, keeping any inflection from his voice.

"I hoped you would warm me."

She glanced up at him, temptation in her eyes. The impact sent savage heat flooding his loins. He could recall a time not too many weeks ago when he would have given most of his fortune to have an invitation like this.

"Why don't you stir the fire," he forced himself to say, "while I close the draperies?"

Tearing his gaze from her lush nudity, Lucian turned and went to one of the windows. Under pretense of shutting the drapes, he tilted his glass behind a table, letting wine trickle onto the carpet. With all his soul he wanted to believe Brynn innocent. Yet he didn't dare trust her.

He could feel her gaze probing between his shoulder blades from across the room. Swearing silently, Lucian moved on to the next window. He was clearly a fool. He was obsessed with his own wife. With her vibrant beauty, her fiery hair, her defiant spirit. She was a temptress who made him ache with desire. The only woman he'd ever met who could drive him so wild that he lost control. She haunted him, even in his dreams. Especially in his dreams.

He would lose her forever if he sent her to prison.

Deliberately spilling more of his wine behind an armchair, he closed the drapery and moved on to the final window, where he stood pretending to drink from his glass. Outside a chill sliver of moon hung low on the black horizon, partly obscured by ghostly, scudding clouds. A blustery wind blew off the sea; he could hear waves beating the rocky shore below.

A good night for treason.

Inside, however, the bedchamber was warm and

hushed. Lucian sensed Brynn before he heard her soft footfall as she came up behind him.

"Are you still angry with me?" she whispered in that low, sultry voice that could tie him in knots.

Yes, he was angry with her. Angry, heartsick, regretful. He had never known a woman who could bring him to his knees . . . until Brynn.

He snapped the drapes shut.

Composing his features into a mask, he turned slowly to face her. Her gaze, he noticed, went immediately to his glass that was now only one-third full. The relieved smile she gave in response ripped at him, but Lucian made himself remain still. He would play her game, would see how far she intended to take her betrayal.

Her finger dipped into his wine, then rose to glide along his lower lip. "How can I assuage your anger, Lucian?"

"I think you know, love."

Her own lips were red and moist with wine, and he fought the urge to crush his mouth down on hers. He forced himself to remain immobile, even when she slowly, provocatively, slid her fingers into the waistband of his breeches.

When he gave no response, she relieved him of his wineglass and set it down along with her own. Then she began to undo the buttons at the front placket of his breeches.

His heart was thudding in his chest when she drew open the fabric to expose the stiff erection that stirred so eagerly between his thighs. With a tempting smile, she closed her caressing fingers around the base of his pulsing arousal and sank down to kneel at his feet.

A muscle flexed in Lucian's jaw as he grimly struggled against the fierce ache she incited in him. He should be pleased that Brynn was willingly taking the lead. Since their first meeting she had fought him. For the three months of their stormy marriage, they had been locked in a contest of wills.

While her fingers stroked, she leaned closer to press her lips along his throbbing shaft. Lucian jerked when she kissed him there. Her lips were warm on his flesh. His skin felt hot, seared by the erotic touch of her mouth as she softly ran her tongue around the swollen head, the sensitive ridge below. . . .

He felt her lips close around his distended length to take him more fully in her mouth. Lucian gave a grimace of pleasure, fighting for control. His now-rigid member thickened still further as she explored him with her mouth and tongue, tasting the slick contours.

Desperately he tried to keep his mind divorced from his senses as she made love to the most intimate part of him. He had been the one to teach her this—how to use her new skills to such devastating effect. He had shown her pleasures of the flesh, led her to embrace her woman's passion.

Lucian shuddered. Her mouth was a firebrand, her teeth softly raking.

She was wrong about his feelings for her. He wanted Brynn for more than a broodmare or a convenient lover. Perhaps it had begun that way, but now . . . Now he wanted to possess her completely.

And yet she seemed more unattainable than ever. She was his wife in name and body, but he could not claim her heart.

He groaned at the thought, and at her exquisite ministrations.

"Am I paining you?" she asked, a smile in her voice.

"Yes," he said hoarsely. "Dire pain." A pain that was more than physical.

"Should I stop?"

"*No, siren.*"

Involuntarily his hands curled in her flaming hair. He felt her moist lips sliding down his aching shaft, and he strained against her mouth, even as his mind battled to resist her spell.

Nothing in their marriage had gone as planned. Admittedly he was mainly to blame for the initial contention between them. He had made countless mistakes with Brynn. Compelling her to wed him despite her fervent protests. Treating her with intentional coldness, keeping himself remote.

With supreme arrogance, he had expected her to fall at his feet, for his wealth and title if not his charm and looks. From the outset she had resisted him, but he'd vowed to tame her and make her his own. And once she became his bride, he'd demanded she share his bed and bear him an heir.

It should have been a fair exchange—a noble marriage for a son. He had wanted a child of his own flesh, some part of him to leave behind were he to die before his time, as his dark dreams seemed to portend.

He felt as if he were dying now. His hand clenched

in her hair as hunger poured in hot waves through his body.

He was as captivated now as ever. Sweet hell, from the first *moment* he had been smitten with her. He couldn't escape her.

She had tried to warn him how it would be between them, but he hadn't listened. Instead his heart had stubbornly refused to abandon its infatuation, his enchantment growing into a dangerous obsession.

Brynn knew it, and she was using it mercilessly against him now.

He had few defenses against her. The more determined he was to deny his passion, the more fiercely his need grew to possess her, until he was willing to do almost anything, pay any price, simply for one of her luxuriant smiles.

Lucian squeezed his eyes shut. Was he actually considering betraying his country to save her? Sacrificing his honor, everything he believed in?

Damn you, Brynn.

He was shaking. He clutched at her shoulders and felt her shudder with pleasure herself. Gazing down into her passion-hazed eyes, he could see she was nearly as aroused as he. Perhaps she only intended to seduce him, but her desire was real.

That knowledge shredded the last of his control. Urgently Lucian drew her to her feet and lifted her up, his mouth feverishly capturing hers as she wrapped her legs around his flanks.

Carrying her to the bed, he lowered her to the silk sheets and followed her down, pressing himself between her welcoming thighs.

For a moment, then, he hesitated. Her face was so

incredibly beautiful in the flickering candlelight. He curved his hand to her throat, wishing he could draw the truth from her. Wishing he could see into her heart and mind.

"Please . . . I want you, Lucian," she whispered hoarsely.

And I'll want you till I die, he thought as he entered her.

She was wet and eager for him. She wrapped her supple legs around his hips, clutching him to her as he thrust into her, driving his engorged phallus deep within her hot, pulsing flesh.

Lucian shuddered, needing her more than he needed air.

How had it come to this? If he had known their marriage would lead to this day, would he still have coerced Brynn to wed him? Would he have made the same mistakes? Would he have blindly ignored his stark dreams of warning?

What had she been thinking that day three months ago when he had encountered her in the secluded cove alone? Could he have changed the outcome had he behaved differently toward her?

Had she known then what would happen between them? Was she plotting treason even then?

He groaned, spilling his seed deep within her body.

If only he knew. . . .

Chapter One

The Cornish Coast, three months earlier . . .

It was not one of her better days. Brynn Caldwell dove beneath the warm surf, trying to drown her simmering anger in the deep tidal pool. Her frustration with her oldest brother, Grayson, had reached the limits of her endurance.

With a muttered oath, she surfaced and rolled onto her back, willing herself to calm. This was not the first time she had futilely argued with Gray and sought refuge in the secluded cove below their house. The inlet was flanked on two sides by jagged boulders and behind by a low cliff that shielded the natural rock pool from prying eyes. She came here whenever she could, or whenever she felt a need for peace, as now.

Here she could be free of the confining restrictions she imposed on herself. Here she could forget the troubles that constantly worried her: how to make ends meet for her impoverished family, how to protect her youngest brother, Theodore, from Gray's dangerous notions of upbringing.

The afternoon July sun was warm on her face as

Brynn floated, the salty seawater soothing her frayed temper. Yet she had never felt so helpless. Gray intended to take Theo out on a midnight smuggling excursion tonight, and despite arguing herself hoarse, she could do nothing to stop him.

"Devil take him!" she murmured, an imprecation she used frequently of late toward her oldest brother. Grayson was very dear to her, but dragging a mere child into their illicit activities was utterly criminal.

It galled her to feel so powerless. She had raised Theo from a baby—ever since their mother had died in childbirth twelve years before—and she was desperate to spare him the danger that had ensnared her four other brothers and herself as well.

Smuggling was a way of life on the Cornish coast. Having grown up here, she accepted the illegal means to which the local folk resorted simply to survive, trafficking goods such as brandy and silk past government revenuers to avoid crushing taxes.

But Free Trading was so very perilous. Her father had perished in a storm several years ago while trying to elude a revenue cutter. And so had numerous other men of the district, leaving behind widows and young children with no means of support.

And now Grayson meant to involve Theo in an upcoming brandy-smuggling foray so he could "learn to pull his weight" and help relieve the oppressive debts their father had amassed. It was enough to make Brynn want to do violence.

She made herself float awhile longer, then swam some more, trying to burn off her frustration—to no avail. She was physically spent by the time she turned toward shore, but her feelings of guilt and anger and helplessness were just as strong as she clambered onto the ledge of the rocky pool.

For a moment she stood dripping wet in her shift, wringing out her long hair. The sea breeze would dry it quickly, for this stretch of Cornish coast boasted one of the warmest climes in England.

When she started to reach for the towel she had left lying on the ground, however, she realized it was gone. Her gaze lifted, searching, then fell upon the intruder in her private sanctuary. Brynn froze, her heart thudding in her chest.

He was leaning casually against a boulder, watching her from the afternoon shadows. He was dressed informally as well in breeches and gleaming top-boots and a white cambric shirt with no cravat. Yet there was nothing casual in his look as his measuring gaze slowly raked her.

Alarmed, she took a backward step. How had he found his way to the rocky stretch of beach below the cliff? Had he discovered the cave below the house with its secret tunnel? He didn't look like a revenuer, but government men sometimes roamed these shores, searching for contraband.

"Who are you?" she demanded in a breathless voice. "How did you get here?"

"I climbed down," he replied, gesturing with his head at the rocks above him.

"You didn't answer my first question."

He was tall and lithely built, she noted, with dark, curling hair worn a trifle longer than fashionable. When he stepped out of the shadows, her gaze riveted on his face. His lean, aristocratic features were strikingly handsome, barely saved from arrogance by a sensual mouth. His heavily lashed eyes were a startling hue, the deep blue of the ocean on a brilliant summer day, and they held her transfixed.

"I'm Wycliff," he said simply, as if she should be duly impressed.

She was, in truth. She recognized the name of the rich and powerful Earl of Wycliff. By reputation, he was a notorious rake and a leader of the infamous Hellfire League, an exclusive club of wicked noblemen dedicated to pleasure and debauchery. Brynn was suddenly keenly aware of a different kind of danger. Simply being alone with him could taint her reputation.

"That does not explain what you are doing here," she replied tartly.

"I am visiting a friend."

"Do you realize you are trespassing?"

His mouth curved in a charming half smile. "I couldn't resist the pleasure of watching a sea nymph cavort in her kingdom. I wasn't even certain you were real."

He held out her towel to her, but Brynn warily backed up another step, every instinct she possessed warning her to flee. She wanted to retreat farther, yet with the pool directly behind her, there was nowhere to go but into the water.

"You needn't fear me," he remarked soothingly. "I'm not in the habit of ravishing beautiful women, no matter how scantily clad."

"That is not what I hear—" Brynn began, then looked down at herself and nearly gasped. The shift she wore had turned transparent, showing her breasts with their puckered rosy nipples and the thatch of auburn hair at the vee of her thighs. Flustered, she crossed to him and snatched the towel from his grasp, then wrapped it around her body, shielding her charms from his interested gaze.

"I won't assault you. I am a gentleman, after all."

"Are you?" she asked skeptically. "A gentleman would go away at once and allow me to dress in private."

A lazy smile filled his blue eyes, but he made no move to accommodate her wishes. Annoyed by his arrogance, Brynn brushed past him and stalked barefooted across the shingle toward the rock where she had left her gown and slippers. She had barely taken four steps, however, when a stinging pain in her left sole made her draw a sharp breath. Halting abruptly, she stood on one leg, cursing her clumsiness. She had cut the pad of her foot on a shell or rock.

"You're bleeding," a concerned voice said behind her.

"I am fine."

When she tried to hobble toward her clothing, though, she suddenly felt herself being swept up in a pair of strong arms.

Brynn gasped in shock.

"How dare you . . . Put me down!" she demanded, and tried to break free, but her struggles were in vain. Not only was Wycliff tall and lithe but surprisingly muscular as well—and altogether too domineering for her taste, both in manner and tone of voice.

"Be still," he ordered. "I only want to see to your wound."

He carried her as if she weighed no more than thistledown and lifted her up onto a boulder so that she sat facing him, her knees level with his broad chest.

Brynn glared repressingly at him, but he only flashed her a wicked smile. When his gaze flickered over her bosom, she realized that her towel had come loose and clutched at it wildly, covering her indecently exposed breasts. There was nothing she could do, however, to hide her legs, which were bare to the knees.

At last he turned his attention to her left foot. He cradled it gently in his elegant hands, turning it slightly to inspect the bloody cut on the underside. His touch was careful as he brushed away sand and probed the wound with his thumb.

"It doesn't appear to be too deep," he murmured.

"I told you, my lord, I am perfectly all right. And I don't appreciate you accosting me."

Instead of answering, Lord Wycliff began pulling the hem of his shirt from the waistband of his breeches.

Brynn's eyes widened in alarm. "What are you *doing*?"

"Tearing a strip off my shirt to bind your wound. I haven't any bandages with me at present, or even a handkerchief."

It was a costly shirt, made of the finest cambric, she noted, the price of which would have fed a commoner's family for weeks. But the Earl of Wycliff was reportedly wealthy enough to destroy a dozen such garments without thinking twice.

"You will ruin your shirt," Brynn protested weakly.

That charming half smile flashed again. "But my sacrifice is for a good cause."

He ripped the fabric at the bottom and tore off part of the hem, then began to bandage her foot.

Biting her lip, Brynn stared down at his dark head as he bent over her. His nearness was affecting her strangely, making her senses swim and her heartbeat quicken ridiculously. His thick, curling hair was deepest brown, the rich color of dark chocolate, and she could smell his clean masculine scent over the pungent brine from the sea.

He seemed intimately aware of her as well, for his touch was lingering and provocative as he bound her foot. After he tied a neat knot over her arch, he went still. When he looked up suddenly, his sapphire eyes had darkened.

Brynn froze. *Sweet heaven.* She had seen that look before in men's eyes. Want, need, primitive male lust. She was sitting there, wet and bedraggled as a drowned cat, and yet this handsome stranger was looking at her as if she was the most bewitching woman he had ever encountered.

It was the Gypsy's curse again, Brynn thought with a sinking heart. The powerful Romany spell that had made men go wild for the females in her family for nearly two hundred years. And she was alone with this wicked lord, wearing scarcely a stitch of clothing.

She shivered, despite the warmth of the sun beating down on her wet head.

"Are you cold?" he asked, his voice suddenly husky.

"No . . . I told you I am quite all right. Or I would be if you would go away and leave me in peace."

"It would hardly be chivalrous of me to leave you in this condition. You're injured."

"I will manage well enough."

"You can't mean to walk home, siren. Where do you live? I'll carry you."

Brynn hesitated. She couldn't possibly allow him to carry her. She couldn't be seen alone with a nobleman of his notorious ilk, especially while in this state of undress. Even if she were to don her gown—which was one of her oldest— appearing in public in his arms was sure to cause a scandal. Simply divulging her identity to him would be courting trouble.

If he would just leave her, she could return home through the cave, which was connected by a narrow passageway to her family home on the cliff top.

Pretending regret, she lowered her gaze to conceal the lie in her eyes. She would do better to encourage him to believe her a servant. Indeed, she suspected he already thought her one, for no true lady would go swimming in her shift. "My master would not like it if a strange man were to accompany me home."

"You have a protector?"

By that he was asking if she were some man's mistress, she realized.

"Yes, my lord." She didn't tell him that her "protector" was her older brother, Sir Grayson Caldwell.

"I should have known." His voice was low and sensual. "A woman as lovely as you would of course be taken."

"Let me go . . . please." She would have climbed down from the boulder where she was perched, but he stood directly in front of her, too near for comfort.

"You haven't even told me your name."

"It's—" *Elizabeth,* she started to say, which truthfully was her middle name. But few servants owned such an elegant appellation. "My name is Beth."

His heavy eyebrows drew together as he studied her. "Somehow that doesn't fit. It doesn't do justice to a sea nymph. I shall call you Aphrodite instead. That's what I first thought when I saw you rising from the foam."

"I would rather you call me nothing at all and say farewell."

His half-lidded gaze was amused as he measured her. "My, what a little firebrand you are. Your protector must have his hands full dealing with you."

"That is hardly your concern, my lord."

"No, regrettably it isn't." His murmur was husky and vibrant. Seductive. It stroked her nerve endings like velvet.

"*Will* you release me?" she responded much too breathlessly.

"Yes. On one condition."

"Condition?" Brynn eyed him warily, trying to summon her defenses. After the frustrations of her day, she was in no mood to be trifled with or eager to become the plaything of a rake.

"You must pay a forfeit." His hand lifted to her face, and with one finger he brushed her mouth lightly. "A simple kiss. Nothing more."

He wouldn't be satisfied with one kiss, Brynn feared. Even a rake as experienced and jaded as the Earl of Wycliff would not be able to resist the damnable Gypsy's curse. To her everlasting dismay, she possessed unique feminine powers. An irresistible allure she had inherited from her legendary ancestor.

Yet she knew she wouldn't be rid of him unless she agreed.

"If I kiss you, then you promise to go?"

"If you insist."

"You give me your word of honor?"

"Absolutely."

His eyes touched her intimately, and she couldn't look away. She only hoped she could believe him.

"Very well," she said with grave reluctance. "One kiss."

Her throat dry, Brynn braced herself as he put his hands at her waist to lift her down from her rock. But instead of simply setting her on the ground, he held her against him. Her breath caught in her throat as he deliberately let her slide down the full length of his body.

His seductive smile was unapologetic. "If I am allowed only one kiss, I must make it good." Still keeping her pressed to him, he bent his head.

His lips were warm, surprisingly soft—and more tempting than she could have imagined. She tried to hold herself stiffly, but found it impossible with the caress of his alluring mouth.

His teeth began tugging at her lower lip, nipping softly, while his hand stroked the curve of her spine.

Brynn felt the first stirrings of a sexual response that she was unprepared for.

Unconsciously she parted her lips, and he took immediate advantage. Delicately, inexorably his tongue slid inside her mouth in a slow and thorough invasion. His taste was incredibly arousing. She shivered at the warm stroke of his rough-silk tongue inside her mouth, feeling a sweet, foreign ache between her thighs.

His kiss became more demanding then, teasing a hunger from her she couldn't believe possible. Every nerve in her body flared and tightened as his tongue played with hers, meeting hers, coaxing, twining in a long sensuous pattern of withdrawal and penetration. A helpless sigh whispered from deep in her throat. She could feel the slow movement of his hips against hers, feel the shameful tingling of her breasts, the brazen heat that uncoiled between her thighs.

Then he pulled her even closer, into the hard heat of his body, fitting her more fluidly against his rigid arousal, and she had difficulty catching her breath. And his hands . . .

Her pulse beat wildly as his long fingers curved over her breast. In some distant part of her mind, she knew she shouldn't allow him such liberties, but she couldn't find the strength to protest. His practiced fingers caressed her, cupping and teasing the furled bud with expert skill.

She was trembling when he finally raised his head, yet he didn't release her. His gaze bored into her, penetrating in a way that was disturbingly intimate.

"I want to taste you," he murmured, his voice a husky rasp.

She knew she should turn and run, but she couldn't move. She was held captive by the unwavering intensity of his gaze.

He brushed a wet strand of her hair away from her temple, then moved his hands to the neckline of her chemise. Her towel fell forgotten to the ground as he freed her breasts to the warm sun and to his heated gaze.

His eyes alight with cobalt fires, he lowered his head. She felt the soft brush of his breath before his lips captured one pouting crest. A whimper sounded in her throat as he tongued her, laving the peaked nipple. Then his mouth closed wet and hungry on the cresting tip, drawing the soft, swollen flesh between his teeth, pulling at it with a hard sucking motion.

The sensation streaking through her body was so excruciatingly violent, her knees went weak. Her hands rose to his hair and clenched in the silky thickness. He pressed her back against the boulder, but she offered no protest, ignoring the voice of reason screaming a warning in her head. He was seducing her, and she didn't care.

His knee rode intimately between her thighs, sending desire knifing through her trembling body. The rough rock bit hurtfully into her through the thin fabric of her shift, yet she found herself clutching his head to her breast, trying to draw his tantalizing, relentless mouth closer.

He went on tasting her, tormenting her, while Brynn's senses went wild. Sweet heaven, what was happening to her? No man had ever affected her this way. She had never felt such intense sensations, such uncontrollable desire. *She* was the one to drive men mad, not the other way around. *Men* were the victims of the powerful Gypsy's spell—

Dear God, the curse.

From somewhere far away dim reason filtered through to her consciousness. This was madness. He was much too fervent. His passionate embrace was careening out of control, spiraling into something dark and dangerous. Brynn knew without a doubt that her virginity was at stake; if she let him continue like this, she would have no claim to innocence left.

"No . . . please . . . you *promised*," she gasped.

Dredging up a vestige of resistance, she tried to pull away. Yet to her dismay, he would not let her go.

Her desperation rose. On the edge of panic, Brynn brought her knee up between his thighs, contacting with the hard ridge of male flesh hidden there beneath his breeches.

The sharp sound he made in response was between a gasp and a groan, but her blow had the desired effect of making him release her with a smothered curse. She caught a glimpse of his face—bewilderment, pain, anger—as he doubled over. He stood there a moment, his hands clutching his knees as he struggled for breath.

Brynn stared at him, her naked breasts heaving. No lady should claim to know about the intimacies of a man's body, but having grown up with five brothers, she knew something about fighting. Grayson himself had taught her to protect herself physically from overamorous suitors, instructing her on the most vulnerable parts of male anatomy.

For the first time in months, Brynn found herself blessing her older brother rather than cursing him.

But she still had an angry, injured male to deal with, she realized when the handsome Lord Wycliff lifted his head. Despite the glazed, spellbound look in his eyes, he fixed her with a baleful glare, his gaze raking her bare breasts.

Desperately she straightened her disheveled chemise and inched away, slipping out from between him and the boulder. She regretted having to cause him such pain, but there had been no other way to break the spell.

"I am sorry," she muttered defiantly, "but you should never have kissed me—touched me—like that."

He was still short of breath when he answered, surprising her. "I know. It was unpardonable of me."

Brynn returned his gaze warily as she moved over to her pile of clothing.

His sensuous mouth twisted in an expression that was halfway between a pained grimace and a self-deprecating smile. "I am the one who should be sorry. My only excuse is that I became carried away by your charms."

His apology amazed her, yet she wasn't certain she could trust it. Scooping up her gown and slippers, she held them to her chest, concealing her breasts from his view.

"I suppose you could not help yourself," she replied grudgingly.

Clutching her garments close, she turned and scrambled up the rocky path that cut across the cliff face, unmindful of her injured foot.

She paused once to glance behind her. Lord Wycliff stood on the shingle beach below, staring up at her. His hands rested on his narrow hips, his powerful legs slightly spread, as if he stood on a mountaintop, surveying his domain.

He did not intend to follow her, she realized with immense relief. Yet she hadn't seen the last of the arrogant earl, Brynn was certain.

Turning, she fled, disappearing behind a scrub thicket that clung precariously to the edge of the path.

When she was out of sight, Lucian let out his breath in a quiet rush. The encounter had left him unexpectedly shaken.

It was a novel experience, being bested by a servant. For that matter, it was novel for any woman to resist his advances—and even more singular for him to lose control the way he had.

Lucian shook his head, feeling an amused, self-mocking smile twist his mouth. He was entirely unaccustomed to being rebuffed. Normally females, no matter their station or claim to comeliness, vied for his attention and favors. Never before had he been *assaulted* by one.

This entire interlude was wholly unforeseen. He was on a mission to uncover vital war intelligence, searching the coves along the seacoast for places where stolen gold might be hidden. The last thing he'd thought to discover was a scantily clad sea nymph with flaming auburn hair and emerald eyes.

Enchanted at first sight, he had watched bewitched when she climbed from the pool, stricken by the untamed beauty he had stumbled upon. When she stood bathed in full sunlight, a soft sea breeze wafting over her body, she had looked like a primitive goddess, and he could barely catch his breath.

But she was no imaginary creature, he'd discovered to his delight. She was intensely real, an alluring, flesh-and-blood woman. Everything about her was profoundly sensual, from the deep blaze of her hair, to her creamy, silken skin, to her slim thighs, naked and dewy from the sea. And those eyes . . .

He could lose himself in those vibrant green eyes.

Who the devil was she? She was too well-spoken to be less than an upper-class servant. A lady's maid, perhaps, or a governess. Except that no governess looked the way she did, or possessed such spirited defiance or so tart a tongue. He was a little amazed at her daring.

Obviously she had the confidence of a woman secure in her position. Her beauty doubtless commanded the homage of a wealthy protector.

She would make a magnificent mistress, Lucian knew—fiery, disdainful, yet sexually responsive enough to meet his intense appetites with those of her own.

He could eagerly imagine sliding deep within her silky body, feeling her wrap those strong, graceful legs around him, that cloud of glorious hair entwining him as he took her in the throes of passion.

It was enough to set his blood on fire. And the thought of her response . . .

She had wanted him, he knew. He had recognized all the signs of an aroused woman, her body growing sweetly pliant as he held and caressed her, her soft whimpers of pleasure as he had tasted her lush, ripe breasts. . . .

Heat surged through him at the mere memory. Lucian found himself swearing a low oath at the ache in his loins. He hadn't been left this tormented with unconsummated desire since adolescence.

So how did he proceed from here? Could she be lured away from her protector—by the promise of riches or some other significant consideration? There was no question that he was intrigued, or that her lush loveliness entranced him.

A pity her station wasn't more elevated. For months he had been searching for a bride to bear him a son. Were her lineage better, he wouldn't hesitate to claim her.

But despite her lack of breeding, he would enjoy a dalliance. No, more than a dalliance, Lucian amended. He felt a restless aching need to possess her. He wanted the fascinating beauty in his bed.

His eyes narrowed as he contemplated the cliff path where she had fled. He wanted her. And Lucian Tremayne, seventh Earl of Wycliff, usually got what he wanted.

Chapter Two

With grave reluctance, Brynn descended from the family carriage and took her brother's proffered arm. A welcoming blaze of lights illuminated the family seat of the Duke of Hennessy, the highest-ranking peer in the district, but Brynn had no desire to attend this assembly, no matter how rare the occasion or prized the honor.

"You might try for a smile, puss," Grayson teased. "You look as if you're being sent to the guillotine."

"I would far rather have stayed quietly home."

"I know. But it has been three years since the duke has issued any invitations to his home. It would never do to snub him—or his illustrious guest."

Brynn's heart sank at the thought of that illustrious guest. *The Earl of Wycliff.* The aging duke was holding an assembly to honor his London visitor.

"Moreover," Gray added seriously, "it will do you good to get out for once. You are at risk of becoming a recluse."

"You know perfectly well why I keep out of the public eye."

"Yes, but you needn't avoid society entirely, only males who show you undue attention. And curse or no curse, I doubt a man of Wycliff's stamp will be in danger of swooning over you. He's one of the most sought-after lords in England. Doubtless he will be attracted only to a great beauty with a fortune and title to match his own."

Yet the bold earl *had* been attracted to her, Brynn thought gloomily.

Other than to warn her brother that she'd seen a stranger nosing around the cliffs, she hadn't told Gray about her encounter with the lustful Lord Wycliff four days ago, nor did she intend to. Gray would be distressed to learn she had so narrowly escaped trouble, perhaps enough to forbid her to swim in the cove, which was one of her few liberties. He was as protective of her virtue as a mother hen.

As they were admitted into the immense foyer of the ducal mansion, Grayson swept a critical eye over her. "I don't think you need worry about attracting male attention, Brynn. You have disguised your feminine charms rather well."

Her ivory gown, which was four Seasons out of date, was of plain muslin and boasted a modestly high neckline, while her blazing hair was scraped back in a severe knot and mostly hidden beneath a feathered chapeau.

"If he does pay you any notice, however, it will not hurt you to make yourself amenable. Wycliff wields a great deal of power in elite circles, and an acquaintance can only be beneficial."

"Beneficial to whom?" Brynn replied dryly.

"To me, of course. To our family."

She heard the note of bitterness in her brother's voice and glanced up at him. Her elder by four

years, Grayson was a handsome man with features similar to her own, although his hair was
much darker than hers, a rich chestnut brown. Despite his looks and title, however, his eligibility was
greatly disadvantaged by the impoverished state of
his finances—a circumstance for which he bore little
blame.

Their family had never been affluent, but after
their father's death three years ago, they were stunned
to learn the extent of their debts. Samuel Caldwell
not only had made several unwise investments, he
had borrowed at usurious rates from a moneylender to purchase naval commissions for two of his
older sons. Simply repaying the interest on the loan
depleted the small income from the entailed Caldwell estate.

As the heir, Grayson was at risk of being thrown
into debtors' prison, yet to his immense credit, he had
shouldered the duty of supporting his five younger
siblings without complaint and striven to keep their
home from going to total ruin. It was a heavy burden, and Brynn had felt obliged to help relieve it,
even to the extent of aiding Gray's illicit smuggling
activities. Although Free Trading was no proper role
for a lady, she had sometimes performed sentry duty
and occasionally even lugged her share of contraband. But her primary contribution was in selling
their smuggled goods. She'd become quite adept at
negotiating with the merchants in St. Mawes and
Falmouth for the best prices.

Grayson regretted her involvement, but he needed
her help, especially after their younger brother Reese
had joined the merchant marine last spring. And she

owed Gray her allegiance. As her oldest brother, he'd always looked after her and fiercely protected her from her lustful suitors. She loved him dearly, despite her current vexation with him and their recent arguments regarding young Theo's welfare.

It galled Grayson to have to toady to anyone, Brynn knew. His pride was even greater than her own, and she understood his bitterness at being drowned in such crushing debt.

"Very well," she said, forcing a smile. "I will be the height of congeniality, fawning over Lord Wycliff as if he were a prince royal."

Her reply dredged a reluctant grin from Gray. "You needn't fawn, puss. Just keep that tart tongue of yours between your teeth and don't purposefully offend him."

Brynn very much hoped the opportunity to offend the earl would never arise. With luck, she could manage to avoid Lord Wycliff this evening. And if she were extremely fortunate, he wouldn't recognize her as the nearly naked mermaid he'd kissed so thoroughly a few days before.

She surrendered her wrap to a footman and allowed Gray to escort her to the ballroom, where much of the local gentry had already gathered. Brynn would have preferred to skip the receiving line entirely and repair to the ladies' retiring room to hide, but her brother insisted that she honor the niceties.

The elderly duke stood with several members of his family and another gentleman whose elegant bearing proclaimed him to be a lord. He was significantly taller than the others and possessed a lean, muscular grace that was missing in his more portly companions. His shoulders filled out his impeccably cut blue jacket to perfection, Brynn saw, risking a glance down the line, before her attention was claimed by her host.

The duke, with his rheumy eyes blinking, greeted her fondly and then introduced her to his houseguest as "the loveliest young lady in all of Cornwall."

At this whisker, Brynn kept her eyes downcast, adopting a mousy manner when she offered her hand to his lordship and murmured a polite greeting. Yet any hope Wycliff wouldn't recognize her died instantaneously; he froze in the act of bowing over her hand.

The touch of his fingers burned, even through her gloves, but when Brynn tried to withdraw her hand, his grasp tightened almost imperceptibly, holding her captive and compelling her to lift her gaze.

His sapphire eyes locked with hers. "Miss Caldwell? I am charmed."

"Th-thank you, my lord."

A ghost of a smile curved his beautiful mouth. "Have we met before?" His gaze boldly flickered downward over her breasts. "You seem vaguely familiar."

"I believe you must be mistaken," Brynn replied stiffly, feeling herself flushing.

"I'm not so certain. I rarely forget a lovely face."

She tried to stare him down, giving him her coolest look, but he affected not to notice.

"You must promise me a dance, Miss Caldwell, so that we might further our acquaintance."

Brynn glanced helplessly at her brother, who was giving her a look that was half warning, half plea. "As you wish," she capitulated. But she snatched her hand away and moved on more quickly than was polite.

She took refuge in one corner of the room among the wallflowers and dowagers, while Gray went in search of his own friends. Brynn was glad for the chance to compose herself—and for the unusually amiable greetings she received, grateful to know she wouldn't be entirely shunned for the evening because of who she was.

The legend of Flaming Nell was accepted fact in these parts. Nearly two centuries ago Lady Eleanor Stanhope had been cursed for stealing a Gypsy woman's lover and doomed to lure innocent men to their deaths. And Brynn, as one of her descendants, was believed to be burdened with the same affliction.

Despite the Gypsy curse and the tragedy in her own past, however, she wasn't quite an outcast with her neighbors. The women welcomed her company, even liked her for the most part. But she was considered a danger to their sons. They kept their menfolk far away from her, especially those of marriage-able age.

After making the requisite small talk, Brynn let the ladies' conversation wash over her as she puzzled out her unusual reaction to Lord Wycliff.

His crystalline blue eyes were just as compelling, his seductive half smile just as devastating as during their first encounter, yet that didn't excuse her behavior. She was still ashamed of the way her body had betrayed her that day in the cove, could still recall the hot, trembling sensations that had rushed through her at his erotic caresses.

What on earth had come over her? No man had ever affected her that way. She had once experienced a girlish infatuation—to her profound regret and sorrow—but never had she even come close to losing control or surrendering to a man's caresses. With Lord Wycliff she had acted a perfect wanton. . . .

But by all accounts Wycliff was a practiced rake who made seduction a sport. She had never been able to afford a London Season, but the duke's granddaughter, Lady Meredith, was her closest friend. Meredith was now a viscountess and lived primarily in London, and her frequent letters were filled with lively *on dits* about the ton, describing in titillating detail exploits of the wicked rakes and dangerous adventurers who made up the infamous Hellfire League. And Lucian Tremayne, Earl of Wycliff, was one of its chief founders.

Notorious for his scandalous conquests in the bedroom, he had cut a dazzling swath through society for years. Brynn could well believe the tales about him. Reportedly he had the power to make strong women weak—and she was living proof.

Her fascination with Wycliff was incomprehensible. She had little respect for such noblemen—rich, idle, shallow, not to mention arrogant and infuriatingly puffed up by their own self-consequence.

Her current companions, however, did not hold the same aversion, apparently.

"Ah, if I were only twenty years younger," the widowed Mrs. Prescott murmured beside her.

"Twenty years still would not do you a bit of good, Honoria," her friend, Mrs. Stobly, remarked with a cattish smile. "Gentlemen like that can have their pick of rich beauties, and you fit neither bill, I'm sorry to say."

"I don't believe you are sorry in the least, Alice."

Following their gaze, Brynn felt herself frown as she watched the earl lead out the aging Duchess of Hennessy for a minuet. Wycliff cut a striking figure on the dance floor, lithe, elegant, yet with the supple, muscular build of a sportsman. He had captured every female eye in the ballroom, including hers.

With a murmur of disgust, Brynn tore her gaze away. She had more admirable concerns than watching a legendary rake conquer feminine hearts.

Lamentably, though, she caught the eye of a young dandy in the crowd, the local squire's son who had fallen victim to her allure some months before.

Alarmed to see Mr. Ridding making a direct beeline for her, Brynn rose quickly to her feet. Yet before she could escape, he hastened to intercept her, bowing before her with a breathless grin.

"Miss Caldwell, I hoped . . . no, I *prayed* you might come. I beg you to honor me with the next set of dances."

When he reached for her hand, Brynn pulled away anxiously, determined to dissuade his pursuit of her. "Mr. Ridding, you know that is unadvised."

"I dreamed of you last night, did you know? You were not so averse to me in my dream—"

Just then his mama came rushing up to rescue him. "Orlan, come away from that young lady at once!"

"Mama, I was only requesting a dance—"

"I won't allow it. You know very well the danger."

Mrs. Ridding tugged insistently on her son's sleeve to draw him away, much to Brynn's relief. And yet she felt her cheeks flush with humiliation and pain as she sensed the accusing eyes of the dowagers. They blamed her for the untimely, tragic death of her one-time suitor so many years ago. She couldn't fault them for their condemnation, since she couldn't forgive herself.

Choosing to retreat rather than prolong the distressing moment, Brynn offered a forced smile and made her way through the swelling crowd and out of the ballroom, searching for the library. Perhaps she could make good use of her time until her brother was ready to leave.

Upon exploring the shelves, she was somewhat heartened to find a copy of Beckford's *Latin Primer*. Next week she was supposed to quiz Theo on the conjugation of verbs, and she still had a great deal of preparation to do; she had to keep at least two lessons ahead of her sharp-witted youngest brother if she had any hope of maintaining his respect for her as his tutor.

As a girl her own education had been typical for a young lady—French, Italian, the use of globes, basic sums. Latin and Greek, history, and higher maths were considered the province of masculine minds, and she'd had to scramble to educate herself in those subjects after her family was forced to let their longtime governess go because of the pitiful state of their finances.

Brynn had settled comfortably on the settee and

was deep in concentration when an intimate male voice sounded behind her.

"So this is where you've hidden yourself."

Giving a violent start of surprise, Brynn straightened and cast a wary glance over her shoulder. "You do have the most vexing habit of startling me, my lord."

Wycliff strolled into the room casually, as if he owned the place. Circling the couch, he stood before her a moment, measuring her. "Miss Brynn Caldwell, the genteel but impoverished daughter of a baronet. Imagine my delight to discover you weren't an apparition after all—and my surprise to discover your true identity."

She felt herself flush, but remained mute.

His intent masculine gaze raked over her, making her keenly aware of her femaleness. His mere presence set her pulse leaping, while that slow, heated look made her suddenly warm.

"Why the deception?" he asked.

"What deception?"

"You told me your name was Beth."

"It is. I am Brynn Elizabeth."

"Why did you conceal it from me?"

"Why?" she repeated warily. "Because I feared a scandal. It was bad enough that you . . . that I allowed myself to be caught in such a compromising position. I saw no reason to compound my indiscretion by advertising my identity."

"So you deceived me, claiming to have a protector."

"I do have a protector of sorts. My brother. Five brothers, in fact. They usually are quite proficient at shielding me from the unwanted advances of strange gentlemen."

A spark of amusement glimmered in his eyes. "An inventive way of shading the truth. But as memory serves, you let me think you a governess or a domestic."

"That was no lie, either. I regularly function in the role of governess. I tutor my youngest brother."

A slashing dark eyebrow rose with skepticism.

"It's true," Brynn insisted. She held up the primer in her hand, showing him the title.

"A Latin grammar?"

"I am endeavoring to teach my brother the classics, although I'm severely disadvantaged, since my own linguistic education did not extend past Italian."

"Why do you not simply hire a tutor?"

"My family, sadly, is not in a position to afford such luxuries," Brynn said stiffly. "Not everyone possesses the fortune of a Midas, as you reportedly do, my lord."

His expression took on a measure of contrition. "Forgive me. That was gauche of me."

She thought—hoped—he might leave her alone then, but she had no such luck; he continued to study her from beneath long, wicked lashes.

"You continually surprise me. First an enchanting sea creature, now a bluestocking. You interest me profoundly."

"I don't intend to, I assure you. I have no desire to provoke your interest."

"How old are you?" he asked suddenly.

Brynn gave him a blank look. "It is hardly polite

to ask a lady to reveal her age, but if you must know, I am four-and-twenty."

"And still unwed? A woman of your obvious spirit and beauty?"

"I am quite content with my spinsterhood."

"In God's name, why?" The question was entirely serious.

She hesitated, reluctant to bring up the curse and her fear of marriage. "Because I am responsible for raising my youngest brother. I have no intention of marrying. At least not until he is safely settled." *And not even then,* she added to herself.

Wycliff shook his head in apparent disbelief. "A determined spinster bluestocking . . . I would never have guessed."

"But then your powers of intuition are not excessively well-developed. Not if you mistook me for Aphrodite."

Rather than Wycliff taking offense, the blatantly suggestive spark in his eyes blossomed into appreciative laughter. Even more to her surprise, he moved toward her. Brynn drew back instinctively, shrinking into the corner of the settee, but he merely seated himself beside her without so much as a by-your-leave.

"I trust the cut on your foot healed well enough?"

"Quite well . . . Thank you," she added grudgingly.

When Wycliff sat there curiously appraising her, she stiffened and eyed him nervously. "You really should go, my lord. The company will be missing you, since you are the guest of honor."

"You promised me a dance."

"Well, I cannot dance with you here."

"Why not?"

"Because . . . well, propriety, for one thing. I should not even be alone with you."

"You didn't object so strenuously the other day."

She took a steadying breath. "I gave you the wrong impression that day, I know. But despite appearances, I am not the sort of female you think me."

"And what sort is that?"

"The kind to welcome your attentions. I am not usually given to acting the wanton."

"A pity."

Brynn ignored the unholy laughter dancing in his eyes. "I am certainly not at all proud of my behavior, but yours was hardly admirable, either. Still, I suppose it was only to be expected from a rake."

"You consider me a rake because I treated you as a desirable woman rather than a lady?"

"I consider you a rake because I know of your reputation. Even in the dull backwaters of Cornwall we have heard of your legendary exploits." Brynn regarded him coolly. "I was not fortunate enough to have a London Season, but I have friends who report faithfully to me, and your wicked past is a common topic of discussion. You are notorious for your conquests among the ladies—and I have no desire to become one of your conquests."

A smile seemed to loiter at his tempting mouth as he shook his head again. "Do you have any notion how unique you are? How many females have tried to orchestrate just that sort of compromising situation in a bid to ensnare me in matrimony?"

Brynn could well guess. The legendary Lord Wycliff would be pursued because of his startling physical beauty alone. And with his wealth and title, he was a prize women would do anything to win. According to her friend Meredith, more than one lady had been known to sneak into his bed in an effort to force his hand.

"Well," Brynn said firmly, "you may put your mind at ease on that score. I am certainly no threat to your bachelorhood. On the contrary, you are the one who is a threat. By singling me out this way, you will only cause me embarrassment, or worse. If we are seen intimately together, I won't have a shred of reputation left."

He lifted his arm, resting it on the couch back behind her. "And your reputation concerns you?"

"Very much."

His hand rose to touch the nape of her neck. "Your hair is the vibrant color of flame. I wondered. It looked darker—almost auburn—when it was wet."

Feeling unsettled, Brynn held herself rigidly. She didn't care for what his featherlight touch on her skin was doing to her senses.

"I liked it better down, though." His voice dropped to a husky murmur. "I would like even more to see it flowing over my pillow."

Vexed by the seductive note in his voice and what she saw as a deliberate attempt to taunt her, Brynn shot up from the settee and turned to face him. "I will not allow you to trifle with me, Lord Wycliff."

His eyes had darkened slumberously. "I assure you I am not trifling, siren. I am merely being honest. I want you in my bed, I fully admit it. I would hardly be a man if I didn't."

Brynn pursed her lips impatiently while she hugged her book to her chest. "I don't doubt you want me. It is a very common sentiment. But there is a perfectly reasonable explanation for your lustful urges."

"Is that so?"

"Yes. I am cursed."

"Indeed?" The word held a wealth of skepticism.

"It is quite true. Ask anyone in these parts and they will confirm it. One of my ancestors was a legendary beauty who stole a Gypsy woman's lover. In revenge the Gypsy put a curse on her. Her female descendants are doomed to have remarkable allure and the power to enchant men, but if they dare give their hearts, their love is fated to end tragically with the death of their beloved."

"And you believe in this . . . curse?"

"Completely," she replied with all seriousness. "There have been too many inexplicable incidents to believe otherwise. Nearly every generation of women in my family has experienced a tragedy in love."

"Including you?"

An arrow of pain lashed through Brynn at the memory. "My first suitor died when I was sixteen, drowned at sea. I am surprised no one warned you about me," she added, unable to quell a hint of bitterness.

His doubtful expression never wavered, and Brynn felt a surge of frustration. "You needn't take my word for it. Everyone here knows of the danger we present. It is indisputable that we cast spells over men. We attract them in droves."

"Droves?" Wycliff's amusement was edged with

cynicism, or perhaps his disdain was merely the result of a natural sense of arrogance bred into him. "Let me see if I comprehend you correctly. Because of a Gypsy curse, I am likely to first lose my head over you, and then my life?"

"Not your life. Not unless I came to love you. But it is certain you wouldn't be able to resist me."

A warm, intimate smile touched his chiseled mouth. "You realize, of course, that you are disparaging my powers of control."

Brynn's fingers clenched around her book. "I can understand why you would be skeptical, but I assure you, it would be foolish of you not to take the curse seriously."

"I think you will have to prove it."

Her eyebrows rose. "Prove it?"

"Yes. We should put this claim of yours to the test."

"And just how do you propose we do that?"

"Kiss me."

Brynn stared at him. "You are jesting, of course."

"Not at all."

"I should think the last time we kissed would have been proof enough. You must remember how it ended when you—"

"I remember quite well," he said dryly. "You tried to unman me."

"Only," Brynn returned, flushing, "because I was forced to save myself from your overamorous attentions. Admit it, my lord, you refused to release me because you became carried away."

"I think I can manage to curb myself this time. Put your book down and come here, love."

When she remained immobile, Wycliff lifted an inquiring eyebrow. "Would you care for your acquaintances to hear how I found you at the cove, Miss Caldwell? Your brothers, perhaps? I doubt they would countenance your parading around in a state of near undress."

Her eyes narrowed in disbelief, then in anger. "That is extortion."

"I consider it merely leverage."

"Why? For revenge?" Her expression turned scornful. "Because I dared to resist you? Because I failed to fall at your feet in a swoon?"

A half smile claimed the corner of his mouth. "I admit you bestowed an incalculable blow to my male esteem, but no, I am not seeking revenge. I am merely interested in conducting an experiment. You've aroused my curiosity with this talk of curses."

She stood there defiantly, regarding him in frustration. Wycliff merely waited patiently with the sort of supreme confidence that set her teeth on edge.

Finally, however, when she refused to do his bidding, his expression changed; his mouth curved in a smile that was slow and tender and all enveloping.

Brynn could well understand why so many women had been seduced by him. His smile held a wickedly irresistible appeal. That, along with his raw magnetism and devastating charm, was a potent force indeed.

Against her will, she felt herself being drawn to him. And she had little doubt that he was ruthless enough to make trouble for her if she failed to do his bidding.

Capitulating with a silent oath, Brynn returned to

sit beside him on the settee, yet she kept her spine rigid and refused to look at him. "I should think a rake of your legendary skill would be able to find more willing females," she grumbled, "instead of trying to ravish me at every turn."

His soft laugh was a velvet rasp. "I hate to disappoint you, darling, but this is not ravishment. Only a kiss."

Only a kiss, Brynn thought wildly. Then why was her pulse so erratic?

Her senses assailed by his nearness, she focused all her effort on resistance, summoning every ounce of willpower she possessed. The earl had leaned toward her, his lips nuzzling her neck . . . her earlobe.

"So sweet," he murmured. "As delicate as spun sugar."

"Will you please simply be done with it?" Brynn said through clenched teeth.

His long fingers came to cradle her cheek as he turned her face toward his. "You will have to unlock your jaw first," he murmured softly, a sensual undertone of laughter in his voice. "How can we test your claim if you won't participate?"

"I have no need to test my claim. I don't consider it in dispute. And I don't *wish* to kiss you."

"Then simply humor me. Part your lips, treasure, and let me taste you."

"I really do not want—" Her protest was cut off by the soft, erotic pressure of his mouth. It touched hers lightly, brushing across her flesh like silken warmth.

She murmured another protest, yet the feelings that rose in her put the lie to her words as his kiss deepened. His fingers drifted over her face and throat, making her quiver, making her breasts feel heated and full. At the glide of his tongue within her mouth, a sigh of surrender whispered from her throat.

He thrust deeper and sent a shocking surge of fire curling hotly inside her. Brynn felt herself weakening, yielding to him. Helplessly she lifted her arms to slide her fingers in his hair. It was soft and satiny and as sensually arousing as his kiss.

She gave him no resistance when he drew her to him. Her senses burned. She was melting against him. He sucked at her tongue until she whimpered a breathy sound of capitulation. Then he eased back on the couch, pulling her with him.

Desire, wild and irrational, lanced through her trembling body as she found herself draped over him. She could feel him beneath her, the warmth of lithe muscles, the supple play of hard masculine flesh. An intense yearning flooded her, as if she were the one caught in the Gypsy's spell. . . .

She gave a strangled moan against his tender mouth. This was wrong. Her hand came up between them, pressing against his chest. She should not, could not let this happen. Yet it was all she could do to push him away.

Summoning all her strength, Brynn sat up with a jerky motion. Her heart was hammering in her chest, her head swimming, yet Wycliff didn't appear to be nearly as affected as she was.

He straightened, watching her intently. Then he reached up with one finger and brushed her lips, still damp and tender from his mouth.

"Whether or not the curse is real," he said, his voice low, husky, "I would still very much like to have you in my bed."

Dazed, Brynn stared at him. When she remained mute, his mouth curled in that slow half smile that had the power to capture female hearts.

She blinked, trying to shake off the force of his spell. Regaining her senses finally, Brynn leapt up from the couch, her book tumbling from her lap.

For a span of several heartbeats, she remained there, staring at him. Then, wordlessly, she turned and fled.

As Lucian watched her bolt for the second time in their brief acquaintance, he felt a strange mix of emotions—puzzlement, desire, exhilaration. . . .

Desire was perhaps the strongest. It would be a consummate lie to say he was unaffected by their heated embrace, as he'd pretended. His carnal urgency was every bit as fierce as the last time he'd kissed her. More so now, since this time he knew what exquisite delights lay beneath her modest gown.

Lucian frowned. He put no stock in Miss Caldwell's claim of being cursed, yet *something* had caused his intense attraction to her. Despite his pretense of control, it had taken all his willpower to restrain his raging lusts. Even now his body was reverberating with the craving he'd felt. His erection was stiff within his satin breeches, pulsing with his still rapid heartbeat.

Yet what he felt for her went deeper than mere lust or physical arousal. *Enchantment* was the word that came to mind. He was utterly spellbound. She was a flame-haired, emerald-eyed enchantress, the kind of woman to haunt a man's dreams. . . .

His lip curling wryly, Lucian shook his head at his poetic flights of fancy. He was indisputably fond of women in general, yet it was unlike him to become enraptured of any one female, even such a beauty as Miss Brynn Caldwell. He'd been intrigued and challenged by her elusiveness, true, but that didn't explain his violent feelings of possessiveness.

He wanted her—badly. And he intended to have her, Lucian reflected with exhilaration.

He had misjudged her the first time, obviously. He'd tasted the innocence in her kiss just now—enough to convince him that she was as inexperienced as she claimed to be.

That was the real reason he'd insisted on kissing her tonight. To test her virtue. If he was to make her his wife, he needed some reassurance that she wasn't playing him for a fool. He owed it to his name and title to demand at least some measure of purity from his countess.

His mouth curved in satisfaction. He had found his bride, he was certain of it. Miss Brynn Caldwell had beauty, birth, breeding, and a family history of fertility—five brothers, no less. And a lively spirit as well, one which he found refreshing after all the toadying, marriage-minded debutantes who had relentlessly pursued him for his title and fortune over the years. Tart tongue or no, she would certainly never bore him.

His bride. The image had a powerful charm to it. And the thought of having that exquisite body beneath him, her lush nakedness warm against him, her slumberous eyes heated with desire, was enough to make his loins ache.

Perhaps he was mad, making such a critical decision so soon after meeting her. Choosing a lifelong mate required careful consideration, logic. And taking a wife just now would play havoc with his duty. He hadn't planned even to think about wedding until after the war had ended and Boney was driven back into his lair.

Yet his deepest instincts were urging him on, telling him to act. He wanted a son, and his enchanting temptress seemed his best chance both to beget an heir and to have a desirable woman in his marriage bed. And arguably, he knew his prospective bride more intimately than most noblemen did theirs.

It was possible Miss Caldwell might object to his plan. She might not want to bear him a son, or even become his wife. She professed to be set on remaining a spinster, which truly would be a crime, Lucian reflected with amusement.

Well then, he would simply have to overcome her resistance. A keen feeling of anticipation rose up in him at the thought of winning her surrender. He had already made a measure of progress. She wasn't nearly as immune to his caresses as she pretended.

He could have taken her right there on the couch, perhaps. In truth, he'd actually considered it for a fleeting moment. If he had summarily seduced her, it would have removed any chance that she would refuse his offer of matrimony. But he didn't want to begin their marriage mired in scandal.

Lucian's elation swelled. He'd thought his stay in

Cornwall would be devoted strictly to business, but he intended to return home with a bride.

A fiery, green-eyed beauty who could stir his blood and give him the son he so fervently wanted.

Chapter Three

The dream was different this time. He lay wounded, dying, as usual, but he was no longer alone. A woman stood over him—an enchanting beauty with flaming hair and flashing eyes, her hands dark with his blood. His killer?

Lucian woke in a cold sweat, not knowing where he was at first. Searching the gray shadows, he felt the tension ease from his body.

He was lying in bed, the sole occupant of the prime guest chamber in the duke's sprawling castle. It was early morning, if the faint light stealing beneath the gold brocade curtains was any indication. There was no sign of his prospective bride, even though in his dream she had seemed so vivid. . . .

"It wasn't real," he whispered, his voice a low rasp. She hadn't tried to kill him.

Sitting up, Lucian rubbed a hand down his face. All her talk of curses had evidently affected his intellect. His sea siren had somehow become entwined with his visions of death. His own death.

With an oath, he threw off the covers and rang for his valet before striding naked over to the washstand and splashing cool water on his face.

There was a simple explanation for his recurring nightmare, Lucian knew. During his last foray into France, on a mission to search for a missing Englishman, he'd had a near brush with death. He'd been forced to kill a man he considered a friend—a stark choice of kill or be killed. Guilt had eaten at him ever since. Guilt and a bleak premonition of his future. He'd been haunted by the same nightmare. He saw himself dying alone, desolate, unlamented, and unmourned.

He was not afraid of dying, precisely, Lucian acknowledged. Better men than he had given their lives in the decades-long struggle to rid the world of the Corsican tyrant. But the experience had undeniably shaken him.

For the first time he'd had to face his own mortality. He was not invincible, as he had somehow believed. The charmed existence he'd always taken for granted would not last forever. Life was, he'd suddenly realized, fragile and precious.

The incident had also made him aware of how little he had to show for his thirty-two years of living. True, he'd played a small role in trying to make the civilized world safe from French domination, working for the Foreign Office, advancing intelligence gathering for Britain. But if he died tomorrow, he would have no real legacy to leave behind.

That was what he wanted most now: a legacy. An heir. A son to carry on his name. The feeling had taken on increasing urgency in recent weeks. It was now a yearning, a hunger deep in his soul.

To sire an heir, however, he must first have a wife.

Lucian's mouth curled wryly as he drew on a robe and pulled the sash taut. This was a novel experience for him, searching for a bride. He'd always fervently resisted the chains of matrimony, preferring instead the dalliances and seductions and brief affaires that had titillated society and earned him notoriety as something of a libertine.

He took great pleasure in his lovers, but the pleasure was mutual, he made certain of that. And the game at which he was so expert was understood by his partners, with no expectations of matrimony. He'd become quite deft at eluding the pursuit of those eager ladies who coveted his title and fortune.

Suddenly changing course—pursuing a marriage partner instead of being the pursued—had felt strange. Moreover, finding the ideal bride was not at all as easy as he expected. Regrettably, the women he most admired and respected were already wed or in a profession that society deemed unfit for nobility. Until he had happened upon Miss Brynn Caldwell . . .

A quiet rap sounded on his bedchamber door. When Lucian bid entrance, his valet stepped into the room.

"You require assistance, my lord?"

"Yes, Pendry. I have an important call to make this morning, and I wish to look my best. The green coat, I think."

"Certainly, my lord," Pendry responded, lifting an eyebrow at his master's unusual concern with his appearance.

Flashing a grin, Lucian settled in a chair so the valet could shave him. His dark mood had shifted rapidly—from disquiet at his nightmare's strange permutation to agreeable anticipation.

This morning's call would be duty as well as pleasure, hopefully dispatching two birds with one proposal. For some time now he'd wanted a pretext to further his acquaintance with Sir Grayson Caldwell. This stretch of Cornish coast was a smuggler's paradise, and Sir Grayson reportedly was the leader of the local ring.

Ordinarily Lucian wouldn't concern himself with simple smuggling, no matter how illegal. The ring he sought, however, posed a far graver threat than usual. The contraband was not brandy and silk, but stolen gold.

Lucian's challenge was to prevent government shipments of gold bullion—payments intended for Britain's allies—from being stolen and smuggled to France to fund Napoleon's armies.

He'd recently received intelligence that Sir Grayson was possibly involved in one of the thefts. If so, the baronet might eventually lead them to the ringleader, one of a dozen suspects who thus far had eluded England's best agents.

That was the sole reason Lucian had come to Cornwall. Ensconcing himself on the duke's estate gave him the opportunity to investigate Sir Grayson Caldwell.

Meanwhile, proposing marriage to Caldwell's beautiful sister would certainly provide an excellent pretext for searching out his secrets.

Brynn woke suddenly, a cry on her lips. She lay there in bed, her heart thudding as the dark remnants of her dream faded. The image had been so vivid. A man—tall, lithe, dark haired, pulse-stirringly handsome—lay dying at her feet. Lord Wycliff? Was that his blood staining her hands?

A feeling of horror washed over her. Freeing her arms from the bedcovers, Brynn stared down at her hands in the early morning light. They were clean, white, unstained. Yet she couldn't shake the needles of alarm crawling over her skin.

Dear God, was it happening again? The one time she had dreamed so vividly about a man, he had died, drowned at sea. Her suitors were often plagued with dreams of her, a result of the Gypsy's curse, but rarely did she reciprocate.

A clammy chill swept her. Was her dream of Wycliff merely a grim illusion? Or was it a deadly premonition?

"You wish to court my sister?" Sir Grayson Caldwell asked, clearly surprised by Lucian's request for permission to pay his addresses.

"Not court, precisely," Lucian replied, sitting across from the baronet in the Caldwell drawing room. "I fear I haven't the time for a lengthy courtship, since I must return to London within the sennight. No, I would prefer to settle the matter as soon as possible. I should like Miss Caldwell's hand in marriage."

Sir Grayson appeared to choose his words with care. "I can understand why you might be attracted to her, my lord. But in all honesty, I feel I must warn you . . . make you aware of what is driving your fascination. Brynn has a strange effect on gentlemen, causing them to lose their heads over her."

"So she advised me."

"She told you of the Gypsy's curse?"

"Yes. Although I must say I find it hard to credit. Men are bound to pursue a beautiful woman. And your sister is extremely beautiful."

"True, but with Brynn, the attraction is inexplicably forceful."

"Then you give credence to her tale of a curse?"

Grayson hesitated a long moment. "I think it unlikely the curse is mere coincidence. Certainly our mother never doubted its power and stuffed Brynn's head full of warnings from the time she was a child. After Mama's death, however, the admonitions faded from Brynn's mind—at least until she lost her first suitor to a tragic drowning at sea. She blamed herself for his death. Ever since she has virtually lived the life of a recluse for fear of repeating the tragedy."

"I am willing to risk the possibility of a curse."

"But she may not be. You should know that Brynn has turned down any number of proposals thus far. I doubt she will receive yours with any more eagerness."

"I'm prepared to make her an extremely generous settlement. And her family as well," Lucian added, glancing around the shabby if immaculate drawing room.

"I admit an infusion of funds would not go amiss," Grayson said with a faint flush of embarrassment. "But you will not find it easy to convince Brynn—or to persuade her to leave our youngest brother. She has the raising of him, you see."

"You have no objection to my suit, though?"

"No, not in the least. I would consider it an honor to claim a nobleman of your consequence as my brother-in-law. I am simply saying that I cannot force her to accept you. My sister has a mind of her own, I fear."

Lucian smiled faintly. "So I have discovered," he murmured to himself.

He found Brynn Caldwell in the unkempt garden where she sat on a bench with a boy who must be her youngest brother, Theodore. For a moment Lucian paused beside a linden tree and watched the two of them.

She wore a faded sprigged-muslin gown and a wide-brimmed bonnet to shield her face from the bright morning sun, yet that alluring aura of enchantment surrounded her, no matter the setting. And her effect on him was the same as before. Lucian felt a rush of heat to his loins that he had rarely felt with any other woman.

Theo was a gangly, bespectacled youth, all skin and bone, with a pale complexion and a shock of red hair that resembled a rooster's plumage. The boy was reading a passage of poetry aloud with obvious reluctance, until finally he gave a sound of disgust and looked up at his sister.

"I do not see how Milton can possibly benefit me, Brynn."

"Because it increases the breadth of your knowledge and widens your view of the world," she replied calmly. "You cannot hope to have a well-rounded education with your nose constantly in a chemistry book."

"But my experiment is at a *crucial* stage."

She had an easy, musical laugh. "I am a cruel sister, I know. You would rather be in your dungeon of a laboratory, blowing things up, than out here in the fresh air."

"I have not blown anything up in weeks."

"For which I am profoundly grateful," she said wryly, ruffling his vivid hair. "But if you will suffer through ten more minutes, you may return to your laboratory until luncheon."

He grinned at that and opened the poetry book again.

Lucian found himself spellbound as he watched their interaction. He could count on one hand the number of genteel ladies who would show such warmth to a younger sibling. It gave him more confidence that she would make a good mother for his son.

He knew the moment she became aware of his presence. She looked up, her green eyes bright as new spring grass. Immediately wary, she came to her feet.

Theo's voice trailed off as he realized there was an intruder in their midst.

"My lord Wycliff," she said with forced politeness. "What brings you here?"

"You, Miss Caldwell." Adopting a relaxed smile, Lucian moved forward. "I would like a private word with you, if I may."

"We are in the middle of a lesson."

The boy piped up. "That is quite all right, Brynn. I don't mind leaving."

Brynn flashed him a repressive glance. "This is my brother Theodore, my lord."

Lucian offered his hand to shake, to the boy's obvious surprise and pleasure. "Do I conclude correctly that you have an interest in chemistry, Mr. Caldwell?"

"Very much, sir."

"I am acquainted with a number of members of the Royal Society," Lucian commented casually, referring to the exclusive club of the country's premier scientists. "And I had the pleasure of attending a lecture at the Royal Institution by Mr. John Dalton earlier this year."

The boy's eyes widened. "Do you *know* Mr. Dalton, sir?"

"I have the honor of being one of his patrons. He wrote *A New System of Chemical Philosophy*."

"Yes! It regards the weight of atoms. I have been attempting to isolate one of the elements he discovered—" The youth flushed and fell silent, evidently flustered by his loquaciousness.

"Mr. Dalton is my brother's hero," Brynn interjected. "Theo practically sleeps with that book under his pillow."

"Then perhaps you would like to meet him," Lucian suggested. "That could easily be arranged when you next come to London."

Theo's expressive face had brightened with anticipation, but then fell just as swiftly. "I will not be able to come to London, sir."

Lucian met Brynn's glance and discovered her

frowning at him. "Perhaps in future you may. Would you permit me to speak to your sister alone?"

"Yes, my lord, certainly," Theo responded without even waiting for his sister's permission.

Brynn held her tongue until the boy had gone before fixing a stern gaze on Lucian. "It is cruel to raise his hopes that way when you have no intention of fulfilling them."

"What makes you think I won't fulfill them?"

"I cannot credit a man like you would concern yourself with a boy you don't even know."

Lucian answered mildly. "Your protectiveness toward your brother is admirable, Miss Caldwell, but I assure you, I am not making idle promises. Theodore seems extremely bright, and Dalton would be pleased to know he has a devoted admirer—and to encourage the boy's interest in chemistry."

Her expressive eyes turned troubled. "Even so, we don't have the funds to afford a trip to London."

"Circumstances can change," he said cryptically. "Tell me," Lucian added before she could reply, "has Theodore always been bookish?"

The question seemed to distract her, for her expression softened. "Always. It takes an exerted effort to lure him out-of-doors for a few moments each day. I don't think it healthy that he locks himself away in a dark chamber with all those fumes and odors. But for some reason Theo finds his experiments fascinating."

"I imagine it isn't easy tutoring him in subjects that are beyond your ken."

The slight flush on her cheeks was charming. "I do wish I were better equipped to teach him. We had to let our longtime governess go several years ago, and are not able to hire genuine tutors or send Theo to school as he would like."

"He truly is eager to attend school?" Lucian asked, amused. "He must be a boy in a million."

"He is," she agreed with evident pride. "His greatest ambition is to become a scientist. He hopes someday to attend Cambridge to study chemistry."

"Actually, that could be arranged."

Her impatient look returned. "You are suggesting I believe in pipe dreams?"

"What if it were not a pipe dream? What if I were willing to fund your brother's education entirely?"

She stared at him, suddenly wary once more. "What is your price?" she said finally.

"Must there be a price?"

"With you, I don't doubt it, my lord. You have stooped to using extortion twice before—both times we've met, in fact. I am not so green as to believe your interest in aiding my brother stems purely from altruism. You would expect something in exchange for your generosity, surely."

Lucian winced wryly at her poor opinion of his character, even though he couldn't dispute her point about their encounters thus far. "Very well, if you prefer bluntness, my sweet firebrand . . . the price of my generosity is your hand in marriage."

She backed up a step, clearly shocked.

Her retreat brought out the primitive male urge to chase fleeing prey in Lucian, but he forced himself to remain still, to keep his expression bland.

"You needn't look as if I have suddenly sprouted horns, Miss Caldwell. I am asking you to marry me."

"Marry you?" Her voice was breathless. "Why ever would you wish that?"

"Because I find myself at the point in life that I must wed and produce an heir," he answered, almost truthful.

"But why *me*?"

"You don't know?" His gaze swept her appreciatively, from her vibrant, momentarily tamed tresses, to her brilliant green eyes and lush mouth, her full, tempting breasts, her empire-waist gown that hid an enticing figure and slender, lithe legs. . . . "You have only to look in a mirror to have your answer."

She shook her head in exasperated denial. "I explained all that, my lord. The attraction you feel isn't real."

Lucian felt himself biting back a smile. The waves of attraction thrumming through him were *very* real. So was the heat, the lust he felt for her.

"I sincerely dispute that. It's true I find your beauty alluring, but you have any number of attributes that are just as appealing. Intelligence and wit, for instance. And I've seen how you care for your brother. You would make a good mother, I think."

Her exasperation only increased. "You have concluded that after, what? Three brief encounters?"

It did seem strange, his conviction that she was the bride he had been searching for. He had only just met her. Yet intuitively he knew a great deal about her. She had a fiery passion that could stir his blood. Doubtless she could be taught to be an exceptional lover. "Call it instinct, if you will."

"I think your instincts have utterly failed you. There are countless reasons we would not suit. For one thing, I am not at all the sort to make a good countess."

"Why do you say so?"

"Because I am not easy in society. I am known as a recluse. And I am indeed a bluestocking, just as you accused me of being. I am considered unconventional, even ungenteel. I regularly help my brother—" She stopped herself, apparently reconsidering her admission.

"Those are crimes indeed," he murmured.

Her chin rose at the teasing note in his voice. "Laugh if you will, my lord, but I assure you, I would not make you a comfortable wife."

No, *comfortable* was not a word he would use to describe her, nor, come to think of it, was *wife*. Rather she was like a prize courtesan, one who made him think of tumbled silk sheets, of hot, exquisite wildness. He had only to look at her and he wanted to stir that wildness.

"I am not interested in comfort . . ." Lucian began, then caught himself. "Or if I am, it's an entirely different sort of comfort. I think you'll suffice on that score. I've kissed you—more than once. I have no doubt you could make a satisfactory bed partner."

Her ivory cheeks took on a becoming flush, although she didn't seem to have a ready answer. Finally she adopted a look of cool indifference. "I should think you would want a chaste bride, Lord Wycliff. If so, you will be disappointed in me. I have a well-earned reputation for promiscuity."

He fixed his gaze on her mouth, remembering the luscious taste of it, the innocence. "Somehow I think you are stretching the truth again."

Her flush deepened. "Well, it is not stretching the truth to say I don't wish to have you for my husband. I have no desire to wed a libertine."

"I think you'll find my reputation highly exaggerated."

"You are a founding member of the Hellfire League, are you not? A band of noblemen notorious for their scandalous exploits."

"I engaged in a few scandals in my reckless youth, I admit, but my exploits have been far tamer in recent years."

"Forgive me if I find that hard to credit," she said tartly.

"I can provide you with countless character references, if you wish," Lucian answered, unable to stem his amusement.

"No doubt."

Taking a measured breath, she regarded him with a frown, as if searching her mind for other arguments to use against him. "I understand that you make your home in London. I am not fond of London."

"Have you even been there?"

"Twice. Although it was a number of years ago," she added reluctantly, as if compelled to be strictly honest.

"Twice isn't sufficient for a fair test."

"Perhaps not, but I like living in the country."

"My family seat is in Devonshire and is charmingly bucolic."

"I prefer Cornwall, the sea. . . ."

"I have a castle in Wales with a spectacular view of the sea."

She pressed her lips together, as if striving for control, which merely made him want to shake it loose. He wanted to slide his hands around her waist and bury his mouth against hers, to explore her, to seek out all the enticing places where her silky, delicate heat flared and burned.

"Well, none of this is to the point," Brynn said finally. "I cannot wed you because I cannot leave here. I will not abandon Theo."

"But if he were to go away to school? Eton, Harrow, Westminster?"

There was a moment of prolonged silence. He could tell by the sudden tilt of her chin that he had struck a nerve.

"That is exceedingly underhanded of you," she said at last, her frustration evident, "to offer such a bribe."

"It is exceedingly common, as well as practical," he contradicted gently. "Particularly for a lady in your circumstances. Marriage in exchange for a fortune and title."

"I am not interested in either."

"You cannot be happy living in genteel poverty."

"I *can*, my lord. I am."

"Your older brother, Grayson, apparently doesn't share your view. He seemed highly interested at the prospect of a generous marriage settlement."

Her eyes flashing with pride, she locked gazes with him. "You think you can *purchase* me, Lord Wycliff? As if I were a broodmare?"

"I had in mind a more honorable position than broodmare," Lucian replied mildly. "That of wife and countess. Most ladies would be flattered by my proposal."

"Then ask one of them."

When he made no response, she took a deep breath. "I thank you for the honor you do me, my lord, but I will not marry you."

Determined not to accept her refusal, Lucian moved toward her. For a moment she looked as if she might bolt, but she stood her ground, even when he took her hand. Yet she was clearly discomposed when he turned her palm over and raised it to his lips, placing a kiss on the sensitive skin of her wrist.

Lucian was gratified to feel her shiver.

"You will want more time to consider my proposal," he murmured, deliberately holding her green gaze.

"I . . . I do not *need* more time. I have given you my answer."

"I still have hopes of persuading you. I will call tomorrow, my sweet. Perhaps by then you will have had a change of heart."

Brynn watched him walk away, torn between disbelief on the one hand, dismay on the other.

His supreme confidence vexed her. It vexed her more that she was so susceptible to his practiced touch. Wycliff was a rake, a man notorious for bending women to his whim. A devil whose sensuality was so potent it was almost a visible force.

She should be able to resist such blatant manipulation. Yet that hadn't stopped the warmth that suffused her body the moment his lips touched her skin, or quelled the longing that had risen in her at the seductive look in his compelling blue eyes. He thought he could vanquish her with the rapier-sharp edge of his rakish charm. Oh, he was arrogant and infuriating. . . .

And yet he could afford to be confident of victory. He held the upper hand and he knew it. If he truly meant to fund Theo's schooling . . .

With a murmur of distress, Brynn sat down on the bench and pressed her hands to her flushed cheeks. She was still in shock over his proposal.

She didn't plan to marry. It simply wasn't worth the risk. She had always known she was different, that her future was not her own. For as long as she could remember, she'd been warned of the danger of falling in love. Not danger to herself but to the man she cared for.

The women of your house will be forever cursed for their beauty. Any man they love will die.

She hadn't wanted to believe in the curse, but there were simply too many macabre incidents over too many generations to doubt its validity.

Her mother had suffered its terrible power. Gwendolyn Caldwell had lost her first betrothed to a bizarre accident—a bolt of lightning on a nearly cloudless day. Vowing never to love again, she subsequently married Brynn's father, bore him six children, and died in childbirth, leaving her twelve-year-old daughter to raise the baby.

Brynn had clearly inherited her ancestor's flame-haired beauty and, apparently, the same legendary allure. But after her mother died, she had disregarded the warnings and developed a girlish infatuation for the first young gentleman to seriously court her. When he'd drowned at sea, she had finally learned to accept her fate.

Afterward she'd gone to great lengths to avoid attracting men. Taming her vivid tresses. Dressing modestly—even primly. Hiding her dangerous allure. Remaining at home, out of the public eye, living an almost reclusive existence. Embracing being shunned. She'd encouraged belief in the curse and her reputation as a danger because it kept potential suitors at bay.

She didn't want suitors. Didn't want gentlemen she scarcely knew losing their heads over her, declaring their undying affection. She could never reciprocate their feelings. She didn't dare accept their suit, for fear of what might happen. It was better not to risk the tragic consequences.

If there were times when she regretted her bleak future, when she felt achingly lonely at facing the prospect of a loveless existence, well then, she had only to recall her own tragedy to be reminded of the stakes. She could never fall in love. Never.

In any event, she was quite happy with her life, Brynn told herself frequently. She had no time for loneliness, no room for such vulnerability. No patience for suffering the dazed, spellbound beaus who pursued her. All her efforts were directed toward tutoring her youngest brother and helping her oldest brother save their family from dire penury—by smuggling and marketing contraband.

Brynn took a deep breath. Fortunately she had stopped herself from divulging her involvement in the Free Trade to Wycliff. She couldn't expose their illicit activities to an outsider who might not understand, a powerful noble who could make trouble for them.

The immediate trouble now, however, was how to deal with her latest unwanted suitor.

Brynn shivered, remembering the heated look in the earl's eyes. He claimed to want her for his wife. And underneath that irresistible, sophisticated charm, she sensed a determination that was deadly serious—and possibly deadly as well.

Just this morning she had dreamed of Wycliff, of his death. Even if she wanted to accept his proposal of marriage, she couldn't simply ignore her dark premonition, could she?

Chapter Four

Brynn couldn't simply ignore Lord Wycliff's proposal either, for Gray questioned her about it that evening after dinner. Theo, as usual, had escaped to his dungeon directly following the sweets, leaving his older brother and sister alone in the smaller dining room close to the kitchen, where they took their meals these days to save work for their few servants.

Brynn could see Gray eyeing her speculatively, as if preparing his thoughts for a discussion beyond the polite small talk that had pervaded dinner. Fearing the subject matter, she sipped her wine and waited. Silence reigned.

Meals were much quieter now without their three other brothers at home. Arthur and Stephen, two years and three younger than Brynn respectively, had joined the Royal Navy shortly before their father perished and their finances plunged so drastically. And last year eighteen-year-old Reese had set out to make his fortune in the merchant marine.

Thus far, of all the brothers, Reese had suffered the most from their father's disastrous investments. There had been no money for him to purchase a naval commission or even attend university, as the older boys had done. Not that that dismayed Reese, however, since he was the least studious of all the brothers. But Theo would be devastated to be denied the opportunity—

"Brynn?"

She gave a start at having her distracted thoughts interrupted.

Gray smiled faintly. "It is not like you to be woolgathering so deeply that you fail even to hear me."

"I'm sorry. What did you say?"

"I asked you twice what answer you gave Wycliff."

She winced as Gray finally introduced the subject she dreaded. "I refused him, of course."

"Did you even give his proposal consideration? Wycliff is one of the most eligible bachelors in England."

"Perhaps so, but I have no interest in marrying him."

"Why not?"

"There are a dozen reasons."

Grayson's jaw tightened, but for a moment he merely regarded her silently over his wineglass. When at last he spoke, his voice held an unusual edge of bitterness. "You might think of your family before you blithely throw away this opportunity to deliver us from debt."

The unfairness of the accusation made Brynn catch her breath. She opened her mouth to respond, but Gray began a strange tirade, all the more forceful for its quiet delivery.

"I for one am tired of scraping for a living, Brynn.

This house is falling down around our ears because we cannot afford repairs. I can barely manage to keep up the fishing ketch and pay the crew, which is our sole livelihood. We owe enormous sums. The moneylender is pressing for repayment of his loans, issuing veiled threats. . . . I could be tossed into debtors' prison at any moment."

Brynn bit her tongue. There was no point in reminding Gray that she was doing her best to help him repay their loans. She understood his desperation. The humiliation of being so deeply in hock, of having to sell precious family heirlooms and dismiss beloved employees. The guilt of being unable to provide for his family. The gnawing worry, wondering how to ensure their survival from day to day.

And Gray had made his share of sacrifices. Most hurtfully, he'd had to abandon his own marital aspirations and watch the young lady he admired wed another gentleman.

"I have turned down other proposals," Brynn said when he was through, "and you never objected before."

"None were as advantageous as this. You will not find a better catch than Wycliff."

"You make it sound as if he were a fish."

Grayson only scowled at her lame attempt at humor.

"You know very well," Brynn pointed out, "that I cannot leave Theo. At least not until his future is secure."

"His future would be thoroughly secure if you married Wycliff. He has offered to fund Theo's schooling. We could hire the best possible tutors or send him to school— Faith, Wycliff is wealthy enough to buy an entire school, for that matter. And you would no longer have to play at being a governess."

That stung, considering the effort she had put into teaching her youngest brother. Brynn drew a steadying breath, willing herself to patience. "I'm not certain Theo is ready to attend school. Boys there can be so cruel."

"Perhaps, but it could be the making of him. He is far too studious as it is. And you cannot keep him sheltered his entire life, the way you've done thus far."

Brynn looked down at her glass. They had frequently argued about her overprotectiveness. She was as watchful of Theo as any mother could be, since she had raised him from his first breath.

"It is easy for you to advocate my wedding Wycliff," Brynn said quietly. "You are not the one who would have to become his wife."

Gray surveyed her with all seriousness. "He seems like an amiable enough sort. And I doubt you find his appeal objectionable, considering how the ladies swoon over him."

"His appeal is a large part of the problem, Gray. I . . . I dreamed about him last night. I saw him dying."

Her brother stared at her. "Perhaps it is only a coincidence."

"You know very well it is not. I don't want the responsibility of causing his death. I couldn't bear the guilt."

"Merely because you wed him doesn't mean you would cause his death. You would simply have to discipline yourself not to develop any affection for him."

That might be easier said than done, Brynn thought darkly. The attraction she felt for Wycliff already was nigh irresistible. "I am not willing to take the risk."

"He seems willing enough."

"I know. He scoffed when I warned him what could happen." She made a sound of frustration. "Why can't he simply believe me? If not for the curse, he would not even be pursuing me. Certainly he would never have proposed *marriage*. He knows nothing about me, nothing about our illicit activities. I doubt he would want a Free Trader for his countess if he knew the truth. But I didn't think it wise to reveal my involvement."

"No, that would have indeed been unwise," Gray agreed, frowning. "I learned only today that Wycliff works for the Foreign Office."

"What do you mean, *works*?"

"He is employed by the British government."

Her eyebrows rose in surprise. "Why would a nobleman with his reputed fortune need employment?"

"I hardly think he needs it," Grayson retorted. "And I have no idea why. For the challenge of it, I presume. Whatever the reason, he is quite powerful in government circles. He's not someone I would like to thwart."

"Well, his sense of power is another thing I find maddening. He very much enjoys throwing his weight around. I've rarely met a man so arrogant. He thinks he can simply command me to wed him and I will eagerly obey."

Gray eyed her with a hint of sympathy. "I can understand that your pride would be offended. Mine is as well. But you cannot forget how dire our situation is."

Chagrined by his gentle tone, Brynn bit her lip. Pride had always been one of her chief faults, and it was humiliating to have to swallow it. She hated being so powerless, so dependent on someone else's whims. "I have not forgotten our situation. But I resent his lordship's presumption that his wealth can buy my submission. He thinks he simply can purchase me to bear his children. I am not for sale."

"He wants sons, Brynn. What man does not?"

She remained stubbornly silent.

"Are you saying that you don't want children of your own?"

She earnestly wanted children of her own, but she had resigned herself to a barren life, telling herself she would be content devoting herself to raising Theo. "No, I am not saying that. But I certainly don't want them to be sired by Wycliff. Just think how I would feel if I murdered my own children's father."

"I expect you could manage to avoid murder," Gray said dryly.

"This is hardly a joking matter, Grayson!"

"Of course it isn't. I'm sorry." When she remained silent, he spoke again. "Did you consider that once we are free of debt, I will no longer have to engage in smuggling? Nor would Theo."

That made Brynn sit up. "You would stop taking him out with you?"

"Yes, of course. You know very well I pressed

him into service only because I needed help managing my crews with all our brothers gone. And it is better to learn the trade at a young age. But I cannot give up our one source of income until I settle our debts." Gray held her gaze steadily. "I thought that keeping Theo from the Free Trade was your most earnest desire."

"Of course it is. I don't want him to have anything to do with smuggling, or the sea. He isn't cut out for such physical danger. He becomes ill every time you take him out—"

Gray cut short her familiar diatribe. "Then you should be grateful to Wycliff for the chance to spare Theo the danger."

Perhaps she should indeed be grateful, Brynn acknowledged. "You truly think I should marry Wycliff?"

"Yes. For Theo's sake if nothing else."

Brynn felt despair well up inside her as she realized the truth of her brother's quiet pronouncement. "Very well, I will consider it."

She pushed back her chair and rose abruptly to her feet, needing to be alone. Without another word, she left the room.

When she reached her bedchamber, she shut the door and went to one of the windows that overlooked the coast. A sense of desperation tightened her chest as she stared out beyond the rocky shoreline to the sea.

Was Gray right? Should she wed Lord Wycliff? Did she dare take the risk?

Unable to remain still, Brynn turned to pace the floor. Wycliff was clearly anything but a gentleman when it came to winning what he wanted, dangling a generous marriage settlement in front of her to compel her acceptance. But he was the last man on earth she should ever marry.

If she were to take a husband, she should choose someone the absolute opposite of him. A quiet mouse of a man for whom she felt no attraction, not someone who stirred her blood with merely a glance. There would be no danger of falling in love then. . . .

Her jaw clenching, Brynn went to her dressing table and brought out her jewel case, which held only a few inexpensive trinkets and one extremely valuable piece. Withdrawing the locket that had been passed down to her from her ancestor, she opened the clasp to reveal a miniature portrait of Lady Eleanor Stanhope—Flaming Nell—the legendary temptress who centuries before had driven men mad with her alluring features and fiery hair and who had been cursed for her profligate sins.

Not for the first time did Brynn wish her ravishing relative could have tempered her wanton behavior and avoided causing her female descendants such grief. But there was no escaping the curse. Wycliff, despite his skepticism, had become so entangled in it, he was disregarding her every objection, all her warnings, in his determination to coerce her into marriage.

Brynn's fist closed tightly over the locket, pressing the gold filigree painfully into her palm. She desperately wished there were someone she could talk to, someone other than Grayson, who had a vital interest in her compliance.

Her mother would have been adamant about her

refusing Wycliff's suit, Brynn knew. But what would Esmerelda advise?

The elderly Gypsy woman was a descendant of the curse's original creator. For the past century her small band had been allowed to camp on the Caldwell estate when they visited the district, in hopes of making amends for Flaming Nell's offense.

When Brynn's first suitor died, she'd gone to Esmerelda to interpret her dark dreams. The Gypsy's cryptic insights had proved both confusing and contradictory, but Brynn had come away with the firm conviction that she was to blame for her suitor's death.

She couldn't consult the old woman this time, however, for she had no idea where to find her. Her band roamed the south of England from Cornwall all the way to London.

Closing the locket, Brynn returned the piece to the jewel case. Perhaps she was mistaken. Perhaps her troubling dream of Wycliff didn't mean he would actually die, but was merely a warning that she had to take care. If so . . .

She didn't want to agree to his marriage proposal, yet did she really have a choice? If she wed Wycliff, she could free Grayson of the threat of debtors' prison. Moreover, Theo would have the education he'd always wanted, the future she'd always hoped for him. If not, he would remain under her inadequate tutelage at home, where his life would be at risk. He would be sucked into the dangerous underworld of smuggling.

Torn by her conscience, Brynn squeezed her eyes shut. For her beloved brother's sake, she would have to concede. She would have to become Wycliff's countess, bear him a son. Sweet heaven.

Opening her eyes, she lifted her chin with grim determination. Very well, she would wed him. She would give Lord Wycliff the heir he wanted in exchange for a marriage settlement that would put paid to her family's debts.

Yet caution was imperative. She would have the responsibility for saving Wycliff from his lust, and from her own. Most critically, she would have to prevent any affection whatsoever from forming between them.

She could manage that, Brynn fervently hoped, drawing a deep breath. She only prayed he wouldn't come to regret entering into such a dangerous union.

Chapter Five

Brynn formally received Lord Wycliff in the drawing room the following afternoon. If she thought to postpone the issue of his marriage proposal, however, she was doomed to disappointment, for he came straight to the point.

"May I hope you have reconsidered my offer?"

"Yes," she replied stiffly. "You know very well that for my family's sake, I cannot afford to refuse."

"Then you consent to become my wife?"

"Yes."

"I am honored," Wycliff said pleasantly, as if he had never doubted her answer.

Brynn felt her frustration return at his certitude. She took a steadying breath, knowing she had to attempt once more to persuade him of the danger he faced in wedding her. "Truthfully, I don't *wish* to honor you, my lord. I would prefer to make you see reason. You would be much wiser to withdraw your suit before it is too late."

"I want a son, Miss Caldwell. A legitimate heir. Unfortunately that requires I wed someone of the female persuasion. Preferably a lady."

"But it needn't be *me*. By all reports, you could have any woman you want."

"I want you. I thought I had made that perfectly clear." The slow half smile that shadowed his mouth was meant to disarm her, but Brynn refused to be disarmed. His attempts to charm her could be fatal.

"And I," she retorted, "made it perfectly clear, my lord, that your lusts are irrational."

"Since we are soon to be wed, surely we needn't be so formal. My name is Lucian."

She stared fixedly at him. "Lucifer, did you say?"

A hint of amusement lit his eyes. "I have been called worse."

Brynn raised her gaze to the ceiling, summoning patience. "I wish I could make you understand the danger of the curse."

"Lamentably, I am not the superstitious sort."

"Perhaps not, but there is proof. If you don't believe me, you should examine the church records. Nearly every generation of women in my family has faced a tragedy in love."

"So you said. But I expect those tragedies can be explained by mere coincidence."

"You dream about me, don't you?"

The expression on Wycliff's face suddenly turned enigmatic, and Brynn could see she had struck a nerve. "Your dreams are not mere coincidence, I assure you. I haunt men's dreams, as did my other female ancestors."

He glanced across the drawing room at a portrait hanging on the wall. "Is that a relation of yours?" The portrait was of an elegant woman with auburn hair and a look of sadness in her dark eyes.

"That was my mother."

"She is very beautiful. It would not have taken a curse to make men dream about her, or even to lose their heads over her."

Clenching her hands together, Brynn exhaled slowly. She was obviously not going to persuade Wycliff. "Very well, ignore the danger, if you will, but don't expect me to. My first suitor died because I showed a partiality toward him, and I cannot allow that to happen again. I won't have your death on my conscience. Ours must be a marriage of convenience, nothing more."

Wycliff hesitated a moment. "A marriage of convenience would be perfectly acceptable on my part," he said lightly. "I am not interested in a love match. I only want a son. But I won't be ruled by fear, either, siren. I am not afraid of your developing a partiality for me."

"But don't you see—"

He held up a hand, forestalling further argument. "I consider myself warned and absolve you of any responsibility."

His easy smile was meant to take the sting out of his dismissive words, but she wasn't mollified. Nor was she pleased when he abruptly changed the subject.

"Now then, perhaps we should discuss our upcoming nuptials. Do you object to marrying by special license?"

It was Brynn's turn to frown. "A special license? It is usual to be married in a church."

"The ceremony can still be held in church. I

prefer not to wait for the banns to be read. I thought Friday next a good date. Six days from now."

"Six days!" Brynn's mouth dropped open as she regarded him in dismay.

"That should allow me sufficient time to send to London for a special license."

"Surely there is no reason for such haste!"

"Regrettably I cannot afford the time away from my pressing affairs."

"An appointment with your tailor, no doubt?"

She saw his eyes narrow momentarily at her barb, but she didn't apologize. She already resented Wycliff's high-handedness, and a dashed, slipshod wedding was one more mark against him.

"A rushed union will only seem rash and give rise to gossip," Brynn pointed out.

"I expect my consequence is great enough to ward off most gossip. Earls are generally accorded more license in bending the rules."

"More than mere mortals, you mean?"

Not responding directly to her tart tone, he rose gracefully to his feet. "Does sea travel make you ill?"

"No. Why do you ask?"

"I came to Cornwall by sea. My yacht is docked at Falmouth. I thought we would return to London that way, since sailing will be faster than traveling by coach, and more comfortable as well."

Brynn felt a surge of panic rise in her at the realization that she would have to travel with Wycliff. Sweet heaven, she would soon become his *wife*. Their marriage was truly going forward.

"Are you agreeable to sailing?" he prodded when she sat silent.

"Either way makes no difference," she murmured, her thoughts distracted.

"Very well." Moving to stand before her, Wycliff reclaimed her attention by reaching down for her hand. Holding her gaze, he brought her fingers to his lips, totally unsettling her composure.

Brynn snatched her hand away, feeling the sensual tingling of her skin.

"Forgive me for leaving you so abruptly," he murmured, "but I should see to the details of our nuptials."

"I don't mind in the least if you go," she declared. "Indeed, the less I see of you the better."

His lashes lowered slightly over his blue eyes as he studied her. "It does not bode well, sweet, for our marital bliss if we are constantly doing verbal battle."

"That presumes marital bliss a worthy goal," Brynn returned coolly. "I told you, I have no interest in a blissful union. A discordant marriage will be much safer for you."

"But not nearly as pleasant," he returned smoothly.

"I will not fall for your practiced charm, my lord Wycliff," Brynn said stubbornly. "You cannot make me succumb."

His beautiful mouth eased into that potent, masculine half smile she was coming to know. "I see I will have to enlist all my powers of persuasion to convince you differently. I must confess," Wycliff added in a wicked murmur, "I look forward to the challenge."

The following six days passed with deadly swiftness. Brynn alternated between dread of her upcoming nuptials and attempting to convince herself that she had exaggerated the possible danger.

The arrogant Lord Wycliff was constantly underfoot at Caldwell House, putting himself out to be charming. By the time the wedding grew close, he had won over both her youngest and oldest brothers.

Theo was eating out of his hand and suffering a severe case of hero worship, in part because Wycliff willingly spent time in the boy's precious laboratory. Even Grayson seemed at ease, despite his humiliation of needing the earl's generous settlement.

Only Brynn refused to relent. She had to maintain a strict aloofness from Wycliff. She couldn't allow any amount of devilish charm or seductive smiles to sway her or to penetrate her defenses.

Although required by the conventions of courtship to suffer his company, she made every effort to avoid being alone with him. In his presence, she endured his admiring, brilliant gaze with as much fortitude as she could muster, pretending to function in a rational way. When he was away, she tried to block from her mind any thought of him or what their impending union would bring.

At least there was one advantage of wedding in such haste, she discovered. Between arranging the details of the service, settling her youngest brother's future, and preparing to totally uproot her life, she had less time to worry.

And just possibly her concern was inflated out of proportion. The women in her family, Brynn reminded herself, could marry without disastrous consequence if they took care not to fall in love. And she was entering into a marriage of convenience, nothing more.

Moreover, her dark dream of Wycliff hadn't returned. Perhaps her feeling of impending doom was mere bridal nerves.

Lucian's dreams of Brynn, however, turned more vivid—visions of his death mingling with erotic images of their marriage bed. The unsettling dreams, along with the warnings he encountered about his future bride, did give him a moment's pause.

His elderly host, the Duke of Hennessy, reacted to the betrothal with surprising distress.

"It troubles me, Wycliff, that you chose Miss Caldwell when you could have countless other brides. There is a history in her family you should know about—"

"I'm aware of the tales," Lucian replied. "But I don't give them much credence. I confess surprise that you do."

His grace looked uncomfortable. "I am not superstitious as a general rule, but I knew her mother. In fact, I courted Gwendolyn myself once. I must say, I consider myself fortunate to have escaped. But if your mind is made up, I suppose I have no right to protest."

"My mind is made up," Lucian asserted.

The duke's genteel neighbors seemed just as disturbed by the news. They eyed Lucian with disbelief and whispered behind his back, although they didn't presume to express their opinions. The villagers, too, seemed dismayed by the turn of events. And Lucian's valet was concerned enough to venture his master's displeasure by relating tales he'd heard from the ducal servants. There were even veiled accusations about Brynn Caldwell being a witch.

Lucian, however, dismissed the tales and maintained his course. He didn't investigate the church records as Brynn had suggested, for he disliked bowing to superstition. And when his betrothed suggested once more that he withdraw his suit, that he still had time to change his mind, he shook off his misgivings.

He didn't believe in curses. He wanted Brynn Caldwell for his wife, and he wouldn't be intimidated into giving her up.

It felt magical, his skillful touch. His lips moved over her flushed face, her throat, her breasts, claiming her nipples, his mouth wet and warm. She arched her back, seeking his gentle torment. As if he understood her desperate need, his hand brushed her loins. She trembled, her flesh burning for him. . . .

Brynn awoke with a start, her body suffused with heat as the remnants of her erotic dream faded. Lucian—Lord Wycliff—had been kissing her, touching her, arousing her to passion.

She shivered in remembrance. Her dream bore no resemblance to her dark nightmare where she'd envisioned his death. This one had been lush, searing, strangely alluring. She could still feel a sweet throbbing between her thighs, still feel a yearning ache in her heart.

Surely her dream wasn't a premonition. She hadn't wed Wycliff yet—

Brynn sat up abruptly, realization dawning. This was her wedding day. She would soon be his bride. A feeling of panic curled inside her as she hugged the covers to her still throbbing breasts, wondering if she was making a terrible mistake.

She tried to put her dream from her mind and treat the day as any other, yet it was all Brynn could do to choke down a morsel of breakfast. Afterward, with the aid of their one maid, she bathed and donned her best gown of pale peach sarcenet.

As she stared at herself in the cheval glass, she bit her lip hard. She had slept poorly, and there were smudges of circles under her eyes, while her face seemed ghostly pale. Yet even her wan appearance didn't adequately show her turmoil.

A wedding day was supposed to be a special— perhaps sacred—time in a woman's life. But for her there would be no joy, no sweet anticipation. Only loneliness and dread.

Even had there been no risk involved in wedding Wycliff, this still was the end of her life as she knew it. Today she would leave behind her girlhood forever. More despairing to contemplate was that she would forsake her home and her family for good. Early tomorrow morning she would set sail with her new husband for London.

"Sweet mercy," she whispered to the insipid person in the mirror.

She was leaving behind everything she knew, everyone she held dear, to wed a stranger. Lamentably, she couldn't even say farewell to her three other brothers, Arthur and Stephen and Reese. None of them would be attending today's ceremony, for there had been no way to get word to their various ships in time, although it was doubtful they would have been able to obtain leave in any case.

Brynn felt a tightness in her throat. She wasn't certain which was worse: the pain of losing her family, or the prospect of spending a lifetime with a man she didn't dare love.

Either way, the irrevocable moment loomed. In less than an hour, Grayson would escort her to the village church, where the ceremony would be officiated by the vicar. The wedding "breakfast"—a feast funded by Wycliff, organized by the Duchess of Hennessy, and prepared by the duke's vast staff of servants—would follow immediately afterward and last most of the afternoon.

The wedding night would be spent at Caldwell House, rather than the duke's castle or Wycliff's ship. Gray had insisted on that detail for her own protection, a demand for which Brynn was grateful.

Until now she had shied away from contemplating exactly what the physical intimacy of marriage would entail, but despite Wycliff's vaunted prowess with the female sex, he was a man like any other. Under the influence of the Gypsy's spell, he might very well let his passions become carried away and require restraint. She felt safer, knowing she could call on her brother should things get out of hand. But she would still have to face her own apprehension about sexual matters—

A quiet rap on her door interrupted her distressing thoughts. It was Theo, wearing his best jacket, which he had long outgrown. His gangly wrists stuck out a good two inches below the sleeves.

His mouth formed an O when he caught sight of her. "You look so beautiful, Brynn."

"I think you must be a trifle biased," she said, trying to strike a light tone as she stepped back to let him enter her bedchamber.

"I came to see if I might help you in any way . . . packing your trunks, perhaps."

She looked at her beloved youngest brother and had to smile. "Since when have you ever been interested in such trifling corporeal matters as packing? If so, I am honored that you plan to bring your head down from the clouds for my sake."

Theo grinned, a grin that slowly faded. "Well, actually I . . . I came because I wanted to give you something." He opened his hand to reveal a small vial of yellowish liquid. "I've made you a potion. Perhaps it will help to ward off the curse."

Accepting the vial, Brynn unplugged the stopper and grimaced at the pungent odor that assaulted her nostrils. "What in heaven's name is in this? Bat's wing and toad's tongue?"

"Only a few chemicals. You should wear it like perfume. I don't believe it will burn your skin."

"I am vastly relieved," Brynn said wryly. "Thank you, darling. This should indeed ward off anyone who decides to become overamorous. Even Wycliff. He doesn't believe in the Gypsy's curse, but if nothing else, I can pour it over him."

"It isn't wise to ignore such things," Theo said seriously. "There are some phenomena even science cannot explain."

Brynn thought her brother would take his leave then, but his face grew even more solemn. "Brynn . . . I know you are doing this for my sake . . . marrying his lordship so I can attend school. And I . . . I want you to know how grateful I am."

"Don't be silly," she said, forcing the words past the sudden ache in her throat. "I've always fancied myself as a countess."

Theo gave her a reproving glance. "You always taught me not to tell plumpers."

"So I did." She feigned a smile. "Don't mind me, love. I'm the one who is being silly. I suppose I am suffering from bridal nerves. They are quite common, I understand."

"Well, if you must marry, I think Wycliff is a good choice. He seems a capital fellow."

"You only say so"—Brynn tried to feign a teasing tone—"because he has bribed you with promises of fresh supplies for your laboratory."

"He has also promised that I may visit you in London on my first holiday from school. Is that all right with you?" Theo had chosen to attend Harrow and would soon be leaving for the start of the term.

"Of course it is all right! I would like nothing better than to see you," she said fervently. "I am sure to be lonesome in London. I know no one there except Meredith, and she repaired to her husband's country seat for her confinement. Even when she returns, she will doubtless be busy with her new baby."

The look her young brother gave her held wisdom far beyond his age. "I don't want you to be sad, Brynn."

She swallowed hard. "I won't be sad in the least. Not if I know you are happy."

Gathering Theo to her, she gave him a fierce hug, unmindful of her gown. Yet she could feel the tears threatening.

With fierce determination she compelled herself to release him and step back. "Now go away," she scolded, "and let me finish dressing in peace. It would be ill-bred to be late for my own wedding."

Fearing she would break down, she pressed a motherly kiss on his brow and ushered Theo forcefully out the door.

Shutting the door behind him, Brynn pressed her forehead against the oak panel, trying desperately to hold back tears. After a moment, she managed to regain control of herself. She would *not* wallow in self-pity. She had made the decision to wed Wycliff for her family's sake, and she would have to live with it.

Lifting her chin, she took a steadying breath, grateful for the cold sense of resignation that crept over her as she turned to finish dressing.

Even so, the numbing chill couldn't deaden the pain in her heart at leaving the family she loved, or the dread she felt about the future.

Chapter Six

The church was filled to overflowing. Many of the attendees were friends and well-wishers. Some were merely curiosity seekers, eager to see a peer of such exalted rank take a bride of such dangerous repute. All of the guests, Brynn reflected as she stood before the vicar with her intended husband, doubtless believed she had enticed the Earl of Wycliff into matrimony with her unnatural powers.

As the ceremony progressed, she avoided even glancing at her tall, wickedly handsome groom. It was safer not to look into vivid blue eyes that were the same hue as his superbly fitting coat, or to contemplate how his pristine, intricately tied cravat set off his striking, aristocratic features. Yet she knew every woman present felt a spark of envy.

At that moment, Brynn would have gladly exchanged places with any one of them. She listened with growing dismay to the vicar intoning words that were ancient and binding. She was being joined in holy matrimony to a stranger.

Brynn winced as Lord Wycliff slipped a gold band onto her finger, yet the enormity of their vows didn't truly sink in until her new husband lightly brushed her mouth with a kiss. His lips were cool, restrained, yet somehow scalding, and they drove home the finality of their union like a blow.

She had bound herself to this man forever, for better or worse. And it was very likely to be *worse*.

Unnerved, Brynn turned away, almost stumbling.

Wycliff's hand reached out to support her elbow, and for a moment her gaze locked with his. To her dismay, the burning look in his eyes held possessiveness, triumph.

With deliberate care, she extricated her arm from his grasp. "I truly hope," she whispered in a hoarse voice, "that you don't come to regret this day."

"I don't intend to," his lordship replied tranquilly, showing none of the inner turmoil she felt.

Her hand trembled as she signed the church register, cementing the marriage. Then, chastising herself for her cowardice, Brynn straightened her spine and plastered a smile on her lips as she accepted the seemingly endless good wishes of the guests.

The Duke of Hennessy's barouche carried the wedding party to Caldwell House, where a feast had been laid out on the terrace by the duke's vast army of servants. The wedding breakfast was torment for Brynn, for it seemed to last for hours. The July afternoon turned so warm, she felt light-headed, despite the cooling salt breeze that blew off the sea. It took all her willpower to serenely endure the countless toasts drunk in the bridal couple's honor, beginning with the aging duke's salute to his good friend Wycliff. The expensive champagne, along with everything else she managed to swallow, tasted like dust.

It was the night ahead, however, that loomed

threateningly in her mind. When the guests began to trickle away, Brynn felt her panic rising at the thought of the obligatory bedding.

As a rule, she didn't consider herself a coward, but she had to acknowledge that she feared the physical aspect of marriage. The concept of surrendering her body to a man—even her husband—felt alien to her. Indeed, she'd spent so much of her life avoiding men, resistance was second nature to her.

Wycliff could so easily become carried away. And what if she couldn't resist him? His mere touch affected her more than anyone else's had ever done. She could be a terrible danger to him if she fell for his practiced seduction.

The sun was low on the horizon when the duke and duchess took their leave, signaling the end of the festivities. Shortly, Brynn found herself sitting at the bridal table alone except for her new husband and her oldest brother. Theo had long since grown bored with the proceedings and escaped to his laboratory.

When Grayson rose to embrace her, Brynn had to fight against the ache of tears, knowing this might be one of the last times she would see him in a great while. She clung to him for an extra moment, drawing on his strength.

Gray kissed her cheek, then stepped back, his gaze fixed on Wycliff, his expression intent. "You will take care of my sister?" he asked, his tone solemn to the point of grimness.

"I won't harm her, I promise you," Wycliff answered easily.

Grayson shifted his gaze to Brynn, who stood

awkwardly beside her new husband. "If you need me, you have only to call."

She forced a smile. "I shall keep that in mind."

Giving her hand a reassuring squeeze, Gray pressed another kiss on her temple and took his leave.

"Your brother is quite protective of you," Wycliff remarked when they were alone.

"For good reason."

"I have no intention of ravishing you, Brynn."

"So you say," she muttered in a low voice. "I only hope you can remember your honorable intentions when the time comes."

Wycliff didn't respond to her obvious concern. Instead, to her surprise, he motioned to the man-servant who was hovering at the terrace doors.

"Thank you, Pendry," he said when the servant presented him with a slim, flat box.

He waited until they were alone again before handing the box to Brynn. "For you, my lady. A wedding gift," he said in response to her quizzical glance.

Brynn accepted the box warily and nearly gasped when she opened it. Inside was an exquisite array of emerald jewelry set in gold—necklace, bracelet, and ear bobs.

"Emeralds to match your beautiful eyes," Wycliff said softly.

She schooled her expression to indifference. If he thought he could breach her defenses by showering her with flattery and jewels, he was much mistaken.

"I do not want your bribes, my lord," she said stiffly, setting his gift on the table.

"My name is Lucian," he merely reminded her.

He glanced beyond the terrace toward the vast ocean sparkling golden in the distance. "It is a lovely evening, and much too early to retire. Why don't you go inside and put on a more comfortable gown? Something older that you don't mind getting soiled."

She stared at him. "Why?"

"I fancy taking a stroll along the shore."

Brynn considered asking if he'd taken leave of his senses, but she was more than willing to postpone the moment of reckoning as long as possible.

She did as she was bid, taking a great while to change out of her gown. She couldn't help noticing that her nightdress was laid out on the bed where she had slept for all of her twenty-four years. Brynn shivered, not wanting to think of the night to come.

When she made her way downstairs, her husband was waiting for her on the lower landing, holding a basket and what looked like several woolen blankets draped over his arm.

"Strawberries and champagne," he replied to her unspoken question.

"You mean to hold a *picnic* at this time of day?" she asked, her brows arching in astonishment.

"Something of the sort. I thought a private celebration was in order. And I hoped perhaps we might call a truce for the evening."

Brynn was uncertain quite how to respond. She didn't want a truce. Didn't want to let down her guard. Yet she made no protest when he took her hand and led her back to the terrace and across the lawn, toward the cliffs.

Beyond them, the sun was a red ball on the horizon, sheening the sea before them with golden fire. At the cliff's edge, Lucian paused for a moment, drinking in the sight. Brynn couldn't fault him for being spellbound; the view was magnificent.

They negotiated the narrow path down to the rocky shore. He was headed for her own private cove, she realized, not knowing whether to be more alarmed or dismayed. When he took her arm, offering unnecessary assistance, Brynn uneasily drew her arm away, although she refrained from pointing out that she could find her way blindfolded.

Near the rock pool where they'd met, he found a short stretch of sand, where he spread one of the blankets. When Brynn was seated, he fished in the basket and held up the bottle of champagne. "Would you care for a glass?"

"Yes, please," she replied, needing any courage spirits could give her to get through this evening.

He poured two glasses, then settled himself beside her on the blanket, stretching on his side, supported by his elbow. Defensively Brynn drew her knees up and sipped her wine in silence.

At least the setting was spectacular. The breeze had died to a gentle caress, while the timeless rhythm of the waves washing up on the rocky shore helped soothe her frayed nerves.

Lucian was the first to speak. "The warmth of the climate here never fails to surprise me."

"Yes," Brynn replied grudgingly. "This stretch of Cornwall is one of the most temperate in all of England. Palm trees grow here, and roses bloom even in December."

"I can testify that the most beautiful roses can be found here. I was fortunate to have discovered one."

He was looking directly up at her, Brynn realized, slanting him a glance. "Flattery will have no effect on me, my lord. I have no intention of falling for your practiced seduction, or becoming another of your legendary conquests."

"I don't think of you as a conquest, siren."

"No?"

"No. I think of you as my incredibly lovely bride."

Brynn winced. "Must I remind you, we agreed to a marriage of convenience? There is no need for you to try to charm me. I am willing to uphold my end of the bargain. As long as you provide for my brother's education, I am prepared to do my wifely duty."

His mouth curved in a slight smile. "I trust you will find our marriage bed a great deal more pleasant than mere duty."

Brynn pressed her own lips together, clamping down on the urge to retort, determined to hold herself aloof. When he offered a dish of strawberries, she declined.

Choosing one for himself, Lucian bit into the juicy fruit. "You seem willing to sacrifice a great deal for Theodore."

Her beloved brother was a subject she couldn't resist. "I would do anything for him," Brynn said fervently.

"There appears to be quite a gap in your ages."

She looked down at her glass. "My mother had difficulty after Reese was born. She was *enceinte* several times—" Brynn faltered, realizing the subject was too personal, and too immodest as well. "She died giving birth to Theo," she finished quietly.

"And you raised him? You could not have been much more than a child yourself."

"I was twelve. Old enough to care for him."

"Theo is fortunate to have you." When she didn't answer, Lucian's voice seemed to soften. "I always wanted a brother or sister. I was an only child."

Brynn deliberately hardened her heart. She didn't want to hear about her new husband's childhood, or anything else that would increase their intimacy. She couldn't allow her emotions to soften toward him. "You are laboring under the serious misapprehension, my lord, that I care to know anything about you."

He only responded mildly to her ungracious reply. "I did not bring you here to fight, sweeting."

"Why did you bring me here, then?"

"I thought you would feel more comfortable in your kingdom."

"More comfortable?"

"You've been ill at ease with me all day. Perhaps here, in a familiar setting, you will be less nervous about consummating our union."

Giving a start, Brynn turned her head to stare down at him. "You intend to consummate our marriage *here*?"

"Can you think of a better place?"

"Certainly I can! A bridal chamber is the usual setting for a consummation."

"But then our marriage is not exactly usual, is it? In fact, I would call it rather unique."

She drew a steadying breath, grasping for arguments to throw in his path. "Do you have any notion the scandal it would cause if we were seen? Or do you simply not care?"

"No one will see us. I intend to wait until it grows dark, of course."

It was nearly dusk now. Brynn took a deep gulp of champagne, hoping the sparkling wine would quell her agitation. "It will still be scandalous," she murmured.

"Not much more so than your swimming nearly nude in this very location."

She shook her head, feeling a bit desperate. It was one thing to swim here in privacy. It was quite another to purposely hold one's wedding night on a rocky beach. "Surely you do not expect me to undress here?"

"Why not? I've already seen a good deal of your body."

"It will be much too cold," she said lamely.

"I brought several blankets. And I will do my best to keep you warm."

He set the dish of strawberries aside and sat up, making Brynn tense. "I thought you would be more adventuresome than this, my sweet."

"I am not as adventuresome as all *that*."

A faint smile curved his mouth at her indignation. "I am your husband now, Brynn. Married women are permitted more freedom than young misses."

He paused. "Do you know what is supposed to happen between us?"

"I am not completely green. My closest friends are married, and one of them told me . . . generally what to expect."

"Then you know that carnal relations are necessary to conceiving a child."

She wondered why a child was so important to him, but she didn't dare ask and give him an opening for even more intimate confessions. "I am well aware of it, my lord."

"Lucian," he murmured. "Say my name, love."

"Lucian," she repeated reluctantly.

"That's better. Would you like more champagne?"

"Yes, please."

She was drinking too much, she knew, but she was not about to stop; she needed the courage if Wycliff meant to go through with his plan.

He refilled her glass, then proceeded to untie his cravat. "You have no cause for worry," he said, catching her look of dismay. "I have every intention of making your first experience pleasurable."

"Certainly I have cause for worry. You may not believe in the curse, but I have no doubt your obsession will only grow worse once we . . ."

"Become lovers?"

"Yes."

"I've always held the opinion that a curse has power only if you give it credence."

"Well then, you might consider my feelings. You obviously have a vast deal of experience, so you cannot understand my anxiety."

"Your virginal trepidation."

She bit her lip, knowing she was blushing. "Yes."

His compelling eyes held sympathy, tenderness, as did his low voice. "I don't expect I could fully understand, since I've never been a woman. But I promise you, the consummation won't be as disagreeable as you fear."

Stiffening, Brynn deliberately looked away. She would have no protection against Lucian whatever if she allowed him to seduce her with tenderness. "I am not interested in your promises, my lord. I agreed to share your bed, nothing more."

"Forgive me, love, but you agreed to be my wife."

She had no reply for that, for she had indeed agreed to be his wife. And to bear him a son. Which entailed sexual intimacy . . .

When Lucian shrugged out of his jacket, Brynn stiffened. His shirt followed, giving her a warm jolt of disturbing awareness. In the fading half-light, his torso was unexpectedly muscular, and made her surprisingly breathless.

"Could we not . . . put off the consummation for the time being? I scarcely know you."

His glance held disarming gentleness. "The sooner you put it behind you, the sooner you'll realize there is nothing to fear."

"I am not afraid, precisely. I simply don't want to be intimate with you."

"Why not? Is there something physical about me that you find disagreeable?"

"You know there is not. Not . . . physical."

"What, then?"

You make me feel far too vulnerable, she thought

to herself. "Your insufferable arrogance. You think all women should fall at your feet."

"I assure you, I don't think that at all." His voice was low, vibrant, stroking her like rich velvet.

When she didn't reply, he reached up to touch a curling tendril of hair that had escaped its severe knot. "Aren't you the least bit curious about the pleasures to be found in lovemaking? What it means to be fully a woman?"

"No, not in the least," she lied.

As if to disprove her claim, he shifted his hand to caress the shell of her ear with a fingertip. Brynn nearly flinched.

"Has your blood never turned hot at a man's touch?"

Only yours, she thought, biting her lower lip as his finger slowly trailed down the back of her neck.

"You won't find lovemaking unpleasant, I'll vow. At least not after the initial time. I think I can safely promise you will enjoy the physical side of marriage."

She wouldn't meet his gaze. And yet it was difficult to remain aloof when his fingertips were moving over her skin with such delectable pressure.

His hand continued caressing her nape. "May I take down your hair, Brynn? Please?"

She hesitated, vaguely disarmed by that "please." She would have liked to refuse him, but as her husband, he had that right. "If you wish."

"I wish very much." Rising partway, he knelt behind her and began to remove the pins from her hair. Brynn held her breath at his tender ministrations. She could smell the warm, clean, musky scent of his skin, feel the heat of his hard, elegant body at her back as he freed the heavy mass and let it fall. When his fingers curled slowly, possessively in her hair, she felt a dangerous softening inside her. His touch was so gentle, so incredibly arousing.

Then, wordlessly, he brushed her hair aside, smoothing the thick tresses over her shoulder, and began unfastening the buttons of her gown. Brynn went rigid. Moments later, she felt the hot, moist tip of his tongue trace the high curve of her spine, and she shivered. He was nuzzling her neck, his teeth strangely arousing against her flesh.

She remained frozen, aware of a disquieting pleasure that uncurled low in her stomach. His soft, persuasive lips continued to kiss her nape as he slid the neckline of her gown down over her shoulders to expose her corset. She could feel him loosening the hooks, feel the restrictive pressure ease. When he lowered the bodice of her chemise, her breasts spilled out.

"Lucian . . ." she protested.

"I like the sound of my name on your lips."

His hands slid around to cup her breasts, and she drew a sharp breath.

"There is no need for shyness between us, my lovely Brynn. Your body likes me touching you. See how your pulse has quickened . . . your nipples are taut. . . ."

His fingers closed around the tight buds, sending hot arrows of pleasure streaking through her, making her arch against the tormenting ache. "Do you like how that feels, Brynn? You will like the feel of my mouth even better. Let me taste your sweetness. . . ."

He took her glass from her and set it aside, then eased her back on the blanket. Brynn felt her senses swimming, her blood pounding thickly with the wine she'd drunk, as he bent over her. He kissed each nipple in turn, laving the swollen tips with his silk-rough tongue, suckling until she gave a breathless whimper. When he blew on a turgid peak that was still glistening from his mouth, she quivered at the erotic shock of it.

Holding her dazed gaze then, he sat back and unfastened the buttons of his breeches, drawing them down around his lean hips.

In the gathering darkness, her gaze locked on his naked loins. He was heavy and aroused. She was faintly shocked to see the huge shaft, pulsing and erect, between his sinewed thighs.

"It is only flesh, love. Touch me and see for yourself."

Taking her hand, he brought it to his groin, letting her explore at her own pace. Brynn swallowed her shock and touched him gingerly, feeling the warm, satiny flesh stretched over granite. He was very male, but not really so frightening. Experimentally, she closed her fingers around the rigid length, and he surprised her by giving a soft groan.

Brynn pulled back her hand at once. "Did that hurt?"

He gave a soft, husky laugh. "A very pleasurable hurt."

His eyes were hot as he bent over her again, but

this time instead of attending to her breasts, he took her mouth. She lay tense beneath him until he murmured against her lips, "Let me in, siren. Kiss me the way I'm kissing you. Give me your tongue."

She opened to him then, absorbing the slow, penetrating motion of his tongue in heated pulses, even as she felt a ripple of despair course through her. He was so very experienced, and she had no weapons to aid her in halting his sweet seduction. Against her will, she was being tantalized by his potent sensuality, his magical kisses.

When he gathered her closer against his aroused body, deepening his kiss, Brynn shuddered, helpless against the surge of warmth that enveloped her. A shivering desire began to grow inside her, tightening her nipples, her thighs, heating her every nerve ending. It was as if Lucian wove some strange spell around her, a spell she no longer wanted to escape. Her arms climbed upward to encircle his neck, and she gave in to the need to return his kiss.

As the tentative thrust of her tongue met his own, Lucian felt an emotion akin to triumph. It was beguiling, the innocence and enthusiasm in her untutored mouth, the excitement, the tender searching. He tangled his fingers in the rich fullness of her hair and drank of her sweetness, showing her how to respond, to give, to take.

She was making small sounds of pleasure deep in her throat when he slowly swept his hand down her body, pausing at the juncture of her thighs that was shielded by her muslin gown. When she stiffened instinctively, he caressed her soothingly.

"Let me touch you, sweeting," he murmured. "An aroused woman feels pleasure when she takes a man inside her body, but you must be ready to receive me. Let me arouse you, lovely Brynn."

In the darkness he could feel her questioning gaze searching his face. "I . . . don't think it's possible," she whispered thickly, "to be more aroused."

He buried his smile against her throat. "Oh, yes, it's possible. And it will be my great pleasure to show you."

She made no protest as he raised her skirts to bare her delicate flesh to the night air, and yet she tensed when he moved his palm along the warm satin of her inner thigh.

Wanting to distract her, Lucian lowered his mouth to her tantalizing breasts, suckling her again as he fingered the soft folds at her damp apex.

She was wet silk between her legs, her body already prepared for his taking. The realization made his shaft clench with savage need, yet he knew he had to take exquisite care in satisfying her for her first time.

Her breathless moan told him he was succeeding. She clutched at his shoulders as he found the nub of her sex. He murmured a soft reassurance when her body jolted in shock, and went on stroking the sensitive flesh. In only moments she had tilted her head back, moving it restlessly against the blanket, straining her hips against his caressing hand.

He felt her tremble, and gently thrust a finger into her silken warmth. Brynn whimpered softly in pleasure. He slid a second finger into her, pushing deeper, and she gasped, clamping her thighs around his hand.

Sucking hard on her engorged nipple, he kept up the arousing rhythm with his fingers, probing and withdrawing, until the motion enticed her hips into an undulating movement she couldn't control.

She arched and twisted, instinctively seeking relief from the feverish passion he was building within her. He could feel the heat rising from her flushed skin, hear her rasping pants as she reached the brink of climax. A heartbeat later, he felt her shatter.

Triumphant, Lucian took her mouth again, capturing her startled moans. He kissed her face and held her until she lay completely pliant in his arms. His erection was a throbbing, painful heat, but he forced himself to remain still, allowing her time to recover.

He sensed her bewilderment as Brynn searched his face in the darkness.

"That was the pleasure you spoke of?" she whispered hoarsely.

He smiled. "Yes. That was the pleasure. But there is more."

"More?" Her voice sounded faint. "I don't know if I can bear any more."

"You can," he promised softly. "You'll find the bliss even deeper when our flesh is fully joined. Let me show you, Brynn."

Her silence, while not welcoming, suggested surrender.

Smoothing a tendril back from her forehead, Lucian slid his thigh between hers, then hesitated.

A strange tenderness filled him as he gazed down

at her shadowed features. This was his wife. The woman he had chosen to be his life's mate. He had made love to countless other lovers, but this time was somehow different. He was burning with lust, desire, need, yet the feelings rioting through him were more powerful than any he had ever experienced.

And more dangerous. Having Brynn beneath him like this—sexually responsive, incredibly alluring— reminded Lucian of his erotic dreams. . . .

He frowned. Was Brynn right? Was he becoming obsessed with her?

Lucian shook his head. For now he wouldn't consider the possible danger. Brynn was his bride. His elusive enchantress. He wanted to taste her secrets and make her his forever.

His whisper brushed close against her ear. "Let me make you mine, sweet Brynn. . . ."

With deliberate slowness, he eased over her, spreading her thighs with his own. When he entered her partway, she drew a sharp breath. He held himself still, allowing her to grow accustomed to his alien hardness stretching her, filling her.

Her breath grew harsh when he pressed in a bit farther. "No, don't tense up, love. Try to soften your body when you take me inside you."

When he felt her tension ease, he progressed slow increments at a time. This time he felt her wince when her fragile barrier rent, but she made no sound beyond a faint gasp as he sheathed himself the final measure.

For a long moment Lucian didn't move, pressing soft kisses over her flushed face, her eyelids, cherishing the lush promise of her virginal tightness.

He could feel her softening, warming around him, feel her heated wetness increasing with her renewed arousal.

"Better?" he asked, his control no longer steady.

"Yes," she said, the word a mere breath of sound.

Lucian forced himself to hold back, to restrain the excitement flaring through his senses. She was moist and hot and insanely inviting, but still innocent and untutored. Calling on all his willpower, he began the slow, exquisite task of bringing her to pleasure, moving gently inside her, using all the skill he possessed to coax a sexual response from her.

She offered no resistance now. When he pressed even deeper, Brynn's thighs parted to accept more of him. And when he drew back, she tentatively lifted her hips, as if to follow. Lucian clenched his teeth, fighting the scorching hunger of his body.

Traces of the same scorching hunger singed Brynn. The heavy, burning ache inside her was growing, yet it wasn't pain. It was heat; it was desire. Her entire body throbbed at the feel of Lucian's hard flesh joined with hers.

Then his mouth dipped to her breasts, kissing her erect nipples, and the twinges of pleasure sharpened. His tantalizing, arousing caresses made her press closer, molding her skin to him as she felt the hot, coiling tension rise, spiraling through her body from the bright center of sensation.

In reward, he sank deeper. She whimpered, wordlessly pleading, helplessly needing. He thrust harder, and Brynn suddenly erupted.

Her senses exploding, she moaned, mindlessly clutching his face to her breasts, frenzied with longing. All she could do was cling to Lucian and endure the storm, a magical whirlwind of fire in the darkness.

Her cries of ecstasy and wonder still echoed softly in the night as he drove himself to his own convulsive climax deep within her. Vaguely she felt his shudders, felt his restrained violence as he moved possessively, forcefully between her thighs. Yet her shaking body seemed to accept his urgency, welcoming him until his final tremors faded.

Dazed, trembling, Brynn fell limply back, shutting her eyes.

It might have been an eternity before she regained enough awareness to feel the gentle kisses Lucian was pressing over her face. He was still buried within her, his breath hot and soft on her skin, while she was still throbbing, pulsing with intolerable pleasure.

"Was that as distasteful as you expected?" he asked, his voice warm with intimacy.

"Not quite," she breathed, reluctant to admit that he had been right.

His laughter was soft and vibrant, as full of promise as the night air around them. Carefully he eased from her body and gathered her in his arms.

Wincing with twinges of pain, Brynn pressed her face into the smooth, muscular wall of his chest. She could feel his warmth, smell the exciting male muskiness of his skin. His embrace felt unbearably intimate, yet after what had just passed between them, it was rather tame, she supposed.

She was glad he couldn't see her embarrassment. The caressing darkness had made her cast away all inhibition and logic, turning her into a wild, lustful creature she couldn't even recognize.

She was stunned by the wonder of a passion she'd never anticipated. She hadn't realized such a degree of wanton feeling existed. But then her new husband was a captivating man, magnificently virile, seductively male. . . .

Brynn drew a sharp breath.

With very little effort, Lucian had breached her defenses. Like every other woman he pursued, she had succumbed to his disarming tenderness and smoldering sensuality . . . heaven help him.

Brynn squeezed her eyes shut. She didn't want to think of the danger. Not now. Not at this incredible moment.

She buried her nose deeper into his chest, wishing she could hide inside him.

"Has any female ever resisted your attempts to charm?" she murmured finally.

"You, love." His tone was gentle and faintly amused. "You're the only one I can recall. Except for my mother, perhaps. She was usually immune to my efforts."

It seemed he could laugh at himself. That surprised her. And worried her. She didn't want to find anything else appealing about Lucian. Didn't want to come to *like* him.

Even so, she was indescribably grateful he had been so considerate of her virginal state, that he had been so gentle with her. He was still being gentle, his fingers drawing lazy patterns on the bare skin of her shoulder. . . .

At last acknowledging that she shouldn't encourage such familiarity, Brynn edged away, then flinched at the tender throb deep inside her where she'd stretched to accommodate his raw power.

"Perhaps we should return," he murmured as if he sensed her discomfort. "You would be more comfortable in a real bed."

Sitting up, she fumbled to straighten her clothing but found it difficult with her mind still in turmoil. In a moment Lucian brushed her fingers aside and helped her dress. Brynn bit her lip at this telltale evidence of his licentiousness. Even in the dark, he knew his way around a woman's undergarments.

She held her tongue, though, and suffered his attention in silence. When he pressed a kiss on her temple, she pulled away and rose to her feet. She was startled to feel a wetness between her thighs. It was Lucian's seed, she realized, reminded of the brazen carnal relations they had just shared.

"Wait a moment," he murmured. "I brought a lantern."

She could hear him opening the basket and then striking a lucifer. The sudden brightness as he lit a box lantern made her wince, but it was the sight of his naked torso that made her avert her gaze. His lean, muscled frame rippled with fluid strength and sent butterflies curling low in her belly, as well as fresh pulses of sensation throbbing between her thighs.

When he had put on his shirt, he returned the champagne and strawberries and glasses to the basket. Then, gathering the rest of his clothing and the blankets, he handed her the lantern.

"Lead the way," he said.

She would not look at him as she negotiated the path along the cliff face, or when she accompanied him across the lawn and onto the terrace, heading for the French doors that led to the dimly lit library.

She had just climbed the marble steps when her husband came to a sudden halt.

"Brynn, wait," he ordered in a low, urgent voice.

She paused, then gave a start of alarm when the dark figure of a man moved out from the shadows of the house, into the lantern light. She hadn't suspected anyone was there.

"My lord, it is I, Davies," the man murmured in a cultured accent.

He was an older, distinguished-looking gentleman, Brynn saw, with graying hair and a tall, somewhat portly figure. Lucian must have recognized him, for she could feel his tension ease beside her.

"Yes, Davies," he said with apparent casualness. "I presume you have a good reason for traveling all this way from London?"

"I do, my lord. I have news, which I fear is not good." The man glanced at Brynn. "Perhaps we might speak in private?"

"Of course. Brynn, this is my secretary, Mr. Hubert Davies. Davies, my new wife, Lady Wycliff."

The man sketched her a deep bow. "I am honored, my lady."

Brynn murmured a polite reply, then glanced up at Lucian, who gave her a brief smile.

"Will you forgive me, my dear? It appears I have some dull business affairs to deal with. Why don't you go upstairs? I will join you shortly."

Short of making a scene, Brynn had no choice but to oblige. She made her way up to her bedchamber, rife with puzzlement and curiosity—and disquietude as well.

When she caught sight of herself in the cheval glass, though, she drew a sharp breath in dismay at her wanton appearance—her hair tumbling wildly down her back, her gown disheveled, her cheeks flushed with color.

Her flush deepened when she realized her husband's secretary had spied her this way. It was shameful to have been caught in such brazen behavior, especially after she had vowed she wouldn't succumb to Lucian's practiced charm.

She washed the vestiges of his lovemaking from her body and restored order to her appearance, pinning her hair up again, and then discovered she didn't know what else to do with herself—whether to change her gown for her nightdress or simply wait for Lucian to come.

At loose ends, she tried to read, but found she couldn't concentrate. Her mind kept wandering to Lucian, both to the incredible passion he had shown her and to darker thoughts of what effect this night would have on their future.

It was perhaps a half hour later when her restlessness grew to a fever pitch. Shutting her book, Brynn rose to her feet and began to pace the floor, wondering what could be keeping Lucian.

She was about to go downstairs in search of him when she heard a soft rap on her bedchamber door. When she bid entrance, she was taken aback to see his secretary, Mr. Davies.

"Forgive me, my lady, but I have a message from his lordship."

"A message?"

"Yes. He regrets being called away on an important matter."

"I'm not certain I understand," Brynn replied, frowning. "What could possibly require his attention at this time of night?"

"Business that cannot be avoided. Lord Wycliff has left for Falmouth, where his ship is anchored. He gave me instructions to escort you by coach to London on the morrow. I am to help settle you in your new home."

Brynn felt herself stiffen. "I wonder that he could not spare the time to tell me himself."

"The matter was urgent, my lady. Lord Wycliff begs your forgiveness."

Brynn wasn't certain she could believe the apology, but she tightened her jaw and bit back a tart comment, saying merely, "When may I expect to see him again?"

"I regret I cannot predict, my lady. Doubtless it will be several days at least, perhaps a week, before he can join you in London. As for tomorrow, it will be best to get an early start as the journey will be rather long. I came in his lordship's traveling coach. If you are agreeable, I will have your trunks loaded at first light."

"Very well, Mr. Davies," she said rather numbly.

With a deep bow, the secretary stepped back and shut the door quietly behind him, leaving Brynn to stare after him, stiff with shock and hurt and welling resentment.

What business, she wondered, was so urgent that her new husband must abandon his bride on their wedding night? And why in heaven's name could he not even do her the simple courtesy of saying farewell?

Chapter Seven

London

"We should arrive at his lordship's town residence shortly," Mr. Davies remarked, speaking for the first time in two hours. "Are you comfortable enough, my lady?"

"Yes, thank you," Brynn prevaricated, shifting in her seat to relieve her cramped muscles. Nearly three days of coach travel, even in a coach as well-sprung and luxuriously appointed as her new husband's, was not her idea of comfort.

The journey had been lonely as well, with only the reserved, impeccably proper Mr. Davies for company. They had set out for London early on the morning following her wedding. The elderly gentleman maintained a formal distance and seemed reticent to answer even the most elementary questions about his employer, Lord Wycliff.

With nothing to distract her thoughts, Brynn found herself dwelling on her feelings of loneliness and trepidation. It had been even harder than expected to say farewell to her home and family. And the ache in her breast at giving up Theo could not have been deeper had she truly been his mother rather than his older sister.

Worse, with so much time on her hands, her reflections kept returning to her wedding night and her new husband. No matter how she tried to push it out of her mind, she couldn't help reliving her one incredible carnal interlude with Lucian. She had expected him to be skilled, but his lovemaking had been more stunning than anything described by poets. The sheer ecstasy he'd aroused in her was beyond what she could have imagined in her wildest dreams. Even now a sharp sense of pleasure curled low in her stomach whenever she remembered him moving between her thighs. . . .

Brynn pressed her lips together, completely vexed with herself. She had intended to hold herself aloof, but at the first challenge, she'd melted into a mindless puddle in his arms. It was small consolation that Lucian Tremayne was a practiced rake whose erotic finesse was as vast as the ocean. She had succumbed to his seduction like the veriest gull.

And then he had forsaken her without a word of farewell, leaving her to be dealt with by his stately secretary as if she were a possession—a horse or a dog—that could be turned over to the care of servants. At the very least Lucian could have had the common decency to say farewell. Or better yet, permit her to remain in Cornwall with her family.

Brynn muttered a silent oath. She shouldn't give a fig that her husband had abandoned her so abruptly after consummating a union she had never wanted. It was irrational for her to feel dismayed and hurt.

Indeed, she should be *glad* to be able to nurse a resentment toward him.

It would be far easier to resist a husband who showed her so little consideration. There would be no danger of coming to care for him—and she had definitely been in danger that night. For a brief while during their passionate tryst on the beach, their intimacy had aroused feelings in her that she didn't dare acknowledge.

But whatever momentary warmth she'd cherished toward Lucian in those moments, whatever fleeting optimism about their life together, was dashed when he decided so abruptly to desert her, leaving her to face a strange future alone but for his properly decorous secretary.

Brynn gave a deep sigh. She was not usually one to give in to despondency, but just now it was a struggle.

Her spirits rose when the coach reached the elegant London district of Mayfair, where the cream of the ton resided. As the coach drew to a halt, Brynn leaned forward in anticipation to peer out the window, wondering what her new home would be like.

She caught her breath at the magnificent sight in the fading evening light. The mansion of imposing gray stone was not quite a palace but nearly so. Unaccustomed to such grandeur, Brynn was filled with both awe and dismay when the coach was met by a cadre of bustling footmen.

Inside, the house seemed even more luxurious, with a vast entrance hall filled with glistening chandeliers

and gleaming marble. The domestic staff resembled
an army and was lined up in the hall according to
rank—first the butler and housekeeper, then upper
servants such as the chef and chief gardener, and finally the liveried footmen and uniformed serving
maids.

The head servants were obviously proper to the
point of stiffness. Brynn didn't catch their names at
first, but she couldn't miss their studied coolness.
Nor did she miss the housekeeper's disapproving
frown when the butler relieved their new mistress of
her bonnet.

Brynn resisted the urge to reach up and smooth
her chignon, which no doubt was disheveled after
the long journey. Her unruly hair was such an untamed color that it took very little to make her look
wild and brazen. She had to forgive the elderly
woman her reaction. And perhaps her stiffness and
lack of warmth as well. Her master's sudden marriage must have come as a complete shock. Moreover, longtime servants would be protective of their
status and would not welcome a new mistress with
open arms.

Brynn allowed the butler to take her gloves and
pelisse, then hesitated, uncertain of the etiquette for
this situation. Had her husband been present, the
task of introducing her to her new home would
likely have fallen to him.

Fortunately Mr. Davies intervened in the awkward silence. "Would you care to tour the house,
Lady Wycliff? Or perhaps you would prefer to rest
first?"

She gave him a grateful smile. "I am not tired, but

I would like to change out of my traveling dress before I see the house."

"Did your maid not accompany you, my lady?" the housekeeper asked, her tone holding a hint of reproach.

"I am afraid not," Brynn answered just as coolly, not wanting to admit that she hadn't been able to afford the service of a lady's maid for years.

At the servant's frosty look, Brynn squared her shoulders and returned an unrepentant gaze, reminding herself that she needn't endure such unspoken censure. She was the Countess of Wycliff now, even if she had been abandoned by her husband. Her rank was one of the few advantages to this unwanted marriage.

The housekeeper was the first to waver. Dropping her gaze, she asked Mr. Davies which rooms her ladyship was to be given.

"Lord Wycliff wishes her to have the gold suite."

"Very well," the housekeeper said, pressing her lips together as if she had swallowed a bitter prune. "If you will come with me, my lady . . ."

As she was led upstairs, Brynn caught glimpses of elegant furnishings everywhere she looked, all superbly tasteful, never ostentatious. When she followed the housekeeper into a magnificent bedchamber, decorated in shades of ivory and gold, she found it hard not to gasp at the exquisite appointments.

"There is a sitting room as well as a dressing room," the housekeeper informed her. "These rooms belonged to the late Lady Wycliff. His lordship's mother, whom I served for many years."

"They are very beautiful," Brynn murmured, "Mrs. . . . ? I'm sorry, I forgot your name."

"Poole," the housekeeper said stiffly. "I am Mrs. Poole."

Her lapse, Brynn realized, was no doubt an unforgivable mistake that only added to the housekeeper's resentment. She would have to do better in future.

She offered an apologetic smile. "Thank you, Mrs. Poole. I can manage from here."

The servant returned a cool stare, but she evidently thought better of outright defiance because she sketched a brief curtsy before withdrawing.

Alone, Brynn took a deep breath. It would require an enormous amount of work if she hoped to win over such stalwart opposition as the housekeeper's— and she wasn't yet certain she even wanted to make the attempt.

Her awed gaze returned to the beautiful bedchamber. Crossing the room to one of the tall windows, Brynn looked down at the elegant square. She had known Lucian was wealthy, but this was beyond wealth; this room was fit for a queen.

She winced at the realization that this would be her new throne. She wasn't cut out for such an exalted position. Nor was she even certain she preferred such formal riches as these. Her former home suffered greatly in comparison, but even with its threadbare furnishings, Caldwell House was more comforting, for it was filled with laughter and affection. . . .

Brynn's despondency returned in full measure as she remembered all she had left behind. How would she manage to cope? She already missed home dreadfully, missed her family, the warmth.

Shivering, she wrapped her arms around herself. It was cold here in London, even in August. Far colder than the south of Cornwall.

After a moment, however, Brynn tightened her jaw and berated herself for falling prey to self-pity. Turning, she was about to shrug out of her gown when a whisper-soft rap sounded on the door.

"Yes?" Brynn said, inviting entrance.

The door opened slowly, and a young, blond-haired woman in servants' attire inched into the room, her gaze focused meekly on the Aubusson carpet.

"I am Meg, milady," she murmured in a thin voice that quivered with nerves. "Mrs. Poole sent me to assist you."

"Thank you, Meg, but you may tell Mrs. Poole that I don't require assistance."

To Brynn's startlement, the maid's lower lip began to tremble. "Is something wrong, Meg?" she asked in concern.

"Please, milady," Meg pleaded, giving her an almost desperate look. "Don't send me away, I beg you. Mrs. Poole will think I have displeased you."

Seeing that the girl's distress was genuine, Brynn felt her heart warm immediately. "You haven't displeased me in the least, Meg," she said gently. "It is only that I have been accustomed to caring for myself. My family has been in rather straitened circumstances lately, so I have had to forgo the luxury of a personal maid. I confess, though, that I would appreciate your assistance."

"Oh, thank you, milady!" Meg breathed, bobbing up and down numerous times as if Brynn were indeed a queen. "I usually serve as a parlormaid and I haven't much experience, but I am a quick study, I promise you, even Mrs. Poole says so, and I will do anything you ask, *anything*—" She stopped abruptly, having run out of breath, and gazed wide-eyed at her mistress. "Where do I begin?"

Brynn managed a smile. "Perhaps with the buttons on the back of my gown."

She offered her back, willing herself to patience as the girl attempted the task with fumbling fingers. She had to make allowances for the cold reception of longtime employees like Mrs. Poole and for inexperienced, terrified ones like Meg.

But still, Brynn reflected, adjusting to her lordly husband's household would be more difficult than even she had imagined.

Dover

The prison cell was dank and stank of vermin, both the animal and the human sort—the condemned souls who had been caged there over the past centuries. Lucian had to stifle the urge to cover his nose with a handkerchief.

He'd sailed directly from Cornwall to Dover after learning that a government courier had been ambushed and murdered. The courier's pouch contained dispatches meant for General Lord Wellington in Spain, most important a schedule of impending gold shipments, detailing dates and locations of delivery to Britain's European allies. Then, before the schedule could be changed, a wagonload of bullion worth nearly two hundred thousand pounds was stolen, all its guards killed, shot without mercy.

An urgent investigation had ensued, with agents combing every tavern and posting inn and dock, searching for possible leads. The man in custody had had the poor judgment to boast about knowledge of the theft, although he claimed to have no responsibility in the courier's murder.

Lucian had come today with one of his best agents to continue interrogating the prisoner.

"You there," the jailer said gruffly, "get to yer feet. You 'ave visitors."

The ragged blanket on the straw mattress moved, then moaned when the jailer kicked it. "This is Ned Shanks, milord."

A hulking brute of a man crawled slowly out from beneath the blanket and climbed to his feet, clutching his ribs.

Shanks was clearly the worse for his imprisonment. In the lantern light, Lucian could see his grimy face was badly bruised and one eye swollen shut, while dried blood matted his greasy black hair.

A look of fear crossed his face when he saw Lucian's colleague, Philip Barton, who was primarily responsible for the prisoner's current damaged condition.

"Leave us, please," Lucian said to the jailer.

When they were alone, Lucian eyed the prisoner for a long moment. As the silence drew out, Shanks visibly grew more nervous, until finally he exclaimed in a voice oddly high and breathless for so large a man, "Gor, I know naught, milord. I don't even know why I been arrested."

Lucian kept his voice gentle. "You have been arrested, Mr. Shanks, because a government courier has been murdered and his dispatch pouch gone missing. And because you have knowledge about how and why it happened."

"I know only what I told that gent, I swear! That's all I know."

"Why don't you repeat your tale to me? My colleague, Mr. Barton, believes it might be helpful to have another, fresh perspective."

Ned flashed the silent Barton a fearful glance. "I 'eard my friend Boots bragging about a job over an ale, saying 'ow 'e was soon to be plump in the pocket."

"At the Boarshead Tavern?"

"Aye, milord. Well, I followed 'im to see who 'e planned to meet with. I stopped around the corner from the mews. It was dark so I couldn't see much, and I could only 'ear part of what was said."

"But you could see his companion."

"Some'at. 'E was a toff, for sure. Boots called 'im a lord. Lord Caliban, or some such thing."

Although expecting to hear the familiar name, Lucian felt himself flinch. Caliban was the monster in Shakespeare's *The Tempest* and the sobriquet of the ringleader the British Foreign Office had been seeking for months.

"And what did this Lord Caliban say?"

" 'E told Boots when the courier would come and what to do—where to lie in wait on the 'ighway. 'E wanted that courier's bag bad enough to pay big. Boots was to get twenty quid if 'e could deliver the bag."

"I wonder if Boots realized what the pouch contained."

" 'Pon me life, I don't know anything more. Only what I 'eard Boots say."

"Are you aware your friend Boots was found garroted in an alley two days ago?" Lucian asked even more gently. "The work of your Lord Caliban, I expect."

Ned's face went white.

"What can you tell me about this Caliban?" Lucian said finally.

"Not much. 'E wore a mask. And a fancy coat, like yerself."

"What of hair color or physical build? Was he short or tall?"

"Medium, I guess. Taller than Boots. But 'is 'air was covered."

"Any distinguishing marks you can recall? Think, please, Mr. Shanks. It would be of great use to us to have even the slightest hint of Lord Caliban's identity."

Ned's grimy brow furrowed. "No marks, but . . . come to think of it, 'e had a ring."

"What sort of ring?"

"Gold. Wore it on 'is left 'and. I remember it glittered red."

Philip spoke for the first time. "You told me nothing about a ring before."

Ned's wary look held alarm. "I only just now remembered. Boots was going on about it, saying 'ow it would be worth a fair plum if 'e could lift it."

"Can you recall anything about the design?" Lucian asked.

"Something like a dragon's head, Boots said. 'Ad red stones for eyes."

"Rubies, perhaps?" Lucian asked.

"I guess, maybe. I really didn't get near enough for a look."

Contemplating the prisoner, Lucian was certain he had nothing more to offer. "Thank you, Mr. Shanks. You have been a great deal of help."

"Milord?" Ned's tone grew anxious as he sent Barton another fearful glance. "What will ye do with me? I 'ave a wife 'oo will be wondering what's become of me."

"So do I," Lucian murmured softly. "You are free to go, Mr. Shanks."

"Go?" Ned looked astonished, as did Philip Barton to a lesser extent.

Lucian fished in his pocket and drew out a handful of guineas. "Here. In remuneration for your trouble."

Accepting the offer reflexively, Ned stared down at the gold pieces in total bewilderment.

"If you should hear of any news," Lucian added, "anything even remotely connected with Caliban or with your late friend Boots, I would hope you will inform the innkeeper at the Boarshead. He can get word to me."

"Aye, milord, of course!"

At his eagerness, Lucian flashed a charming half smile. "You might also be interested to know a reward is being offered for the capture of this Lord Caliban. Two hundred pounds."

Shanks's mouth gaped open. It was still set that

way when Lucian left the cell, followed closely by Philip Barton with the lantern.

Neither of them spoke until they were seated in Philip's closed carriage and headed toward the inn where they both were staying.

"You think it wise to let him go?" the younger man asked.

"Wiser than frightening him out of his skin," Lucian replied mildly. "Or beating him to confess knowledge he doesn't have. Greed can sometimes prove a better method than pain."

"I shall keep that in mind," Philip said stiffly.

"That was not a criticism, my friend. You did an excellent job simply finding Shanks. Because of you, we are one step closer to unearthing our traitor. But Shanks can be more useful to us alive than dead. And this way, if he hears even a whisper about our chief nemesis, I expect he will jump at the chance to tell us."

"You're certain Caliban is the traitor you are looking for?"

"I'm certain of it," Lucian said grimly.

He had a large score to settle with his elusive enemy. Murder, theft, treason only headed the list of crimes. Even more personally galling was Caliban's practice of luring young bucks of the ton into betraying their country. Lucian's grimmest task had been to kill one of his boyhood friends who had turned traitor at Caliban's behest. The memory still haunted him.

"He must have an accomplice within the Foreign Office," Philip muttered. "How else would he know when to intercept the courier?" He clenched his fists. "It rankles to know a traitor is directly under our noses and we cannot do a bloody thing to stop him."

"Indeed," Lucian agreed succinctly, feeling but not visibly displaying the same corrosive self-torment that was eating his subordinate inside.

Philip turned his troubled gaze to Lucian. "My lord, I would not blame you in the least if you were to dismiss me. I should have thought of changing the transport schedule. If I had, then the last shipment of gold would still be safe, the guards still alive."

Lucian shook his head. Philip Barton was one of his brightest agents, but even the brightest made mistakes. And the young man was not entirely to blame. Lucian was suffering his own harsh brand of guilt, his own private anguish. Had he been in London instead of dallying in Cornwall, courting his bride, he could have acted when the courier's murder was first discovered. In all likelihood he could have prevented the gold theft and the deaths of half a dozen more innocent men, a lapse in judgment he would forever have to live with.

Whether or not the shipment had been smuggled to France yet was anyone's guess, for the trail had gone stone cold. Lucian had immediately sent men to Cornwall to scour the coast in the event that Sir Grayson Caldwell was involved, but he doubted Cornwall was the transfer point this time. The gold was likely in France by now, bankrolling Napoleon's armies instead of those of the Triple Alliance—Austria, Prussia, and Russia.

Lucian was seething with helpless fury inside, his gut and heart both aching with dismay. But long practice at concealing his feelings behind a sophisticated mask allowed him to answer evenly. "If I dismissed you, Philip, then I would have to dismiss myself. I was off attending to my own personal affairs, I recall."

"It is not the same thing, my lord. Your wedding nuptials should come before duty."

"No." His resolve hardened. "Nothing should come before duty."

Lucian turned his head to gaze out the carriage window. Lusting after a woman, even his own wife, was no excuse for forsaking his grave obligations. A few vital infusions of gold into Napoleon's military machine could prove pivotal in the outcome of the war—the difference between a Europe subjugated under a tyrant's boot heel and the allies finally being able to crush him once and for all.

Winning the war, putting an end to the death and destruction and devastating misery the Corsican monster had caused, was far more crucial than any one man's personal considerations, Lucian reflected darkly. He might have regretted having to leave his marriage bed—virtually being dragged away on his wedding night—but his own private desires could not be allowed to matter.

And in truth, he'd been glad for the opportunity to gain some distance from his new bride. It unsettled him, how enamored he'd become with Brynn in such a short time. He didn't believe in such things as curses, but admittedly he found it hard to explain the driving urgency he'd felt to possess her, the stunning satisfaction of making love to her . . . his dark dreams.

He'd sent his secretary to make his farewells that night, rationalizing that had he gone to Brynn himself, he would have had to offer some explanation as to his purpose. He had no intention of disclosing his investigation of the gold thefts when her brother might very well be up to his neck in treason.

But the real reason he'd sailed away without a word, Lucian acknowledged grimly, was because of fear: if he went to her, if he touched her again, he might not be able to leave her at all. Away from her, he could try to forget her vibrant beauty, her defiant, intriguing spirit . . . the dark images that filled his mind.

Or so he'd mistakenly hoped.

Since he'd wed her, Brynn had obsessed his thoughts. Obsessed even his sleep. His dreams were filled with her now. Never before had he dreamed about any specific woman, but since making love to Brynn, he couldn't stop seeing her whenever he closed his eyes.

Lucian cursed silently. This was not the sort of marriage he'd planned—becoming foolishly enchanted with his beautiful wife. But he couldn't, wouldn't indulge his growing obsession for her.

Brynn was no doubt offended that he'd abandoned her so abruptly after compelling her to wed him. But he couldn't worry about placating her wounded sensibilities. Not when so many men had died as a result of his negligence.

His jaw hardened with determination. For the

moment he had to put his country before his marriage and focus every ounce of his attention on
his duty.

London

"Of course she will receive me!" a cold feminine
voice intoned from the lower reaches of the house.
"You will inform her to come down at once!"

Brynn, hearing the imperious command all the
way from her upstairs sitting room, gave a start of
surprise to think she had a caller. This was her second afternoon in her new home, and thus far her
only companions had been loneliness and boredom.
She wasn't accustomed to such inactivity, or to having servants cater to her every whim.

After quickly smoothing her simple blue muslin
gown and checking to see that her hair was still
tamed, Brynn descended the grand staircase to find a
tall, regal, silver-haired lady awaiting her impatiently.

"I should like a word with you in private, miss,"
the dame snapped. Turning, she swept from the
grand hall and into the adjacent salon, obviously
expecting Brynn to follow.

Brynn sent the butler a bewildered glance. "Who
in heaven's name is that?"

Naysmith's usually stern expression came surprisingly close to a grimace and, more surprisingly,
held a hint of sympathy. "Forgive me, Lady Wycliff, but she would not permit me to announce her.
That is his lordship's great-aunt, Lady Agatha Edgecomb. Do you wish me to tell her you are not
receiving?"

"No, thank you, Naysmith. I will speak to her."

Squaring her shoulders, Brynn made her way to the salon. Lady Agatha was facing the door, her spine ramrod straight, as if girded for battle.

"What is the meaning of this outrage?" she demanded at once, brandishing a newspaper in her hand. "I was left to learn of my nephew's marriage from the society pages, of all things!"

"Our marriage was very sudden," Brynn answered as calmly as she could, considering the woman's rudeness. "I expect there was not time for you to be informed."

"Why the need for such haste? Are you *enceinte*?"

Brynn blinked at such bold speaking. "No, I am not, my lady. Although I fail to see how that could be any of your concern."

"Certainly it is my concern! I am head of this family!" Lady Agatha's gray eyes narrowed in dislike. "What sort of impertinence is this, missy? I will not countenance such disrespect! My nephew will hear of this, I can assure you."

"You may tell him whatever you wish, Lady Agatha. Indeed, if you have objections to our marriage, you must take them up with my husband."

"*If* I have objections! Of course I have objections! Wycliff has completely disregarded what he owes his family and his title. Who are you? Who is your family? Tell me that!"

"My father was Sir Samuel Caldwell of St. Mawes, Cornwall. My mother, Miss Gwendolyn Vaughn."

"Just as I thought! Wycliff has gone off and married a nobody. And that hair of yours. Only a jezebel would have hair that wild color!"

Brynn drew herself up to her full height. "If you have come simply to harangue me, Lady Agatha, you may take your leave. Otherwise, I would be pleased to invite you to stay for tea."

The lady's face turned purple. "I would sooner take tea with a Hottentot!"

Deliberately Brynn stepped aside, making way for her unwanted guest to leave.

Lady Agatha glared in indignation, the feathered plumes of her bonnet all aquiver with rage. "I feared the worst and now that I see you, I realize I was right. Wycliff was seduced by a hussy! A scheming interloper! Well, I am here to tell you, you will not succeed!"

With that dire prediction, she swept from the room in a rustle of silk skirts and creaking stays.

In her wake, Brynn stood rooted to the floor, unable to move. She was unsurprised to find herself trembling with fury and perhaps even a little shock.

It was a long moment before she realized she was no longer alone and that someone stood behind her at the salon door. Stiffening, Brynn turned and looked up, her expression tight with the strain of holding her temper.

"Oh my, I see you have met Lucian's great-aunt Agatha," the young woman there said in a low, husky voice.

She was an absolutely stunning beauty, Brynn saw, with raven hair and intensely blue eyes.

"If it is any consolation," the visitor added, offering a smile, "Lady Agatha treats everyone that way. Please don't let her distress you. She can be perfectly dreadful—almost as difficult as my own aunt."

Her smile held a genuine warmth that Brynn hadn't felt since leaving Cornwall, and Brynn felt her anger easing.

"May I come in?" the young lady asked. "I should have waited for Naysmith to announce me, but I heard the contretemps and thought you might be in need of reinforcements."

"Yes, of course, do come in. Forgive my manners."

"I am Raven Kendrick." Stepping into the room, she held out her gloved hand. "A friend of Lucian's. You might say he is my guardian in absentia, since my true guardians recently returned to America. I have been staying with my grandfather in the country for the summer, but when I heard Lucian had married, I had to come to London to welcome you. . . . Which seems fortuitous," Miss Kendrick added wryly, casting a glance over her shoulder where Lady Agatha had disappeared, "considering the reception you are likely to get from Lucian's relations. I'm afraid few of them are likely to greet you with open arms, at least at first. They're eager to claim a part of his fortune and hoped he might remain a bachelor forever."

"I didn't expect them to welcome me, but after meeting his great-aunt, I see I should be prepared for outright hostility."

"At least Lady Agatha is the worst. Lucian calls her a battle-ax."

"I cannot say I disagree."

Raven's laugh was musical and sweetly infectious, and her blue eyes danced when she regarded

Brynn thoughtfully. "I heard you were a beauty, and I feared you might be the arrogant sort, but you aren't in the least, are you? I think I am going to like you."

Brynn couldn't help but smile. "You can conclude that after barely meeting me?"

"Oh, I'm an excellent judge of character. And I don't care at all for the starched attitude of London society. I was raised in the West Indies, where everything is much less formal and conventional."

"Perhaps you should be concerned that you might be contaminated by a hussy and a jezebel."

"If you are a hussy, then we will be well-matched. Lady Agatha considers me an utter hoyden. I confess, I have been aching for eons to put her nose out of joint as you just did. No one else dares speak back to her except Lucian."

Brynn laughed. "Would you care to sit down, Miss Kendrick?"

"Thank you, but do call me Raven. And I would love some tea, if your offer is still open."

Brynn glanced toward the door to find Naysmith hovering respectfully just outside. He gave a brief nod to indicate that he understood and then disappeared.

When they were settled—Raven on the chintz settee and Brynn in a chair opposite—Raven said with a frown, "Lucian is still out of town, I take it? It was really too bad of him to abandon you so soon after your nuptials, leaving you to face the wolves alone, but I suppose his job requires him to be away. Where is he this time?"

Brynn hesitated, not liking to admit she had no

idea where her husband was. "He didn't say, exactly. Just that he had urgent business to attend to."

"Well, he is always gallivanting over the globe." Raven gave Brynn a considering look that was both shrewd and sympathetic. "So you should not take his neglect personally."

Brynn refrained from replying to that comment, finding it hard to repress her bitterness.

Evidently observant, Raven said in a firm voice, "Well, you needn't think yourself all alone, for I intend to make up for Lucian's despicable negligence."

"Are you always this forthright?" Brynn asked, both bemused and charmed by her visitor's frankness.

Raven laughed. "Ordinarily I am worse, but I am striving to be on my best behavior with you. Truthfully, though, I can get away with more scandalous behavior than many debs. I am engaged to wed the Duke of Halford, and my grandfather is an earl—which gives me more license. And I am not really showing conceit when I say I can help establish you in society. I mean to try, so consider yourself warned. I intend to take you under my wing."

"Very well, then," Brynn said with an answering laugh. "I am warned."

"London is rather thin of company at present, but there are plenty of other pastimes. Do you ride?"

"Not well, I'm afraid."

"I customarily enjoy a gallop in the park early each morning, but I won't mind curtailing my speed for the pleasure of having your company, if you will join me. Our first outing, however, must be to Oxford Street to shop for my bride clothes. My aunt has been helping me prepare for my nuptials, but her taste is vastly different from mine. Your opinion would be greatly welcome."

"I would be happy to accompany you, if you think I can help."

"And of course you must have a new wardrobe. You will need to maintain the height of fashion if you mean to establish your place as the Countess of Wycliff."

Brynn frowned. "Perhaps I do need a new gown or two, but I cannot see any reason for the extravagance of an entire wardrobe."

"Trust me, you will need it in order to stare down the despots of the ton such as Lady Agatha. You cannot have them saying Lucian refuses to dress his lady and add even more fuel for gossip after your unexpected marriage. In any case, Lucian can certainly afford it, and he *truly* should be made to pay for his dreadful treatment of you."

Brynn felt her lips curving in a smile, finding herself in complete agreement. She was supremely grateful to have found a new friend among the hostile populace of London. And for the first time since coming here, she could look forward to something other than aching loneliness.

Chapter Eight

Despite his best intentions, Lucian felt his heart-beat quicken with anticipation as he mounted the front steps of his London residence. His desire to see Brynn was a powerful yearning inside him—a yearning he had vowed to crush. He wouldn't allow his craving for his beautiful wife to make him shirk his duty again.

"Welcome home, my lord," his butler intoned, stepping back to permit him entrance.

"Thank you, Naysmith." Lucian glanced around him as he handed the servant his hat and gloves, repressing an unreasonable disappointment that Brynn wasn't there to greet him. "Where is my wife?"

"Her ladyship is not at home," Naysmith answered.

Lucian raised an eyebrow. His secretary had sent him two different reports of Brynn over the past week, but there had been no mention of any social functions that would keep her out at this late hour.

"She is attending a soiree with Miss Kendrick, I believe," was the butler's explanation. "At the home of Lord and Lady Sinclair."

"Ah." Damien Sinclair was one of Lucian's

closest friends and one of the few peers who usually remained in London during the warm summer months. Like Lucian, Damien had governmental responsibilities he couldn't forsake simply for personal convenience, although Damien's skills lay in the area of finance, not espionage.

"Will you be joining Lady Wycliff, my lord? Shall I order your carriage?"

Lucian considered a moment, then shook his head. It was nearly ten o'clock, and he'd sworn he would try to distance himself from Brynn, try to quell his obsession. It would hardly be in keeping with his new resolve to go running after her the moment he arrived home. "No, I won't be going out again. I'll spend the remainder of the evening in my study."

"Very well, my lord."

Naysmith preceded him into the study to light the lamps and pour a glass of brandy. He left the hearth untouched, since the August evening was too warm for a fire.

Accepting the crystal snifter, Lucian dismissed the butler and settled in his favorite leather armchair. Yet his thoughts were too restless for him to enjoy the peace and comfort of his home.

His fury and frustration had only grown over the past week. The investigation into the murders and missing gold had reached a dead end, while his search for the elusive mastermind, Caliban, had been just as fruitless.

His ineffectiveness galled Lucian. He had vowed to find and punish the ringleader, but meanwhile the only action he could take to prevent further thefts was purely defensive. He'd ordered a new schedule of gold transfers drawn up, a schedule that only a handful of people would be privy to this time. But that still couldn't guarantee the gold would be safe in the future, or that he could avert further murders.

For a moment Lucian shut his eyes, unable to drive away the images in his mind—the bodies of the dead guards littering the road like refuse. The slaughter had left him shaken.

Lucian took a deep swallow of brandy, welcoming its fierce burn. Guilt was a familiar companion to him, he reflected darkly. It had driven him to join the intelligence section of the Foreign Office nearly six years ago, eschewing the self-indulgent, frivolous life of a wealthy nobleman. He'd taken that unusual course to relieve his conscience; he'd felt a vague shame that he had lived while so many others had not.

Many of the dead had been friends—some killed in battle against the French while serving in the army or navy, others while engaged in the dangerous business of espionage. And then, during his last visit to France, he'd experienced the ultimate guilt: killing his friend Giles with his own hands.

Lucian flinched at the memory, even as his mouth curled with cynical self-reproach. He had always possessed the devil's own luck. He'd been involved in any number of dangerous situations and escaped entirely unscathed—until he'd confronted Giles, barely eluding death himself. Since then his luck had changed radically. He felt it in his soul. *And in his dreams.* The dreaded nightmare had recurred last night: the stark vision of his own death, Brynn standing over him, her hands wet with his blood.

Lucian stared into his glass, scoffing at his own fanciful imagination. Brynn was no assassin. She was merely a dangerous enchantress who would cause him to shirk his duty if he allowed it.

But he wouldn't allow it. He would keep his distance emotionally, maintain a cool reserve even in their most intimate moments. He still badly wanted a son, but enjoying the physical pleasure of getting her with child didn't necessarily mean succumbing to her unquestionable allure.

Even so, Lucian realized as he recklessly downed the last of his brandy, he found it impossible to quell his sense of anticipation at the thought of seeing her again, of crossing swords with her, of surprising a quick smile from Brynn, perhaps even winning a laugh. He missed her rapier wit and her tart tongue. He missed her vibrancy.

His near brush with death had made him yearn for life, to feel *alive*. Brynn made him feel alive. Everything about her set his nerve endings singing, from her sensual beauty to her spirited defiance to her fiery hair.

A dangerous sentiment, he knew. Brynn was an unmistakable danger to him, curse or no curse.

Yet despite his vow to remain detached, he couldn't stop himself from wanting her, craving her, or from fantasizing about taking her in his arms and rousing her to passion.

"His lordship awaits you in his study, my lady," the butler said, admitting her to the house.

Brynn froze in the act of surrendering her wrap. Lucian was *here*? Feeling a moment of panic, she thought about fleeing upstairs and taking refuge in her rooms. But he would know she had returned home, and she was not ordinarily a coward. . . . Not that these circumstances were ordinary. She had to face a husband she barely knew, one who had coerced her into marriage and then promptly deserted her.

All the resentment Brynn had kept banked during the past week came surging to the fore.

Steeling herself for the encounter, she made her way to his study and found Lucian sitting before a cold hearth. When he looked up and met her eyes, Brynn felt her heartbeat falter. The impact of his crystalline blue gaze was as breathtaking as she remembered, his stark handsomeness just as riveting—devil take him.

For an instant she thought his eyes brightened with welcome, perhaps even joy, at seeing her again, but then a mask descended over his face, and he raised a crystal goblet to her in salute. "Greetings, my sweet."

His voice was slightly unsteady, she realized, while his appearance was more disheveled than she'd ever seen it, lacking its usual elegance. He had removed his coat and loosened his cravat carelessly, and the dark glitter that reflected in his eyes made her wonder if he was in his cups. She halted just inside the room, determined to keep her distance.

"Aren't you going to give your husband a proper welcome?" he asked, his tone low and silken.

"Not by choice," Brynn responded, her own tone

determinedly frosty. She had no intention of encouraging any intimacy between them. She had dreamed of Lucian again this past week, dark dreams that frightened her. She wouldn't let her premonitions become reality by falling blithely into his arms.

He sent her a brooding look, but then his eyes narrowed, sweeping the bodice of her pale blue silk evening gown, which left a good deal of her neck and arms bare.

"Is that a new gown?"

Brynn stiffened as his probing gaze fixed on her breasts. "I trust you don't object. Raven said I am badly in need of a new wardrobe if I am to fulfill the role expected of me as your countess. And you left before giving me any indication of how much I could spend—"

He waved a dismissive hand. "I don't object in the least. I won't have my wife in rags."

Brynn pressed her lips together, refraining from defending the former lamentable state of her attire.

"Did you enjoy yourself this evening?" he asked when the awkward silence drew out.

"Somewhat."

"Somewhat?"

She gave an uncomfortable shrug. Her new title and Raven's sponsorship had afforded her entrée into the glittering salons of the ton, but she didn't like admitting to Lucian that she found the lavishness a bit overwhelming, or that in Cornwall she was accustomed to a much simpler life and far more humble trappings.

"Some of your friends are very agreeable," she finally said. "Vanessa Sinclair, especially. But others . . .

have been more judgmental. If it weren't for Raven, I should have been at a grave loss this past week. I am supremely grateful to her for coming to my rescue when I found myself thrown into a lion's pit."

His lashes lowered, hooding his eyes. "I apologize for having to leave you so abruptly."

"Your apology is hardly adequate," Brynn said coolly. "You might have sent me word sometime during this past week, perhaps informed me of your whereabouts."

"Davies knew where to find me."

"How flattering. The servants know far more about your activities than does your wife."

Lucian remained stonily silent, his expression inscrutable. Brynn dared to stare back at him, but her stance was one of false calmness. This man was far different from the enticing lover who had seduced her on their wedding night. She could find no trace of his celebrated charm or beguiling warmth. Instead he was cold, detached, distant. He had already given her ample cause for resentment, and absurdly his remoteness only wounded her further.

"Is your business concluded?" she forced herself to say in an emotionless tone.

His features hardened. "For the most part."

"A pity. I won't mind in the least if you take yourself off again."

She had struck a nerve, she could see from the glittering glance he shot her. His sensual mouth tightened in a grim line, yet she wouldn't back down. Their future dealings together depended on her resistance now. If she began by allowing herself to care when he came and went, she would have no hope whatever of keeping their relationship on safe ground.

Having scored a hit, though, she thought it wiser to make a dignified retreat. "You are evidently in a poor humor, and I am rather tired. I believe I will retire. If you wish, we can continue this discussion in the morning."

"I think not," he said softly.

She had started to turn away but his quiet retort brought her up short. She gave Lucian a sharp, questioning glance.

His eyes were as brilliant as sapphires and just as hard. "Go upstairs and prepare for bed. I will join you shortly."

Brynn's hands clenched into fists at his imperious order. "If you think I will welcome you into my bed after the way you treated me—"

"I don't believe I require a welcome, sweeting," he replied, his mouth curling in a humorless smile. "I am your husband, you will remember."

"How could I forget?" she muttered bitterly before turning abruptly and leaving the room.

Alone, Lucian sat staring moodily into the golden depths of his suddenly tasteless brandy. He had not handled that at all well. He should have expected such belligerence from Brynn, but he'd been too occupied erecting his own defenses to be concerned with soothing her wounded pride.

He hadn't been prepared for seeing her in the flesh. The instant she entered the room, his groin had tightened. All he could think about was having her, pulling her down with him before the hearth and possessing her body.

Bloody hell. He'd been hot to have her from the first moment he laid eyes on her, but the heat he'd felt just now, the lust, was more dangerous, more compelling than mere attraction.

Lucian swore again under his breath. She was his *wife*, not his mistress. Once a man was wed, he wasn't supposed to find his wife so enchanting, so incredibly bewitching. Or be filled with such a fierce longing to possess her.

It was going to be harder than he'd imagined to hold himself aloof, Lucian realized with a groan. Somehow, though, he would have to find the will to clamp down on his obsessive urges. His life had no room for wildfire passions raging out of control. He would have to harden his heart toward Brynn, or more appropriately, soften his loins.

Perhaps he was unwise even to press the issue just now. It might be more judicious to wait for her resentment to cool before insisting upon his marital rights. But then, that might take a great while. He still wanted a son. And he couldn't shake the dark premonition that time was running out for him.

No, he couldn't afford to wait, Lucian told himself.

Grimly he took another long swallow of brandy, needing the additional fortitude to face his beautiful wife and make love to her without losing himself in her powerful enchantment.

A bundle of angry nerves, Brynn sat at her dressing table while a sleepy Meg brushed her hair. They both jumped when Lucian spoke from behind them.

"That will be all," he said, dismissing the maid-servant. "I wish to be alone with my wife."

He had come through the connecting door that linked their suites, Brynn realized. Any hope that Meg would shield her died a swift death as the girl dropped the brush and scurried from the room.

Alone with her husband, Brynn averted her gaze from his tall, lithe form. He wore a brocade dressing gown of midnight blue that accented the sapphire color of his eyes and proclaimed very clearly his intent to sleep with her.

She kept her back to him, refusing to look at him or even to acknowledge his presence. She could feel his gaze raking her through her concealing nightdress.

Brynn gave a start when she felt his hand linger-ingly touch her hair. She hadn't heard his soft foot-fall over the heavy beating of her heart.

"What do you want?" she demanded, stiffening and pulling away.

"I should have thought I'd made that clear," he said quietly. "I want a son."

She turned her head to glare up at him. "What is clear is that I'm nothing more to you than chattel. You think you can simply command me and I will leap to do your bidding."

"You are not chattel. You are my wife."

Rising to her feet, she faced him fully. "I am hardly your wife. Admit it, I am nothing more to you than a broodmare. A convenient means to slake your lust."

"That isn't true."

"If not, then why are you here in my bedchamber against my wishes?"

"I intend to sleep here tonight, Brynn."

"And you are giving me absolutely no choice in the matter?"

His features remained enigmatic. "Must I remind you of the vows we spoke before the altar?"

"Ah, yes, our holy vows. I'm certain you respect those so highly."

Ignoring her sarcasm, he met her hot gaze levelly. "Come to bed with me, Brynn." His words were soft, imperious, and made her go rigid.

"And if I refuse?"

There was a moment of silence. "You haven't the right to refuse. You're my wife."

Her jaw clenched. She had always been proud, perhaps to a fault, but even though she despised being thought of as merely Lucian's possession, she knew she was fighting a losing battle. Under English law, a man's wife was his property to do with as he saw fit. She didn't have the legal right to deny him her bed. But that didn't mean she had to welcome him.

She gave Lucian a scathing look, which she saw had no effect. His face could have been carved from granite for all the emotion he showed.

The silence lengthened, gathering tension with every drawn-out moment. As she stood defiant before him, he spoke again, this time in a voice that was low and silken.

"I think you've already proven you don't have the willpower to resist me, any more than I can you."

Brynn felt sudden despair well up in her. That was the problem. She found Lucian irresistible. But she couldn't give in to her urges. All she could do was try to protect them both with cold indifference. She lifted her chin, giving him an icy stare.

Lucian viewed her chill expression with feigned apathy. A sharp longing knotted his insides as his gaze swept over her. Her vibrant hair shimmered, cloaking her shoulders in a mass of fire and silk. He had to set his teeth to keep from dragging her into his arms. It would be wiser, he reminded himself, to get this over with at once, before the hunger burning within him eroded the last of his self-control.

"You had best accustom yourself to my visits," he said, keeping his own tone cool. "I intend to sleep with you each and every night, at least until you conceive."

"Until I conceive?" Brynn narrowed her gaze, finding a glimmer of hope in his declaration. "And then you will leave me alone?"

There was a long pause. "If you wish it. Once you present me with an heir, there will no longer be any urgent need for me to 'slake my lust,' as you put it."

"I shall hold you to that promise."

Regally she went to the bed, then slid beneath the covers, giving him her back. Moments later she felt the mattress shift as he sat beside her. She stiffened when his fingers plucked the sleeve of her nightdress.

"You won't need this."

"I prefer to keep it on," she said tightly. "It isn't necessary to remove it to do what you intend to do."

His voice was low, compelling, and darkly masculine as he replied, "There is no reason to make this difficult, Brynn. Conceiving a son should be pleasurable for us both."

"I don't wish it to be pleasurable. I only wish you to be done with it."

"Very well."

She heard a quiet rustle as his dressing gown fell to the floor. He pulled down the covers before joining her in the bed.

Brynn shivered. She could feel him at her back, feel his hot skin as his body pressed against hers. His heavy arousal was obvious through the fabric of her nightdress.

When his hand moved to her arm, she tried not to flinch. She kept herself rigid, even when he began stroking her . . . her arm, her waist, her stomach . . . touching her purposefully, silently. After a moment, his hand rose to her breasts hidden by her nightdress. His fingers splayed over the sensitive mounds, deliberately brushing her tingling nipples until they peaked and thrust against the delicate fabric.

Brynn drew a sharp breath, finding it difficult to remain unresponsive. There was no warmth, no real tenderness in his caresses, but he was arousing her all the same, despite her effort to resist.

Eventually his hand swept lower, and he drew up her nightdress, baring her body to the waist. Brynn bit her lip hard as his palm skimmed her buttock, then slowly slid over her hip around to her belly, seeking her woman's mound. When he touched her there, she clamped her thighs together, knowing he had found her cleft wet. Not accepting her resistance, he urged her thighs apart and slid two fingers deep into her.

Heat seared through her. Brynn shuddered, involuntarily arching against his tormenting hand while his thumb rubbed the tiny bud of femininity with her own sleek moisture. It was impossible to remain passive.

Her breath quickened audibly in the silence.

Finally he left off arousing her and grasped her shoulder, rolling her toward him so that she lay on her back.

"Look at me, Brynn," he urged hoarsely.

She did look—at his chiseled face dark and grim with concentration, and lower, at his hard, lean, graceful body with its powerful, swollen erection. Brynn shivered, despite the mildness of the August night. Lucian had possessed her body once before, but he was still a stranger, one who was prepared to invade her with his foreign hardness.

Shifting his position, he mounted her, lowering himself till their bare loins just touched. Impossibly, the muscles of her lower body tightened and clamped down in eager anticipation of his possession.

He entered her then, thrusting slowly into her with a detached control, relentlessly filling her. Brynn gasped, tremors moving through her body at the shock of his uncompromising maleness inside her.

Squeezing her eyes shut, she averted her face. She felt helpless lying like this, impaled by his flesh, totally at his mercy. Yet when he began to move, the traitorous warmth in her began to blur the edges of her resistance.

As he withdrew, her quivering inner flesh clutched helplessly at his thick length, not easing until he sheathed himself fully again.

He kissed her then, covering her mouth firmly

with his. He tasted of brandy, hot and sweet and potent. She tried to turn away, but he thrust his tongue deeply into her mouth, penetrating the way his engorged shaft was doing between her spread thighs.

Against her will Brynn felt herself responding wantonly to him. When he withdrew only to thrust harder, she found it impossible to remain still. In spite of her fierce determination, she whimpered.

His kiss grew more forceful, and so did his rhythm. When her hips began to writhe, he gripped them firmly with his hands to still her and plunged into her again and again, devastating her control. Moaning now, she wrapped her arms around his shoulders, clutching him tightly to her as he drove into her. Spears of searing heat lanced her as his hard flesh went deeper and harder, ravishing her with pleasure.

Then suddenly wave after wave of shuddering tremors began to ripple remorselessly through her. Brynn cried out as she shattered in ecstasy.

She was scarcely aware when Lucian permitted himself his own harsh release. When he finally went still, she was gasping for breath. His heavy weight lay sprawled across her, his own ragged breath loud in her ear.

Burning with resentment and worse, passion, Brynn squeezed her eyes shut. He had forced a response from her that was deeper and far more powerful than her first incredible time. Far from simply enduring his emotionless sexual attentions, she had *welcomed* them. He was indeed Lucifer, a devil who could arouse her body at will.

Frightened that he could have dredged such a response from her, she tried to push him away.

"Please get off me," she ordered tightly, as if she'd never come apart in his arms and burned with desire. "You are crushing me."

He raised his head slowly, as if not believing her hoarse command. A span of several heartbeats passed. When she stared coldly at him, though, Lucian obliged her, easing from between her thighs.

Abruptly Brynn pushed her nightgown down to cover her naked limbs and drew the sheet up over her. "I trust you are finished," she ground out.

There was another long pause before his hand reached for her. Relentlessly he cupped her chin in his fingers, his blue eyes cold.

"Don't pretend you didn't enjoy my lovemaking, sweeting," he said softly. "You were hot enough to melt a glacier."

She flinched as the words set themselves like tiny barbed arrows into her flesh. "Pray don't call what you did *lovemaking*."

"Fucking, then," he said, his voice even lower, dangerously hard. "Is that an adequate description? Well, be prepared, love, for I intend to have you like that every night—and make you enjoy it."

Not giving her a chance to reply, he rose and caught up his dressing gown, shrugging it on before he crossed the bedchamber. Moments later she heard the door between their rooms shut with harsh finality.

Brynn rolled over, clutching the sheet to herself as a wave of hurt coursed through her.

She suddenly felt lonelier and more wretched

than in recent memory. She had wanted to wound Lucian, to drive him from her bed. So why was she the one aching with misery?

Fighting back tears, she gazed up at the canopy overhead, cursing her husband. *Fucking, then . . . I intend to have you like that every night—and make you enjoy it.*

Wincing, Brynn drew a quavering breath. She very much feared he would make good his promise to make her enjoy it, and then what would happen?

Chapter Nine

Except for his nightly visits, Brynn saw little of Lucian the following week. She was perfectly satisfied, however, to live separate lives. As far as marriages went, theirs was not an unusual arrangement for the upper classes and the nobility, although her reason for their distance—the danger of a curse—was rather unique.

During the days, her husband spent a great deal of time away from home, presumably at his work, Brynn concluded from conversations with Raven. Lucian reportedly had offices at Whitehall, where he toiled for the Foreign Office.

The first inkling she had of Lucian's unusual job came one afternoon when she accompanied Raven shopping for bride clothes. After inspecting a bolt of ivory lace, Brynn rejected it, saying the quality was inferior.

"How can you tell?" Raven wanted to know.

"See the dropped stitches here? And the dye? The pattern isn't uniform. We can do better, I'm certain."

As they left the shop, their footmen following dutifully behind carrying parcels, Raven asked Brynn how she knew so much about lace.

"I have sold a good deal of it to modistes and milliners over the past few years."

Raven raised an eyebrow in surprise. "Your family is in trade?"

Brynn hesitated, wondering how much of her background to reveal. "Of a sort," she replied, realizing Raven could be trusted not to be judgmental. "But not the merchant trade. In Cornwall, when we speak of trade, we mean the Free Trade."

"Smuggling?" Raven's eyes brightened with curiosity. "How intriguing." Glancing over her shoulder then to see who might overhear, she evidently remembered she was on a public street and lowered her voice. "Do tell me about it."

Brynn returned a wry smile at her friend's delight. "I don't consider smuggling to be intriguing. Actually, it is very hard work, and rather dangerous. But it is a fact of life where I come from, a way to make ends meet. I know of few families who aren't involved in some fashion or another."

"And you take part yourself?"

"Not often. Mostly I handle disposing of various kinds of contraband."

"I think it would be gratifying," Raven said almost wistfully, "to be able to engage in adventures forbidden to women. Still . . . I wouldn't advertise your connection to Lucian, if I were you."

It was Brynn's turn to be curious. "Why not?"

"Because he has a great aversion to smugglers. I've heard him express his opinion in no uncertain terms. Smuggling cheats the government of badly needed tax revenue that Britain and the allies must have to vanquish the French. I can understand his point of view, even if I don't share it. Lucian has spent years trying to bring down Napoleon. He takes pride in his work—even though spying is considered a vulgar enterprise by most of the ton."

"Spying?"

At Brynn's quizzical look, Raven added, "Lucian is a genuine spymaster, did he not tell you?"

Brynn felt her heartbeat quicken with alarm. "My brother said he worked for the Foreign Office."

"He does. In intelligence. It is all very clandestine and hush-hush. Sometimes Lucian disappears for weeks at a time, no doubt on some mission or other. He won't discuss his work, but in fact he is considered something of a hero."

Brynn scarcely heard that last remark, for she was still recovering from the shock of her friend's revelation. Disquieted, she thought back over her various conversations with Lucian, wondering if she had ever said anything in his presence to implicate her brother in the illegal act of smuggling. She hadn't considered Lucian as a danger to her family, only to her, but now she realized he could very well be a threat to Gray.

And Lucian hadn't mentioned a word about his occupation to her, Brynn thought, vexed. His secretiveness and lack of candor was yet another cause for resentment, while the danger was one more reason to be wary of her new husband.

"Forgive me, Brynn. . . ."

She shook herself mentally when she realized Raven had spoken to her. "I'm sorry, I was woolgathering. What did you say?"

"I know it is none of my business, but is something wrong between you and Lucian?"

"No. Why would you think so?"

"You are scarcely ever together, for one thing. You don't behave at all like newlyweds."

Brynn forced a smile. "Ours was a marriage of convenience, nothing more. I am perfectly content with our arrangement."

And even if that was a lie, Brynn reflected, she was glad she seldom encountered Lucian.

Other than his work, several other business enterprises apparently occupied his time, including the vast Wycliff shipping concerns. When he was home, he was often closeted with his secretary as well as numerous business mangers and clerks.

And according to the Wycliff butler, Lucian regularly engaged in the typical gentlemen's sports of riding, fencing, and fisticuffs. In the evenings he frequently dined at his club. And afterward, well . . . Brynn suspected Lucian was carousing with his Hellfire colleagues, since he never returned until late at night.

The evenings were the worst for her. After lonely dinners with only herself for companionship, she would lie in wait for him, dreading his visits, although she had usually fallen asleep by the time he came to her bed. Emotionless, silent, he would awaken her with his dispassionate caresses, arousing her as if performing a perfunctory and not particularly pleasant chore. Just as silently, he would return to his own rooms, leaving her burning with the pleasure he had given her.

Brynn fought his carnal mastery with fierce determination. He might possess her in the flesh, but she would never allow him to touch her spirit.

The days were more pleasant, at least. Not surprisingly, Lucian possessed an extensive library, and Brynn discovered countless subjects within the shelves of leather-bound tomes that interested her. Additionally, she spent hours reading the newspapers to which her husband subscribed, catching up on the events of the world, events that were rarely even discussed in the backwaters of home.

And thankfully Raven proved a delightful companion. Brynn thought she might be truly miserable without their friendship. They rode in the park each morning and paid calls or visited the shops each afternoon. Raven was grimly determined to assemble a trousseau befitting her impending marriage to a duke. And she proved to be a stern taskmaster in demanding that her own advice regarding Brynn's apparel be followed.

Brynn found her wardrobe growing at a shameful rate—dresses for morning, afternoon, and evening, walking and riding and traveling, shoes and bonnets and reticules to match, spencers and pelisses . . .

She regarded the expense a shocking waste, especially when she considered how much good she could do at home with even a tiny fraction of what she was so nonchalantly spending. The centuries-old stone church of the St. Mawes parish was crumbling. Her own home badly needed repairs. Most of the fishing vessels owned by the villagers were held together by prayers. . . . It was dismaying to realize that a single one of the new gowns Raven insisted she purchase could lift a Cornish family out of squalor into relative prosperity.

Yet beautiful gowns were necessary for the role she must play. Raven was right, Brynn conceded; she needed to be fashionably attired if she intended to stare down the despots of the ton. And while she had no profound desire to enter Lucian's aristocratic world of luxury and license, or to become a useless ornament for his earldom, she did indeed want a place in society for Theo . . . and for her possible future children, if it came to that.

Moreover, Brynn admitted only to herself, after being shunned for so many years, it was gratifying to be accepted into a group where no one knew anything of her past, instead of being treated like a leper.

As the week passed, she found it harder to allow herself to mope and wallow in loneliness. The moments when she longed for even a Latin grammar to help occupy her thoughts were gone.

She gradually began making acquaintances as she allowed Raven to coax her out of seclusion. Perhaps it was time, Brynn rationalized, to stop hiding at home like a prisoner, letting the curse rule her life. But she made a concerted effort to dull her demeanor, remaining polite but distant in company, speaking only when spoken to.

She liked most of Raven's friends, and some she even found clever and fascinating. Raven, with her own brand of beauty and lively allure, proved a potent draw, and handsome young gentlemen regularly flocked around her like honeybees—gentlemen who regrettably soon turned their attention to Brynn, despite her earnest attempts to act the wallflower.

Lucian wasn't pleased to find his wife the object of such ardor, either. One afternoon he came home to discover Brynn surrounded by a half dozen young bucks gathered in his drawing room, with only Raven providing female chaperonage.

A dandy with an outrageously high cravat was reciting a sonnet praising the lure of Lady Wycliff's emerald eyes, but since the verse didn't quite rhyme, it was received with winces and convivial laughter.

"No, no, I am being unjustly maligned," the poet protested amiably.

Brynn's low voice held a smile when she agreed. "Indeed, Mr. Pickering. You should be commended for your effort."

Lucian felt an unreasonable shaft of jealousy as he paused in the doorway. For the most part he'd succeeded in resisting his desire for Brynn this past week, but seeing her looking so fresh and lovely in a jonquil-shaded gown aroused him, while the presence of so many admiring beaux incited an uncustomary instinct of primitive male possessiveness.

The company grew suddenly quiet when Lucian moved into the room. Clamping down on his jealousy, he kept his expression bland as he crossed to Brynn and bent to kiss her cheek.

"Why don't you introduce me to your friends, my dear?" he said lightly, ignoring her flush and the way she visibly stiffened.

Raven stepped in to perform the duty, however, while Brynn fell silent. It was soon clear that the lively mood of the company had changed to reserved formality. And when Lucian settled himself beside his wife on the settee, he found himself the recipient of continual wary glances.

After a short while the gentlemen began to excuse themselves. When the last one had gone, Raven gave Lucian a disapproving frown as she rose to her feet. "I am sorry that we have seen so very little of you lately, Lucian."

"Regrettably I have been busy."

"You seem to have forgotten that you are recently wed. I would not have expected you to neglect your bride so."

He glanced at Brynn. "My bride doesn't seem to be suffering. Not when I find her holding court for admirers who compose sonnets to her emerald eyes."

Brynn returned her husband's gaze with a cool look before she rose from the settee. "You needn't champion me, Raven. I am quite content. Come, I will show you out."

She started to follow her friend from the room, but halted when Lucian called softly to her, feeling a warm shiver run down her spine. It disturbed her that just the sound of his voice could affect her.

"Need I warn you, love, that you have a position to uphold in society now?"

Wincing at his implied criticism, she glanced back at him. "I have done nothing wrong."

"Perhaps not, but encouraging the attentions of those wild young bucks could give the wrong impression."

His accusation stung, yet she knew Lucian was right. She had indeed forgotten herself this afternoon. She would have to take greater care to remember the dangers of becoming too friendly with her admirers.

Squaring her shoulders, Brynn sidestepped his charge with an indirect reply. "Is there a reason you deigned to grace us with your company this afternoon, my lord?"

"Must I have a reason to return to my own home?"

"You have been here so seldom, I thought perhaps you might have one."

"Actually I wanted to deliver an invitation to you. My great-aunt, Lady Agatha Edgecomb, is holding a garden party in our honor Saturday next."

Brynn stared at him in surprise. "In our honor? When I first met her, Lady Agatha swore she would never acknowledge our marriage. She thinks me nothing but a tart."

Lucian's mouth curved dryly. "I persuaded her to reconsider. She understands she has no choice but to accept you as my wife if she doesn't want me to cut the connection."

"That does so relieve my mind," Brynn said with false sincerity. "Your aunt will make such a delightful acquaintance."

A muscle in his jaw flexed at her facetious tone, but he answered mildly, "I don't care much for my relatives, particularly Aunt Agatha, but I trust you will behave with circumspection and give them no cause to impugn our marriage."

Brynn smiled coolly. "They will doubtless impugn our marriage, no matter how I behave. And if you wanted a model of circumspection, you should have considered that before you wed me," she retorted before walking from the room.

She had to pause to compose herself, however, before joining her friend. It vexed her that Lucian should take her to task for her behavior. Despite appearances, she hadn't purposefully encouraged the reckless ardor of her admirers. A few poems were nothing compared to what had happened in the past.

Indeed, she wondered what Lucian would say if he saw gentlemen *truly* losing their heads over her. It would serve him right, Brynn reflected with indignation, if she allowed it to happen. Perhaps then he would believe her.

Still, she reminded herself, she wasn't willing to risk the danger for a few moments' satisfaction of thumbing her nose at her autocratic husband.

She was dreaming again, another dark dream of Lucian. This time the danger came not from her, but from a man wielding a deadly rapier.

Caught off guard by the unexpected attack, Lucian leapt back, barely eluding the slashing blade. His opponent followed, thrusting viciously, a look of feral rage on his face.

Unarmed, Lucian spun away defensively, trying to avoid becoming a target in the uneven contest. When he took refuge behind a table, the man reached out and sent it thudding to the floor, then lunged again.

This time Lucian was ready. Sidestepping, he

caught the hilt of the rapier and held hard, trapping the weapon between their bodies.

The man tried to wrest it free, to no avail. For an endless moment, they stood locked together, straining in a desperate struggle for control, teeth bared, breath coming harshly. Finally the man gave an anguished cry and launched himself against Lucian, throwing them both off balance. Grunting, they fell together, crashing over the table.

Instinctively Lucian rolled to one side and sprang to his feet, firmly in possession of the rapier. Yet his opponent lay there on the floor, groaning, blood seeping from a mortal wound in his chest.

Dropping the blade with a clatter, Lucian went down on his knees beside the dying man, cradling his head almost tenderly.

"Giles ..." he whispered, his face taut with agony.

"Forgive me, Luce. ... It is better this way. ... Please ... don't tell ..."

His last rasped words were lost in a violent fit of coughing as blood bubbled up from his throat.

Brynn came awake suddenly, her heart strangely aching for Lucian. She felt his torment, his despair, in killing his friend.

"No ... !"

Hearing the muffled groan, she gave a start and turned her head on the pillow to find Lucian lying beside her. They must have both fallen asleep after he'd made love to her, she realized; her inner thighs were still wet with his seed, while her body still throbbed from his possession.

He was in the throes of a nightmare, it seemed.

Her heart wrenching with compassion, Brynn reached out to touch his shoulder—a mistake, she discovered when Lucian jolted awake. She gasped as he grasped her wrist in a fierce grip.

His blue eyes fixed wildly on her before he finally recognized his surroundings. She could see his confusion in the dim light of the bedside lamp. Usually he left her bed directly afterward.

Releasing her wrist as if burned, Lucian ran a hand roughly down his face. Then, pushing the covers away, he sat up abruptly, giving Brynn his naked back as he swung his legs over the side of the bed.

"Lucian," she asked quietly, needing to know. "Who is Giles?"

He flinched visibly. His voice was hoarse when he finally spoke. "Who told you about Giles?"

"No one told me. I saw him in my dreams."

His back remained so rigid, Brynn knew he didn't believe her.

"You must be mistaken," he said finally. "Giles is dead."

Without another word, he rose from the bed and snatched up his robe, then crossed the bedchamber. The door shut softly behind him, leaving her alone.

Brynn lay there unmoving, her thoughts still whirling. Her dreams could be deadly premonitions, but somehow she was certain her dark images of Giles were part of Lucian's past, not his future. And she was just as certain that she had probed an open, festering wound in his conscience.

*   *   *

Despite her professed indifference, Brynn did care deeply about how she was received by society. By the time Saturday arrived, she felt as if an army of butterflies had taken up residence in her stomach, for she knew she would be on trial at her first major public appearance.

The day of the garden party dawned bright with sunshine. At the appointed hour of two, she found Lucian awaiting her in the entrance hall.

His eyes followed her as she descended the grand staircase. There was nothing in her costume to earn his disapproval, Brynn knew; her high-waisted gown of pale jade jaconet, with a floral-patterned shawl draping her arms, was almost modest. Her hair was sedately tamed in a chignon, except for a few errant curls wisping at her temples, and mostly hidden by a jaunty, close-fitting hat adorned with knots of jade ribbon.

Brynn endured his inspection silently, mentally daring him to comment, but he merely offered her his arm in silence and escorted her to the waiting carriage.

Only when they were settled did she really notice Lucian's appearance. He was dressed with his usual damn-your-eyes elegance in a blue coat and buff breeches, and his striking features were so handsome that she found it hard to catch her breath in such close quarters with him.

There was little conversation between them at first, until Lucian bestirred himself to tell her about the guests she was likely to meet, particularly his many relatives. He had more than a dozen cousins in London alone.

Brynn found her curiosity aroused, despite her re-solve to keep their relationship impersonal. "Raven says your favorite cousin isn't even English."

Lucian's mouth twisted in a wry smile. "No, Nicholas Sabine is American. He was here in England this past summer, in disguise."

"Why in disguise?"

"Because he was accused of piracy. Nick is an ad-venturer who ran afoul of the British navy and wound up marrying an Englishwoman."

"Raven told me of his marriage, but nothing about why."

"It is an interesting story, but I was out of the country during most of Nick's visit, so I'm not privy to the details. I expect you should ask Raven. The two of you seem to be growing close."

Brynn fell silent at Lucian's suggestion, remem-bering her vow to have no intimate interaction with him other than what was strictly necessary to main-tain civility.

She gave a cool, curt reply, and turned her atten-tion to the passing landscape outside the carriage window. If she saw the way his lips tightened, she ignored it.

The Edgecomb estate was on the outskirts of London, near Richmond, and along the bank of the Thames River. Brynn felt her nervousness rise as they drew closer, wondering how she would endure the scrutiny of Lucian's scornful relatives and dis-dainful acquaintances.

By the time they arrived, a goodly number of guests were milling about the grounds to the rear of the estate. The elegant gardens bore a formal design, with stately rows of yew trees and myrtles lining the smooth gravel paths, interspersed with occasional statuary and giant urns. Beyond, an immaculate lawn led down to the river. Brynn could see rowboats on the water and an archery range that had been set up to provide entertainment.

Lady Edgecomb received Brynn with the same frosty stare as before, yet unlike during their last meeting, the lady seemed prepared to bite her tongue. She extended a stiffly courteous welcome, even though her mouth puckered as if she were sucking lemons.

After a moment of polite conversation, Lucian took Brynn's arm to stroll the garden avenues and meet the various guests. Several of his cousins were present—both genders and of varying ages. If he disliked any of them, Brynn couldn't tell, for he exchanged pleasantries with every evidence of his usual charm and appeared to overlook their obvious fawning.

Much to Brynn's surprise, Lucian seemed almost proud to proclaim her his wife. Even more surprising, he was oddly protective of her. She felt the heat of his body as he stood close beside her, the strength of his hand that rested so casually at the small of her back, but for once she accepted his possessive touch with gratitude rather than dismay. Despite the cold reserve that existed in their marriage, he apparently had decided to shield her from the sniping and criticism of his relatives.

Brynn was quite aware that they were the center of attention—not just herself, but Lucian as well. Other women followed him with their eyes, hunger evident in their expressions, a hunger Lucian appeared not to notice.

The first half hour passed without incident, even when they encountered Lady Agatha again. The dowager's chill seemed to thaw marginally, but when Lucian ushered Brynn toward another group, she audibly let out her breath.

"Relieved?" he murmured, as if understanding.

"Yes. That wasn't as bad as I feared. At least your aunt didn't swallow me alive."

Lucian's mouth curved in a wry half smile. "I never expected her to. I'm certain you can hold your own with Lady Agatha or anyone else."

His praise unaccountably warmed Brynn, but just then she caught the reflection of sunlight off the river. The pastoral scene could have been an oil painting, with willows growing along the bank and fleecy clouds scudding overhead.

"How lovely. May we walk that way?"

"As you wish, my lady."

When Lucian offered his arm, she took it and strolled with him down toward the river.

"This is nothing like the ocean," she said wistfully, pausing to view the scene. "But I miss having a view of the water. I miss being able to swim whenever I wish."

"That doesn't surprise me. A sea siren should be allowed to cavort in her kingdom."

She heard the amusement in his tone and glanced up at Lucian to find him regarding her with an intimate warmth in his eyes.

"I'm afraid you cannot swim just now," he added,

"but if you like, we can return here at another time so you can indulge your secret vice."

Brynn felt herself tense at the unwanted tender moment between them. Her pleasure faded, as did Lucian's smile.

"Come," he said evenly, "there are more guests to meet."

He had just turned her back toward the house when a fair-haired gentleman crossed the lawn to intercept them. Lucian's features showed genuine affection as the two men greeted each another.

"My dear, let me make known one of my closest friends, Dare North, Earl of Clune—and now the Marquess of Wolverton. Dare came into the title recently when his grandfather passed away."

Wolverton flashed a wickedly charming smile as he bowed over her hand. "A pleasure, my lady. I heard Lucian hung himself in the parson's noose, but after seeing what a lovely lady he chose, I can almost understand why. The rumors of your beauty don't do you justice."

Brynn kept her own answering smile curt. She had no intention of arousing male attention, certainly not that of a rake like Lord Clune—or Wolverton, she amended. He was a rogue of the first order and one of the founders of the Hellfire League. News of his outrageous exploits had penetrated even to Cornwall.

"I have heard of you as well, my lord. Your reputation precedes you."

His grin was slow and lazy and in its own way as powerfully magnetic as her husband's. "I am not nearly as wicked as the gossips make me out to be."

Lucian's laugh held amusement. "Don't believe it for a minute, my dear. Dare has half the ladies in England swooning over him, and the other half quaking in outrage at his scandals."

Wolverton actually winked at her, which made Brynn struggle to swallow a smile. She could well understand his dangerous appeal to the ladies.

"I don't suppose you have any sisters?" Wolverton asked in a leading tone.

"I have five brothers, my lord."

"A pity—"

Just then Raven came up to them. "Clune!" she exclaimed after pressing cheeks with Brynn in greeting. "Or I should say Wolverton. . . . When did you get back from inspecting your new family seat?"

Surprisingly, he bussed her cheek with a kiss that held more brotherly affection than ardor. "I returned just this morning, vixen. I trust you have missed me."

"Most certainly. No one but you appreciates a good gallop in the park. I'll wager half the female population has found London impossibly dull without you."

"I should hope so. Where is Halford?"

Raven waved in the direction of the house. "Speaking with some of his friends. He has no skills in archery, and I am dying to learn." Her betrothed, the Duke of Halford, was some twenty years her senior, Brynn knew, and had no interest in most of Raven's activities. "Do come with me, Brynn. Pickering has offered to teach me to shoot, and I don't wish to be the only novice."

After glancing at Lucian, Brynn nodded and excused herself.

Both noblemen followed her progress as she and Raven joined a group of gentlemen at the archery butts. Lucian didn't much like seeing Brynn consorting with the same young bucks who had written poetry to her last week, but he could hardly forbid her participation in an innocuous sport, held in public and in broad daylight. Especially when she could claim so few acquaintances in her new life.

He felt a measure of guilt over that. He hadn't made the transition easy for Brynn, leaving her alone so much of the time. But he'd thought it best to avoid her, for her sake as well as his own. Being in her company made his own dilemma that much more difficult. His fierce need to visit her bed each night was growing out of control. He was becoming obsessed—and that knowledge disturbed him deeply.

When he heard a throat being politely cleared, he realized Dare was watching him with an unusually somber expression.

"You always did have exquisite taste in women, Luce, but *marriage?*"

Lucian shrugged. He could hide his thoughts from most people, but not his closest friend, so he didn't even try. "I want a son."

"I thought you went to Cornwall to sniff out traitors."

"I did."

"But you were seduced into marriage, as rumor says?"

"Quite the contrary. I was the one who insisted we wed."

"Well . . ." Dare returned his gaze to Brynn. "I can certainly understand why you would wish to claim her. There is something about her. . . . A quality beyond beauty. It's quite bewitching."

It was a rare statement coming from a true connoisseur of women, Lucian knew. "She is unlike anyone I've ever known," he said in a low voice. "Since meeting her, all I've done is think with my loins."

"I would never have guessed it from the gossip. Word is you've been avoiding her, spending all your evenings at your club. This is the first time you've even been seen together in public. Rumor has it that yours is not a happy union."

"That much is true. I essentially had to coerce Brynn to the altar, and she hasn't forgiven me for it yet." He felt his friend's penetrating gaze. "But I can at least put the rumors to rest about my not wanting her."

The marquess grimaced. "I hope you don't mean to curtail your activities with the League? When Sin wed, he forgot all about his Hellfire companions, claiming he was stricken by the hopeless malady called love."

Lucian nodded at the memory. Damien Sinclair, known as Lord Sin to the ton, had been one of their leading members before he fell hard for a beautiful widow who had acted as companion to his invalid sister.

"I'm afraid I've already begun to curtail my activities," Lucian said.

"In the name of respectability?"

"Primarily. I owe it to my name and title to put my wilder days behind me."

Dare gave a deep sigh that was only slightly exaggerated. "This is a dark day for libertines. We will miss you, Luce."

Trying to shake off his somber mood, Lucian glanced pointedly at the other nobleman. "I needn't warn you to keep away from my wife, do I, Dare?"

"Certainly not." He flashed an amiable grin. "I would never poach on a friend's private preserve. I have that much honor."

Lucian nodded. Dare's devil-may-care charm hid a surprising depth of intellect and feeling, though he seldom revealed it. And while he might not flinch at cuckolding an adversary, he would never betray a friend—Lucian would have wagered his life on it.

"Your wife seems to be quite the center of attention at the moment," Dare mused aloud.

Lucian followed his gaze to find a knot of gentlemen gathered around Brynn. From the looks of it, they were publicly vying for her favors.

He felt himself stiffen. He couldn't blame them for being entranced by her vibrant beauty, but it incensed him all the same. As did his inability to control his jealousy.

Just then the crowd suddenly parted, and Lucian realized an altercation had sprung up between two of the archers. Even from a distance, he could see Brynn was in the thick of it.

Frozen by incredulity, Lucian watched as the fight showed no signs of abating. One gentleman struck the other, then was felled to the ground with a reciprocal blow. When Brynn stepped between them, she was nearly bowled over—

Lucian felt a surge of fear that shook him from

his stupor. Lunging into action, he sprinted across the lawn, intent on protecting her. When he reached the two combatants, he grasped the first one by the scruff of the neck and hauled him to his feet.

Hard on Lucian's heels, his friend Dare took hold of the second brawler, while Raven began chiding both fighters in a fierce undertone.

"Stop this nonsense at once, both of you! You should be ashamed of yourselves, causing such a spectacle."

"But I wanted to be the one to teach Lady Wycliff," Lord Hogarth said plaintively, wincing in pain as Lucian's choking hold tightened on his collar.

"She said I could have the honor," Pickering muttered.

Brynn stood to one side now, looking shaken. When Lucian eyed her narrowly, her cheeks flushed with guilt and she turned away, refusing to meet his gaze.

Lucian felt a swell of anger. His first instinct was to pummel both young bucks with his fists for fighting over his wife. His second was outrage at Brynn herself for being the cause of their brawl.

When Hogarth began to cough, however, Lucian forced himself to release his grip.

Raven was still venting her fury on the hapless miscreants. Both gentlemen appeared chastened now, and both sported wounds: one a bloody lip, the other an eye that would doubtless turn black and blue.

When she fell silent, Dare spoke up, making light of the situation in an evident attempt to ease the tension. "Perhaps this might be the ideal time to re-turn to the house for refreshment."

"Yes," Raven agreed, still fuming. "We have had quite enough entertainment for one afternoon."

The crowd dispersed then, one of the gentlemen limping, the other carrying himself rigidly as if nursing a grudge.

Brynn would have followed, but Lucian caught her arm and said in a dangerous voice, "I thought I warned you about the need for propriety."

She stiffened at his touch. "I was simply learning to shoot," she replied, her chin lifting with a mea-sure of defiance.

Lucian had to clamp down on his own anger. "If you care to shoot, I will be the one to teach you."

"How curious. I suddenly find I have lost my ap-petite for archery."

Pulling her arm from his grasp, Brynn turned and walked away.

Lucian swore under his breath, struggling against the urge to follow her and drag her back to him. He wasn't normally given to fits of jealous rage, but his possessiveness where Brynn was concerned was ut-terly savage. Bloody hell, he had to get control of himself.

Bending, he snatched up a bow and notched an arrow, then drew it back and let the missile fly with a whooshing thud. It struck the target dead center.

When he turned, however, he realized he wasn't alone. Dare was regarding him with something akin to sympathy.

"I must say, I don't envy you," his friend said

softly. "If this is what marriage leads to, I believe I shall pass."

Only when Lucian was alone with Brynn in the carriage, driving home, did he have the chance to mention the fray on the archery range that had caused a minor scandal among the company. "Would you care to explain how you managed to create a sensation less than an hour into the party after you agreed to behave with circumspection?"

Brynn gave him a wounded look that was edged with indignation. "You cannot believe I deliberately encouraged that dispute?"

Lucian found himself gritting back a reply. Perhaps she wasn't entirely to blame. Perhaps she hadn't purposefully orchestrated a public fight over her attentions. But she could certainly have prevented a spectacle by simply keeping away from those two young hotheads and not giving them cause to drool over her. "Can't I? I think you deliberately encouraged those pups to make fools of themselves over you."

"You are quite wrong. I've told you before. The curse makes men do foolish things when they are around me."

"Then I suggest you not allow them to be around you."

"Are you saying I must shun their company?"

"I am saying I would like you to avoid scandal. I don't enjoy seeing my countess become a public spectacle."

"Then you should never have wed me," Brynn said stiffly. "I warned you how it would be."

Annoyed, Lucian frowned. "What are you about, Brynn? Is this your means of revenge for having to wed me—to disgrace me and our marriage before the ton?"

"No, of course not. It is merely the curse at work."

"I don't believe in such things as curses."

"Perhaps you should."

His eyes narrowed. "I have been tolerant until now," he said finally, "but my patience can be stretched only so far."

She gave him an arch look. "And what will you do when it breaks, Lucian? Beat me? Lock me away with nothing but bread and water?"

"I can think of far more pleasant ways to control a recalcitrant wife."

Brynn flushed but lifted her chin. "I may be your wife, but you do not *rule* me," she retorted before lapsing into chill silence.

Lucian set his jaw as he surveyed his beautiful wife sitting rigidly in her corner of the carriage seat. How had their relationship deteriorated to this? This icy contention wasn't what he had planned when he had taken her in marriage.

The urge to melt Brynn's coldness, to destroy her aloofness, surged through him. How satisfying it would be to draw her into his arms, push up her skirts, and thrust deep inside her, giving her pleasure while taking his own. . . .

Swearing at himself, Lucian forced his mind away from the thought. Passion could succeed in turning Brynn's ice to fire, at least momentarily, but it would do nothing to help him overcome his dangerous attraction to her.

Determined to regain his control, Lucian turned to gaze out the carriage window, his face as coldly aloof as Brynn's own.

Brynn took a steadying breath as she paused at the door to Lucian's bedchamber. When they arrived home, he had repaired to his rooms to change his attire for the evening. She'd waited several moments, debating what to do. Finally she pulled the pins from her hair, then crossed through her sitting room into his. But she hesitated as she reached for the door handle.

Lucian claimed not to believe in the curse, but she could prove to him that it was very real. Yet did she dare risk the danger of a demonstration? If she purposely sought to arouse him, there might be no controlling the outcome.

Still, the incident on the archery range this afternoon had only bolstered her belief in the Gypsy's spell. Her behavior had actually been quite modest, not in the least alluring, certainly not compared to Raven's charming demeanor. But the two gentlemen hadn't fought over her friend, Brynn reminded herself. Only her. She was a fool to have hoped she could simply ignore the curse's power.

She needed to convince Lucian of its potency, though. She had to show him that he was just as vulnerable as any other man—more so, in fact, because of his intimate conjugal demands. She had to make him understand the danger so he would help her avert the dire consequences.

Knowing it was better not to allow time for her courage to wane, Brynn opened the door and stepped inside his bedchamber. She had never been in her husband's room before. It was decorated with masculine elegance in rich dark colors of forest green and gold. A massive bed dominated the room. Her gaze was drawn to it, then skittered away to find Lucian at the washstand, toweling his face dry.

Brynn came up short. He was shirtless. The sight of his sleekly muscled torso made her breath catch in her throat.

He hadn't heard her enter, fortunately, which gave her time to recover her composure. She shut the door softly behind her.

Lucian looked up then and froze, surprise flickering in his blue eyes before he quickly masked his expression.

"Have you lost your way?" he asked coolly.

"No. I need help with the buttons on the back of my gown. Will you do me the kindness?"

Lucian eyed her with suspicion. "Why don't you call your maid?"

"I don't want to trouble her."

"But you want to trouble me?"

She merely smiled, a slow, sultry smile that made his features visibly harden. "Do you mind?"

His gaze raked her, taking in the sight of her hair loose and falling around her shoulders. Without answering, he crossed to her. When Brynn gave him her back, he pushed her hair out of the way almost roughly.

At his evident impatience, Brynn couldn't help

but feel a measure of satisfaction, but she held her
tongue as he unfastened the buttons in grim silence.

"Thank you," she said when he was done, keeping her voice low and husky.

She turned to face him. He was so close, she could
feel the heat of his body. He felt the same heat, she
knew. The same taut sexual awareness. She could
see it in his eyes that were glittering like sapphires.

"What game are you playing, Brynn?"

"No game. I am simply proving a point."

"And what point is that?"

"That the curse is extraordinarily potent. I did
not purposefully try to arouse those gentlemen this
afternoon. If I had wanted to, I would have behaved
far differently."

"Like you're behaving now?"

"Yes."

Holding his gaze, she bit her lower lip provocatively and raised her hand to the neckline of her gown.

Lucian went rigid as she drew the silk fabric down
to expose the lush swell of her breasts beneath her
chemise. She meant to undress in front of him, he
realized, and deliberately incite him. He felt his loins
tighten with a savage ache.

"That is far enough," he said tightly, determined
not to respond.

"I don't think so."

She didn't stop with the bodice of her gown.
She pulled her chemise down, freeing her exquisite
breasts, high and firm with rose-hued nipples. His
mouth went dry at the thought of tasting them.

"Do you truly think you can resist me?" she
asked, her husky voice wicked and tempting.

He sucked in a harsh breath. He damned well should resist her. A man could grow addicted to a body like Brynn's and forget everything else that mattered. Already he wanted her with a fierceness, a longing that stunned him.

"You are playing with fire," he warned, his voice thick with desire.

"Perhaps. But I suspect you are the one who will be burned."

He *would* be burned, he had no doubt. Her hair was an abundance of pure flame, flowing around her ivory shoulders and naked breasts with shimmering life. And yet even knowing the danger, he couldn't stop himself from reaching for her.

"Take care, Lucian—"

She never finished her sentence. His hungry mouth swallowed her words as his arms crushed her to him.

He kissed her fiercely, anger and arousal making his blood surge hot. She tasted like fire. Flame seared him as he thrust his tongue deeper into her mouth, while savage possessiveness burned inside him.

He felt her involuntary response. She had gone rigid at first, but suddenly Brynn opened to him, her lips parting to accept his thrusting tongue. His hardened shaft cramped beneath his breeches with primal need.

He groaned against her mouth, the sound thick and raw. He wanted more of her, needed more. . . .

His hands grasping her shoulders, he bent to her breast, capturing a taut nipple. She arched instinctively, pushing herself against his hot mouth. When he drew hungrily upon the peak, sucking hard, her hands clutched in his hair.

He heard her hoarse breath through a haze of passion. "Don't you see?" she gasped. "You can't stop yourself. . . ."

He jerked backward. With a fierce effort at control, Lucian tore himself away. He stood staring at her, drawing in deep gulps of air, passion making him shake.

The struggle was clear on his chiseled face, Brynn realized, feeling clashing emotions of triumph and despair. His eyes glittered with arousal and something darker, a primal lust that was almost savage.

Reaching for her bodice with trembling hands, she covered her naked breasts, which were still heaving at his explosive kiss.

"Do you see now, Lucian?" she asked softly, praying the lesson had sunk in. "You can't escape the power of the curse. You won't be able to resist me unless we keep our distance."

His fists clenched. "I think you underestimate my willpower. I won't surrender to your spell, siren. I'll prove to you the curse isn't real. I won't touch you again."

It was precisely the response she had been hoping for—for Lucian to determinedly fight her allure. So why did she suddenly feel such a loss?

Moreover, his newfound resolve created a fresh dilemma. Brynn forced herself to smile tauntingly while her eyes widened with skepticism. "Does that mean you won't make love to me any longer? If so, then how can I fulfill my wifely duty and conceive a child?"

Smoldering silence met her question, while his virile face hardened.

Brynn took a steadying breath. "That *is* what you want, is it not? A child? Well, I've begun to want the same thing. You promised that when I conceive an heir, I no longer must endure your carnal attentions. So the sooner I comply, the sooner we can be free of each other. I trust after this, however, when you do visit my bed, you'll make an exerted attempt to control your lustful urges."

Having delivered that blow, she turned and forced herself to walk regally from the room.

Alone, Lucian stood shaking as the vestiges of passion began draining from his body. What in hell's name had come over him? He had been wild to have her. If she hadn't taunted him about his lack of control, he would have stripped her naked and taken her right then, ravishing her without any thought to tenderness.

He could have raped her, his hunger had been that raw, that explosive.

Lucian clenched his teeth, willing his muscles to unlock, willing the fiery ache in his groin to dissipate. He had never been so powerless, so mindlessly out of control.

He swore a vivid oath. And what of next time? If he touched her, would he be unable to resist the flame-haired, green-eyed witch who was his wife?

Chapter Ten

She dreamed of Lucian again. His tongue was on her, gently plying her sex between her thighs, softly licking, arousing, savoring. His tenderness was exquisite.

She arched against the pleasure, whimpering at the sharp sensation that rippled through her. His caresses brought her to the edge of explosion, yet he drew back, leaving her unfulfilled, aching with excitement.

"Lucian . . . please . . ." She wanted them joined, yearned for his possession.

He understood her craving.

His kisses moved upward, his breath searing on her naked skin . . . her belly, her breasts, the curve of her throat. Her body shuddered in welcome as he covered her. His swollen hardness slid into her yielding, wet flesh, deeply penetrating . . . but then he held himself still.

With unbearable sweetness, his lips brushed softly over her face, dredging a sigh of joy from deep in her throat. When he smiled down at her, his poignant tenderness made her want to weep. Helpless with desire, she molded herself to him, heat and desperate need welling up in her.

Then he began to move inside her, a rhythm that was ancient, mindless, elemental. Her longing built as he loved her, blossoming to a sweet anguish that made her shake, until with one final thrust he unleashed a storm of fire and she cried out at the piercing ecstasy. . . .

Brynn stirred awake, her body throbbing with need in the darkness. Beside her the bed was empty. She was alone.

She had only been dreaming. Lucian wasn't with her, arousing her with his soul-stirring caresses. She had driven him away with her coldness.

She reached up and touched her face, surprised to find it wet with tears. In her dreams she had found the tenderness she craved from Lucian, the warmth, the joy.

Squeezing her eyes shut, Brynn clutched a pillow to her breasts, remembering her dream and her desperate longing to cherish him.

She couldn't allow herself such indulgence, though. She might deplore the cold reserve between them, but she knew it could be no other way.

Lucian didn't visit her bed that night, or at any time during the following week—a reprieve for which Brynn told herself she was grateful. His avoidance, however, only renewed her sense of loneliness.

Her strained relationship with her husband wasn't her sole cause of despondency, either. Eager to prevent a recurrence of the recent contretemps with her gentlemen admirers, Brynn deliberately cut back on her social engagements. When she did go out, she was careful to keep a crowd of female friends around her, and she refused to speak to Pickering and Hogarth altogether.

Her efforts only made her feel more isolated. Yet she found herself experiencing a strange melancholy that couldn't be attributed simply to loneliness. Her courses came and went, which meant she hadn't conceived, which meant the unsettled state of her marriage would continue. Even though Lucian was avoiding her bed at the moment, that would have to change.

At least her loneliness briefly abated toward the end of her first month as a countess when Grayson paid her a visit on his return from Harrow.

So glad was Brynn to see him that she flew down the stairs and practically launched herself at Gray as he awaited her in the entrance hall.

"Lord, don't choke me, puss," he said, laughing as he pried himself loose from her stranglehold on his neck.

Realizing she was being observed by the butler and several footmen, Brynn took her brother's hand and pulled him into the nearby salon, shutting the door behind them for privacy.

"I hope you've brought me news of Theo. I've received scarcely a word from home since I left."

"Because we have all been busy trying to run the household. I never realized how much you contributed to making the place comfortable, Brynn."

She turned aside the compliment impatiently. "What of Theo?"

"You'll be pleased to know he is safely and happily

ensconced at Harrow. I left him debating the effica-
cies of certain acids with one of his new masters."

"Happily? He truly seemed happy?"

"Ecstatic." Grayson's gaze turned searching.
"What of you, Brynn? Are you at all happy?"

She shrugged, not wanting to discuss her marriage. "I never desired happiness. Now, please, tell
me more about Theo."

She settled with Gray on the settee and interrogated him for half an hour over their youngest
brother's reaction to school and the details of his attendance, down to how many pairs of stockings he
had packed. Finally satisfied, Brynn sat back and let
Gray enjoy his tea, which the attentive butler had
delivered some moments before.

When eventually they got around to discussing
Gray's plans, he responded by looking oddly self-
conscious. "I hoped I could wrangle an invitation to
stay here, if Wycliff doesn't object. I would rather
not waste funds on taking rooms at an inn."

"But of course you must stay," Brynn declared,
adding in a defiant undervoice, "whether or not
Wycliff objects."

She rang for the butler and made arrangements to
have the ancient Caldwell carriage and horses sta-
bled, then showed Gray to a guest bedchamber herself. Her relationship with the housekeeper, Mrs.
Poole, was still strained, and she didn't want the
woman's sour remarks to spoil her reunion with her
brother.

Intending to allow Grayson time to refresh himself and rest, Brynn suggested they meet for dinner

at six. "It is unfashionably early for London, I know, but I prefer to keep country hours."

"Will Wycliff be joining us?" Gray asked with a studied casualness.

"I doubt it," Brynn replied. "I usually dine alone. Lucian doesn't spend much time at home."

That brought her brother's searching look again, but he didn't comment directly on her marriage. Instead he asked her an odd question. "Brynn, what do you know about Wycliff's work at the Foreign Office?"

"Not much. We have never discussed it."

"I heard he is involved in national intelligence—spying, if you will."

"So I've been told." Her eyebrows lifted in puzzlement. "Why do you ask?"

Gray shrugged. "Just curious. I will see you at dinner, then."

"Very well."

Returning to her sitting room, Brynn read for a while, then changed for dinner and went in search of her brother. When she didn't find him in his bedchamber or the drawing room, she extended her search to the lower floor. He wasn't in the salon or dining room, either. When she finally found him, it was in the study, of all places. He was sitting at the desk, rummaging through one of the drawers.

"Gray?"

He gave a start and looked up, a guilty flush on his face.

"What are you doing? That is Lucian's desk."

"I . . . was looking for writing implements."

"You can find paper and pen in your room."

"Can I? I didn't think to look there."

He reached farther into the drawer, then shut it and rose to his feet. Brynn stiffened when she saw him slip something into his pocket. She moved toward him, wondering if he thought she was blind. "What did you take, Gray?"

His flush deepened. "Nothing important, really."

"Grayson Caldwell," Brynn said, feeling as if she were scolding her youngest brother when he misbehaved. "Let me see."

He hesitated a long moment before drawing the object from his pocket. "It's nothing of significance."

Brynn caught a glimpse of a ring that bore the Wycliff seal. "Lucian's seal ring?"

"Yes. I merely wanted to borrow it."

"Why?"

"Because I need his stamp on a letter."

"Why don't you simply ask him to stamp it for you?"

"Oh, certainly," Gray replied with an edge of sarcasm. "I should present him with bald proof that I'm trafficking in contraband cargo. How do you think he would react, Brynn? He's an official of the British government. Do you really think he would turn a blind eye if I were to divulge my illegal activities to him?"

Brynn frowned. "Why are you still involved in illegal activities? You told me you would stop smuggling as soon as our debts were paid. The settlement Lucian gave you should have been more than sufficient. . . . Wasn't it?"

"Not quite," Grayson said, refusing to meet her gaze.

She took a deep breath. "Gray, I won't beg Lucian for money. It was bad enough that I sold myself to him in marriage. I refuse to become any more obliged to him—"

"It wouldn't matter if you did. Money cannot help me out of this difficulty."

She placed a hand on his sleeve, her eyes searching his face. "Gray, what is wrong?"

"Nothing is wrong. I simply need Wycliff's seal on a letter of authorization to ship a load of brandy. It will allow me to elude the revenuers if I am caught."

"But why must you even take the risk? Can't you just stop smuggling?"

"I do intend to stop, Brynn. Very soon. But I still have obligations. I cannot quit until I make one final shipment. This will be my last smuggling venture, I swear, but it will be more dangerous than most."

The plea in his eyes took her aback. She had never seen her brother so troubled.

Disturbed by his intensity, Brynn stared at him a long moment before finally shaking her head. "Gray . . . you cannot use his seal without permission. It wouldn't be right. You must put it back."

His expression hardened. "Please, Brynn, don't ask me to do that. I have no choice."

"I am not asking you, I am telling. If you insist on taking it, I will have to inform Lucian."

He stared at her for a long moment. "You cannot go to him, Brynn. He could ruin me. I think Wycliff already suspects me of being a Free Trader. He could order the excise men to hound our shores until I am caught. I could wind up in prison, despite your marriage to him. Is that what you want?"

"No, of course not, but—"

"It isn't only my own skin that concerns me. It is yours and Theo's as well."

Brynn felt her heart quicken in alarm. "Theo's? What are you talking about?"

Taking a deep breath, Grayson shook his head. "Nothing. I only meant it would reflect poorly on you if I were imprisoned. Don't worry. I intend to deal with my problems. But I need this ring, just for a few moments."

"Grayson . . ."

"Please, Brynn, you have to trust me."

She searched her brother's face until finally he averted his gaze.

"There is no other way," he said in a low voice. "Please believe me, I wouldn't stoop to this if I weren't desperate."

Brynn started to reply, but then froze when she heard the murmur of masculine voices out in the hall. Giving a start, she spun to find Lucian standing in the doorway.

She felt herself flushing with guilt, much as her brother had done moments before. They shouldn't even be in here.

Wondering how much of their conversation he had overheard, she watched him warily as he greeted Grayson pleasantly and shook hands. She could see no sign of suspicion in his demeanor, but still she found it hard to maintain her composure when Lucian turned his attention to her.

"I was just giving m-my brother a tour of the

house," she stammered. "We were about to go in to dinner."

"Excellent. I hope you won't object if I join you."

"No . . . of course not," Brynn said, forcing a smile.

For the rest of the evening she had no opportunity for a private word with her brother, either to question him about his cryptic comments or to demand that he return her husband's ring.

Somewhat to her surprise, Lucian put himself out to play the charming host, carrying much of the conversation since Brynn had little to say with her thoughts so distracted. She merely toyed with her food as she debated what to do. Smuggling brandy was one thing, but purloining Lucian's property was unquestionably wrong.

Still, if Gray was in trouble, Brynn argued with herself, she couldn't simply abandon him. And if Theo was possibly in danger . . . She had to discover what was worrying him so.

The chance to speak with her brother never came, however. At the end of the meal, Brynn left the gentlemen to their port and repaired to the drawing room alone, where she wound up pacing the floor. But when the two men joined her, the conversation remained centered on male sports.

Finally realizing Gray meant to outwait her, she gave up and retired to bed, leaving Lucian to entertain him at billiards late into the night.

She woke earlier than usual the following morning, just as dawn was breaking. Hearing the clop of horses' hooves on pavement outside, Brynn threw a wrapper on and raced downstairs to find Gray preparing to leave.

He looked up as she reached the front entryway.

"Grayson," she said tersely, "I believe you are forgetting something."

He smiled, glancing pointedly at the butler, who was directing baggage to be carried out to the waiting carriage. "Ah, yes, puss. I didn't say goodbye." Leaning toward her, he kissed her forehead even as he whispered in her ear, "Don't scold, Brynn, especially in front of the servants."

"I *will* scold if you don't immediately tell me what is going on," she replied in a harsh whisper of her own. "What sort of trouble are you in?"

"Nothing I can't handle. I didn't mean to alarm you."

"Grayson . . ." she repeated, her frustration welling. "What about the . . . object that doesn't belong to you?"

He reached into his pocket and pressed the ring into her hand. "Here, take it."

Her fingers closing over the cold metal, Brynn pasted a sweet smile on her lips for the benefit of the footmen. "If you ever do anything like this again, dear brother . . ." she murmured.

"I know, you'll have my head for fish bait." He gave her a forced grin. "But this has saved my life, whether you realize it or not."

He kissed her cheek again and took his leave. Brynn shivered as she watched him go, wondering if Gray could possibly be serious about his life being at stake.

The moment the front door had shut behind him,

Brynn turned and slipped into the study, intending to restore the ring to its proper place.

She had just reached for the desk drawer when Lucian spoke behind her. "Can I help you find something, love?"

Brynn jumped in alarm and spun to face him. Meeting his blue eyes always jolted her, but this time they were particularly penetrating. She stared back at him, wondering with a sense of desperation what excuse she could possibly give him for being here.

"I'm curious to know what has you so fascinated with this room."

"N-nothing," she replied, knowing she was stammering again. "I . . . I am missing an earring. I thought perhaps I might have dropped it here yesterday."

When Lucian moved toward her, she took a step backward. His gaze raked over her, taking in her dishabille, from her hair tumbling wildly over her shoulders, to her wrapper that she had donned over her nightdress, to her bare feet.

"Perhaps you should have put on shoes," he murmured, coming to stand before her.

She swallowed hard. "I . . . didn't have time. I wanted to say farewell to my brother."

"Weren't you concerned you would drive the footmen wild, roaming the house in that state of undress?"

"I am perfectly well concealed," she replied much too breathlessly. "More so than when I wear evening attire."

Lucian's chiseled mouth curved in a smile. "For evening, you don't normally wear your hair loose and flowing like that, looking as if you've just left your bed. You might give a thought to us poor mortals, siren," he added before his smile suddenly faded.

His charming remark had been automatic; part of the habitual seductive manner of a rake, Brynn realized. But he had evidently remembered whom he was addressing.

His expression was solemn as he reached up to smooth a curling tress back from her face, but when his fingers brushed her temple, Brynn flinched. She was certain he hadn't meant his touch to be arousing, but it seared her as if it were a brand.

Uneasily she returned his gaze. Lucian was very, very still. Spellbound. She recognized the carnal haze in his eyes.

She drew a sharp breath, knowing she would have to act to break the enchantment.

When his gaze dropped to her mouth, she forced herself to smile coldly.

As if he had no control over his actions, he reached up to caress her lower lip with his thumb. His voice was incredibly husky when he murmured almost to himself, "You play the ice maiden so well. It dares a man to try melting you."

He could melt her quite easily if she allowed him, Brynn knew, feeling her pulse quicken wildly.

It took all her willpower to maintain her pretense of chill disinterest. "You aren't alone," she replied, injecting frost into her voice. "Any number of gentlemen feel that way."

His hand dropped as if he had touched hot coals, while the seductive warmth abruptly left his eyes.

"I will be away for the remainder of the day," he said tersely before turning on his heel and quitting the study.

Brynn let out a shuddering breath. Suddenly remembering her purpose, she turned back to the desk and dropped Lucian's seal ring into the drawer as if it were poison. Then she shut her eyes, feeling the violent thud of her heart.

It dismayed her, having to lie to Lucian. She despised deception. But she'd had little choice. She couldn't expose her brother for fear of how Lucian would react. Grayson might be engaged in something illegal, but he was still her flesh and blood. Certainly she owed him more loyalty than she did her new husband.

Didn't she?

Chapter Eleven

Lucian dodged a blow and returned a punishing one of his own as he battled Gentleman Jackson himself. A crowd had formed around the ring, most of whom were watching in silent awe.

Jackson's Rooms on Bond Street was one of the finest pugilist clubs in England. Stripped to the waist and breathing hard, the two opponents had already gone six rounds with their bare fists. Lucian's shoulder muscles ached, and he was sporting various new bruises, but he'd had the upper hand for some time now.

Then he let fly another deadly punch, connecting with Jackson's jaw and sending the former champion of England stumbling backward against the boundary ropes.

Regaining his footing with difficulty, Jackson wearily held up his hands and grinned. "Pax, my lord. I know when I've had enough."

Nodding, Lucian hid his disappointment and shook hands, brushing off the Gentleman's praise and the spectators' accolades with strained patience. He was still hungering for blood as he picked up a towel and wiped the sweat from his brow.

Primal violence was supposed to relieve sexual frustration, but it had had little effect on his lust. Nor had it improved his mood in the least. He wasn't sleeping well or concentrating on his work. He spent his nights tortured by his aching loins, burning to possess his elusive, tormenting wife. His days he filled with mind-numbing work or spent in places like this, soliciting punishing physical activity.

Despite his resolve to keep up his guard, he'd become much too bewitched by Brynn. And now he was suffering from another kind of arousal altogether: suspicion.

When he'd found her in his study this morning, he wondered if he was badly mistaken about her. He had thought Brynn uninvolved with her brother's suspected treasonous activities, but after seeing them together—the guilty looks on their faces—he had to seriously question if he could trust her.

Lucian swore under his breath. It was grating enough that his agents in Cornwall had nothing untoward to report about Sir Grayson—no evidence whatsoever that his nocturnal activities went beyond simple smuggling. Worse, they had no further leads regarding the gold thefts or the alleged mastermind, Caliban. Such impotence galled Lucian, but the possibility that he would have to keep an eye on his own wife in his own home filled him with anger.

It was that dark thought that had driven him beyond his normal range of endurance when he'd fought Jackson, but he still hadn't worked off his frustrations.

Clenching his jaw, he tossed the towel on a bench.

As he reached for his shirt, though, he looked over and spied the Marquess of Wolverton moving toward him. Dare wasn't smiling.

"What brings you here?" Lucian asked when his friend reached him. "I thought you considered fisticuffs barbaric."

"I do. Rapiers are far more civilized."

"Well, if this is a social visit, I should warn you, I'm in the devil of a foul humor."

"Then I regret to make it worse. I've heard a rumor I thought you would wish to know about."

"A rumor?"

"Do you recall the contretemps that began at your aunt's garden party?"

Lucian winced at the memory. "How could I forget? Two young whelps quarreling over who could best teach my wife to shoot."

Dare nodded. "Pickering and Hogarth are still quarreling. The poet has challenged Hogarth to pistols, and they aren't even planning to wait properly until dawn."

"A duel?" Lucian said, raising an eyebrow. "What does that have to do with me?"

"They are fighting over your wife, Luce. It seems the two young sap-skulls have accused each other of impugning her honor. They are dueling over her as we speak."

To save time, Dare drove, since his curricle was immediately available. They took the North Road, heading toward a field just outside London.

Lucian sat silently, his muscles rigid, his thoughts

churning. They would likely arrive too late to prevent the duel and avert a scandal, but he had to try.

When they drew near, a sinking feeling claimed
him. They might indeed be too late. Several car-
riages had stopped beside the road, and a crowd
had gathered alongside the field.

What knotted his gut, however, was when he recognized a landau that bore the Wycliff crest on the
door panels. Apparently it had only just arrived, for
as it ground to a halt, a woman spilled out and
began running toward the crowd.

Brynn. Dear God.

Riveted, Lucian watched as she pushed her way
through the spectators and onto the dueling field,
plunging directly into the fray barely an instant before shots rang out—

Fear slammed into his chest.

Leaping from the curricle even before it came to a
stop, Lucian sprinted toward the crowd, terrified of
what he might find.

They were hovering around a prone figure, he saw
with dread. Upon reaching them, he shouldered his
way through, then skidded to a halt, shock taking the
place of fear. Brynn was there on the ground, kneeling
beside a man's body, holding his bloody hand.

For a moment Lucian felt his mind reel. The image
was so much like his nightmare visions . . . except
that in his nightmares, *he* was the man dying.

He moved closer, his heart pounding. The prone
figure was Pickering; the poet had clearly been shot
but didn't appear to be dead. An elderly man, evidently the surgeon, was inspecting his shoulder
wound and elicited a groan.

Young Pickering grimaced in pain at the prodding of his raw, bloody flesh, even as he gazed up at Brynn. "My lady . . ." he rasped, biting his lower lip.

Tenderly she brushed a lock of hair from his brow. "Hush, don't speak. Save your strength."

Lucian gritted his teeth, relief and jealous fury welling inside him. He wanted to wring Brynn's neck for endangering herself that way, for scaring him half out of his mind, for gazing down so tenderly at another man, wounded or not—

When Lucian moved possessively to stand beside her, though, Brynn looked up, as if sensing his presence. She was crying; he could see pale streaks on her face, anguish in her green eyes. Lucian felt something twist painfully in his chest, warring with his darker emotions.

She froze for an instant when she saw him, but then the wounded man claimed her attention.

"I would endure ten times the pain," Pickering murmured hoarsely, "for but one of your smiles."

Brynn swallowed in a visible effort to hold back tears and might have answered, had not the doctor brusquely interrupted.

"He should recover, but I must take him away to remove the bullet. Stand back, please," he said to the crowd that was pushing in to gape at the wounded man.

One young gentleman stood slightly apart—the poet's opponent, Lucian realized. When Brynn rose unsteadily to her feet, Lord Hogarth stepped forward to address her in a pleading tone.

"Please forgive me, my lady. I didn't mean to hurt him, truly."

She whirled on him, her eyes heated through her tears. "I am not the one you should be begging for forgiveness!"

Hogarth first looked startled by her vehemence, then wounded. He opened his mouth to protest, but Brynn cut him off. "This must stop, Hogarth. It *will* stop. I never wish to see either of you again."

"My lady . . ."

"Please just *go*."

He looked stricken, but he seemed to comprehend her sincerity, for he took a step backward, then another, before turning and stumbling blindly away.

Dashing tears from her eyes, Brynn watched as the injured Pickering was carried to the surgeon's carriage. The crowd dispersed then, sending surreptitious glances at Lucian.

Swallowing hard, Brynn risked a glance at him herself and felt her heart sink. His blue eyes were glittering dangerously.

She didn't protest as he took her arm in a firm grip and escorted her to the Wycliff landau. From the corner of her eye she saw his friend Lord Wolverton waiting beside his curricle, but Lucian gestured toward the marquess, indicating he meant to ride with his wife.

He handed her into the landau, then settled beside her, shutting the door forcefully behind him. She could feel his simmering fury as the carriage began to move.

"What are you doing here?" she murmured, wiping tears from her cheeks.

"What do you think I'm doing? I've come to fetch my *wife*. And I'm the one who should be asking that question. What in *hell* were you thinking, running onto a dueling field like that? You could have been killed!"

"I wasn't thinking. . . ."

"Obviously not!" His voice dripped sarcasm. "What did you intend? To watch with glee while your beaux annihilated each other?"

"No, of course not. I was endeavoring to stop them."

His eyes were brightly blue, furious, beautiful. For a moment Lucian held himself rigid, as if struggling for control. "You might have employed a bit more discretion," he finally ground out. "Didn't you at least think to take an unmarked carriage?"

He was referring to the Wycliff crest emblazoned on the carriage panels, Brynn realized. All of London would soon know of her presence on the dueling field.

She turned to stare out the window, biting back her hurt, knowing Lucian had a right to scold. She had been horrified to learn from another admirer about the impending duel. Her only intent had been to intervene before someone was hurt, but she had been too late. She bit her lip, guilt gnawing at her.

"I trust you're satisfied," Lucian said in a tight voice. "The scandal sheets will have a field day. What a spectacle—two fools trying to killing each other over my countess." He reached across her and drew the shade down to cover the carriage window, then did the same on his side, as if to shut out prying eyes.

"I didn't want this to happen," she murmured.

"Don't insult my intelligence by claiming you

cared whether you turned me into a laughing-stock."

Brynn shook her head miserably. She couldn't blame Lucian for being angry that she had sullied his name and her reputation. Even though she hadn't purposely precipitated the scandal, she had known where the curse could lead. "I . . . I'm sorry, Lucian."

"Sorry is hardly adequate. Either of those witless whelps could have died."

"I know," Brynn whispered, aching inside. "I am to blame. I knew what could happen."

"Apologies will serve you little purpose, even if I believed them," Lucian gritted out, unmollified.

When she didn't reply, he said even more harshly, "Mark me, Brynn, I won't allow you to continue like this. You will behave with discretion, or I will remove you from London altogether." He cursed under his breath. "Perhaps it was a mistake, bringing you here in the first place."

Brynn swallowed her tears, her chin lifting defensively. "Our entire marriage was a mistake. I tried to tell you, but you wouldn't listen."

"It is far too late now to undo it. And I won't tolerate your continued wantonness."

"I have not been wanton."

"What do you call luring helpless young bucks to pant after your skirts?"

"I call it the effects of the curse."

"I can more easily believe you've been dallying behind my back." Her husband grasped her upper arm tightly, forcing her to look at him. "I warn you, Brynn. I intend my heir to resemble me."

Taken aback, she stared at Lucian in genuine shock as she comprehended his meaning. "I would never be unfaithful to my marriage vows."

"No? You draw the line at driving fools wild?"

Brynn felt a measure of alarm at the dark glitter in his eyes. She had seen Lucian angry before, but she had never been treated to the full force of his temper or his outraged sense of pride and male jealousy. He was wrong about her, though. She would never dream of cuckolding him. Nor would she be his doormat.

Brynn reined in her anger and hurt and stared at him rebelliously.

The atmosphere was suddenly charged with a new tension. Danger and desire.

He wanted her, she could see it in the fierce blaze of his expression. Against her will, Brynn felt a now-familiar curling sensation stirring in the pit of her stomach: sexual longing.

Their gazes clashed; hers defiant, his heated with primal emotion. His hands closed over both her shoulders in a tight grip.

"Don't touch me," she warned, trying to pull back.

The blue of his eyes became deeper, stormier. "Are you daring me, wife?"

She shivered, knowing the peril of challenging him, yet she couldn't stop herself. "What if I am?"

Something dark and thrilling flared in his expression. In a single smooth motion, he raised the skirt of her gown.

"I shouldn't think you would want to risk any more scandal," she taunted.

His expression was hard and sensual, his eyes dilated and dark with arousal as he insinuated his hand between her thighs.

Brynn suddenly felt breathless, stunned by her body's instinctive response. Lucian had only to touch her and she grew wet for him. A scalding heat flared between her thighs while her nipples tightened to rigid peaks. She had no doubt he could feel her readiness, smell her musky scent.

His finger brushed the bud of her sex and she had to stifle a moan. His bold touch inflamed her senses, igniting the explosive emotions simmering between them.

She drew a sharp breath as he released her to unfasten the buttons of his breeches. His erection sprang long and thick and hard from the base of his groin.

He was going to take her right there, she knew, yet she didn't want to stop him.

Lost in the blaze of his eyes, she began to tremble, wild arrows of sensation shooting through her body, excitement coursing through her veins. There was an inevitability about it that frightened and thrilled her.

He reached for her again, pulling her against him. When his mouth slanted down upon hers, passion flared instantly between them. His tongue was wet and scalding as it thrust into her mouth, the turbulence of their clashing wills only adding to the heat.

Then his fingers found the center of her femininity and slid deeply inside her, as his tongue was doing to her mouth. Brynn forgot everything else in a fiery burst of pure, erotic hunger.

As did Lucian.

His temper had turned to burning fever. He wanted to shatter that cool control of hers with passion, wanted to turn her determined resistance to heated surrender.

Not giving himself time to think, he lifted her up and set her astride him, crumpling her skirts around her waist. Brynn gasped as he slowly impaled her, yet her body accepted him easily, sheathing him in silk fire.

And suddenly they were kissing with frantic intensity, all the tension of the past weeks exploding in the heat of animal hunger. His hands slid up her back to twist in her hair, while the rock and sway of the carriage drove him deeper into her.

His tongue delved into her mouth, devouring and demanding, the taste of her making him wild. He had expected a fight and instead found the fury of a consuming desire sweet on her lips. He kissed her more fiercely, stoking the fire that flamed between them.

She wasn't feigning her desire; he felt it in her kiss, in the frantic, melting way she clung to him, in the hoarse sounds of pleasure she was making. Their tongues mated in a fever of need, and he arched his hips, burying himself even deeper inside her quivering body. He was feverish, but no more so than she. She matched the primitive force of his passion, moving with him in a frenzied rhythm.

Her eagerness shattered Lucian's restraint, shredded any remnant of self-control. He was helpless to resist—but so was she. Breaking off their kiss, she threw back her head and gave a raw cry.

She was beautiful, hot and wild, her face flushed with passion, her mouth open. It was only an instant later when Lucian followed her in a fiery climax.

His chest rising and falling as he gulped air, he came slowly to his senses. Brynn had collapsed in his arms, her face buried in his throat. He was shuddering in the aftermath, roiling with the turmoil of emotions he'd felt—still felt—tenderness, fury, fire.

It was shocking how swiftly he had lost control. His explosion was the culmination of weeks of frustrated lust, and of jealousy as well. He'd been driven by possessiveness, by the primal need to stake his claim to her. . . . Yet his violent reaction had been stronger than mere possessiveness, Lucian knew. It was stark fear that Brynn could have been hurt. That he could have lost her. Once she was safe, all his feelings had come spilling out. He'd taken her with primal urgency, not even knowing when anger had turned to desire, to ravenous hunger.

Devil take it, he knew better. He knew how to be gentle. Knew how to rouse her slowly, to make his caresses so sensual she would nearly die of pleasure before he took his own.

He drew a ragged breath, fighting for control. His muscles still trembled with the burning need to possess her. And Brynn . . . She would no doubt regret their explosive passion even more than he did. God, but he wanted to turn that regret to willing surrender.

His lips grew soft on her face, his fever mellowing

to tenderness as he held her and stroked her, sliding his palms slowly down her naked thighs. . . .

"You're a witch," he whispered huskily against her hair. "A beautiful, sweet witch."

It was clearly the wrong thing to say. He felt Brynn's sudden stiffening, as if he'd doused ice water over her heated body. Pushing against his chest, she detached herself from his embrace and scrambled off him.

Retreating to her corner of the carriage, Brynn smoothed out her disheveled skirts with trembling hands.

"I am *not* a witch," she murmured unsteadily, hating that designation. For much of her life she'd attempted to live down that tainted label.

"No, of course not," he replied in a low voice that was unexpectedly conciliatory. "It was merely a figure of speech . . . an endearment spoken in the heat of the moment."

Brynn sent him a despairing glance, feeling the silky wetness of Lucian's seed slicking her inner thighs. Shame, desire, hurt, dismay all swirled in her breast. Her gown was rumpled and stained, yet Lucian hadn't even wrinkled his perfectly tailored coat. And he thought her a witch.

Forcing back the pain, she tried to respond with indifference. "You just informed me that you wouldn't countenance my wantonness, Lucian. It is hardly fair of you to demand unimpeachable conduct from me and then promptly contradict your own commands."

"Wantonness with me," he said carefully as he fastened his breeches, "is not the same as wantonness in public, Brynn. I am your husband, after all."

"Perhaps so, but I prefer not to be mauled as you have a penchant for doing."

His blue eyes narrowed. "Mauled? You can't pretend you were an unwilling participant, siren. Your raw cries of pleasure would argue otherwise."

Brynn felt dark color flush her cheeks. She hadn't expected that wild hunger in herself. Lucian had turned her into a wanton creature, little different from her passion-crazed suitors. He had a deplorable talent for drawing intense reactions from her, whether passion or fury. Her heart twisted with despair. Whatever had happened to her plan to remain totally unmoved and indifferent to him?

"Well, you are hardly better than those fools you profess to disdain," she retorted, forcing coolness into her voice.

It was all she could do not to wince at the darkening expression on Lucian's handsome features. Brynn averted her gaze from the scorching intensity of his eyes. He was regarding her with disdain, as if they hadn't just made forbidden love with frantic, explosive need. A sudden ache welled up in her throat.

Just then she felt the landau rolling to a stop. They had arrived home, she realized, blinking back tears. Thank God they hadn't a few minutes earlier.

Without waiting for a footman, Brynn reached for the door handle, intending to descend from the carriage on her own. But Lucian put a hand on her arm to detain her.

"I meant it, Brynn. I'll send you to my family seat to rusticate in the country if I must."

The burning ache in her throat intensified, but she locked her jaw, determined not to cry in front of him.

"Then do so," she replied. "I would welcome the respite."

She fled then, before her tears threatened to spill over.

Lucian found himself biting back an oath as he watched his wife run up the entrance steps and disappear inside his house. The hurt he'd seen in her eyes flayed him with guilt.

Against his better judgment, he found himself following her, all the while arguing with himself over the wisdom in prolonging their latest battle.

He received no reply when he rapped softly on her bedchamber door. When he opened it, his heart leapt in alarm. Brynn was on her knees, her face buried in a chair before the hearth, sobbing as if her heart were broken.

For a long moment, Lucian stood there, wondering if he had been the cause of such anguish. Finally he shut the door behind him and crossed to her.

When he reached down and touched Brynn's shoulder, she gave a violent start and looked up, her tears arrested.

She wiped furiously at her cheeks, as if ashamed of being caught by him. "What do you want?" she asked hoarsely.

"Did I hurt you?"

She looked away. "No . . ." She took a shuddering breath. "Yes. That horrible name . . ."

"What name?"

"Witch. The village children used to call me that.

Even my friends . . . I heard their whispers behind my back after James died."

Feeling his defenses crumble, Lucian withdrew a handkerchief from his pocket and sank down beside her. "James?" he murmured gently as he wiped her face.

"My suitor. I killed him." Her eyes welled with fresh tears and spilled over before she covered her face with her hands.

Lucian hesitated, recalling what Brynn had once told him. "I thought you said your suitor drowned at sea."

"He did."

"That isn't an uncommon fate for a Cornishman, is it?"

"No. But he died because I came to c-care for him."

When her voice broke in a sob, Lucian felt his heart melt. Brynn was agonizing about something she had absolutely no control over, yet she clearly believed she was to blame for causing a man's death. She must have lived with her burden of guilt for a great while, he realized—

Lucian felt himself flinch as he recognized the parallel to his own situation. He understood guilt. He'd killed one of his closest friends with his own hands. But Brynn was condemning herself without real cause.

Almost against his will, Lucian reached for her. He knew the danger of touching her, but his need to comfort her was stronger than his need for self-preservation.

Drawing her into his arms, he settled back against the chair and pressed her face into his shoulder, offering solace. It was a measure of her distraction, he knew, that she permitted such closeness.

"I suspect his death was just an accident," Lucian said quietly into her hair. "You can't hold yourself responsible for an act of nature."

"I wish I could believe that." She was silent for a long moment, and when she spoke, her voice shook. "Perhaps I am a w-witch. Those two men today . . . they could have died . . . because of me."

He could feel her tremble, and his arms tightened instinctively around her. "I doubt you were to blame for that, Brynn. Those witless hotheads fought over you because you're a beautiful woman. If not you, they would have found another reason to duel."

"But you said—"

"I know what I said, but I was angry . . . and concerned for you. You could have been hurt, intervening the way you did."

She drew back, studying his face. "You don't believe in the curse at all, do you?"

He managed a smile. "I've told you, I'm not the superstitious sort."

"Then how do you explain your dreams, Lucian? How do you explain mine?"

He didn't immediately reply, having no explanation for his disturbing dreams of Brynn. "You have dreams?" he asked finally.

"I dreamed about James before his death. And you . . . sometimes I see images of you."

He saw the helplessness in her eyes, the vulnerability, and he reached up to touch her cheek—

Abruptly Brynn drew back, as if suddenly becoming aware of the impropriety of his tenderness. Averting her gaze, she rose to her feet and crossed her bedchamber to the door between their rooms. She hesitated for a long moment. Then, opening the door, she stood to one side, clearly inviting him to leave.

"I think you should go," she said, her tone once more holding a distinct chill.

Rising more slowly, Lucian went to her, but then paused, reluctant to abandon their unsettling discussion. "I'm certain there is a logical explanation for our dreams," he said finally.

Brynn tilted her head, her look almost one of sadness. "Oh? And what about Giles?"

Lucian flinched involuntarily. "What about him?" he asked, suddenly wary.

"In my dreams I saw you fighting him, Lucian. I saw what happened between the two of you."

You saw me kill him.

Lucian forced himself to relax his rigid muscles. "I have nightmares about Giles sometimes, I admit. No doubt you heard me calling his name in my sleep."

Her smile was bleak. "Perhaps. And then perhaps I am a witch after all."

Chapter Twelve

Entirely unaroused by the night's entertainment, Lucian shifted restlessly in his seat. This was the first Hellfire gathering he'd attended since his marriage— a musical performance by a dozen bare-breasted "Muses" who were partially garbed in diaphanous Grecian robes, their nipples rouged to entice and delight. The music was surprisingly good, but he found the Cyprians' charms sadly wanting in comparison to Brynn's. Breasts not as tempting and firm, limbs not as long and slender, hair lacking the untamed, vibrant luster of hers, eyes nowhere near as bright. And most critically, none of the intriguing spirit that Brynn possessed in such irresistible measure . . .

Lucian mentally voiced an oath. He'd come here to escape thoughts of his beautiful wife, not to be reminded of his frustrations.

Rising, he took his snifter of brandy and stepped through the French doors of the salon, out onto the terrace. A chill edged the September night air, presaging fall. Welcoming the coolness against his heated body, Lucian leaned against the stone balustrade, his restless reflections centered around Brynn.

Their strained union was not what he wanted of his marriage—a contentious dance of mutual lust and resistance. They were fighting each other and themselves. More baffling was the strange matter of their dreams. He couldn't explain the haunting bond he had with Brynn, why their night visions seemed intertwined. Unless the Gypsy's curse was somehow real. . . .

Hell and damnation, he wouldn't be ruled by a damned curse he didn't even believe in—

"What the devil are you doing out here alone?" he heard his friend Dare ask behind him. "You don't find the entertainment to your liking?"

"Nothing is wrong with the entertainment," Lucian prevaricated.

"It must be women troubles, then. Your wife, I take it?"

"You might say that." His tone was mocking.

Dare joined him at the terrace balustrade. "How novel. I don't believe I've ever seen you at a loss with a woman before, Luce."

Perhaps, he thought darkly, because he had never been at such a loss before. He had frequented the lavish and licentious courts of Europe and had lovers beyond counting. Women had come easily for him . . . until Brynn. "You forget that I've never faced such novel circumstances before."

"Marriage?"

Lucian's mouth twisted. "Exactly. My marriage of convenience has turned out to be anything but convenient. The consequences of taking a reluctant bride, I surmise."

"You can always lose yourself in the arms of someone more willing. Acquire a mistress."

"That is your answer to every problem, isn't it?" Lucian asked impatiently. "Moving on to another woman."

"It usually works," Dare said softly.

Lucian shook his head. "I'm not in the market for a mistress. Nor do I intend to supply the gossips with more fodder for scandal. My marriage is the talk of the ton as it is."

Leaning a hip against the railing, Dare stared out into the dark garden. "Well, I certainly am no expert on matrimony. Only once in my life did I ever consider becoming leg-shackled."

Surprised by the admission, Lucian sent his friend a sharp glance. "I never knew you contemplated marriage."

Dare shrugged. "It was a long time ago, and I've done my damnedest to forget it."

"What happened?"

"I was foolish enough to think myself in love. I went so far as to propose before discovering my mistake." His tone hardened. "My innocent young betrothed wasn't quite as pure as I thought her." Dare gave a brusque shake of his head and flashed his charming grin, as if dismissing his dark thoughts. "But I've had some small amount of experience with women," he added with his customary wry humor. "I think I might be qualified to advise you in winning over a lady."

Lucian had to smile at this understatement. Dare could melt stone if he wished to. "All right then, what do you advise? I am all ears."

"You could start by showing your bride more consideration. From what I hear, you've been a touch high-handed with her. Dragging her into a whirlwind union so you could get an heir upon her, then disappearing and leaving it to your servants to transport her to London, where she had to face society's wolves alone. Rather arrogant of you to believe she might welcome such treatment, don't you think?"

"Perhaps. It wouldn't be the first time I've been accused of arrogance."

"Even so, you should never have left her so soon after the wedding, Luce. Not at all chivalrous of you. Or astute. Neglecting your new lady is no way to win her heart." Dare paused. "Are you interested in winning her heart?" he asked curiously. "Or in giving yours?"

It was odd to hear Dare North, London's most notorious bachelor, speaking of love, Lucian reflected. His own feelings about the subject were nebulous. He had never loved any of the soft, willing beauties who'd shared his bed, but he envied other men who had managed the feat. He'd recently seen his American cousin Nick Sabine fall deeply in love. And his friend Damien Sinclair was madly enamored of his wife. . . .

Lucian grimaced. Falling in love with Brynn would be the height of lunacy. He'd been smitten since he first set eyes on her seductive beauty, and his condition had only grown worse with time. When she was near, the passion he felt for her was never far beneath his surface—

He muttered a low oath. The emerald-eyed siren

had quite bewitched him, tied him in knots. He wasn't even certain he could trust her. For all he knew, Brynn could be mired knee-deep in treason with her brother. It would be dangerous to risk giving her even more power over him. And yet the idea of ending the strain in their marriage . . . of truly winning her . . . had a definite appeal.

"I honestly don't know," he finally answered. "Love was never part of my plan. I only wanted a son."

"Perhaps your plan was too logical. Too calculating. The heart doesn't follow logic." Quite suddenly Dare made a scoffing sound in his throat. "What the devil—listen to me waxing poetic. I must be growing maudlin in my waning years."

"Ah, yes, you're quite ancient," Luce said with an edge of sarcasm. "You're a year older than I, Dare. You'll have us in invalid chairs before the night is through."

His friend eyed him steadily. "No need to take your foul temper out on me."

"Just so. My pardon."

Dare slapped him lightly on the back. "Forgiven." Then he turned and lazily rested his elbows on the railing. "One thing I do know," he added with more seriousness. "If you neglect your wife, others are bound to step in."

"Others already have stepped in," Lucian responded, his tone turning dark again. "That is a large part of the problem, or hadn't you noticed?" He took a long swallow of brandy. "Fools losing their heads over her all because of a curse."

"Curse?"

"My wife claims to be cursed, didn't I tell you? Men lust after her because a damned Gypsy put a hex on one of her ancestresses. She even haunts their dreams."

"How intriguing," Dare said, grinning.

"It's not the least intriguing if you're the poor sap in danger of being cuckolded."

"Is that what troubles you?"

Lucian hardened his jaw. "Brynn claims I needn't worry on that score."

"And you believe her?"

"Oddly enough, I think I do. In Cornwall she went to great lengths to avoid provoking male interest, even mine. Especially mine, in fact. When she first came to London, I thought she might be encouraging her admirers out of revenge, to repay me for the way I treated her, but I no longer think her provocation was deliberate. She was undoubtedly virginal when I first took her."

There was a long pause while Dare considered that. " 'A virtuous woman is a prize beyond rubies,' " he quoted softly.

"Perhaps so, but it's damned uncomfortable, having a wife every man jack sees as a prize."

"Well then, perhaps you should enter the lists. Join the competition for her favors."

"What are you suggesting? That I challenge those witless young whelps to a duel?"

"Not at all. Why don't you simply try your hand at seducing her? Use that vaunted charm of yours. The best way to conquer a woman is to woo her. I'll wager you haven't seriously tried that approach."

"Not seriously. Not since we wed."

"You should have. I own myself astonished, Luce. You never properly court your bride and then you essentially abandon her? Any female with an ounce of pride would be put out by such conduct. Can you blame her if she isn't content with her lot?"

No, he couldn't blame her, Lucian admitted. He had made numerous mistakes with Brynn from the first, violating his normal sense of fair play with a vengeance. He had demanded her submission, then deliberately treated her coldly, too worried about himself and fighting his obsession to show her the consideration she deserved. He'd been possessive and jealous, and when her admirers fought over her, he'd reacted like an outraged husband, accusing her of playing the wanton, which had only wounded her and roused her resentment further. He'd harbored suspicions about her possible involvement in treason without any real proof. . . .

His behavior indeed was inexcusable, Lucian admitted.

"You're right," he said quietly. "I've made a shambles of it."

It was Dare's turn to raise an eyebrow. "Surely you don't mean to accept failure so readily— legendary lover that you're reputed to be? I doubt it's too late for you to repair the damage, in any case."

Was he too late? Lucian wondered. Their marriage had begun shakily and plunged in a downward spiral with each icy clash. He had welcomed Brynn's resentment, indeed purposely cultivated it, deliberately destroying any chance for warmer relations in their marriage. He regretted that the most, the coldness between them.

Yet he wasn't totally powerless when it came to changing the current state. He had a measure of physical control over Brynn. He knew how to command her passion, how to make her body respond with desperate hunger. . . . But he wanted more than that. He wanted her willing and eager in his arms. He wanted peace between them, and trust, perhaps even friendship. He wanted to know her better, her thoughts, what she felt. He wanted to be able to share his thoughts, his feelings, his hopes and fears. . . .

"No woman has ever resisted you for long," Dare observed, watching him closely.

"I can see you don't know my wife very well," Lucian said almost with wistfulness.

"Perhaps not, but I certainly know women. I suggest you take yourself home and devote yourself to your bride. Spend some time with her. Take her off to the country, perhaps. With all the distractions you've faced pursuing traitors, you've had no chance to become intimate or put your powers of seduction to the test."

Lucian shook his head. "I can't leave London just now."

"Why not? What is more important—saving England or ending this wretched misery you've let yourself wallow in? Besides, I don't imagine you'll be much good to your country until you settle this situation with your wife."

Dare had a point, Lucian realized, frowning. Until now, his country had always come first for him; duty was more important than personal desire. Yet for weeks now his conflicting feelings for Brynn had proven a relentless distraction, despite his vow to the contrary. He would do well to settle the strife between them before it rendered him totally ineffectual.

Perhaps he *should* try a different approach with Brynn: wooing her.

It would be difficult to win her over. She would likely spurn his advances after the way he'd acted, especially given her staunch belief in the Gypsy's curse. Certainly he wouldn't change her convictions overnight, yet he could take small steps that wouldn't arouse her alarm or provoke her to tears. . . .

The vivid image of Brynn crying in his arms yesterday made Lucian wince. He wanted very much to dispel her fear that she was a witch. He wanted still more to end the coldness between them, to repair the tattered fabric of their relationship, perhaps establish a bond of trust. It was even possible they could have a marriage with mutual affection, if not love. . . .

Tilting his head back, Lucian drained the last of his brandy, not certain if embarking on a new course with Brynn was at all wise. Yet for the first time in the weeks of his contentious relationship with her, he felt a sense of eager anticipation.

It startled Brynn when her husband joined her in the breakfast room the following morning. Usually Lucian had left for the day by the time she rose.

She stared when he greeted her amiably, her cup of chocolate raised halfway to her lips. While she watched, Lucian filled a plate from the sideboard, accepted coffee from the hovering footman, and then dismissed the servant. He gave Brynn a brief smile before settling back in his seat and opening one of the morning papers that she wasn't reading.

She found herself at a total loss.

He'd arrived home late last night, she knew, for she'd lain in her lonely bed tossing and turning, listening for him. But he hadn't visited her bed. Most likely it was because he had found other pleasures to occupy him. Absurdly it hurt to think of Lucian in the arms of another woman—

Forcing those foolish thoughts away, Brynn made herself chew her suddenly dry toast and concentrate on the editorial before her.

Silence reigned for a time. Eventually Lucian closed his paper and applied himself to his breakfast. Brynn nearly jumped when he addressed her moments later.

"You aren't wearing a riding habit. You don't mean to ride this morning?"

He knew of her customary early morning rides in the park with Raven, Brynn supposed, but she was surprised he had noticed her attire.

"No," she answered carefully.

"Why not?"

She gave him a wary glance. "I never plan to go out again."

"Why?"

"Because it is safer."

His eyebrow lifted. "Isn't that a rather drastic measure?"

She tried to flash an arch smile but feared it merely came out bitter. "You were the one who insisted I keep away from the young bucks 'panting after my skirts.' The only way I know how to accomplish that is to avoid them entirely."

"I expect you'll find such confinement restrictive," he said finally.

"Certainly I will. It is lonely having to do without company, but I am accustomed to it. And remaining quietly at home here is better than being forced to rusticate at your country estate, where I know absolutely no one."

She felt his light gaze examining her face. "You needn't do without company entirely. Do you enjoy Shakespeare?"

Brynn eyed him warily. "Yes, why?"

"I thought we might attend the theater this evening."

"*We?*"

A smile flickered at his mouth. "I should like to escort you, if you will allow me."

"Why?"

"I hoped you might accept it as an olive branch."

She considered that for a moment. "I can't imagine why you would want to offer an olive branch."

"Because I don't enjoy this constant state of antagonism between us, Brynn. I would like it to end. We cannot spend a lifetime like this, fighting each other."

She didn't enjoy their antagonism, either, or the explosive results. The memory of their rash, brazen lovemaking in the carriage still haunted her. But keeping discord between them was the safest thing for Lucian.

"I never wanted our marriage to become a battleground," he said when she was silent, his voice dropping to a soft murmur. "I regret that more than you know."

Brynn caught her breath, unable to look away from the unwavering intensity of his gaze. She wished his eyes were less compelling and not quite so blue.

His voice lowered even further. "I know I haven't been the most ideal husband, Brynn. I would like to try to make it up to you."

She couldn't answer, not with the sudden tightness of her throat.

Finally he gave a soft sigh. "Whatever our private disputes, I would prefer to present a more amiable image in public. It will help quiet the scandal for us to be seen together and pretend to enjoy each other's company."

"Yes . . . I suppose that would help."

He rose then and came around to her side of the table. Taking her hand, he raised it to his lips. "Until this evening, then."

Brynn shivered, feeling the tingle of his hot mouth all the way down her arm to her loins.

She stared after Lucian long after he was gone. Finally she felt her breath escape in a sigh. She had her own regrets about their relationship; she yearned for an end to hostilities as Lucian claimed he did. Yet she didn't dare lower her defenses.

It worried her, this contrite, gentle side of him. If he were to begin treating her with tenderness and consideration, he would be impossible to resist.

Brynn shook her head, desperately fighting the emotions he unleashed in her. How had her feelings for Lucian become so complicated? Their relationship would be so much safer if she could simply hate him. But she feared that was well beyond her power. It wasn't hate Lucian woke in her, but hungry longing.

As they entered their box at the Drury Lane Theatre, Lord and Lady Wycliff were the focus of all eyes. A sense of excitement claimed Brynn as Lucian took his seat beside her. It was a treat for her to attend a performance of skilled actors. The country troupes that toured southern Cornwall were the dregs of their profession, so watching actual masters was sure to be a delight.

But it was Lucian himself who caused the involuntary lightness of her spirits. He had dined at home with her, playing the role of solicitous husband—a performance, she knew. Yet he acted as if he were truly enjoying her company instead of fighting his attraction to her. Clearly he was making an effort to begin anew.

The change in him was profoundly appealing—and unquestionably dangerous. In return, Brynn did her best to maintain a cool demeanor and subdue her own appeal. She wore her fiery hair sedately tamed, while her ivory slip with its overskirt of silver tissue was modestly cut for an evening gown. Yet she could tell by the sudden darkening of Lucian's blue eyes that he admired the effect.

He continued his exhibition of amiability when they reached the theater. The moment Lucian was settled beside her, he took her hand and brought her fingers to his lips to kiss, gazing deeply into her eyes, just as if he were in love. His amorous gesture was for the benefit of the audience, Brynn presumed, but the sheer intimacy of it made her soften inside. . . .

Abruptly she scolded herself for her susceptibility; Lucian well knew the power of his sensuality, and she would be wise to keep up her guard.

They were barely seated when visitors started arriving at their box, wanting to be introduced to his lordship's new lady. Lucian showed all the heart-melting charm and rakish wit that had so fascinated her when they'd first met, as well as a possessiveness that was as curiously gratifying as it was disturbing. He remained so close she could feel his body heat, his arm lightly draping her shoulder, as if staking his claim on her. And when they were left alone once more for the start of the play, he kept hold of her hand.

Despite her resolve to keep him at a distance, to protect him with her indifference, Brynn found herself loath to pull away; his touch felt so right. All through the first act, her nerves were alive and acutely tuned to him.

Almost as distracting were the whispered conversations in the neighboring boxes and from the pit below. Few in the audience were actually watching the stage but had turned their opera glasses on herself, suggesting their fascination with the woman who had claimed the elusive Lord Wycliff's hand in marriage.

Even with all the disturbances, however, Brynn found the performance riveting. When the first intermission came, she gave a sigh of delight.

"Your eyes are fairly sparkling," Lucian murmured in her ear. "I take it you approve of the performance."

"It's marvelous," Brynn said with heartfelt agreement. "Although I suppose I sound rather provincial to admit it."

A breathtaking, whimsical smile tugged at the corner of his mouth. "Perhaps. A pretense of ennui is certainly considered fashionable. But I think your candor refreshing."

"Thank you for bringing me here, Lucian," she said sincerely.

He bowed gallantly. "Your enjoyment is my pleasure."

"You don't find the play enjoyable?"

"Somewhat. But I've seen this performance a half dozen times. It isn't difficult to become jaded on the entertainments London has to offer."

"I can't imagine becoming so jaded that Shakespeare begins to pall. If that is the consequence of your wicked life, then I will gladly pass."

His lashes veiled his sapphire eyes, and Brynn could have bitten off her tongue. She hadn't meant to spoil the moment by reminding him of their discord.

She was relieved when a new visitor appeared in their box. Brynn felt nervous about meeting so illustrious a personage as the Foreign Secretary, whom the papers frequently vilified. But Lord Castlereagh apparently was a close friend of Lucian's. Although his lordship initially displayed a stiff reserve toward her, he conversed easily with Lucian and soon had Brynn admiring his sharp intelligence.

The admiration became mutual when she quizzed him about the Duke of Wellington's progress on the battlefields of Spain, which she had been reading a great deal about. Castlereagh had long been a champion of Wellington and shed any trace of aloofness when he spoke proudly about his confederate's stunning victory at Vitoria.

"You've done well choosing your bride, Wycliff," Castlereagh said as he was preparing to leave the box. "It is surprising that you found her in the wilds of Cornwall. I'll wager you're glad you decided to mix pleasure with business."

"Very glad," Lucian said, giving Brynn a glance so warm, she felt herself blush.

"And you, Lady Wycliff," Lord Castlereagh added, "have snared one of the keenest minds in Britain. I trust you won't object if I keep your husband in my employ for a while longer, until we win the war. We can't do without him. Boney would be ruling the world by now if not for heroes like Wycliff."

"I am hardly a hero," Lucian said dryly.

"You're far too modest, sir. And I believe March would argue strenuously with that." Castlereagh turned to Brynn. "He saved the Earl of March last spring from the Frogs—stole him right out of their damned jaws at considerable risk to his own skin. You should persuade your husband to tell you about his adventures sometime."

Brynn raised an eyebrow. "I fear my husband doesn't share his secrets with me."

"Wise, I suppose. Loose lips have been known to change the course of history—and not for the better. But since Wycliff won't allow himself to be lauded, I must. I cannot tell you how thankful I am to have him on our side. I wish I could have a dozen of him."

Such praise did not come lightly, Brynn was certain, and it strongly renewed her curiosity about the depth of Lucian's involvement with the war effort.

It was only when they were driving home, however, that Brynn had the opportunity to satisfy her curiosity a small measure. She could barely see Lucian sitting beside her; the carriage lamps were unlit, leaving his perfect profile in shadow.

She studied him silently a moment before venturing to ask the question that had been burning in her mind ever since hearing Lord Castlereagh's praise. "What do you actually do for the Foreign Office?"

"Whatever needs to be done," Lucian answered cryptically.

"Including risking your life?"

"Rarely that."

"The Foreign Secretary obviously disagrees. Castlereagh called you a hero. And I know Raven considers you one."

"Raven is somewhat biased," he replied, his tone dry.

"But you still took a risk in rescuing Lord March."

"I was merely doing my duty."

Brynn shook her head. "Few noblemen would consider it their duty to work for the government— or work, period. I wonder how you became involved in such an endeavor."

Lucian turned to gaze at her in the darkness. "Do you want the polite version or the honest truth?"

"The truth, please."

"To be frank, I was bored with my wicked life."

He let that sink in before adding lightly, "There

was nothing heroic about my decision. I was raised in privilege and ease and came into my inheritance young—my parents succumbed to a fever while traveling abroad just after I reached my majority, leaving me with more wealth than I knew how to spend. My greatest victories were winning at faro or wagering on a horse race. For a long time I felt . . ."

Lucian hesitated as if searching for the right words. "I felt something missing in myself. I scarcely knew or cared what was happening to Europe. And then six years ago, my closest friend was killed in a naval battle, fighting the French. His death made me realize there was more to life than choosing what tailor I should patronize or which entertainments I should attend in an evening."

Brynn could hear the pain in his voice at losing his friend, as well as his self-condemnation.

Lucian's tone was quieter, more reflective when he continued. "I offered my services to the government, thinking the occupation would help to fill the days . . . the emptiness. But it became much more. I finally found a worthy challenge," he said softly. "A sense of purpose. Whatever I've risked, I have gained far more."

Brynn was taken aback to hear him sharing such confidences with her. Perhaps it was due to the darkness, or to the truce they had declared between them, but Lucian was actually divulging something intimate about himself.

She digested his admission in silence. Evidently she owed him a sincere apology. She'd thought him a rake and a wastrel, when he was really risking his life saving others. She'd accused him of neglecting

her when he had had matters of national importance at stake.

The remembrance made her feel rather . . . small.
A sense of regret pierced Brynn for the petty resentment she had felt toward Lucian these past weeks.

"I didn't realize," she said quietly, "that what
you were doing was so . . . vital."

Lucian shrugged. "I haven't exactly been
forthcoming."

"Is that why you left me on our wedding night?
Because of your work?"

His gaze found hers in the dim light. "Yes. Believe
me, nothing else could have dragged me away that
night." He paused. "Had I better explained the reason, would you have forgiven me?"

Brynn felt her breath catch at the gentleness in his
tone. Yet even knowing the danger of encouraging
any intimacy between them, she answered honestly.
"If I recall, I was in no mood for forgiveness. But I
believe I would have understood that your duty
came first."

Lucian laughed softly, without amusement. "De-
feating Napoleon is no longer merely a duty with
me, love. It's a driving passion. I admit, I have no
objectivity when it comes to winning the war. Not
after losing so many friends and countrymen. I
want Boney to pay for the destruction he's wreaked
on England, on all of Europe. And I'll do whatever
is necessary to achieve his downfall, even if it means
taking on tasks no true gentleman would ever
consider."

"What sort of tasks?"

She felt rather than saw him go still. Then Lucian

shook his head abruptly, as if recollecting who she was. "They aren't tales for a lady's ears." His tone had turned suddenly grim, but she could sense his despair.

Perhaps they *were* ugly tales, yet Brynn would have liked to hear them, to better understand this surprisingly complex man she was bound to for life.

She fell silent, contemplating his unexpected revelations. When the carriage drew up before the Wycliff mansion, however, she was filled with a disturbing new awareness. Thus far the evening had been disquietingly pleasurable, but what would the remainder of the night bring? Most pointedly, did Lucian intend to share her bed again and resume claiming his rights as her husband?

Her heart quickening with nervous anticipation, she entered the house on Lucian's arm and surrendered her satin cloak to the butler. Yet, just as on their wedding night, a visitor was waiting for his lordship.

Informed that Mr. Barton was in the study, Lucian gave Brynn a brief glance, knowing it could only be bad news this late in the evening. "I'm sorry, my dear, but I must speak with him."

She returned a slight smile that actually seemed relieved. "Of course," she said quietly.

Lucian watched her ascend the grand staircase, her back slim and straight, hips swaying gently beneath her elegant ivory-silver gown. He had never regretted an interruption more.

Cursing the poor timing, he strode quickly to his study, where Philip Barton rose immediately to his feet.

"I regret the intrusion, my lord, but I knew you would wish to hear the news. The last shipment of stolen gold reached France, there is no longer any doubt. It landed in Boulogne."

Lucian cursed again. "Where was it taken?"

"That isn't known, for the trail ended abruptly. It seems to have disappeared into thin air."

"How can an entire wagonload of bullion," he demanded with angry rhetoric, "simply disappear?"

"Perhaps it was split up. Regardless, my men lost track of it. I am very sorry, my lord."

Lucian clenched his teeth, forcing back his anger. "You aren't to blame, Philip."

"It is the work of Lord Caliban, most likely."

"Was he sighted?"

"No, not this time. I thought you might wish to travel to France to investigate yourself."

Lucian hesitated, considering. He wanted to apprehend Caliban so fiercely, he could taste it. But he wanted to remain in England just as badly. Leaving Brynn now just as he was trying to cultivate a new relationship with her was out of the question. He couldn't possibly woo his bride if he was slinking across France in search of illusive contraband and its treacherous thief. In any case, by now the gold had most certainly reached Napoleon's coffers. Even sending Philip to France might be pointless; the cunning Lord Caliban would be long gone.

Then again, they might learn some vital crumb regarding the traitor's identity.

"No," Lucian replied, "I won't be going to France this time. But I would like you to go in my place, Philip."

"I, my lord?"

"This is one of our few leads to Caliban. We can't risk letting even a scrap of information go unsought. And I cannot leave London just now."

An eager light brightened the young man's dark eyes. "Very well, my lord. I will make arrangements to depart at once."

Seeing his enthusiasm, Lucian added a pointed warning. "Philip, don't be discouraged if you unearth nothing. You will likely hit another dead end."

"I understand. And it is quite possible Caliban never went to France at all, but left the gold to be delivered by his lackeys." Barton frowned, looking disheartened once more. "It's damned galling to know he is right under our very noses, performing his treason."

"Indeed," Lucian agreed darkly. "That's why I have been thinking . . . perhaps it's time to modify our course and begin searching for him here."

"Here, my lord?"

"London society. Lord Caliban could be any of a hundred men. All we know is that he's wealthy and that he possibly possesses a title. But when the Little Season starts, he may well take part in the activities. I'm considering asking Wolverton to help us discover Caliban's identity."

Barton frowned. "I realize Lord Wolverton is a close friend of yours, but he does not strike me as the sort of man who cares a fig about anything but—" He came to a stammering halt, his features coloring at his boldness.

"But his own pleasures?" Lucian finished.

"Yes, my lord. Forgive my bluntness, but can

Wolverton really be entrusted with matters of such importance as espying a traitor?"

"Dare can be trusted, believe me. He doesn't seem serious, but he moves about the ton with ease—goes everywhere, sees everyone. He could help us narrow down the field of suspects at the very least. And while he will doubtless consider it a lark, it may give him a sense of purpose he's been lacking thus far."

"Then I suppose it would be wise to employ his assistance," Barton said, though sounding reluctant.

Lucian bit back a grim smile. This would not be the first time Philip had questioned his unorthodox methods, but they'd been proven right far more often than not.

He saw his visitor to the front entrance, then slowly mounted the stairs, finding it hard to dispel his suddenly bleak mood. The report that the stolen gold was now in French hands was a taunting reminder that he had failed in his duty, that men had died because of his negligence while he was off seeing to his own personal affairs, acquiring a bride. . . .

Tearing off his cravat angrily, Lucian entered his bedchamber, then came to a halt, remembering that bride. The doors that connected their apartments were ajar, with soft lamplight coming through.

To his surprise, he found Brynn in her sitting room, still fully dressed, as if she had purposefully waited up for him.

When she looked up from her book, her eyes met his, giving him the same jolt of sexual excitement as always. Yet the emerald brilliance was more subdued than usual, her wary gaze questioning.

"I trust the news was not too bad?" she murmured.

Here was a chance to extend their intimacy, Lucian knew. Yet he hesitated, his instincts at war with his longings.

On the one hand, if Brynn understood the reasons for his dark moods and his necessary absences, she would likely be more yielding toward him. She was already softening a finite degree, Lucian could feel it. But he couldn't totally ignore the possibility that she might be involved with her brother's nefarious activities. If so, he would be taking a dangerous risk to say anything at all. Sharing information with the enemy could be deadly.

Are you my enemy, Brynn?

Still, he could sound her out about her knowledge without divulging any crucial details.

"Bad enough," he answered, keeping his tone even.

He settled in the wing chair across from her, casually stretching his long legs out before him. "A shipment of stolen contraband was recently smuggled to France."

"Contraband?" Her eyebrows rose politely as she waited for an explanation.

"This isn't the usual trafficking in black-market goods, but gold belonging to the British government. For some months now a band of smugglers has been stealing shipments of gold bullion and clandestinely transporting it to France."

"Why France?" Brynn frowned, looking genuinely perplexed, Lucian noted with keen interest.

"Because Boney needs gold to fund his armies. French paper currency has been virtually worthless for years." Lucian felt his mouth twist humorlessly. "These thefts are doubly galling. Not only does it deprive our government of the gold needed to pay our troops and allies, which is vital to Britain's war effort, but Boney uses it to finance their slaughter."

She digested this intelligence in thoughtful silence.

"This smuggling ring is particularly vicious," Lucian continued. "They don't hesitate to kill to achieve their ends." He gave Brynn a pointed glance. "You grew up in Cornwall. Surely you must be familiar with the Free Trade."

Her lashes lowered over her striking eyes. "A little. Most families there are involved in some fashion. It is a way of life."

"Well, we have no good leads as to the perpetrators or their leader. Perhaps your brother could advise me on how to go about searching."

"My brother?" she asked cautiously.

"Sir Grayson seems a savvy sort. He might have knowledge that could lead us to apprehend the gold smugglers." At her wary expression, Lucian offered a slight smile. "I'm not interested in ending the livelihood of your fellow Cornishmen, Brynn. Only in keeping the gold out of French hands. If we hope to stop the bloodshed and put an end to the war, these smugglers must be caught."

She suddenly looked troubled, distracted even. Lucian felt a sinking weight in his heart.

"I don't know if Gray could be of any help," she said finally. "I suppose it couldn't hurt to ask him."

Lucian forced a smile. Her reply was not the one he had hoped for—that she would disavow any knowledge of her brother's activities. Rising, he crossed to her, then bent and pressed his lips to her brow. "Sleep well, siren."

Taken off guard, Brynn eyed him warily. It had been a tender gesture, as if there were real affection between them.

"You don't intend to stay?" she asked.

"Are you inviting me to stay?"

Their gazes locked. A long moment passed while he studied her. Eventually, though, Brynn looked away, uncomfortable with his penetrating scrutiny.

"Well then," Lucian said lightly, "I see I had best summon all my willpower." When she didn't respond, he reached out to brush her cheek with a knuckle. "Don't worry, love. I intend to wait for an invitation. I won't press my unwanted attentions on you."

"You must do as you please," she said, her voice low.

"Must I?" he asked softly.

Brynn watched him turn away, still surprised and unaccountably disappointed that he hadn't remained.

When he was gone, she let out an unsteady breath of relief. Yet her inner turmoil wasn't caused solely by her husband's potent masculinity. This time Lucian had given her too much to think about—and raised a disturbing possibility.

She'd always believed Grayson was smuggling wine and brandy and silk; never had she dreamed he would become involved in something treasonous such as stealing gold and delivering it to the enemy. Brynn bit her lip. Surely she would have known if Gray were engaged in so wicked a crime. He would not be able to keep such a secret from her—and yet she hadn't been home in weeks.

And Gray *had* been unusually troubled during his last visit, agitated even. Brynn suddenly recalled the questions he had put to her then . . . his keen interest in Lucian's connection to the Foreign Office, particularly Lucian's role as a spy.

And what of her husband's enigmatic comments just now? Did he somehow suspect Grayson?

A stab of fear shot through her as she realized the possible danger to her brother. She had greatly underestimated Lucian. He wasn't a bored nobleman playing at being a hero. After losing close friends to the war, he was personally driven to prevent further bloodshed, even at the risk of his own life. Admittedly, his revelations tonight had given her a new respect for him. Yet she had also gained a new wariness. Lucian was keenly intelligent, intuitively clever. And he was determined to find the gold smugglers. If he were to suspect Grayson—

Another frightening thought struck her. Had he suspected Gray all along? Had that been Lucian's purpose for coming to Cornwall in the first place? Even more damning, had he courted her to get closer to her brother? Had he *used* her that way? Just as he was using her to sire a son?

And something else . . . Gray's desperate interest in Lucian's seal ring. Her breath caught in her throat. Sweet heaven . . . Was Gray truly involved in treason? And had she unwittingly aided him?

It was a horrifying thought.

Brynn shook her head, pressing her lips together in a tight line. She wouldn't jump to conclusions just yet, condemning her brother without a fair hearing. But she would certainly have a great number of questions to put to him when she wrote to him first thing in the morning.

Chapter Thirteen

For an endless moment they stood locked together in a death grip, straining for control of the rapier. Then with an anguished cry, Giles twisted away and flung himself full-force at Lucian, sending them both crashing over the table to the floor.

Struggling for breath, Lucian rolled free and climbed to his feet, firmly in possession of the weapon. Yet his opponent lay still, groaning, blood seeping from a mortal wound in his chest.

Dropping the blade with a clatter, Lucian went down on his knees beside the dying man, cradling his head.

"Giles..." he whispered, agony ripping through him.

"Forgive me, Luce..,. It is better this way.... Please...don't tell..."

His last rasped words were lost in a violent fit of coughing as blood bubbled up from his throat.

"No...!"

The hoarse cry woke her. Brynn sat up in bed, her heart pounding. Her bedchamber was dark, filled with an uneasy silence.

When she heard another muted moan of pain

coming from beyond the door to her sitting room, she hastily fumbled to light a candle and made her way cautiously to Lucian's apartments. He lay sleeping in the huge canopied bed, tossing his head restlessly on the pillow. His body was nearly bare, the rumpled linen sheets scarcely covering his loins.

He groaned again, a tortured sound that wrenched her heart. Bending over him, Brynn laid a gentle hand on his arm and realized he was covered with cold sweat.

At her touch, he woke abruptly, staring at her with a wildness in his eyes. Then his hand shot out, grasping her wrist with an unexpected fierceness.

Startled, she tried to draw away. "I'm sorry. . . . You were having a bad dream."

The savage light slowly faded from his eyes. "The same nightmare," Lucian said hoarsely. "I killed him. . . ."

She knew exactly what he had dreamed, yet she refrained from admitting to seeing his same dark visions. Lucian hadn't believed her when she'd confessed to sharing his dreams, nor did she like to remind him of her powers of witchery.

"Are you all right?" Brynn asked when he shuddered.

Slowly he raised himself onto one elbow, running his hand raggedly down his face. "Yes."

"Well then . . ." She started to turn away, but he stopped her with an abrupt plea.

"Don't go . . . please."

Brynn hesitated. She was standing barefoot in her revealing cambric nightdress, her hair tumbling wantonly down her back. Yet Lucian's mind was obviously not on seduction or carnal matters, for he was staring unseeingly at the shadows of the room, not examining her scanty attire.

Gingerly she set the candle on the nightstand. She couldn't simply abandon him if he needed comforting, even knowing the danger of remaining in such close proximity.

"Do you want to tell me about it?" she asked. "Theo used to be troubled by nightmares, and talking about them seemed to help ease his fear."

Lucian's gaze searched her face intently, before he looked away. "You don't want to hear about something so ugly." His voice was low, taut.

She perched on the edge of the bed, keeping as much distance between them as possible. "I do, Lucian. It obviously disturbs you greatly."

A long moment passed before he answered. "I killed a man. Someone I counted as a friend."

"Giles?" When his gaze flew to her face, she prevaricated, "You cried his name in your sleep."

Lucian stared at her. "Yes, Giles," he said at last, his voice hoarse.

Brynn felt the despair in him. "But you didn't kill him in cold blood."

"No, not in cold blood. He was a traitor. . . ." There was another long pause. From the conflicting emotions on Lucian's face, she knew he was debating how much to reveal to her.

"What happened?" she prodded gently.

He exhaled in a sigh. "Last spring . . . when I was in France searching for March . . . I uncovered a plot. My friend Giles was making deals with the French, selling secrets. Divulging the identity of our agents. When I confronted him, he begged me not to expose him."

Lucian's features twisted in anguish. "I couldn't let him go free, not when several of our men had died because of his betrayal. Giles was like a cornered fox. He drew a rapier and attacked me. . . . I managed to defend myself, but he . . . I killed him with his own blade." Lucian looked down at his hands. "I keep seeing his blood on my hands," he said in a voice so low, it was almost a whisper.

He lay back, shutting his eyes. Brynn could see the pain etched in his face. She ached to offer him comfort, to soothe the darkness and despair he had let her glimpse.

Reaching out tentatively, she touched his curling hair, feeling the sleek, silky texture beneath her fingertips. To her startlement, Lucian reached out and dragged her down to him, holding her against his body so tightly that his heartbeat shivered through her.

For a long moment, Brynn remained frozen in his desperate embrace. She might have consoled a child similarly, only she didn't feel in the least motherly. The heat of Lucian's hard body was arousing, the intimate pressure making her breath catch. She wanted to pull away, and yet he needed the comfort she could give. After a moment she let her arms slide around him. He responded by burying his face in her throat, as if in despair.

She reluctantly held him that way for a long while, a storm of emotion quietly roiling inside her.

"You're horrified," he murmured.

"No . . . No," she answered more firmly. "You had no choice."

"*True.*" She felt Lucian's fury in that single uttered word. "Giles left me no choice. Just as he felt he had no choice. He was being blackmailed for his . . . sexual propensities. To hide his shame, he let himself be drawn into a far worse crime."

"Treason."

Lucian let out his breath in a hoarse sigh. "There is someone preying on young bucks of the ton—a nobleman, most likely—luring them to betray their country either through bribery or blackmail. What I wouldn't give to bring him to justice. . . ."

She felt Lucian's hand clench in her hair. "So Giles was driven to desperation?"

"Yes. In the end, he was down on his knees to me, sobbing. When he charged, I was caught off guard. Even now I'm not certain if he truly wanted to kill me or if he wanted me to end his torment. I concealed his treachery from the world, for what it's worth. I put about the tale that he had died on the road, set upon by bandits. But I wish to God the result could have been different."

"You cannot blame yourself, Lucian," she said quietly.

He gave a muffled, humorless laugh. "Logically I know that. But my nightmares don't seem to understand logic." He paused. "Sometimes I see my own death."

"Your death?"

She felt him shudder. "My hands are covered with Giles's blood, and then it becomes my own blood. I'm dying. I deserve to die, because I killed him."

"Lucian . . . you had no choice. You have to forgive yourself."

"Believe me, I've tried. . . ." His voice lowered to a hoarse rasp. "I never expected my brush with death to affect me so deeply, but it changed me somehow. . . . I suppose because for the first time I realized that I was actually mortal. I see myself dying, with nothing to show for having lived. No legacy. No heirs."

Brynn felt her breath catch as she finally understood. "That is why you want a son so badly."

He drew back, capturing her gaze with his dark, intense one. "Yes. I would like to leave something behind, so my life won't have been in vain."

She returned his gaze with dismay, lamenting the tenderness she suddenly felt for him. His rare vulnerability touched her more than any seductive charm could have done.

"Lucian . . ." she murmured, not certain she should encourage this intimate discussion or divulge her own secrets. Should she explain that she understood? That she harbored similar fears? That she had always dreaded dying alone, unloved, because of the curse?

His fierce hold on her loosened. Drawing away slightly, he lifted a strand of her hair from her breast and rubbed it between his fingertips. "It was arrogant of me to think you would want to bear my son. Small wonder that you opposed my suit."

Brynn shut her eyes, wishing she could deny the sudden flood of emotion that welled up in her. "Perhaps it was arrogant," she said at last, "that you thought to purchase me as your broodmare. But the prospect of bearing your son wasn't why I opposed you. I simply didn't want a husband."

His gaze searched her face. "You don't consider having my child repugnant?"

"No. I wouldn't mind having a child, not at all . . . although . . . I suppose my reasons might be selfish."

"How could having a child be selfish?"

Brynn looked away, grappling with her own misgivings. This quiet night seemed a time for sharing secrets; revelations of the heart came more easily in the dark, with only the glow of a candle to illuminate the intensity of Lucian's expression. But confidences were less dangerous without having to meet his intimate, penetrating gaze.

"A child would ease the loneliness," she said at last.

"Loneliness?" he asked softly.

"The loneliness I've always lived with. I don't think you would understand."

He put a finger under her chin, compelling her to look at him. "I understand loneliness, Brynn."

"Do you?" She gave him a doubtful frown. "How can someone who has led such a privileged life know what loneliness is? You have countless friends."

"Not close friends. Being surrounded by sycophants doesn't qualify. I can count on one hand the people I truly care about. I've felt alone most of my life."

She lowered her gaze. "It still isn't the same. You are able to choose the people you love. I am afraid to be near any man, to smile or talk or offer friendship, for fear of killing him."

Lucian reached up to brush her cheek with a tender forefinger. Brynn winced at his gentleness, finding the intimacy of this moment excruciatingly painful. Until Lucian, she had never shared her deepest secret with anyone, not even her family. Only her mother would have understood the depth of the anguish the curse had caused her: the fear of destroying someone she loved.

"Brynn . . ." His voice dropped. "You just told me I should forgive myself for Giles's death. Well, you will have to do the same—forgive yourself for James's death."

"That is different."

"Certainly it is. You don't have his blood on your hands. You were in no way responsible for his drowning."

She stared at Lucian a long moment, struggling with her own inner demons.

"As for loneliness . . ." he said finally, his voice a whisper of velvet. "You needn't feel alone any longer. We can console each other . . . drive away the loneliness together."

Her throat tightened, leaving her unable to answer.

"I realize this marriage hasn't been pleasant for you," Lucian murmured. "Nor is it what I intended. I should never have left you alone so much of the time. I've been unforgivably cold. . . . Concerned with my own wants, my own needs." He gave a low laugh. "How is that for selfishness?"

Swallowing thickly, Brynn shook her head. "That wasn't selfishness. You wanted a son."

"But I could have been more considerate of your happiness. I am sorry, Brynn, for the way I treated you. I want you to be happy. . . . Or if not happy, then at least content."

His apology shredded her resolve to resist him. When he brushed her lower lip with his thumb, her breath faltered.

"We made such a poor beginning, Brynn, but it isn't too late to start anew, is it? Our union can be more than a cold-blooded arrangement. We could have a real marriage rather than a battleground. I could be your husband in truth."

Heat spread through her, catching hurtfully in her stomach. "No, Lucian. You are ignoring the danger of the curse. We can't have a real marriage. If I came to care for you, you would die."

His seductive mouth twisted. "I don't believe that, love."

"Lucian—"

His fingers pressed against her lips, hushing her. "I am willing to risk it. Curse or no curse, I'm done fighting you."

He gave her a heart-ravaging smile, and Brynn felt herself melt inside. Her gaze dropped from his beautiful mouth to his bare chest, rippling with muscle in the candlelight. How could she resist that elegantly chiseled face, that hard, lean, graceful body? How could she resist his tenderness? How could she *not* resist?

She could feel herself dangerously softening toward Lucian. This tender, vulnerable side of him was so beguiling. It was too easy to care for him, too diffi-cult to withstand his male allure. Her heart was too susceptible. If she let down her guard, she could go too far. . . .

His thumb slowly stroked her lip, heightening her turmoil. "Don't fight me any longer, Brynn. . . ."

She felt his touch like flame, her senses had become so painfully acute. In desperation, Brynn glanced toward the door that separated their apartments, contemplating escape.

She heard Lucian's quiet sigh, as if he realized he had gone too far. "You needn't decide right now, love. I won't press you."

Gratefully Brynn started to sit up, intending to return to her own rooms, but Lucian put an imploring hand on her arm. "Please . . . don't go. Stay with me tonight. Help me keep the nightmares at bay."

She glanced down at him in despair, struggling with her conscience. She shouldn't risk staying, yet she didn't want him to suffer those terrible nightmares, either.

"I won't assault you, I promise you." His half smile was wistful, slightly mocking. "Although having you in my bed without touching you will likely be a torment." When she still hesitated, his voice dropped to a rough whisper. "Stay with me, just for tonight. I need you, Brynn."

Her heart wrenching at his plea, she lay down again. He leaned across her to snuff out the candle, and darkness instantly enveloped them. Brynn tensed when he drew the sheet up over them both, but at Lucian's silent urging, she turned over, giving him her back. She lay there stiffly, willing her defenses to remain strong, even as his naked heat warmed her taut body.

"Sweet," he murmured, nuzzling his face in her hair.

At length, she felt Lucian relax, felt his breathing grow soft and even. Eventually she realized he had fallen asleep holding her.

It was a long, long moment, however, before Brynn could feel the tension begin to drain from her own body. The quiet night was soothing, the darkness deeply sensual—and yet she found sleep impossible. It was painfully arousing, indulging in this closeness with Lucian, listening to his even breathing, his heat and hardness at her back. The physical intimacy only intensified her inner turmoil.

Her heart felt torn by longing. Lucian's proposal was so tempting. He was offering her something deeper than the cold-blooded compact they had entered. A new start for their relationship. A real marriage. An end to loneliness.

But at what price? His life? How could she dare accept? She would be devastated were Lucian to die. She could never bear the heartbreak, the guilt. She had already begun to care for him too much. . . .

Brynn shut her eyes tightly. Until now she had managed to withstand his powerful magnetism. Angered and hurt by his high-handedness and neglect, she had purposefully nursed her darker feelings to shield herself from her attraction, to protect Lucian from danger. And in truth, nothing had changed.

A sharp feeling of despair coursed through Brynn. She had no business letting herself even contemplate accepting his offer of a deeper relationship. Desires of the heart had no place in her life. She was a fool to be feverishly yearning for the elusive promise of love.

And yet how could she deny the hunger he woke in her? Just now his hand slid upward, nestling possessively on her breast, arousing her even as he slept. A small moan surfaced from deep in Brynn's throat, and she stirred restlessly, her body craving his heat and strength.

Easing away, she turned over, watching Lucian slumber in the dim moonlight. His masculine beauty was so compelling, even more so with a shadow of stubble darkening his jaw. She longed to reach up and caress his face, to feel the rough texture, so different from her own softness. She longed to press even closer to him, to stop fighting the passion he aroused within her, to surrender to his tempting allure. . . .

An aching sense of sadness filled her as she acknowledged the hopelessness of her longings. She had no choice but to refuse his offer of a real marriage. Perhaps they could indeed end the turbulent dance of anger and defiance that had characterized their union from the first, and she would be grateful for that. But she couldn't allow any deeper feelings to develop. For her, love would have to remain an unfulfilled dream. She had to keep her distance from him, emotionally at least.

Yet it would be so much easier if she could keep apart physically as well. If they could live separate lives . . .

Brynn drew an unsteady breath, struggling to bury the tangle of unwanted emotions that knotted inside her. Lucian had promised he would leave her alone if she conceived a child. She could hold him to his word, but first she would have to produce the son he wanted so badly. Only when he gained his heir would he be satisfied enough to let her go her own way.

She could make her escape then. She could demand that he honor his promise.

And if he wanted more than she dared give? Then she would have to drive him away. No matter what her own feelings, she had to protect him.

Renewing her resolve, Brynn let her eyes close. She dozed for a time, but the strangeness of sleeping in an unfamiliar bedchamber, next to the man who was her husband, kept her sleep restless.

Fingers of dawn were filtering beneath the brocade draperies when she came fully awake. She lay there, indulging in the guilty pleasure of watching Lucian, studying the chiseled planes and angles of his beautiful face.

It was still early when he stirred awake. His eyes opened abruptly, fixing on her in startlement. Then recognizing her, he gave her a slow smile. "Are you watching over me, guardian angel?" he asked, his voice a husky rasp.

Embarrassed to be caught staring, Brynn blushed and sat up, giving him her back. This would be hard enough without having to face him directly.

"Thank you for staying with me, love. My dreams were only pleasant ones."

She felt his hand stroke her back lightly and winced. Clutching the sheet to her breast, she drew her knees up, girding herself for what she would have to say.

"I have been thinking about your offer, Lucian," she began in a low voice.

There was a brief silence. "And?"

"And I agree it would be good to stop fighting, but . . . I prefer we adhere to the original terms of our arrangement. You promised you would leave me alone if I gave you an heir."

"I said that, yes. But I think perhaps our circumstances have changed." His fingers were warm at her back, distracting her.

"Not really." Brynn turned to glance down at him. "I never wanted this marriage, and nothing has occurred to convince me otherwise."

She was watching his face and saw his disappointment before a mask fell over his eyes.

"You said it was my choice," she reminded him.

"It is," he replied evenly.

"Well, I would like to keep our relationship strictly business."

"Because you fear the curse."

"Primarily."

Lucian studied her for a moment. "You realize that for you to conceive," he said finally, "we will have to resume carnal relations?"

"Yes, I realize that. And I intend to do my part. I will submit to you whenever you wish."

"It's not submission I want, love," he murmured. "I want you hot and twisting in my arms, as you were the last time. Do you remember how wild you were in the carriage, Brynn?"

She felt herself blush. "You will have to be satisfied with submission."

"I don't believe that is possible any longer."

Brynn gave him a questioning glance. "Why not?"

"Because the thought of forcing myself upon you

to get you with child has become supremely distasteful to me."

"You would not be forcing me. I told you, I am willing to bear your child."

"I'm afraid that isn't good enough, Brynn. You're suggesting in effect that I stand at stud. But to service you, I will have to be aroused enough to perform. And your reluctance is the surest way to kill my interest." His mouth twisted wryly. "Regrettably, love, you can't conceive without my full participation."

Brynn dropped her gaze to his mouth. She could remember the feel and the taste of it on hers. "I would not be reluctant," she assured him in a low voice.

"You will have to convince me otherwise." When she lifted her gaze, he expounded. "I told you, I am not going to force myself on you again. You will have to take the lead."

"What do you mean, take the lead?"

"If you want me to make love to you, you will have to be the one to initiate it. You will have to arouse me, siren, rather than the other way around."

Her heartbeat quickened at the thought of arousing Lucian to passion, while her face flushed. "I'm sure I wouldn't know where to begin."

"I would be willing to instruct you." Lucian paused, surveying her. "Perhaps you had best get started."

Her eyes widened. "You want to make love *now*?"

"Can you think of a better time?" He gave her a flicker of a smile. "If I'm to get you with child, we should make love frequently, to improve the likelihood my seed will take root."

Brynn remained totally mute.

"Very well," Lucian said, grasping the sheet as if preparing to get out of bed. "It's your choice."

"No, wait!" She looked at him, their gazes locking. "What do I have to do?"

Chapter Fourteen

He cocked his head, contemplating her with tender amusement. "Do you actually need me to tell you what to do? The legendary siren who can inflame a man with merely a glance?"

Brynn flushed, reluctant to initiate their lovemaking as Lucian demanded. It would be too wanton, and she had spent most of her life quelling any trace of wantonness.

"You could begin by taking off your nightdress," he suggested helpfully. "It's very arousing for a man to see a beautiful woman's body."

In all the weeks of their marriage, she had never undressed fully for him. "It is broad daylight," Brynn muttered in protest.

"It is barely dawn. And making love at all hours of the day or night will help us achieve our aim.

"Come now, love," Lucian prodded when she hesitated. "A bride can claim shyness for only so long. You will have to shed some of your inhibitions if you hope to keep me interested."

Gathering her courage, Brynn drew her nightdress off and let it drop to the floor. His gaze fixed on her breasts, making her throat go dry.

"That's better," he murmured, his eyes sweeping her peaked nipples, then lower to the dark curls between her thighs. "Now then . . . I believe you were about to arouse me."

She glanced down at the sheet, which barely draped his loins. The large ridge beneath clearly evinced the huge size of his erection. "I would say you are aroused quite enough already."

He flashed a smile as tempting as sin itself. "Not nearly enough." With a casual thrust of his leg, he pushed the sheet aside, exposing his magnificent body.

Brynn felt her breath catch at the sight of him. He was beautiful and lithe and strong, his shaft already darkly engorged. The thick swollen length rose nearly to his navel.

Moving his hands behind his head then, he laced them together at his nape. "I'm waiting, wife."

His brazen attitude about his nakedness still flustered her, but it was the heat he roused in her that she deplored. "You don't intend to help me?"

"Not at all. I intend to lie perfectly still and allow you to have your wicked way with me."

Her flush deepened. "You cannot expect me to behave like a tart."

"I can, love. I am your husband, remember? You needn't be shy with me. You've seen my cock before, felt it. You've had it inside you, pleasuring you."

She felt her inner muscles spasm at the thought of having that hard length inside her again, pleasuring her. Yet she couldn't bring herself to move.

"Shall I show you?" he finally asked.

"Yes," she whispered.

He reached down and touched himself. "Watch what I'm doing, Brynn." He took his rigid length in his hand, curling his fingers around the base, slowly stroking the huge shaft, mesmerizing her with his boldness. Her gaze remained riveted on him as he moved lower, cupping the swollen sacs, which made his erection jerk and tighten against his groin.

His voice was a bit huskier when he spoke. "Now it's your turn. Touch me like that. You can arouse me with the slightest caress."

Taking a deep breath, she moved her hand to his thigh. It was rock hard to the touch, dusted with silky hair. "I am still not certain what to do. . . ."

"Use your instincts. You are totally in command."

This beautiful, elegant man was her husband. She had the right to touch him, indeed, the duty. She reached for him.

He tensed when her own fingers curled around his rigid flesh. Brynn felt a strange sense of triumph as the thick shaft surged in her hand, hot and hard and pulsing with life. She explored him with her touch for a moment before he urged her to greater boldness.

"Use your mouth, love. Taste me."

She bent to him, tentative as she touched him with her tongue. He was hot and silken and so very fascinating. She smelled the hot musk of his arousal.

"You taste silky . . . and mysterious," she whispered.

The raw sound from his throat might have been a laugh or a groan. "You can investigate the mystery for as long as you wish, sweet."

Experimentally, she let her lips slide down over the swollen tip. Lucian gave a soft groan and closed his eyes. Gaining courage, she took more of him in her mouth, gently suckling him while her fingers stroked his heavy testicles. She might have gone on for some time, but he suddenly pulled away, his hand tangling in her hair.

"You had best stop," he said, his voice rasping, "before I spend myself in your mouth."

Brynn felt another surge of triumph to realize Lucian wasn't as complacent as he pretended. But then neither was she. Her skin was fevered; her flesh ached to be even closer to him. When he drew her up to straddle him, she went willingly, almost melting against him when he took her breast in her mouth.

As he suckled her quivering nipple, Brynn gave a gasp and arched against him.

"I believe I'm aroused enough. Are you?"

"Yes," she breathed. She was incredibly aroused. The ache between her thighs was a fiery throbbing, while her nipples had hardened to stiff crimson buds.

"Don't fight it then. Come here and let me taste you."

He held her hips, almost lifting her up so that her thighs straddled his shoulders. "Even closer, Brynn."

She shivered at the raw demand in his voice.

Drawing her nearer, he raised his head to press a hard, hot kiss to her soft mound. Brynn felt a shaft of liquid fire shoot through her.

She clutched at his hair as his tongue deliberately

delved into her quivering cleft. The incendiary sensation of his mouth stunned her. Aching with delight, she tried to pull away, but Lucian refused to allow it. He had taken control in some wild and thrilling way and would not be denied.

Gripping her hips with both hands to steady her, he tasted and nipped and licked, running his long, rasping tongue up and then down her swollen folds, stroking the engorged bud of her femininity. Intense pleasure shot darkly through her like spears of flame, its white heat searing her.

Brynn gasped, writhing restlessly against the unrelenting caress of his tongue. She was hot and feverish . . . and suddenly she could no longer remain still. She arched and exploded in a shuddering climax, grinding her pubis against his blazing, eager mouth.

She was still moaning helplessly as the savage ripples died away, but no sooner had she started to sag limply in Lucian's arms than he shifted her bodily, lowering her onto his swollen shaft. Gritting his teeth, he thrust urgently into her, forcing her to yet another fierce climb toward brutal, exquisite sensation. In only moments she was writhing again. She bucked against him as he plunged even more deeply, almost sobbing. Soon wave after wave of rapture racked her quivering body, until finally he relented and sought his own shattering explosion.

Brynn collapsed bonelessly on his chest. She lay dazed, her hair tumbled and wild around them, Lucian's ragged breathing harsh in her ear, the taste of him lingering on her lips.

"That was adequate enough for your first effort,

wife," he murmured wryly, "but you will have to do better than that in future."

The barest hint of laughter edged his passion-weary voice, making her realize he was deliberately provoking her. Yet Brynn could barely find the energy to retort. "Perhaps it was your tutelage at fault, rather than my efforts."

"Perhaps. I see I should teach you other ways to arouse me."

She lifted her head from his bare shoulder. "There are other ways?"

His mouth curved in a rakish smile. "Indeed. There are any number of methods."

"What is wrong with what I just did?"

"Nothing was wrong—in fact, it was very right. But you don't want me to grow bored, do you? If you learn to keep me satisfied, it stands to reason I will be more willing to accommodate your sexual needs, and that you will be more likely to conceive. Isn't that what you want? To conceive a child so you can be done with me?"

Brynn gazed down into his blue, blue eyes. She could feel him swelling again inside her, huge and hot and potent. "Yes," she lied. "That is what I want."

"Well then, wife," he said huskily, drawing her mouth down to his. "We had best move on to the next lesson."

Lucian proved quite serious about requiring Brynn to initiate their lovemaking. He insisted that she come to his bed and wouldn't allow her to confine their frequent sessions to merely the dark hours of night.

He also made good on his pledge to teach her to arouse him, showing her how to move, how to caress, how to pleasure. Brynn was sometimes shocked by the intimacies he suggested, but he had only to coax her with his tantalizing brand of charm, and her body melted to his touch. She was helpless against such overwhelming sensuality and raw magnetism. Thus it relieved her greatly to develop defensive weapons of her own to use in their erotic battles.

She had always possessed the power to incite masculine desire, but under his tutelage, Brynn developed the skills to purposely drive a man wild. Her newfound mastery worked even on Lucian, whose legendary tastes had become jaded and acutely discriminating.

Within a few days of commencing her lessons, she was able to demonstrate the extent of her expanded powers. They lay in his bed, with Brynn draped over her husband, lazily pressing kisses along his naked chest, his hard, flat belly, his swelling erection. When she eventually took him in her mouth, Lucian quivered like a stallion. Moments later, he clenched his teeth and drew away with a groan.

"What is wrong?" she asked curiously, though not with any real concern.

"You know very well what is wrong, wife. Enduring your torment is an agony."

Brynn smiled, triumphant to know this man trembled for her. Deliberately she smoothed her hands up his torso and drew her tongue along his throbbing sex, teasing the sensitive ridge. "Pray tell, how do I torment you?"

Taking her by surprise, Lucian rolled over her, pinning her lightly beneath his weight. His eyes dark with desire, he gazed down at her with unexpected seriousness. "Your very remoteness, love. Even when you are provoking me to savage hunger, you remain distant." His frown deepened as he brushed a flaming tendril from her forehead. "You hide your passion behind a deliberate coolness, which only makes a man burn for you all the more."

Brynn forced a smile, not at all convinced that her attempt at coolness was succeeding. "Is that not what I am supposed to be learning? How to make you burn for me?"

"Devil it is. And it's damned effective," he murmured against her lips.

Drawing him down, she surrendered to his kiss, eager to distract him from his probing scrutiny. She was indeed desperately struggling to repress any emotion, any feeling for Lucian, yet maintaining a strict detachment was proving lamentably arduous.

Making love to him was no longer a duty she resented. No longer merely a means to achieve her goal of conceiving his child. She wanted Lucian. She wanted to arouse his hunger. Wanted to feel the hot rise of his desire, the hot tremor of his flesh between her thighs, moving inside her. She had begun to crave his touch with a dismaying intensity.

If she managed to hide her response, it was only due to years of practice, presenting a chill facade to her admirers. But he had only to caress her to send blood rushing through her veins, filling her with hot yearning. She had only to glimpse the passion flaming in his eyes to feel an answering passion burning deep within her own body. She could feel his enchantment, drawing her ever closer, tugging on her heartstrings, pushing her toward the dark inferno of an impossible dilemma.

The magnitude of the danger became even clearer a fortnight later when her dearest friend, Meredith, finally arrived in London with her husband, Viscount Audley, and their new infant son. Meredith had retired from society when her pregnancy became obvious but had returned in time for the Little Season.

For a duke's daughter, Meredith was not at all arrogant or highbrowed. In both disposition and looks, she resembled a cheerful, pretty Cupid, with her pleasantly plump figure and laughing mouth and short blond curls. Brynn called on her at the first opportunity and received a fervent welcome. After catching up on Meredith's account of her pregnancy, they went upstairs to admire the napping baby Rupert, who promptly woke and began fussing.

"May I hold him?" Brynn asked.

"Of course. Although don't be upset if he spits on your gown. I cannot tell you how many bodices he has ruined."

"I won't mind. Theo regularly spit up on me when he was a baby."

Brynn took the mewling infant in her arms and immediately began rocking him, reminded of the countless hours she had soothed her baby brother after their mother's untimely death in childbirth. To

Brynn's delight, Rupert shortly stopped his fretting and gave her a gurgling smile.

She winced, unprepared for the sweet, responsive pangs in her breast as she cradled the darling child or the powerful maternal instincts he stirred. Perhaps her reaction was because she missed her youngest brother so dreadfully. Or perhaps because the thought of conceiving Lucian's child had been so much on her mind of late . . .

"You should see yourself, Brynn," her friend observed quietly. "You are positively glowing."

Pressing a tender kiss on Rupert's silken forehead, Brynn smiled. "I have always wanted a child of my own."

"But not a husband?"

"No, not a husband."

"Well, marriage obviously agrees with you."

Brynn didn't reply.

"So do you ever mean to satisfy my curiosity? I was never so shocked in my life as when I received your letter informing me you had wed Wycliff. I gather he proposed because of the curse, but I thought you meant never to marry. I am simply dying to know how it came about. Especially since he was considered such a profoundly elusive prize."

Brynn bit back a sigh, knowing she couldn't avoid her dearest friend's pointed questions, no matter how intimate. "I did not have much choice. My family's financial circumstances had grown dire. And Lord Wycliff offered to fund Theo's education."

"Are you happy, then? I couldn't deduce a thing from your letters."

"Happy?" Brynn went still, dismayed to realize

her feelings of late had indeed bordered on happiness. Dangerously so.

"I am happy enough," she murmured. "At least now. The initial weeks were . . . exceedingly disagreeable. We fought all the time. Lucian purchased me for a broodmare, and I resented his high-handedness—so much that I fear I became a shrew. We were both miserable."

"But it is better now?"

She looked away. "We no longer quarrel, thankfully. We came to a truce of sorts."

"Well, you could not expect two strangers to get along perfectly. And I should think you wouldn't find the marriage bed in the least unpleasant. Wycliff is rumored to be quite a passionate man, for all his elegance and sophistication. You don't mean to tell me the rumors lie?"

Brynn felt herself flush. "No, they don't lie."

"And that is what worries you?" Meredith asked. "It's only natural that you would be swayed by his legendary charm. Wycliff has never had the least trouble winning female hearts. But there is real danger if you come to fall in love with him."

"Yes," Brynn agreed. She was finding it more and more difficult to battle the unexpected threat to her heart. She was becoming ensnared in Lucian's potent spell, just as she'd feared she would be. "I admit," she said in a low voice, "that terrifies me."

Meredith gazed at her in sympathy. "So what do you mean to do?"

"I don't know," Brynn murmured. "I don't dare let myself become too enamored of him. That is why I . . . We made a pact. Lucian agreed that after I bear him an heir, we can go our separate ways."

Meredith's expression showed dismay. "Separate ways? Does that mean you would have to give up your child to him?"

Brynn felt her heart lurch. Absurdly, she hadn't considered that far into the future, although she certainly should have. Lucian wanted a son so badly, he would never allow her to keep their child if she left him.

"Could you endure that?" her friend asked quietly.

Brynn's throat tightened. "I'm not certain I could."

"Well," Meredith said with sudden cheerful briskness, "there is no use stewing over that bridge until you must cross it. And perhaps by then you will have found a way to break the curse."

Brynn stared, struck by her friend's casual remark. Was it possible the curse could be broken?

"Perhaps so," she murmured slowly, not daring to let herself hope.

Her defenses, however, suffered yet another blow the following week. Brynn was about to descend to breakfast when she heard a commotion issuing from the floor above. Curiously mounting the service stairs, she followed the din to the serving maids' dormer. To her dismay, she found her maid, Meg, on her knees, sobbing, while the housekeeper stood over her, railing at the frightened girl.

Both women ceased their clamor when they caught sight of Brynn, but almost instantly Meg burst into renewed weeping.

"Oh, milady," she pleaded, "don't let her turn me out!"

"Be quiet, you disgraceful girl!" Mrs. Poole snapped.

"What seems to be the problem?" Brynn asked coolly.

"She is in the family way." The housekeeper pointed at the maid's stomach, adding in a revolted tone, "Look at *that*!"

The thin nightdress did nothing to disguise the girl's thickening belly, while a chamber pot stood beside an unmade cot, attesting to at least one bout of morning sickness.

With effort, Brynn swallowed her shock. The sweet, timid Meg was the last person she would have suspected of bearing a child out of wedlock. She had never noticed the girl's condition until now, perhaps because she'd been so wrapped up in her own affairs.

"I found her lazing abed, too ill to work," the housekeeper went on. "Then I discovered this and dismissed her."

"I beg you, milady," Meg entreated, "don't let her—"

"I told you to hush!" Striking savagely, Mrs. Poole slapped Meg's face, making her cry out.

Outraged, Brynn moved between them. "That will be quite enough, Mrs. Poole!"

"A box on the ears is not nearly enough! She deserves to be soundly thrashed for her wicked behavior."

Brynn narrowed her eyes. "If you dare strike her again, you will be the one dismissed."

Mrs. Poole pointed again at the quaking maid. "I won't have this shameless wanton in my employ!"

"I don't believe that is your decision to make."

The housekeeper drew herself upright, quivering with rage. "Choosing the household staff has always been my purview. Mine and Mr. Naysmith's."

"Perhaps it was, but I am mistress here now." Brynn glanced down at the girl. "Do get up, Meg. The floor cannot be comfortable."

Trembling, Meg obeyed. "Please, milady . . ." She latched desperately on to Brynn's arm, evidently seeing her as a savior. "What will become of me if I'm thrown into the street?"

"You will not be thrown into the street," Brynn assured her.

The housekeeper made a rude, scoffing sound. "She will not even disclose the father of her bastard—if she even knows his name."

Meg's shoulders stiffened, while her weeping subsided the slightest degree. "Certainly I know it. I just won't tell *you*."

"You disgraceful jezebel," Mrs. Poole interjected, "luring some man into sin—" She broke off suddenly, flushing as she glanced over Brynn's shoulder, toward the doorway. "M-my lord . . ."

Lucian stood there, surveying the three women curiously.

Brynn felt herself stiffen. It reflected badly on all three of them that not only had his lordship's peace been upset, but that he was required to visit the servants' quarters to investigate the cause. Yet discomfiting Lucian wasn't what worried her; rather, his presence roused her protective instincts.

She had no idea how he would react to such a major transgression by one of his young servants—whether he would endorse Meg's dismissal or show leniency because of his own rakish past. It would be better for the girl, Brynn realized, if she could handle the problem herself. She would no doubt have a fight on her hands with the housekeeper, though.

"That will be all, Mrs. Poole," Brynn said before the woman could speak up. "You may go."

The housekeeper raised her chin stubbornly. "I should like to hear what his lordship has to say about the matter, my lady."

"We needn't trouble his lordship." She sent Lucian a faint smile. "I regret the disturbance. It will not happen again."

He raised an eyebrow and gave her a long look, then glanced at the housekeeper, who had pursed her lips as if she had swallowed vinegar.

"I trust you understand, Mrs. Poole," Lucian said mildly, "that Lady Wycliff is mistress here. She commands household matters."

His implied threat made the housekeeper's starch wilt. "Yes, of course, my lord," she answered meekly.

As rigid as stone, Mrs. Poole turned away, daring only a brief, scathing glance at Meg before she left the room.

Brynn flashed her husband a genuine smile this time, grateful that he had chosen not to undermine her authority. Her influence was shaky enough, given that her marriage to Lucian had been so contentious in the past. The servants could not have failed to see the chill between them.

Lucian was still watching her. "I had hoped I

might have the pleasure of your company for breakfast, my love," he said lightly.

"I will be down directly, but . . . I would like a few moments here first."

"Certainly. I shall see you shortly."

When he was gone, Brynn took one look at Meg and urged her to lie down.

"Thank you, milady," Meg replied, looking green around the mouth.

"Perhaps I should summon the doctor."

"I am fine, truly. This will pass. My sister always had this trouble when she was breeding."

When the girl curled up on her mattress, Brynn went to the washstand. Wetting one corner of a cloth, she glanced around the austere chamber with its rows of cots. It was not a particularly pleasant place to live—cold in winter and sweltering in summer. Certainly Meg could not remain here to bear her child. Not only would it set a poor example for the other servants, but a baby could not be raised here. Some other solution would have to be found.

Returning to sit beside the invalid, Brynn applied the damp cloth to the girl's sweating brow. After a moment Meg's nausea seemed to pass, and she opened her eyes.

"You are so kind, milady."

Brynn returned a smile. "Would you care to tell me what happened?"

Meg dropped her gaze. "I am weak and wicked, I know, but I did not seduce him as Mrs. Poole said. It is just that he was so handsome. . . ."

"Who is the father, Meg?" Brynn asked gently. "You should not have to bear this difficulty alone."

The girl's lower lip trembled. "I would rather not say. I don't want to get him into trouble."

"Meg, I cannot help you if I don't understand your situation."

"It makes no matter, anyway. He doesn't want to wed me. But . . . it's . . . John, milady. John Hotch-kiss. He's underfootman for Lord Bonamy, across the square."

Brynn hesitated. "Does your John know about the child?"

"He knows." Fresh tears welled in her eyes.

"And what does he have to say about it?"

"He fears dismissal if he were to offer for me. . . . Even if he could gain permission, he has no money to afford a wife. I don't think he wants to be leg-shackled." Meg covered her face with her hands. "It only happened twice. I never thought . . ."

She didn't believe she would be so fertile, Brynn mentally concluded the unspoken sentence.

"And I never thought I would have a by-blow," the girl moaned. "My mum would die of shame if she were alive to see it. And my sister . . . she is sure to disown me."

"Do you have any other family you could live with?"

"No, milady. Just a brother who works in the mills."

Brynn patted her shoulder, wanting to offer com-fort. "Well, we will think of something."

Looking up abruptly, Meg grasped her hand and

gave it a fervent kiss. "Milady, you are truly an angel."

Flushing, Brynn rose to her feet. "Try to get some rest, Meg. I need a little time to consider what to do."

She summoned the butler and asked him to send for the doctor, then joined Lucian in the breakfast parlor. When he looked up from the morning paper, Brynn was struck again by the intense blue of his eyes.

"I gather peace has been restored?" he commented when she was settled at the table and the footmen had withdrawn.

"Yes, at least for now." She could have allowed the subject to drop, but felt a need to express her gratitude. "Thank you for supporting me with Mrs. Poole. She tends to question my authority."

Lucian gave an elegant shrug. "It was nothing. You are mistress here. You may run the household as you see fit—for as long as you remain."

He was alluding to their bargain, she realized. Brynn lowered her gaze to her coffee cup.

"I trust the difficulty is not of great magnitude?"

"Nothing that cannot be resolved."

"Would you care to discuss it? Perhaps I can help."

She gave Lucian a questioning glance, wondering at his sincerity. "Is the pin money you allotted me mine to spend as I wish?" she said finally.

"Of course. And so is the household allowance. Why do you ask?"

Brynn took a deep breath, gambling that she could trust him. "Because my maid is with child by one of the footmen across the square, and I should like to help her."

"I see," Lucian replied, his expression enigmatic.

Despite her determination to remain calm, Brynn felt herself growing defensive. "I will *not* have her turned out, as Mrs. Poole intended, Lucian. What Meg did was wrong, but she should not be the only one to suffer. The sin was her lover's as well. I strongly suspect he seduced her, but even if not, it isn't fair that the girl must be punished while the man can evade the consequences with complete impunity!"

"No, it isn't fair," Lucian agreed mildly. "I will give you no argument there."

When a wry smile curled his mouth, Brynn regarded him with suspicion. "I fail to see how my poor maid's dilemma could be cause for amusement."

"I wasn't thinking of her dilemma but of your bluestocking tendencies. I was picturing how your notions of equality would sit with most of my peers."

"Most of your peers are pompous stuffed shirts who believe women were put on this earth merely to serve them!"

"Calm down, love. We are not at odds here. Your passion is admirable."

Her cheeks flushed, but her hackles settled down. Perhaps there was no need for belligerence after all.

"There is a simple answer to avoiding an illegitimate child," Lucian observed. "The couple can marry."

"Meg doesn't think her footman would be allowed to wed without losing his position with Lord Bonamy."

"I have influence with Bonamy. I'm sure I can

persuade him to intervene. Her footman can be compelled to marry the girl, if need be."

"But I don't want her to be compelled to accept marriage against her will the way—" Brynn broke off. *The way I was,* was what she meant to say. Seeing understanding register in his blue eyes, Brynn bit her lip.

"I know," she explained more diplomatically, "you might find it hard to understand, given your gender and your exalted rank, but for a woman, marriage can be worse than servitude. You have no idea what it is like to be subject to someone else's every whim, to have no rights other than the ones your husband chooses to bestow upon you."

His eyebrows rose. "Have I been so overbearing, then?"

"No . . . not entirely. But it isn't pleasant to be totally at your mercy. How would you like it if you were dependent on me for every morsel of food, every scrap of clothing? If I could arbitrarily overrule your smallest decision, such as what friends you associated with? Or if I threatened to send you to the country if you disobeyed me?" *As you threatened me.* She could see Lucian's comprehension.

"I wouldn't care for it at all," he murmured.

"Of course not. And Meg should not be made to wed her lover if she doesn't wish to. I'm not certain she is in love with him, and I seriously doubt he is with her. He might resent having to pay for his transgressions, and Meg would bear the brunt of his anger. She would be better off alone than being pressed upon a husband who doesn't want her, being forced to endure a bitter union."

Thoughtfully, Lucian shook his head. "I'm not convinced even a bitter union would be worse than rearing a bastard alone."

"Perhaps not, but the choice should be hers. I intend to provide for her, Lucian. At the very least to make certain that she has somewhere to live."

"A better solution would be to dower the girl. Sweeten the pot, so to speak, so her lover will see her as a prize rather than a burden."

Brynn pursed her lips in contemplation. Lucian's suggestion did have practical merit. If finances were the major impediment, then dowering the maid would certainly smooth the path to a happier union. And it would allow her to avoid rearing a bastard alone, which would prove incredibly difficult. . . .

"That might be a solution," Brynn replied slowly. "But I will have to see what Meg says first."

"Speak to her, by all means. But in either case, there is no reason for you to use your pin money. My pockets are deep enough to provide a dowry for a serving maid."

"You would do that for her?"

"Not for her. For you."

When she was silent, Lucian gave her a long look. "I'm not quite the villain you think me, love," he said softly.

"I don't think you a villain," Brynn replied. Indeed, he was far kinder than she wanted him to be. And it was becoming increasingly impossible to remain impervious when Lucian wielded such weapons to assault her defenses.

She averted her gaze from his quietly measuring one. They might have determined a solution to her maid's difficulty, but her own dilemma was becoming more profound by the minute.

If Brynn was torn by the incident, Lucian was more so. Their conversation rang in his head long after it had ended. Her passionate insistence that her maid be allowed to choose her future only drove home how he'd wronged Brynn when he bought her in marriage against her fervent protests, denying her the same choice.

He'd seen her as a prize to be claimed, thought only of his own wishes, determined to use his vast wealth or any other means necessary to assure victory.

He greatly regretted his arrogance now. He had underestimated Brynn from the first, viewing her merely as a temptress and a prime receptacle for his seed. But she was far more than a tempting, fertile body. It wasn't surprising that she would be protective of her brothers, especially her youngest, but that she actually cared what happened to her dependents . . .

Lucian knew how unusual such compassion was. While beauty and good lineage—and even brains and spirit—were not uncommon attributes among the ladies of his acquaintance, a kind heart was a rarity.

Admittedly, Brynn's unexpected depth made her all the more alluring. He'd never met another woman whose touch produced such a blaze of desire in him, and yet he had come to admire his bride as well as lust after her. He wanted her more deeply with each passing day.

Despite his fevered dreams of Brynn, wakening next to her was an unaccountable joy. Wrapped in flaming drifts of her hair, enveloped by her warmth and feminine scent, he felt a contentment that he had never before experienced. She was the most elusive woman he'd ever known—and her sheer elusiveness only strengthened his primitive urge to bind her to him in any way he could.

Getting her with child might provide that bond. Yet he wanted Brynn to want their child. To want their marriage. He wanted to win her affections.

It required every ounce of willpower he possessed to allow Brynn to dictate the pace. He had hoped that given time, she would realize that her fears were primarily in her mind. Yet he didn't seem to be making much headway.

Dare was right, Lucian knew. He would have far better success in courting Brynn if he could get her alone. His London house was simply too full of servants and hangers-on to allow the kind of privacy that was conducive to courtship. His country seat would perhaps allow them more opportunity to be alone, but he couldn't leave London just now when word of Caliban might come at any moment.

Thus far his best agents had failed to discover any further leads regarding the mastermind of the gold-smuggling ring. Philip Barton had returned from France empty-handed.

At least Dare had been enlisted to help flush out Lord Caliban's identity. Dare had initially laughed at the notion of becoming a spy, but rather quickly he'd decided to view it as a challenge; pitting wits against an elusive, dangerous traitor was the ultimate game for him.

With Dare searching for Caliban, Lucian could

devote himself to wooing his bride with a trace less guilt. And suddenly wooing Brynn had become the most important thing in the world to him.

Chapter Fifteen

Much to Brynn's relief, her maid's dilemma was easily solved. A generous dowry proved to be an excellent inducement for the girl's lover to propose, while his employer was soon persuaded to give permission for the marriage. Meg expressed delight with the arrangement, for she wished to give her child a name. And her enthusiasm satisfied Brynn that the girl wasn't being forced into an unwanted union.

Brynn's own dilemma proved far harder to solve. In the days that followed, she found herself more conflicted than ever as she struggled against the desire assailing her heart. Lucian was wooing her, there was no doubt about it. What had started as a war of wills had become a determined courtship, simmering with a fiery passion that set their cold-blooded arrangement aflame.

Her husband, Brynn continued to discover, was a man of smoldering sexuality and insatiable appetites. He made love with tender savagery, for all his sophistication, but his untamed wildness only drove her to greater heights of rapture. And even in a mansion filled with retainers, he found opportunities for intimacy. He had only to touch her and the burning heat of his passion drove all thoughts of caution and curses from her mind.

It wasn't solely Lucian's passion, however, that she found so difficult to resist. Nor was it even his charm or warmth or tenderness. It was that he showed a genuine interest in her—quizzing her about her likes and dislikes, probing her dreams, asking about her life before meeting him.

Brynn tried to keep their conversations brief and unemotional, but Lucian's perceptiveness was as keen as his persistence. He obviously noticed her melancholy when she spoke of her family, especially her youngest brother.

"You miss Theo, don't you?" he asked one morning as they lay in bed after an exhausting bout of obligatory lovemaking.

She nodded. The frantic gaiety of the Little Season had begun in earnest, and she found plenty to occupy her time. And yet she did miss Theo dreadfully. "Very much."

"Would you like to pay him a visit?"

Her eyes widened as she lifted her head from Lucian's shoulder. "I would like that more than anything, Lucian. And I expect Theo will enjoy a holiday from his studies. His letters are cheerful enough, but I suspect he feels a trifle homesick."

"I will be happy to escort you. We can travel next week, if you wish."

"That would be wonderful," Brynn exclaimed, sitting up in bed. "I shall write his masters at once."

Lucian laughed at her eagerness, and yet he was

true to his word, escorting her to see Theo at school. Harrow was located only a short drive north of London, and after collecting the boy, they made a full day of it, enjoying an alfresco luncheon in Epping Forest and returning to wander the shops on the narrow, winding streets of Harrow Hill and take tea.

Lucian acted the ideal host, putting himself out to make the experience delightful for both Brynn and Theo, and neither of them wanted it to end. Theo was especially awed by Lucian, hanging on his every word, and more than once expressed gratitude for enabling him to attend school.

"Don't thank me," Lucian replied easily. "It was your sister's doing."

Theo sent Brynn a solemn look. "I know, sir. And I will try to prove myself worthy of her sacrifice."

Seeing Lucian wince, Brynn swiftly changed the subject.

The visit, however, proved to be the happiest time for Brynn since her marriage. And once she had reassured herself that her young brother was content, her heart was lighter than it had been in months.

Even when they returned to London, her feeling of optimism remained. She no longer felt quite so lonely—how could she be when Lucian was determined to act the ideal husband? And she was busier than ever. She still frequently assisted Raven with her upcoming nuptials. And with London's fall social season in full cry, the Earl and Countess of Wycliff were much in demand. They chose from among a dozen invitations each night—fetes and balls, soirees and musicales, routs and supper parties. Lucian provided Brynn escort to any function she expressed a desire to attend.

"You don't have to accompany me every evening," she remarked once when they were perusing the stack of invitations.

He smiled. "Ah, but I do, love. As your husband, it is my duty to protect you from the lecherous males of our fair city."

Despite his teasing tone, she felt her heart sink to be reminded of the danger. "I don't wish to deprive you of your usual pursuits," she replied, skirting the issue.

"You aren't."

"You don't miss your Hellfire League entertainments?"

"How could I miss such mundane affairs when I have my delectable wife to keep me satisfied?"

She doubted those wicked affairs were at all mundane, although she didn't press the point. Yet while Brynn disliked admitting it, she was secretly glad Lucian had deferred his participation in the League. She didn't care to think of him consorting with the brand of females that entertained the dissolute Hellfire members.

Indeed, she didn't care to think of Lucian with any other female at all. He was as much sought after by the fairer sex as she was by her suitors, and dismayingly, Brynn found herself stung by jealousy each time a beautiful woman looked at him with lust. She was aware that Lucian had had any number of mistresses before his marriage, and she found herself scanning the crowds, wondering which ones had enjoyed his patronage.

Yet he seemed interested only in her for the moment, and wholly dedicated to his pledge of getting her with child.

A week following their visit to Harrow, Brynn was sitting at her dressing table, having her hair arranged, for they planned to attend a ball later that evening after dining at home. When she sensed Lucian's presence, she looked up to find him leaning indolently against the door from her sitting room.

Her heart started beating in that slow, heavy way it did whenever he was near—and accelerated when she saw he wasn't at all prepared to go to the ball. He wore only a dressing robe of forest green brocade, which clearly told her he had more than dancing till dawn on his mind. He stood there a moment, so handsome that Brynn realized she was forgetting to breathe.

Then, with a brief nod, he summarily dismissed her maid, vexing Brynn somewhat with his presumption.

"Meg was not finished with my hair," she protested when the girl had scurried from the room.

"She can finish later. I ordered dinner served in your sitting room, and the dishes won't remain warm for long. Will you join me, love?"

All he had to do was smile that lazy, entrancing smile, exactly as he was doing now, and Brynn's vexation melted.

He offered her his hand and escorted her to the adjacent sitting room, where delicious aromas assaulted her senses. The scene was staged for lovers, Brynn realized. A fire burned lazily in the hearth, and the table that had been set up for their repast groaned with sumptuous dishes—braised duck and ragout of veal, tomato aspic, potatoes in Hollandaise sauce, and artichoke hearts, with desserts of Geonese cakes and raspberry cream.

Lucian took it upon himself to serve her, and when they were done, he sat back and eyed Brynn over his wineglass, his gaze lingering brazenly on her bosom.

She felt herself flush at his lascivious look. "Must you ogle me that way?" she said finally. "Every time you look at me, I feel ravished."

"Perhaps because every time I look at you, I want to ravish you."

She glanced at the clock on the mantel. "Shouldn't you begin dressing for the ball?"

"My appetite hasn't been satisfied yet."

"After that delicious fare, what more could you possibly be hungry for?"

"You, love. I have a vast craving to taste you with the sweets. I've been imagining how much I would like to set you on the table, lift your skirts, and bury my head between your thighs."

Brynn felt her blood heat at the suggestive image. "On the table? You aren't serious."

His smile was tantalizing, tempting as sin. "Ah, Brynn, how little you know me." Leaning forward, Lucian lifted her hand and turned his mouth into her palm.

"Someone could come," she said breathlessly.

"Someone could," he agreed. "But I should be allowed to enjoy savoring my wife in private."

Rising, he crossed the room and locked the door

to the hall. Then he cleared most of the dishes from the table to the hearth, leaving the silver bowl of raspberry cream.

"We will be late for the ball," Brynn said, making one last attempt at being sensible.

"It's fashionable to be late. Besides, that gown you are wearing is worse than being naked," Lucian replied, coming to stand behind her chair.

Brynn frowned, knowing her jade, empire-waist gown was elegantly cut but modest as far as evening attire went. "What is wrong with my gown?"

"It's far too provocative." Bending, he nuzzled aside her tresses and found her ear, touching it with the tip of his tongue. "I can't possibly permit you to go out in public dressed like that, looking so lush and tempting. I shall have to remove it."

He reached down to slide his hands beneath her bodice, caressing her nipples. Brynn arched against his touch wantonly and bit back a moan.

"Lucian . . ." she murmured finally.

"Yes, my love?" he asked, nibbling at her ear.

"This is scandalous."

"No, it isn't. It is merely your duty, which you've neglected outrageously of late, wife. You haven't properly aroused me today."

With effort, Brynn opened her dazed eyes. "I think you should be the one to arouse me for a change."

"I would be more than happy to oblige, love."

Her heart began to race as he unfastened the hooks at the back of her bodice. Helping her to her feet then, he pushed the fabric off her shoulders, letting her expensive gown slide to the floor. Lucian made short work of her corset and chemise, drawing it over her head, leaving her wearing only stockings and garters and slippers.

The heat of his gaze burned her to the core as he stared at her breasts gleaming pale and bare. Opening his robe, he brought her full against his hardened frame, letting her feel his desire. Brynn shut her eyes, hot tension radiating from her loins in waves as his thick, pulsating member nestled between her thighs.

He didn't take her, though. Instead he lifted her to the table and pulled the pins from her hair.

"Your hair is incredible . . . like fire," he whispered, tangling his fingers in the long tresses, "aflame around you." Holding her still, he began a hot exploration of the inside of her mouth. His kiss was relentless in its demand, twisting, bruising, insisting, stirring.

Her senses felt dazed as he eased her back upon the table, spreading her thighs for his appreciation. His eyes roamed freely over her, just as his lean, strong hands were doing. For a moment his hands covered her breasts, his palms working her stiffened nipples, but then Lucian drew back.

The curve of his lips was darkly sensual as he dipped his finger into the bowl of raspberry cream, anointing the twin peaks of her breasts standing taut and high. Brynn shivered at the chill sensation, even as the fire of his gaze heated her flesh. His finger dipped again, and he traced a sweet path along her body, painting her navel with the sweet cream, and lower, drenching the lips of her sex. Brynn had to grit her teeth at the warm shock that went through her.

He let his own robe drop to the floor, standing above her, his magnificent body bare. Then, easing his powerful thighs between her spread legs, he bent to lick the cream from her nipples.

Brynn gasped as he suckled the tight, wet crests, feeling pleasure spiking downward toward the pulsing core of her body.

"Delicious," he murmured, his rasping tongue working his way along her skin. Holding one breast in each hand, he moved his mouth even lower, burying his head between her thighs as he'd threatened earlier.

She went rigid, scarcely believing the incredible sensations as he tasted her. Lucian was so powerful in the way he took control. He licked and savored, setting her nerves awake with each flick of his tongue.

She was whimpering now. The lash of pleasure was almost cruel, the searing wet heat almost unbearable. Desperately she threaded her fingers tightly through his darkly burnished hair and clung to him.

"Lucian . . ." she pleaded finally, restlessly twisting her head from side to side.

"Not yet, wife. You're not hot enough. I intend to pleasure you until you beg me to end it."

"I am hot enough," she vowed. She was willing to beg him if need be. She was shamelessly willing to do anything he wanted of her.

Lucian wasn't convinced. He left off savoring her and raised his head to watch her. She looked deliciously wanton, her bare breasts wet from his mouth, her back arching in arousal. Desire pulsed at his groin with a hot, fierce ache.

"I'm not going to take you," he taunted, "until your body is quivering, until you scream for me to come inside you. Then I'm going to slide into you so deeply, you won't know where I end and you begin. . . ."

A responsive shudder went through her, but it wasn't enough for Lucian. He wanted her vibrant and writhing with need for him. He would make her burn for him, make her feel the same fire, suffer the same torment he was feeling.

Slowly he thrust two fingers inside her, and her hips shot upward off the table, sending a jolt of desire surging through his body. When he deliberately stroked her slick bud with his thumb, she groaned.

"Lucian, damn you," she panted, trying to get closer. "You're tormenting me."

"But I want to torment you. Just the way you've tormented me of late." Pressing her thighs wide, he held her still, guiding her hips with purposeful intent as he positioned the cresting head of his erection at her silken entrance.

"Watch while I take you," he demanded, gazing down at where their bodies joined. Even as he spoke, he sank home into the slick, heated wetness, driving a thready sigh from her. She was wet and fiery hot around him, and so tight he thought he might burst. But he controlled his need with desperate strength. When he withdrew, his swollen shaft glistened with her juices.

Brynn tried to take command then. Her arms locked around his neck, and she wrapped her legs around his waist, clutching at him. Understanding

her need, he thrust again, forcing himself deep,
dredging a raw moan from deep in her throat.

Her plea was unnecessary; he felt the way she was
shaking.

"So beautiful, so wild, so ready for me," he
rasped.

"Now, Lucian . . . oh God, please . . ."

Obligingly his intensity quickened, and he drove
into her with a ravishing, penetrating rhythm, his
own body on fire. He wanted her with a hungry urgency that threatened his sanity.

He clenched his jaw as she arched against him.
She was utterly wild and glorious, with her head
thrown back, her bare breasts heaving from the
force of her panting breaths, so near to orgasm that
the slightest friction would push her over the edge.

He braced his legs and plunged into her sleek passage one last time, so deep he could feel the very
mouth of her womb.

She did scream then, a high keening pleasure
sound that sent a spiking rapture through him. Her
frantic cry was taken from her by his kiss as she
erupted, her inner muscles convulsing around his
erection with a force that nearly made him explode.
Lucian shook with triumph as he feverishly ate her
mouth that tasted sumptuously like raspberries.

Finally the rippling convulsions slowed.

Long moments later, Brynn came to her senses.
Drowsy and replete, she lay sprawled wantonly on
the hard table, cool air brushing her overheated
skin. Lucian was still buried hard and deep within
her, magnificently filling her.

"You didn't find your pleasure," she murmured weakly.

His expression was primitively male, sexual and possessive, as he gazed down at her. "Not yet. But the night is still young. We're going to make each other wild, exhausted, siren."

"We will miss the ball," she replied, a drained smile curving her lips.

"Do you really want to go?"

"Not at all."

It was all the answer Lucian needed. Still impaling her, he lifted her up and strode with her to his bed, his hungry mouth ravaging hers as he bore her down to the soft mattress.

If Lucian's passion was crumbling her defensive walls bit by bit, Brynn found her heart torn even further a few days later. Before she left to ride in the park with Raven, she stopped by Lucian's study to bid him farewell. When at his command she bent to kiss him, he handed her a wooden box tied with a green satin ribbon.

"What is this?" she asked curiously.

"A wedding gift. You didn't care for the emeralds I gave you. I thought perhaps you might like this better."

Setting her gloves on his desk, she opened the box and found an old parchment inside. "A deed? To . . . Gwyndar Castle?"

"One of my properties in Wales. The coastal waters are warm enough that you can swim almost year-round. I've signed it over to you." When Brynn's expression turned troubled, Lucian scrutinized her. "You don't seem pleased."

Wondering if she should answer honestly, she took a deep breath. "I am not pleased that you are trying to buy me, Lucian."

"Buy you?"

Her eyes met his steadily. "You are so wealthy that you've grown accustomed to purchasing whatever you want. But you cannot win me over with extravagant presents. Allegiance cannot be bought."

His blue eyes grew hooded. "I don't deny trying to win you over, or that I would like you to be content in our marriage. But you mistake my motive in this instance. I was merely considering what you said about being dependent on me, about how powerless it made you feel. I thought having a residence to call your own would allow you a measure of independence. If you still wish us to go our separate ways once my heir is born, you can retire there and be free of me."

Brynn stared at him, realizing she had misjudged Lucian once again. Rather than trying to win her affections with expensive gifts, he was offering her at least some small measure of choice for her future.

"I am grateful for your thoughtfulness," she murmured finally. "Lucian . . ." She hesitated, trying to determine how to ask the question that had been burning in her mind for days. "If I fulfill my duty, will you allow me to retire to Wales alone?"

"I would want you to remain in London for your confinement since the best doctors are here, but afterward, you may go anywhere you like."

"And leave our child with you?"

His eyes were unwavering. "Giving up my son is more than I'm prepared to do, Brynn. I would hire the best nurses, of course."

"Of course," she murmured more bitterly than she intended. She glanced down at Lucian's gift, her heart aching at the choice she would have to make . . . wondering if it really was any choice at all. Could she possibly abandon a child of her flesh?

"What if I were to bear a girl instead of a boy?" she asked finally.

He was silent for a long moment. "Our agreement was for a son, Brynn."

"So it was." She closed the box carefully and set it on the desk. "Thank you for your gift." Giving him a wistful, almost sad smile, she picked up her riding gloves and turned away without another word.

Lucian watched her go, grappling with his own tangled emotions. He no longer felt so adamant about wanting his child to be a son; a daughter might be just as satisfying. And if Brynn bore him a girl, he would have every right to demand that she remain with him until she fulfilled their pact to give him an heir. Admittedly not a selfless sentiment.

She wasn't entirely mistaken, either, about his motives in gifting her with the castle. Whether consciously or not, he was attempting to buy her contentment. If Brynn no longer felt dependent on him, at his mercy, then she might willingly choose to remain with him.

And God knew, he wanted her to remain. More than he'd ever wanted anything in his life. He took a determined breath. Somehow he had to find a way to win Brynn's heart. Love could bind them together more eternally than any marriage vows. Love could—

Lucian froze, startled by the alien notion that had crept into his thoughts. *Love?* Was that the name for his affliction? This all-consuming desire for his wife that gnawed at the roots of his being?

There was no question that he was obsessed with Brynn. Cursed or not, her beauty made him ache, her passion drove him mad with wanting. But love?

It had always been an elusive concept for him, yet he was undoubtedly behaving like a man caught in the throes of love. He'd seen two of his friends suffer the same torment. Both Damien and Nick had found passionate love when they least expected it.

He keenly envied the happiness they had found with their wives, Lucian admitted. And he wanted it for himself. For Brynn.

Lucian squeezed his eyes shut. Whether or not he loved her, she was a fever in his blood. He desperately wanted to make her feel the same fever. He wanted to bind her to him with primal need, to brand her soul with the fire that was searing him. And yet . . .

Opening his eyes, he stared down at the box. Considering her unenthusiastic reaction to his gift, his goal of winning Brynn seemed as far away as ever. And not because of any real incompatibility between them. His greatest enemy was a damned curse he didn't even believe in.

"Is something troubling you, Brynn?" Raven asked a short while later as they rode together in Hyde Park.

Brynn forced her attention away from her dark thoughts and managed a brief smile of apology. "Forgive me, what were you saying?"

"Nothing of importance. I merely asked if you might like to attend a fair." She pointed to a hand-bill nailed to a tree, advertising an upcoming fair to be held in Westminster.

Brynn edged her mount closer so she could read the touted list of entertainments: Jugglers, Puppeteers, Rope Dancers, *Gypsy Fortune-tellers*— The last words leapt out at her. She frowned, wondering if the band of Gypsies she knew from Cornwall would be performing at the fair. She seemed to remember they were usually in London this time of year. . . .

Brynn drew a slow breath. If Esmerelda truly were here, perhaps she might be able to offer some advice. Perhaps she might even, Brynn reflected hopefully, help explain her dark dreams of Lucian.

Before she could reply, however, Raven gave a faint sigh. "No matter. I don't suppose Halford would approve of my attending. He has very narrow opinions regarding the conduct of his future duchess, and I doubt a fair would fit into the acceptable category." Her tone held a perceptible note of disappointment in her betrothed, but then she shook her head. "Still, Halford did loosen his starch enough to agree to my request for the balloon ascension this week." With a determined smile, Raven spurred her horse on.

Brynn followed, although she cast a glance over her shoulder at the handbill, noting again the dates and location of the fair. If she could manage it, she would try to attend in the hopes that Esmerelda might be found there, for she desperately needed advice about her future with Lucian from someone who knew the deadly history of the Gypsy's curse.

The curse remained the dark blot on Brynn's horizon. She had attempted to repress the warnings of her conscience, yet she was brutally reminded of the danger a few days later when Lucian escorted her to the balloon ascension held by the Duke of Halford in honor of his betrothed.

Several brightly colored balloons awaited flight, Brynn saw with delight upon reaching the field on the outskirts of London. Her attention claimed by the spectacle, she accepted Lucian's assistance from the carriage and was crossing the road on his arm when she heard the sound of galloping hooves. Brynn looked up to see a team of straining horses hurtling directly toward them, apparently out of control.

She froze in her tracks, her mind registering the specter of a driver in a hooded cloak wielding a savage whip.

Lucian, fortunately, didn't share her paralysis. With a desperate lunge, he shoved Brynn out of the path of the lethal threat and flung himself after her, a bare instant before the coach thundered past.

Both of them lay on the ground stunned, staring after the runaway vehicle.

Lucian recovered first. Uttering a low curse, he climbed to his feet and helped her up. "Are you hurt?" he asked, both his gaze and hands examining her for injuries.

Her face was white as she regarded him numbly.

"You could have been killed," she whispered, her voice raw.

"Either of us could have been killed," he replied, his own tone grim. "But it most likely was an accident. A bolting team isn't uncommon."

Yet she didn't believe him, Lucian could see clearly from her petrified expression.

And in truth, he didn't have total faith in his own reassurances. It wasn't implausible that someone had just attempted to kill him; in his line of work, he tended to make enemies. But he doubted a centuries-old curse was to blame for the near-fatal accident.

Yet convincing Brynn of that, Lucian reflected darkly, was as unlikely as their ascending to the skies without the assistance of a balloon.

Chapter Sixteen

After the ominous carriage incident, Brynn's feelings of dread returned with a vengeance. So did her dark dream of Lucian dying while she stood over him, her hands stained with his blood. Her sense of urgency, however, deepened to near panic when she actually found herself with child.

It was her maid, Meg, who first recognized the symptoms. Brynn was dressing for her morning ride when she began to feel strangely nauseated. When she pressed a hand to her stomach, Meg took one look at her face and went to fetch the chamber pot.

"You should sit, milady. Put your head down, between your legs. . . . There, that's it."

Sinking down into a chair, Brynn obeyed, wondering what was wrong with her. She was rarely ill, and she had eaten nothing to cause this bilious sensation. She covered her mouth with her hand and tried to take slow, deep breaths as her maid ordered.

"It will pass in time," Meg said soothingly, stroking her mistress's forehead. "Once your stomach starts to swell, you'll not feel ill. I scarce feel it now."

"Swell?"

"With the babe."

Startled, Brynn stared down at her abdomen. Was it possible? Was she carrying Lucian's child within her body? But of course, considering their determined efforts to conceive. And somehow she knew it was true.

A ripple of joy flowed through her, followed by a sharp pang of dismay. A child only made her dilemma more difficult. Lucian had promised they could live separate lives in exchange for her giving him a son, but heaven help her, she didn't want to leave her child behind.

Brynn raised a hand to her temple. In all likelihood, she would have no choice. She had to protect Lucian, whatever the personal cost. Indeed, if she were wise, she would leave him now, immediately, before the risk to his life grew any greater.

"Will his lordship be pleased, do you think?"

Brynn nodded slowly. Lucian would be elated when she gave him the news, but what then? Once he knew of her pregnancy, there would be no chance of her evading him. He would insist on her remaining by his side, under the care of the best doctors. She would have to endure his tenderness day and night. . . .

She doubted she could be strong enough for so long a duration. Each day that passed, her feelings for Lucian grew ever more acute. She couldn't envision keeping her heart's defenses intact until she gave birth. Certainly she could never spend a lifetime with Lucian and maintain an emotionless detachment. Perhaps she should indeed leave him at once, before it was too late. . . .

No, Brynn reflected, she didn't dare tell him about her pregnancy. Not until she had decided her course of action.

"I don't intend to inform him just yet, Meg," she murmured, trying to swallow her nausea. "Not until I'm certain I truly am with child. Please, I would like to keep it between ourselves."

"Of course, milady. Whatever you wish."

Brynn went to him that night, her emotions in turmoil, the wonder of having part of Lucian growing inside her body battling her fear of the future. But he kissed her with a slow, soul-destroying tenderness, sending passion, sweet and heavy, flowing through her, shattering her reticence. She melted against him, welcoming him with all the longing within her.

The intensity of their mating was stunning. Lucian took her body with fierce hunger, muttering hoarse, unintelligible words against her throat as he demanded her surrender, but he gave her indescribable pleasure in return. Her sobs of rapture were not only physical, though. Brynn felt a bond with him she had never experienced with any other human being.

Afterward she lay in his arms, her breath tangling with his, his fingers caressing her bare skin with soft strokes. She could feel the solid beat of his heart beneath her palm, feel her own heart aching. What they had shared had been, for her, beyond words.

He had made her feel thoroughly possessed, utterly desired, truly cherished. She had never felt so defenseless, so vulnerable. So filled with longing.

She wanted the child inside her, without question, but what was far worse . . . She wanted her child's father. She wanted Lucian as her husband, wanted a real marriage. She wanted his love, wanted to love him in return. . . .

Dear God, Brynn thought, shutting her eyes in dismay. She dared not love Lucian or he would die.

She sat at her dressing table the following morning, clutching her mother's locket in her hand. Her nausea was just as strong today, dispelling any lingering doubts that she was carrying Lucian's child—and strengthening her dread. What if their child was a daughter? If so, the curse would be passed down and the whole terrible cycle would begin all over again.

Please God, no, Brynn thought fiercely. Let it be a son. She couldn't bear to think of her daughter suffering her fate.

She knew now how her mother had felt. Blindly Brynn stared down at the locket her mother had given her as a reminder of the peril she faced. Inside was the miniature portrait of her legendary ancestor, Flaming Nell, but it was her beloved mother's face Brynn saw. A face ravaged by the pain of a fatal childbirth.

You cannot give in, her mother had whispered hoarsely on her deathbed. *Promise me, Brynn. Swear to me you won't let yourself love any man. It will only bring you terrible heartache.* Though weak from the loss of blood, she had forced the locket into Brynn's hand. *Look at this . . . whenever you feel tempted. Look and remember.*

Brynn felt tears burn her throat now at the memory. Her mother had succumbed to the temptation of love—and suffered untold grief as a result. Her final words had been of warning, a plea to beware. Gwendolyn Caldwell had understood all too well the unquenchable hungers of the heart. The aching need to love and be loved.

The soul-deep longing that was tearing at Brynn now.

She felt her fingers clench reflexively over the locket. She had sworn solemnly that day never to let herself love, but she was in danger of breaking her promise. She very much feared she was falling in love with Lucian. Her desire for him was becoming a torture she could no longer endure. No longer *wanted* to endure.

Setting her jaw, Brynn dropped the locket into her jewel case, banishing it from sight. She would have to leave Lucian at once, unless . . .

She went still. Unless she could find some way to fight the curse. She drew a slow breath, remembering the handbill advertising Gypsy fortune-tellers at the upcoming Westminster fair. Was it possible that Esmerelda was in London? Could the Gypsy woman offer her any hope?

Years ago she'd gone to Esmerelda, grieving over her dead suitor, seeking any sort of comfort, perhaps even some measure of absolution. At the time she had been too distraught by the tragedy to question the possibility of breaking the spell. Indeed, just the contrary, Brynn reflected. Because of James's death and her own ominous dreams foretelling it, she'd finally accepted the destructive power of the curse and resigned herself to her fate.

But she was desperate enough now to grasp at any straw. If there was any remotely possible way for her to remain with Lucian without causing his death, she had to try.

Not wanting to give rise to scandal by attending a fair alone, Brynn seriously considered asking Raven to accompany her. Yet she would feel awkward discussing such intimacies as her marital relations and pregnancy with her virginal, unmarried friend. Besides, Raven was close to Lucian, and she might feel obligated to reveal the secret. And Meredith was too happily engrossed in her own family, Brynn felt, to become involved in her troubles. She took Meg instead, knowing it wasn't totally uncommon or beyond the pale for an adventurous lady and her maid to enjoy such an escapade.

Fortunately the autumn day was overcast and chilly enough for her to wear a cloak without arousing comment. Brynn kept the hood drawn close around her face to prevent being recognized and hired a hackney to take them to the fairgrounds in Westminster.

The fair, she discovered, was typical of other ones she'd attended in Cornwall with her brothers, with jugglers and puppeteers vying with vendors hawking oranges and gingerbread and hot meat pies, as well as dealers in finer wares—satin ribbons and gloves and knives.

The grounds were not yet crowded so early in the day, but finding the Gypsy fortune-teller was more difficult than expected. Brynn passed numerous stalls and performers before finally reaching a tent at one end.

She was greeted eagerly by a young beauty garbed in scarves and bangles and colorful skirts who immediately offered charms and dried herbs for sale. Requesting instead to have her fortune told, Brynn left Meg to await her outside and entered the tent.

The interior was dimly lit with a golden glow cast by a handmade oil lamp. When her eyes adjusted, Brynn could see that an old woman sat on a carpet before a low table. It was indeed Esmerelda, Brynn realized, her heart beating faster.

The Gypsy was gray haired and nearly toothless, with a swarthy complexion the texture of leather. Her black eyes, however, were sharp as daggers.

"My lady," she said in a cackling voice. "I heard of yer good fortune. Ye've become a countess."

"Yes, Mother," she said, using a term of respect the Romany people employed when speaking to their elders. "And yourself? Are you faring well?"

"Well enough," Esmerelda replied with a grin. " 'Tis a good year for gullible Gorgios." With a sweep of her bony, silver-beringed fingers, she invited Brynn to be seated before her at the table.

When the Gypsy reached for her hand, however, Brynn shook her head. "I have not come to have my palm read, Mother. Rather, I have a specific question." Taking a deep breath, Brynn drew several guineas from her reticule and placed them on the table. "A matter of grave importance."

"Yer dreams have returned," the Gypsy replied

solemnly, even as her eyes glinted at seeing the gold coins.

"Yes."

"I see. And what is yer question, my lady?"

"I hoped you might tell me if . . . Is there anything I might do to end the curse?"

"Ye fear for yer lover," the old woman surmised.

"Yes," Brynn replied. "My husband."

Picking up a coin, Esmerelda bit down on it with her few remaining teeth, testing. " 'Twill not be easy. The curse on Flaming Nell was wondrously powerful."

"But can it be broken?"

For a long moment, the Gypsy scrutinized her. Finally she nodded. "Do ye love 'im, yer 'usband?"

"I . . . I am not certain," Brynn replied quietly, not wanting to face that question. "If I allowed that to happen, I would be endangering his life. I cannot bear the thought of causing his death."

"But are ye ready to die for 'im? That is what ye must ask yerself."

"Die for him?"

"Aye, m'lady. Ye must love 'im enough to sacrifice yerself. 'Tis the secret of true love. Are ye ready to give yer life for 'is? Only ye can know yer own 'art."

Brynn stared at the wizened Gypsy, her thoughts spinning. Could she love Lucian that much?

Finally she shook herself. "You are saying I must die for him?"

Esmerelda gave her a sympathetic look that held a touch of sadness. "Perhaps 'twill not come to that."

"But you cannot tell me what I must do to save him?"

"No, I cannot tell ye that, my lady. Only what I ken for certain. A love that is true can battle the most evil spell."

It seemed a contradiction, Brynn thought with growing frustration. If she loved Lucian, he would die—yet she must love him deeply enough or he would die.

"Take 'art, my lady," Esmerelda said, reaching across the table to grip Brynn's hand. "All is not lost."

"Thank you, Mother," she murmured, offering a distracted smile.

Rising slowly, Brynn left the tent, feeling somewhat numb. She had been given an answer of sorts: she must be willing to sacrifice her own life to save Lucian's. And yet . . .

Could she actually credit Esmerelda's enigmatic counsel? And if so, how could she initiate such a sacrifice, even if it was the key to breaking the curse?

Surprisingly, Lucian was at home when Brynn arrived. She found him descending the grand staircase as she entered with her maid.

As Meg scurried past him toward the rear of the house, Lucian bent to kiss Brynn's cheek. "There you are. I wondered where you had gone. I trust you had a pleasant morning?"

Brynn hesitated. She didn't want Lucian to know she had visited the Gypsy fortune-teller; she couldn't have him asking disturbing questions about her reasons. If he probed too deeply, she would have to acknowledge her growing feelings for him, which alone might be disastrous.

"Yes," she said finally. "I went with Raven to the lending library."

She saw his eyes narrow a fraction. "Odd. I encountered Raven just now on my way home from Whitehall. She was bemoaning the fact that her aunt had required her attendance all morning."

Brynn found it hard to contain her flush. "How scatterbrained of me. I meant, my friend *Meredith*. I visited the library with Meredith."

Lucian glanced down at her empty hands. "You must not have found any books to your liking."

"No, nothing," Brynn replied, trying to appear undismayed as he searched her face. She gave him her most brilliant smile. "If you will excuse me, I must change for luncheon."

Lucian watched her go, remembering the guilt he'd seen flash in her green eyes. Brynn had lied to him just now, he had no doubt.

His fists clenched involuntarily as he followed her retreating back. She had never shared her secrets with him in the beginning of their marriage, but lately, with the evolving of their relationship, he'd come to expect a measure of honesty between them. Perhaps he was a fool.

Lucian felt his features harden. He'd once suspected Brynn of complicity in her brother's unlawful activities, but he'd determinedly quelled his suspicions, resolving to make a new start between them. Had he been too hasty? Why would Brynn lie to him? More critically, was this the first time? Or was it merely the first time he had caught her?

*   *   *

If Lucian was troubled to discover her lie, he was more disturbed the following morning when he encountered Meg hurriedly leaving his wife's room with a chamber pot.

"Is something amiss?" he asked of the maid.

"No, milord. Nothing to fret about. Her ladyship is feeling poorly because of the babe, 'tis all."

Lucian felt shock run through him. "Babe?"

Seeing him stare, Meg clapped a hand over her mouth in dismay. "Oh my, I wasn't to tell. Her ladyship didn't want you to know."

He willed himself to smile. "Well then, it will be our secret that you told."

After the maid was gone, Lucian stood in the corridor a long moment, feeling stunned. Was he truly to be a father? Was he one step closer to achieving the goal he had desperately longed for?

His emotions ran the gamut from pride to possessiveness, to wonder, to anger that Brynn would purposefully keep such a revelation from him. Why hadn't she told him? Why had she permitted him to learn secondhand that she was pregnant with his child, especially when she knew how much it would mean to him?

And yet . . . perhaps there was a reasonable explanation. Perhaps Brynn simply wanted to tell him herself.

Forcing his suspicions aside, he rapped softly on her bedchamber door. When there was no response, Lucian entered quietly. Brynn was sitting before the fire, staring into the flames, a faraway look on her beautiful face.

Tenderness filled him as he watched her. A child bound them together in a way their marriage vows never could. Perhaps now Brynn would come to accept their union. . . .

Lucian drew a slow breath. Only now was he realizing how desperately he wanted her acceptance. She had become increasingly precious to him, more precious even than the child she was carrying.

"Brynn?" he murmured.

She gave a start and looked up.

"Meg said you were feeling ill."

Flushing, Brynn shook her head. "It's nothing really."

Feeling a sudden chill sweep over him, Lucian gave her a measuring look. She intended to keep silent on a matter of such import? Even when he gave her an obvious opening? "You're certain you are all right?"

She tried to smile. "I'm fine now. Perhaps something I ate at dinner last night disagreed with me."

Disappointment, sharp and bitter, stung Lucian, before another, more dreaded explanation occurred to him. Was it possible she planned to escape before he could learn about her pregnancy, so that he wouldn't claim her baby? He'd warned Brynn he meant to keep his son with him, even if she wanted to live apart. Was that why she was determined to remain silent? She was planning to leave him?

Grimly Lucian forced his thoughts away from such a possibility. He couldn't believe Brynn would serve him such a devastating blow, not when she knew how much siring a child meant to him.

Yet he found his trust greatly strained. Perhaps he

was merely searching for excuses to exonerate her. What did he really know about his bewitching wife after all?

"Very well, then." Willfully Lucian schooled his expression into passivity, but inside his thoughts were roiling.

Brynn was deceiving him, there was no question. And if she could conceal something as momentous as her pregnancy, what other secrets—perhaps even sinister ones—was she keeping from him?

Chapter Seventeen

Lucian stared blindly down at a dossier compiled about a dangerous French agent, not comprehending a word. Much of his intelligence work involved poring over boring reports, routinely searching for anomalies, coincidences, odd recurrences, clues—but he had never resented the tedium as much as now. He had weightier issues on his mind than enemies of the state: namely, his wife.

For the past week he'd spent a good deal of time at his offices, trying without success to distance himself in some measure from Brynn. He had yet to determine what to do about her lies. She still hadn't told him of her pregnancy, which only served to underscore the shaky foundation of their marriage and rekindle his misgivings.

Adding to his disquiet was his recurring death dream. The nightmare had become more vivid and powerful than ever—of Brynn watching him die, perhaps even causing his death. What the significance of that grim image held, Lucian wasn't certain, but it did nothing to allay his growing fear that he couldn't trust her.

Realizing suddenly that he wasn't alone, Lucian

looked up from his desk to see Philip Barton standing in the doorway. Lucian forced a smile and invited his subordinate to enter.

To his surprise, rather than taking a seat as usual, Philip remained standing, his expression tight-lipped, his fingers agitatedly working the brim of his beaver hat.

Finally Philip spoke. "I greatly regret disappointing you, my lord. If you wish me to resign, you have only to say so."

Lucian heard the misery in the younger man's tone, but had no idea what might have caused it. He raised an eyebrow in puzzlement. "What the devil are you talking about? You haven't disappointed me, as far as I know."

"You didn't trust me enough to divulge your changing the date of the latest gold shipment."

Lucian felt a cold chill squeeze his chest. Events had been quiet of late, perhaps too quiet. Two shipments of gold bullion had been safely delivered to the allies on the Continent, and nothing had been heard from the treasonous Lord Caliban.

"I never changed the date," Lucian said slowly. "Suppose you explain yourself."

For the first time his subordinate looked confused. "But the letter . . ."

"What letter, man?" Lucian demanded impatiently.

"The letter you wrote authorizing the change in schedule."

"I wrote no such letter."

"My God . . ." An expression of horror seized Philip's features. "The gold is gone, then. . . . It was retrieved yesterday, on your order."

Lucian rose to his feet, feeling dread boil up inside him. "I think I should see this letter."

Delivering gold to fund the war effort was not a complex process: the London mint issued gold coinage, which was conveyed to the Bank of England and then shipped out under heavy guard to the Continent to meet troop payrolls and make payments to the countries of the Triple Alliance so they would continue to fight on Britain's side. The transfer process had rarely failed until now.

The bank manager was unnerved to see Lord Wycliff and alarmed to think the gold had been consigned into the wrong hands. "But . . . but the l-letter of authorization seemed absolutely g-genuine," he stammered.

"Allow me to see it, please," Lucian demanded tersely.

With a murmur of distress, the manager signaled for an underling to fetch the letter. When it was presented in short order, Lucian grimly scanned the contents.

For purposes of national security, I am authorizing a change in date of the next scheduled shipment of gold. My agents will call the morning of October 5th at ten A.M. to receive the strongboxes.
Lucian Tremayne, Earl of Wycliff

His stomach roiling, Lucian passed the letter on to his subordinate. There was no question in his mind, though. The shipment was gone. Three strongboxes of new sovereigns—over a hundred thousand pounds' worth—stolen effortlessly, without a drop of bloodshed or strife. No bloodshed *yet*, Lucian amended, his mouth tightening with fury. Such a sum would permit Napoleon's armies to continue their slaughter of the allied forces for weeks.

"This does appear to have been written by you, my lord," Philip said, his tone flat with dread.

"Yes," Lucian replied through gritted teeth. "An excellent forgery."

The manager wrung his hands in misery, looking as if he might cry. "I confess I thought the change odd, my lord, but the letter seemed to be in order— and it bore your seal."

Taking the letter back, Lucian inspected the now-broken wax wafer, which had indeed been imprinted with the Wycliff seal. An imprecise warning thought teased the back of his mind, but before he could make sense of it, the manager launched into a spate of profuse apologies.

Brusquely Lucian thanked him and dismissed the man with a curt wave.

"Do you suppose it is the work of Caliban?" Philip asked when they were alone.

"Who else?" Lucian retorted grimly. "But he obviously had assistance from someone within our offices. Only two people besides you and myself knew when the next shipment was to take place, and I would trust both of them with my life."

"Then who could have gained access to the schedule? And pulled off such a precise forgery?"

Lucian frowned. "One of our clerks might have accomplished it," he said slowly. "Who wrote out the copy of the schedule?"

"None of the clerks, my lord. On your orders, I myself copied the original, but I had not yet delivered it to the bank. Both schedules are locked in my desk."

"Locks can be picked, Philip. Which clerk usually performs such tasks?"

"Normally Jenkins," Philip murmured, clearly dismayed.

"So he would have known the plans for the gold shipments that were stolen earlier this year? Before we took the responsibility from him?"

"It would seem so."

Lucian turned abruptly on his heel.

"Where are you going, my lord?" Philip called after him.

"To hunt down our traitor."

Evening had fallen by the time they researched an address and located the flat of Mr. Charles Jenkins, a senior clerk employed in the intelligence section of the Foreign Office. Lucian planned to withhold judgment until he could conduct an interrogation, but any doubts about the clerk's complicity were dispelled the instant the door was opened; Jenkins took one look at his callers and bolted.

He reached a window and managed to raise the sash partway before Lucian caught him. Spinning the man around, Lucian threw him up against the wall and took hard hold of his cravat.

"Did no one ever tell you it is bad form to turn your back on visitors?" Lucian queried, his silken tone edged with steel.

Jenkins's face contorted with fear as he panted out a question. "What . . . do you want, my lord?"

"I believe you have something to confess."

"Confess? I don't . . . know what . . . you mean—"

His grip tightening, Lucian twisted the cravat. Jenkins clawed at his throat but was no more forthcoming.

"Who paid you to forge the letter?" Lucian demanded, losing patience.

"What . . . letter?"

Enraged by the clerk's brazen equivocation, Lucian hauled the man back to the window and shoved his head through the opening, giving him a good look at the dark cobblestone alley three floors below. "You'll find it a long way down."

Jenkins made a mewling sound.

"Tell me who hired you."

"I can't! He will kill me. . . ."

"What do you think I intend to do to you?"

When the clerk only whimpered and shook his head, Lucian lifted him by the belt and shoved; his torso went through, then his hips. Lucian stopped shoving at midthigh, holding his victim solely by one ankle.

Jenkins screamed in terror as he found himself dangling over the precipice. "All right! I will tell you what I know!"

Lucian waited another moment before pulling the terrified clerk back inside. Jenkins sank to a trembling heap on the floor, holding his throat and eyeing his assaulter with dread.

"I advise you to keep to the truth," Lucian said after a moment, when his rage was better under control. "You'll be hanged for treason unless I can be persuaded to show leniency."

The clerk visibly swallowed and nodded his head.

"Was it you who divulged the schedules of gold shipments months ago?"

"Y-yes, my lord."

"I suppose you have an excuse for betraying your country and sending countless good men to their deaths?"

The clerk's expression twisted into agony. "I never meant . . . I needed money badly to pay my debts . . . and my mother . . . They threatened her life, said they would kill her if I didn't obey. I swear I didn't realize the gold would end up in French hands."

"You didn't realize?" Lucian repeated contemptuously.

"No, I did not! I was only told to supply the schedule."

"But you understood your crime quite well after the first theft, considering the uproar at the Foreign Office."

Jenkins hung his head in shame. "Yes," he whispered. "But by then it was too late. I was in too deep."

"Very well, tell me who is masterminding the gold thefts."

The clerk's expression turned earnest. "I don't know, my lord. I was merely an underling. I heard his name mentioned once—Lord Caliban—but I never saw him."

"*Someone* must be giving you orders."

"Someone did, yes. I received my instructions from a gentleman . . . Sir Giles Frayne . . ."

Lucian felt his heart lurch at the name, but he was spared from answering when Philip spoke for the first time. "Sir Giles has been dead for months."

Involuntarily Lucian met his subordinate's gaze. Philip was one of the few people who knew how Sir Giles had met his ignominious end.

Lucian glanced down at his hands that were suddenly unsteady. The memory of that bleak moment would always be etched in his mind. Killing his friend had unleashed something dark and primal within him, an ugliness he longed to forget. Yet he was prepared to kill again if it meant stopping the treacherous Caliban and his cohorts in treason.

"A convenient claim," Lucian said finally, "now that Sir Giles is no longer alive to defend his name. How can you honestly expect me to believe you?"

"I have proof, my lord . . . if you wish to see it?"

"Yes."

Keeping a wary eye on Lucian, the clerk struggled to his feet and went to one corner of the room. Lucian spared a glance around the spartan chamber, which held a cot, a desk, a chair and reading lamp, and a cabinet with a brazier for cooking. If Jenkins was being paid for treason, there was little luxury here to show for it.

Bypassing the desk, the clerk knelt and dug up a loose floorboard. Retrieving a leather pouch, he turned it over to Lucian. "They're all here—all the instructions Sir Giles gave me for the past year."

Lucian thumbed through the scraps of paper. "I see nothing to connect these to Sir Giles. You could have forged these just as you forged my letter."

"But I didn't, my lord, I *swear* it! I still have nearly

all the money he gave me from the first time. A hundred pounds. Once I realized . . . I couldn't spend it. I told Sir Giles I would no longer help. I *pleaded*— but he insisted. He said Caliban would kill my mother if I failed to do exactly as he asked."

His expression held such sincere misery, Lucian was inclined to believe him. Moreover, he knew very well what treachery Giles had been capable of.

"If your contact is dead, how do you communicate now?"

"My instructions are left anonymously . . . in a flowerpot outside my door. I never see who leaves them."

Lucian stared at him for a long moment, using his most intimidating scowl. The clerk visibly quailed but did not retract his story.

"Very well," Lucian said at last. "Tell me about this letter of authorization you wrote. You forged my hand?"

"Yes, my lord. I obtained some of your correspondence and practiced for weeks."

"How did you manage to get my seal?"

"I did not, exactly. I was supplied with several wax wafers with your seal already imprinted on them. It wasn't difficult to transfer one to the letter. It requires only a hot brick and a razor-thin knife."

"Someone must have acquired your seal ring," Philip observed.

He kept a seal at his offices, Lucian reflected, and another in his study at home— He felt every muscle grow rigid as his mind flashed back to a morning some weeks ago when he'd found Brynn in his study with her brother. And the following day she had returned alone, claiming to be searching for a lost earring.

God's mercy . . . Was that yet another lie? He wouldn't put it past Sir Grayson to have stolen his seal, but Brynn? Was she involved in treason?

Lucian drew a sharp breath. His first instinct was to deny the possibility; his second, a desperate desire to shield her from discovery. She was his *wife*, the woman who carried his child. The one who owned his heart. It would devastate him to have to choose between her and his duty.

Lucian clenched his jaw, knowing he no longer had any objectivity where Brynn was concerned, yet he didn't want Philip to know he suspected his wife of treason. At least not until he had proof. He would have to discover the truth from Brynn. Meanwhile her brother might very well be preparing to transport the gold to France. . . .

Shaking himself from his stupor, Lucian eyed the trembling clerk. "You understand, I trust, the seriousness of your crime against the Crown? That the best I can do for you is to see that you are imprisoned or transported rather than hanged?"

"Yes, my lord," Jenkins whispered. "I understand. I . . . I would be grateful if you would spare my life."

"Mr. Barton here will see to your arrest. I suggest you gather whatever belongings will help ease your incarceration until your trial."

"Th-thank you, my lord."

When the clerk turned away, Lucian drew Philip aside. "I have a notion who might have had access to my seal," he said in a low voice. "Sir Grayson Caldwell."

Philip stared. "But that is . . ."

"My wife's brother, I know. If Sir Grayson is the culprit, it's possible this latest shipment of gold was taken to Cornwall, to be transported to France from there. Following him may be our only hope in finding it."

"Yes, I concur," Philip said slowly.

"I want you to take a half dozen of your best men and ride to Cornwall. Observe Sir Grayson from a distance, but do nothing to alert him that he is suspect. I don't want you to show yourself at all, do I make myself clear?"

"I understand, my lord. You will be coming to Cornwall, as well?"

"Yes, I'll follow you shortly. But I have a matter to resolve first," Lucian said grimly. "One that can't be delayed."

It required all Lucian's acting skills to rein in his emotions and refrain from confronting Brynn the moment he returned home. He wanted to shake the truth out of her, to plead with her to deny her complicity. Yet given her propensity for lies, he knew he was wiser to observe her reaction, to see if she would reveal her guilt. He could only pray she would allay his dark suspicions.

When he arrived, he went straight to his rooms and began to pack, not calling his valet because he didn't want an audience.

He sensed Brynn's presence even before she spoke;

she had entered his bedchamber through their connecting door.

"Is something wrong, Lucian? You are so late, I had begun to worry."

"Yes, there is something very much wrong," he answered tersely, scarcely giving her a glance. "Another shipment of gold has been stolen."

She frowned. "Another one?"

Lucian stopped his packing and gave her a level look. "The circumstances are different from the earlier times—actually worse. My seal ring was brazenly used to forge a letter that authorized handing over the gold to the thieves."

"Your seal ring?" Her voice dropped to a mere whisper.

He forced his expression to remain impassive. "Yes, mine. It implicates me in treason."

Her hand went to her throat. "Surely not . . . No one would believe you had anything to do with stealing government gold."

"Perhaps not, but it will behoove me to catch the thieves as soon as possible."

It was a clear opening for her to confess. Lucian felt his heart contract as he waited for Brynn to speak.

She took a step toward him, her beautiful features wrought with dismay. But then she stopped and visibly collected herself.

"Are you leaving tonight?"

A sinking, hollow feeling clenched Lucian's insides. "We have no real leads. I will make for Dover tonight. That seems to be the likeliest point for the gold to be smuggled to France. It will take some time to investigate. Forgive me, but I may be gone for several days."

"I . . . understand."

"Will you be all right here alone?"

"Yes," she murmured. "There is still a great deal to do to prepare for Raven's wedding."

Closing his valise, Lucian gave Brynn a brief kiss on her forehead, not trusting himself to do more, but she seemed too distracted to notice his lack of intimacy or to return the salute.

He had stepped back and picked up his valise when she apparently recovered.

"Lucian, please . . . take care," she said, sounding sincere.

"I will," he replied. "You take care as well, love."

Then, feeling a numbing chill, he turned on his heel and quit the room.

Brynn stood where he had left her, fear and fury gripping her. Gray never had answered any of her letters questioning his dubious behavior during his visit some weeks ago, but she no longer had any doubt her brother had betrayed her. He had *lied* to her about the ring, claiming he needed the Wycliff seal to authorize transporting a load of brandy so he could elude the tax revenuers. Instead he had orchestrated an enormous theft, stealing a fortune in gold to smuggle to his country's enemies!

Even worse, his crime could implicate Lucian in treason. Dear God . . .

Her mind and heart in chaos, Brynn returned to her own bedchamber, where she began pacing the floor as she tried desperately to think what to do.

Lucian was determined to apprehend the traitors. If he couldn't find the gold in Dover, he would look elsewhere. And the trail might very well lead to Cornwall and Gray. . . .

Brynn shuddered to think what would happen when Lucian confronted her brother. He would show no mercy. His duty was almost an obsession with him. Her brother would be arrested and possibly hanged. . . . Or what if Grayson resisted Lucian as Giles had? It was an easy leap to imagine the two of them locked in mortal combat like in her dark dreams. But this time Lucian might not escape with his life. Or her brother might not.

An icy rivulet of fear ran down her spine. It terrified her to think of either one of them dying.

She didn't want Gray to be hanged, yet if he had committed such a crime, he deserved some measure of punishment. He was still her brother, though. Her flesh and blood. She had to try to save him if she could. *But how?*

She couldn't throw herself on her husband's mercy. Even if she were to plead with Lucian to save her brother, she couldn't believe he cared for her enough to sacrifice honor and duty for her sake. He had killed one of his closest friends who had committed treason, so why would he spare her brother?

And in any case, Grayson had to be stopped. She didn't want the stolen gold to fall into French hands any more than Lucian did.

Sweet heaven, why had she not tried harder to stop Grayson weeks ago? She would never be able to assuage her own guilt. She was to blame for giving him access to Lucian's private study. She should have insisted Gray return the ring at once, even if it had meant making a scene in front of her husband. At least then she could have prevented it from being used for treason.

She had to do something. If only she could persuade Gray to abandon his plan and return the gold—

Brynn stopped in her tracks. That was the only possible way. She had to try to reason with her brother, to convince him to change course.

Shaking herself into action, Brynn turned to tug the bellpull for her maid and another for the butler, intending to summon a traveling carriage. She would have to go to Cornwall at once; there was no time to lose.

She couldn't divulge her true destination, however. Lucian would be suspicious if he discovered where she had gone. She would have to make up some other story—perhaps that Theo was ill. That was it. That lie would have to serve: she was going to Theo's bedside. By the time Lucian learned of her absence, she would have confronted Gray—

Brynn felt another shiver sweep through her. She didn't want to think about how Lucian would react when he discovered what she'd done, or what would happen if she failed.

Her sense of desperation rising again, she went to the clothespress and drew out a traveling costume.

Farther along the darkened street, Lucian watched his residence from the shadows of an unmarked carriage. Stone lay where his heart belonged, yet he was driven by the sick need to learn the truth. To know whether or not Brynn would reveal herself as a traitor. With all his soul, he wanted to believe her innocent.

He hadn't long to wait before she emerged from the house and ran down the steps to the waiting Wycliff traveling coach. As it drew away from the curb, Lucian rapped on the roof of his own vehicle, ordering his driver to follow.

He held his breath as they wound their way through the dark streets of Mayfair. When Brynn's conveyance eventually turned southeast onto the London Road, Lucian had to concede she was making for Cornwall.

He gritted his teeth, his emotions twisting from savage pain to raw fury. Fury at his lovely, scheming countess. Fury at himself.

He had allowed himself to be bewitched by Brynn's exquisite beauty. By the powerful sexual attraction that burned between them. By his growing feelings of love for her.

He had wed a virginal young lady, hoping to sire a son. But Brynn wasn't what he'd thought her to be, wanted her to be.

He didn't know the beautiful deceiver at all.

Chapter Eighteen

Cornwall

Dusk was falling when Brynn arrived home. Although weary and travel-stained after the long journey from London, she immediately sought out her brother, fervently hoping to end the dread that had knotted her stomach for the past three days.

She found Grayson in his study, staring morosely into a meager hearth fire.

When she spoke his name, he gave a start of surprise. "Brynn? What the devil are you doing here?" He came up out of his chair. "Is something wrong? Theo . . . ?"

"Theo is well, to my knowledge," she replied, her tone grim. "But something is definitely wrong, Grayson."

He stared at her a long moment.

Studying him in turn, Brynn realized his face was flushed as if he'd partaken of too much wine. "As for my reason for being here," she added more quietly, "I came to stop you from committing treason."

Gray made no reply, merely raised a hand to his forehead and sat down again wearily.

Her heart contracted with pain. "You don't deny conspiring with the French against your country?" she whispered, praying she was mistaken, that her brother would refute her terrible accusation.

"No, I don't deny it," he said dully.

"Dear God, Grayson . . ." Crossing the room, Brynn sank down onto the sofa, sick with disbelief. "How *could* you?"

His mouth twisted in a sardonic smile. "To be honest, I'm not certain of that myself. God knows, I never intended to become a traitor."

"What . . . how did it happen?"

Gray gave a heavy sigh. "Do you really want to know the sordid details?"

"Tell me," she murmured hoarsely.

Before speaking, he took a long swallow of wine, as if seeking courage. "It began nearly a year ago. I was approached by a gentleman who offered me a large sum to rendezvous with another smuggling vessel and transfer a cargo. At the time I was desperate for funds. You can't have forgotten the dire state of our finances then. How crushing our debts were? How we stood to lose this house? I feared being unable to pay and being thrown in debtors' prison. And then what would happen to you and the boys?"

She hadn't forgotten those dark days when they'd faced their father's increasingly relentless creditors. "So you accepted the offer, even though you knew it to be suspect?"

"I suspected shady dealings, I suppose, but I ratio-nalized that breaking the law smuggling unknown goods was better than being incarcerated for debt and leaving you all to fend for yourselves."

"Gray, was the cargo government gold?"

"Yes . . . although I didn't realize it then. I didn't want to ask. Later . . . they used it to blackmail me. They vowed to expose me as a traitor if I didn't follow their orders."

"They?"

"An unholy alliance of spies and smugglers. I know little about them, except that some of the members are Englishmen of high social standing. The leader is supposedly a nobleman."

"A nobleman? Are you serious?"

"Deadly serious. He's referred to as Lord Caliban. My initial contact was a baronet."

"Was?"

"Yes. He has since died—due to his nefarious activities, I have little doubt." Grayson gave a short, bitter laugh. "Another man took his place. This one is a Frenchman, I'm certain of it, even though he speaks excellent English and calls himself Jack. Jack called on me shortly after you married. He ordered me to obtain your husband's seal ring and make several wax imprints of the Wycliff seal. I refused, but Jack said I had no choice if I wanted to continue living."

"And you believed him?"

"Yes, I believed him!" He eyed her sharply. "These are vicious men, Brynn. They tortured one of the fishermen who refused to aid them. Removed his skin piece by piece as an example to the rest of us. It took the poor bastard two days to die. I think I would rather face hanging than that fate."

She took a shuddering breath. "Do you realize they used Lucian's seal on a forged letter to steal another shipment of gold?"

"I feared something like that might happen." Gray's expression twisted in a grimace that was almost agony. "I wasn't told their purpose, but I can't deny I suspected sinister dealings."

"What of the gold, Gray? Do you know where it is?"

"Here, in the caves below the house. Three strongboxes were delivered last night, which I hid among some other contraband. I am supposed to turn them over to Jack tonight."

"Grayson," Brynn said hoarsely, "you can't deliver the gold into French hands. Napoleon will use it to fund his armies. Think of all the men who will die fighting when the war drags on because of that gold!"

"I have no choice, Brynn. I can't get out. I'm in too deep. Believe me, I've tried. As long as Caliban exists, I am trapped."

"But think of what you are doing! Treason . . ."

"I know." Gray took a gulp of wine. "You cannot say anything worse than I've said to myself a thousand times. I hate myself for what I've done. For what I must do. But I have to comply, or they will kill me—or worse."

"Worse?" Brynn repeated.

He gave her a long, bitter glance. "I wasn't the only one they threatened. After I gave them imprints of Wycliff's seal, I told them I was through, but Jack said they would kill my entire family if I deserted them. Theo, you, our brothers . . ."

"Theo?" Her voice held a note of alarm.

"Yes, damn it, Theo! And you. Why do you think I'm so terrified? They proved their point very clearly recently. A carriage almost ran you over in London, didn't it? Jack said it was a warning to me, Brynn."

She stared at her brother. That potentially fatal accident had been *deliberate*? She had thought Lucian's life was in danger from the curse, never that she was the target of Gray's enemies. Or that Theo was. Dear God.

"The British government may hang me for treason," Gray added, his voice almost fierce, "but at least my family will be spared. I couldn't live with myself if one of you were to die when I could have saved you."

Horrified, Brynn swallowed convulsively, still trying to digest his revelation.

"There must be something we can do," she murmured finally in desperation, searching Gray's face.

His eyes glittered darkly. "There is nothing! Don't you think I have tried?"

"But you could be hanged for treason. . . ."

With a shrug, he stared down into his wineglass. "Do you know what I dread even more than hanging? What Theo would think of me, seeing me dishonored before the world. But I would rather hang than risk him being killed."

She raised a hand to her mouth, pressing back a cry, wondering what in God's name could be done. "Perhaps . . . Is there no one we could ask for help? Lucian . . ."

Gray's mouth twisted. "I'm certain he would be delighted to aid me after my betrayal."

"You could throw yourself on his mercy."

"I would land in prison at the very least."

Brynn wanted to argue that Lucian might be persuaded to show leniency, but she had already discarded that hopeless option herself. Lucian would be the last person ever to feel sympathy for a traitor.

"Besides," Gray added grimly, "that still wouldn't prevent Caliban from carrying out his threat to kill you."

Before she could think of a response, her brother set his jaw and gave her a dark glance. "To be frank, you haven't done me any favors by coming here, Brynn. Wycliff is bound to be suspicious when he discovers you've returned home."

"Lucian doesn't know I'm here. He has gone to Dover, searching for the gold."

"Well, I sincerely hope he keeps away." Grayson took a final swallow of his wine. "If he tries to intervene, he will likely be killed."

Brynn felt her heart clench. "What do you mean?" she demanded hoarsely. "You wouldn't kill him. . . ."

"Of course I wouldn't. Not I. Jack. Caliban's followers. They consider Wycliff their chief nemesis. If he shows his face, I have no doubt what will happen."

She must have looked stricken, for Grayson gazed at her with sudden sadness.

"You love him, don't you." It wasn't a question.

Brynn sat in frozen silence, wanting desperately to refute the accusation. Yet she could no longer deny the truth. She didn't want Lucian to die, not only because he was her husband and the father of her unborn child, but because she *loved* him.

Dear heaven . . .

"Did you forget about the curse?" Gray asked quietly.

"No," Brynn whispered. "I didn't forget." She had tried desperately to isolate her heart from Lucian, had refused to acknowledge her feelings in hopes of protecting him. To no avail.

Cold fear knifed through her. Her love had the power to destroy. By admitting her feelings for Lucian, had she given him a death sentence?

Just then a maid came to the study door and bobbed a curtsy. "Milady, his lordship has arrived."

"His lordship?"

"Your husband. Lord Wycliff."

Gray rose abruptly to his feet, looking stunned, while Brynn's heart froze in her chest. Lucian was *here*? What in God's name was he doing in Cornwall when he'd set out for Dover only a few days ago? How had he known where she'd gone? How had he followed her so quickly?

For a long moment, brother and sister stared at each other in shock.

"Show him to the drawing room," Grayson finally commanded the maid. "We will join him there." When the girl was gone, his voice dropped to an urgent whisper. "Do you think he suspects me?"

"I . . . I don't know."

"Brynn, you cannot divulge a word about the gold to him. I beg you, keep silent."

"Gray—"

"You will have to find a way to keep Wycliff occupied tonight. A few hours at least—long enough for Jack to fetch the gold. They intend to wait for full darkness, but they can't delay too long or the tide will be too low for them to make a retreat."

"Grayson, I can't—"

"You *can*. You must. Unless you want your husband to die. I tell you, Jack won't hesitate to kill him, Brynn. Or me, either."

Setting down his glass, Gray turned on his heel and strode from the room.

After a long pause, Brynn followed more slowly, feeling as if she were being swept helplessly, inexorably along by a rushing current, toward a destiny of murderous peril.

Brynn paused at the door to the drawing room, drinking in the sight of her husband's beloved face. He was busy accepting her brother's greeting, but as soon as Lucian spied her, his blue gaze locked with hers across the room.

Brynn's heart suddenly began to pound as they stared at each other. Lucian's expression remained enigmatic, yet she wondered if he could see completely through her. If he could possibly know what she was contemplating.

Desperation filled her, but she forced herself to hide her dismay and trepidation and ignore her painfully thudding heartbeat. Schooling her own features to surprise, she moved forward, offering her hands and then her cheek for him to kiss. "Lucian, whatever are you doing here? I thought you intended to travel to Dover."

"I did intend to, love," he replied coolly. "But as I changed horses at a posting house, a messenger caught up with me, bearing the news that your brother was ill and that you had gone to his bedside. The timing of the emergency struck me as rather ominous. I have a number of enemies, Brynn, and I worried that they might be plotting to harm you. So I turned around immediately and made for Harrow. My suspicion rose even more when I found Theo quite well and no sign of my beautiful wife. I could only hope you had come here."

"I'm terribly sorry to have worried you unnecessarily, but"—she faltered, nearly choking on the lie—"my plans must have been misunderstood. When I said my brother was ill, I meant *Grayson*."

Lucian glanced at his brother-in-law, who, except for a wine-flushed complexion, appeared the picture of good health.

"I summoned Brynn here," Grayson interjected quickly, supporting her tale. "I feared I was on my deathbed, but it seems I was only suffering a bilious stomach. The new cook I hired after Brynn wed you served a fish that violently disagreed with me. But I am quite recovered now."

"How fortunate," Lucian replied with a brief smile.

"You must be tired and hungry after your long journey," Grayson added in a stronger voice. "Despite that one instance, Cook can be trusted to produce an excellent dinner."

"I have only just arrived myself," Brynn interjected, "and I admit I am famished, now that I'm assured Gray is well."

"We keep country hours here," her brother informed Lucian smoothly now, "usually dining at half past six. But I will have dinner pushed back so you can refresh yourselves. I'll see to it as soon as I have a servant gather your baggage and show you to your rooms."

Preferring not to share the same quarters with Lucian, however, Brynn overrode her brother's orders and claimed her childhood bedchamber for herself, while giving Lucian a guest room farther down the hall. She didn't believe she could endure such enforced intimacy, at least until she gained better command of her unstable emotions. Surprisingly Lucian didn't protest the arrangements, but merely said he would collect her for dinner in an hour.

Brynn was grateful for the chance to compose herself as she washed and changed her gown. By the time Lucian rapped on her door to escort her downstairs, she had managed to get her nerves under tenuous control.

Her composure faltered again, however, when he greeted her with cool reserve; the current strain between them reminded Brynn of the early weeks of their stormy marriage.

"I apologize again for the misunderstanding," she said as they descended the stairs, wishing she could placate him.

A muscle in Lucian's jaw tightened, but he remained silent.

"Are you angry that I came home?"

"I would have preferred to know your intentions. You might have saved me a good deal of worry. As it was, I could only hope that nothing untoward had befallen you—not to mention that I was compelled to abandon my mission."

"I am sorry, Lucian, truly."

"Are you, love?" He didn't sound convinced.

Brynn eyed him warily, but Lucian merely ushered her into the drawing room where her brother awaited them.

Dinner was more congenial than she expected, with Gray putting himself out to play the charming host. And the dishes were more tempting than Brynn had tasted at the Caldwell table since her childhood: hare soup, hot raised game pie, poached turbot in lobster sauce, boiled cauliflower, fillet of pheasant and truffles with a remove of plum pudding, and for the sweets, custard and hothouse strawberries.

She was too agitated, however, to enjoy the delicious fare. With the knots roiling in her stomach, she might as well have been dining on sawdust.

Her tension rose to a dangerous level at the conclusion of the meal. When Brynn would have repaired to the drawing room, leaving the gentlemen alone to their port, Gray spoke up.

"I fear I must leave you. I have an engagement later this evening that I cannot avoid."

Brynn gave a start, then forcibly pressed her lips together to avoid demanding what her brother was up to.

Lucian replied for her. "Don't concern yourself, Sir Grayson. I for one will be glad for the privacy with my wife. I have missed her after so long a separation. These past three days have seemed an eternity." His sapphire eyes met Brynn's, sending a jolt of shivering awareness down her spine, along with unmistakable alarm.

"Well then, if you don't mind . . ." Gray rose

from the table. "I will repair to my rooms to change. Brynn, if you can spare me a moment, I require your advice on a matter of the heart." When she gave him a puzzled frown, his skin flushed as if in embarrassment. "During your absence I have been courting Miss Uxbridge, and I expect to encounter her tonight."

Miss Uxbridge was one of the local squire's pretty daughters. Brynn suspected her brother was telling yet another lie, but she politely excused herself from Lucian and followed Gray down the hall and into the dimly lit library.

"Here," he whispered, fishing in his jacket pocket and handing her a vial of cloudy liquid. "Use this to keep Wycliff occupied tonight."

"What is it?"

"Sleeping drops. Like laudanum, only stronger. You will have to slip it into his wine."

She stared at the vial as if it were poison. "You are asking me to drug my own husband? Grayson, I couldn't possibly—"

"You must, Brynn, if you want him to live. If you want Theo to live. If you care anything at all for them . . . for me . . . you will do as I ask."

Her fingers closed reflexively around the vial. As Gray walked away, she remained frozen in place. Finally she squeezed her eyes shut.

How had she come to this? Torn between the terrible choice of protecting her brothers and betraying her husband, the man who owned her heart.

Chapter Nineteen

Lucian stared down at his wineglass as he waited for his beautiful wife to return, wondering if his worst fear would be realized. Was Brynn in league with her brother? Was she a thief and a traitor? He had little doubt she'd permitted his seal ring to be used by Sir Grayson, thus abetting Caliban and his cohorts in illicitly making off with the gold shipment. Was she also aiding her brother in smuggling the stolen gold to France?

Bleakness washed over Lucian at the likelihood of her betrayal. Bleakness and fury. He was infuriated at Brynn because of the choice she was forcing him to make. He'd always considered himself an honorable man, but honor didn't seem particularly important when weighed against the possibility of losing her to prison—or worse, to the gibbet.

He couldn't allow that to happen. He couldn't allow Brynn to be imprisoned, especially not when she was carrying his child.

Lucian clenched his teeth. It enraged him to think that she would risk their son or daughter's future by engaging in treason. It enraged him even more that

Brynn would destroy the promise of happiness they had found together.

He had wanted to cherish her, damn her. He'd wanted to love her, to build a future with her, beget a family. He had made mistakes with Brynn, he freely admitted. He'd wed her with no regard for her wishes, seeking to end the emptiness in his life, demanding that she give him a son to fill the gaping hole inside him. But he'd believed—hoped—they had moved past his mistakes.

Brynn herself had filled that dark void within him, Lucian acknowledged. For a few short weeks he had found bliss in her arms. Now, however, all he could feel was an emptiness inside him as vast as all eternity. And a rage that ate at him like poison.

Lucian raked a hand through his dark hair, fully aware of his own madness. He was a goddamned fool to have hoped for more from Brynn. He had blindly fallen for an alluring temptress, a radiant beauty with flaming tresses and an enchanting spirit. He was *obsessed* with her. She would haunt him till he drew his last breath. But he was done hoping.

Even so, he had to try to protect her. His men had Caldwell House surrounded. If her brother left for an assignation, Philip Barton had orders to follow at a distance on the possibility that Sir Grayson would lead them to the gold.

Lucian himself would take responsibility for keeping Brynn occupied. He wouldn't allow her to endanger his unborn child. Much like probing a wound, however, on some dark, desperate, gut-deep level he needed to know how far she would go.

If she was engaged in treason, he had to see the evidence with his own eyes. He intended to let Brynn take the lead tonight—to figuratively give her enough rope to hang herself.

And if she was guilty? Then he would have to deal with her and the shattering aftermath. He would have to save her, no matter what it took. Even if it meant sacrificing his honor.

Lucian squeezed his eyes shut as a savage ache clenched his chest. The gash in his heart was not a mortal wound, but near enough. He could only hope that someday the searing pain would be a little duller. But somehow he doubted it ever would be.

Since her dinner gown had no pockets, Brynn slid the vial of sleeping drops between her breasts, where it rested cold and heavy against her flesh. Then, with grave reluctance, she returned to the dining room.

Lucian was lounging at the table but looked up when she entered. It required every ounce of acting skill she possessed to force a smile and pretend she wasn't about to betray him.

When he held out his hand, she went to him and let him draw her down onto his lap to hold her loosely.

"I am sorry Grayson had to leave," she said, keeping her tone carefully neutral.

"I'm not. I am glad to have the evening to ourselves." The words were warm, and yet his expression remained emotionally cool, Brynn realized.

"Do you want to repair to the drawing room?" she asked.

"I can think of a far more pleasurable way to occupy our time."

He bent forward and pressed a light kiss on her collarbone, a suggestive act that told her very clearly what he had in mind. Brynn shut her eyes, deeply affected by even this casual contact. But then Lucian's every touch had always tormented her with desire.

When his lips moved lower, however, over the swell of her breast, she tensed. She couldn't allow him to undress her here, not when he would discover the vial on her person. Resting her palms on his shoulders, she gently pushed him away. "Not here, Lucian. The servants . . ."

"Then where?"

She would have to find a way to administer the draught, she knew. Brynn glanced at his wineglass that was nearly empty. "Will you come to my room?"

"I thought you would never ask." His hands gliding to her waist, he set her on her feet. "Go ahead, love. I will join you shortly."

Grateful that he'd accepted her invitation so easily, Brynn detoured through the kitchens to fetch more wine. Her brother's new chef was delighted to tap a new keg and supply her with a full crystal decanter and two goblets.

When she reached her bedchamber, Brynn carefully shut the door behind her and set her tray down on a side table. Then, retrieving the vial from her bosom, she hesitated a long moment, her emotions in turmoil: despair, regret, heartache, fear for Lucian, all churning inside her.

Taking a deep breath, Brynn opened the vial. She had no idea how much to use, but the dose needed to be strong enough to make Lucian sleep for at least a few hours. Murmuring an anguished prayer, she added six drops to one goblet.

It was only when she began to undress that she realized she hadn't packed a wrapper. Feeling chilled, Brynn donned her gown again, shivering as the silk pressed coolly against her nude body.

Then she sat waiting. She wished Lucian would come, for anxiety and uncertainty were slowly shredding her nerves. She could hear the faint crackle of the dying fire, along with the painful pounding of her heart.

It was utterly wrong to betray Lucian this way, Brynn knew, and yet she had no choice. She harbored a terrible dread about tonight. His life was in danger, she felt it in every bone in her body. If he tried to apprehend the traitors, he would be killed, it was as simple and precarious as that.

She was desperate to save Lucian, even if it meant seducing him and drugging his wine to prevent him from carrying out his duty. Once he was safely asleep, she would somehow have to try to stop Gray herself, though how she would manage that feat she had no idea. She sat wracking her brain for the next several moments, a suffocating tightness in her chest, feeling trapped between the ties of blood and the ties of love.

When the door finally opened, Brynn gave a start and rose to her feet. Lucian was still dressed for evening, she realized as he entered, although he had removed his jacket and cravat. His shirt hung open, exposing a smooth expanse of chest.

Her breath caught in her throat at the picture he made. He was still one of the most sinfully beautiful men she had ever met, with his lean elegance and muscular grace. When the door shut, he leaned indolently against it, his expression enigmatic as he met her gaze.

Brynn swallowed hard, trying to summon the courage for her performance. Slipping the bodice off her shoulders then, she let her gown fall to the floor in a whisper of silk, leaving her completely nude to his view.

She heard Lucian draw a sharp breath, yet his smile seemed forced as his bold gaze roamed over her. "Is this a seduction, my love?"

She tried to make her own smile provocative. "Merely a welcome. I am glad you have come."

For a long moment she met his sapphire eyes, but he made no move to join her. Time stretched between them like a taut wire. At length, however, the soft snap of the fire in the hearth broke the spell.

Determined to appear nonchalant, Brynn shrugged her shoulders and went to the mahogany side table, where the tray bearing the crystal wine decanter and goblets rested. When she had poured two glasses, she crossed the bedchamber to Lucian and offered him the drugged one.

For another endless moment, he stared at the bloodred wine. She could feel her heart pounding as she waited for him to drink. Why did he hesitate?

Relief flooded her when he took a sip, and Brynn

silently cursed herself. She had to strive for composure or her agitation would give her away. Unlike
Lucian, she was an amateur at intrigue. He had
matched wits against countless traitors and would
certainly grow suspicious if she couldn't behave
naturally, as if she wanted to make love to him.

As it was, he regarded her with evident gravity,
and there was a fine tension in his lean, muscled
body—or was the tension merely in her because of
what she was about to do?

When Lucian continued to watch her, Brynn
averted her gaze, unable to meet his eyes any longer.
She loathed herself for her betrayal.

"Is the wine to your taste?" Brynn made herself
say, forcing herself to sip from her own glass.

"Yes. But then the French do make the finest
wines."

She glanced up sharply, not knowing why he had
mentioned the French. Did he suspect her perfidy?
Brynn wondered. Or was he referring to her brother's
smuggling? Lucian's eyes glittered with sexual interest yet hid every other emotion brilliantly.

She shivered.

"Are you cold?" he queried.

"I hoped you would warm me."

She saw his gaze darken responsively at her provocative reply, and for the first time in her life Brynn
was glad for the curse that made her irresistible to
men. She would need every advantage she possessed
if she intended to use Lucian's lust for her own purposes, for despite his obvious sexual attraction for
her, he didn't seem in an amorous mood.

"Why don't you stir the fire," he said, "while I close the draperies?"

Nodding, Brynn crossed to the hearth while Lucian turned and went to one of the windows. She knelt there, feeling the heat from the glowing flames on her bare skin, wishing it could warm the frigid ache in her heart as well.

Glancing over her shoulder, she watched from across the room as Lucian closed the drapery and moved to the final window, where he stood looking out and drinking from his glass. Brynn hesitated, wondering exactly how she should distract him until he succumbed to the drug.

Steeling herself, she rose and went to join Lucian, coming up behind him. Outside the window, a chill sliver of moon hung low on the black horizon, partly obscured by ghostly, scudding clouds. A blustery wind blew off the sea; she could hear waves beating against the rocky shore below.

A good night for treason.

Inside, however, the bedchamber was warm and hushed.

"Are you still angry with me?" she murmured in an effort to capture Lucian's attention.

He snapped the drapes shut and turned to face her. Involuntarily her gaze went to his glass that was now only one-third full. Her relief was profound, yet she still had a role to play; she couldn't stop until Lucian was sleeping soundly.

She pasted an enticing smile on her face. Her finger dipped into his wine, then rose to glide along his lower lip. "How can I assuage your anger, Lucian?"

"I think you know, love."

Her focus dropped below his waist. The stockinet fabric of his evening breeches clung to his powerful thighs, stretched taut over his erection. An immediate, quivering response rippled through Brynn, along with a momentary spark of elation. He might still be angry with her, but he wanted her.

Determined to arouse him further, she slowly, provocatively slid her fingers into the waistband of his breeches. When he gave no response, Brynn relieved him of his wineglass and set it down along with her own. Then she began to undo the buttons of the front placket.

Her heart was thudding in her chest when she opened his drawers to expose the stiff erection that stirred so eagerly between his thighs. With a tempting smile, she closed her caressing fingers around the base of his pulsing arousal and sank down to kneel at his feet.

His jaw was set rigidly, Brynn saw when she glanced up at Lucian. He was still fighting her, and yet he was blatantly aroused, the rigid rod thrusting high, the rampant head gleaming in the lamplight.

Wanton heat coiled through her body to throb inside her, contrasting strangely with the ache in her heart.

Letting her fingers stroke him, Brynn leaned closer to press her lips along his shaft, tasting the marble-smooth skin. Lucian jerked when she kissed him there, and a flaring excitement ignited inside her at the familiar, erotic feel of him.

She attended him lingeringly. His skin felt hot, searing, as she softly ran her tongue around the swollen head . . . the sensitive ridge below. . . . Then her lips closed around his shaft to take him more fully in her mouth.

She felt Lucian tense with pleasure as she suckled him. He was obviously fighting for control now.

His now-rigid erection thickened still more as she explored him further with her mouth and tongue, tasting the slick, velvet contours, making love to the most intimate part of him. Lucian had been the one to teach her this—how to use her carnal skills to such devastating effect. He had shown her pleasures of the flesh, led her to embrace her woman's passion. . . .

She felt him shudder, but she continued deliberately to arouse him, her teeth softly raking. She knew a moment of triumph when he groaned at her ministrations.

"Am I paining you?" she murmured tauntingly against his flesh.

"Yes," he said, his own voice hoarse. "Dire pain."

"Should I stop?"

"*No*, siren . . ."

When her lips slid down his shaft again, his hands curled in her hair and he strained against her mouth, his breathing harsh and ragged. His desire for her had always been fierce, and she used it mercilessly against him now.

She heard her name hoarsely whispered, felt him shaking. When he clutched at her shoulders, Brynn shuddered with pleasure herself. She was nearly as aroused as Lucian, her body pulsing, her feminine hollows wet with desire, yearning to merge with his hard male flesh. She had intended to seduce him, but she was caught up in her own game. When she glanced up at him, she knew his passion-hazed eyes mirrored her own.

"Lucian," she breathed, shredding the last of his control.

Urgently he drew her to her feet and lifted her up. His lips came down upon hers with hot, wet heat, his mouth feverishly capturing hers as she wrapped her legs around his hips.

Carrying her to the bed, he lowered her to the silk sheets and followed her down, pressing himself between her welcoming thighs. For a space of several heartbeats, then, he hesitated, holding Brynn's rapt gaze.

His face was so incredibly beautiful in the flickering candlelight, his features taut with desire and what strangely looked like pain. When he curved his hand to her throat, Brynn stirred restlessly beneath him, wondering why he delayed.

"Please . . . I want you, Lucian," she whispered hoarsely.

He obliged her, sliding the engorged crest of his erection into her pulsing cleft slick with the liquid evidence of her own need.

She was wet and eager for him. Hungrily she wrapped her legs around his, clutching him to her as he thrust into her, driving his powerful member deep within her hot, throbbing flesh. Her arms tightened around him, and she opened to him fully, desperate to take him deep, to fill herself with his essence, even as she battled her heart.

The blaze between them erupted into a firestorm, violent, fierce, raging. Lucian shuddered again and groaned, his body contracting savagely as he spilled his seed deep within her body. His explosion shattered Brynn. She arched helplessly beneath him, convulsing wildly as wave after wave of ecstasy hit her, cries of bliss tearing from her throat, tears of anguish dredged from her eyes.

She was weeping, Brynn realized when her brutal climax at last subsided. Shaking with love and pain that mingled into a tangled, razor-edged knot inside her.

In the turbulent aftermath, they lay together, gasping for breath. Their lovemaking had never been so potent, so powerful . . . so agonized.

His lips pressed against her hair then, and Brynn felt her heart break. When Lucian eased his weight to one side, her arms tightened around him almost desperately while she buried her face against his shoulder, trying to stifle her tears. Dear God, how she loved him. It was a torment, knowing her love might lead to his death.

She lay there a long while, struggling with remorse, with regrets. If only she didn't have to betray him. If she could have kept her heart detached. If she had never wed him in the first place . . .

When eventually Lucian's breathing grew even, Brynn drew back so that she could see his face. His eyes were closed, as if he were in a drugged stupor.

"Lucian?" she whispered.

She waited several more long moments before finally untangling her limbs from his and easing away. Lucian lay there, unmoving, as if dead to the world. But at least he wasn't *dead*. She couldn't bear to lose him to death.

Wiping the tears from her face, Brynn dragged in a deep, steadying breath and forced herself to leave the bed. She couldn't think about Lucian any further now. Nor did she dare tarry. She had to try to stop her brother from committing treason, to try to foil the real traitors.

Her plan was desperate, but it might just work. Grayson had told her the gold was hidden in the caves below the house, that the smugglers planned to retrieve their contraband tonight. She doubted they could act without Grayson's presence, though, or even be able to find the strongboxes without his direction, for surely he would have concealed them well.

If she could just keep Gray away until after high tide, then the gold would be safe tonight. She could reveal its location to the local authorities on the morrow, without implicating her brother. Then Lucian could recover the strongboxes without risking his life, and Gray could escape his vicious blackmailers—

He and Theo would have to go into hiding, of course, and she would go with them. She and Gray could leave tonight. They would collect Theo from school and flee somewhere safe. . . .

Please, please, merciful God, let her plan work. And help her make Gray see reason. She would have to use dire means to convince him, she had little doubt.

She dressed quickly in her usual smuggler's attire— an old pair of breeches and boots and a warm woolen jacket. Then she caught up her vivid hair and stuffed it under a seaman's cap. Finally, with one last, lingering look at her slumbering husband, Brynn put out all the lamps but one. Carrying it with her to light her way, she slipped from the room.

She went directly downstairs to her brother's study and the cabinet where Gray kept his finer weapons. Setting down her lamp, she withdrew a small wooden case from the cabinet and opened it, expecting to find a matched pair of double-shot pistols.

The case was empty, Brynn saw with alarm, realizing Gray must have taken the weapons. But there was an older pistol toward the rear of the cabinet. With shaking hands, she spent a few precious minutes priming and loading the gun; Grayson himself had taught her how so that she might defend herself against her overamorous suitors if need be.

She had just stuffed the pistol in her belt and shut the cabinet when a beloved voice spoke behind her, freezing the blood in her veins.

"Would you care to explain why you left our warm bed and dressed yourself up as a Free Trader, love?"

Chapter Twenty

Her startled gasp loud in the silence, Brynn whirled to find her husband standing in the doorway.

"Lucian," she rasped.

"You didn't answer my question, love." He stood waiting, his features as cold and hard as she had ever seen them.

Brynn stared at Lucian in horror, unable to speak.

When she remained mute, he crossed the room toward her. "Was it poison or something else, Brynn?" His tone was deadly calm.

"W-what do you mean?"

"Don't dare lie to me." His voice held a savage edge. "I've had enough of your lies. What did you put in my wine?"

She swallowed hard. "It wasn't poison."

"What then?"

"Only a sleeping draught."

"*Only* a draught? You attempted to drug me."

"Y-yes." Yet Lucian obviously had only pretended to drink, Brynn realized.

A muscle in his jaw clenched. "I had hoped I was wrong." He stopped before her, his face so dark with anger that she took a step back. "Fool that I am, I prayed you weren't guilty of treason."

He moved toward her, his shadow slipping over her as he grasped her arm in a painful grip. Reaching down, Lucian took the pistol from her belt. "Forgive me if I don't trust you with a weapon."

Numbly she shook her head, trying to recruit her wits. "Lucian, it isn't what you think—"

"No?" He gave a sharp laugh. "Then tell me."

Pulling her arm free, Brynn moved over to a chair and sank down heavily. "I drugged you to keep you safe. I was trying to save your life."

"Indeed?" His features were set like granite. "You'll understand if I don't believe you. You were aiding your brother in treason—keeping me out of the way so he could dispose of the gold."

"No. I don't deny I wanted you out of the way, but it was solely to save your life. Grayson said those men . . . they would kill you if you interfered tonight. I didn't want you to die. I . . . I love you, Lucian."

His very stillness sent a shiver through her. "I told you not to lie, Brynn."

"I am not lying. I swear it. I fell in love with you, even though I tried desperately not to."

"How convenient that you just now realize your feelings when you're seeking to mollify me."

She closed her eyes wearily. "I didn't just realize my feelings. The change has been coming over me for weeks. You must believe me, Lucian."

"Must I? You won't convince me, Brynn. You've lied once too often."

She shook her head. "If I lied, it was because I had no choice."

"You had no choice." The comment held contempt.

"Won't you even listen to my reasons?"

"Very well. Try to explain your lies. Tell me about my seal ring. You gave it to your brother so he could arrange to steal the gold shipment."

"That isn't true! Gray took the ring from your study, yes, but they threatened to kill him if he didn't comply with their demands."

"They?"

"A smuggling ring. Gray says they're vicious. He became involved unwittingly at first, because he needed money to repay our father's enormous debts and to stave off our creditors. My brother isn't evil. He just desperately wanted to save our family from penury or worse. He agreed to smuggle a cargo for them, not knowing it was gold. And then they began blackmailing him. He had to give them your seal or they would kill him."

"Why didn't you simply tell me?"

"I couldn't take the risk that you would arrest him. Or that one of you might be hurt if you tried. After what happened between you and Giles . . ." She saw Lucian wince and continued more quietly. "I admit I wanted to protect my brother, but surely you can understand my feelings. You felt the same way about your friend Giles, you told me so. You grieved for his death. Well, I didn't want Gray to die, any more than I wanted you to. Or Theo. They have threatened his life as well. And mine, for that matter."

From the rigidity of Lucian's jaw, she could tell

he had no intention of trying to understand her dilemma.

Her voice dropped to an anguished murmur. "I didn't know what else to do, Lucian. It has been terrible, feeling torn between people I love."

He didn't respond at all to her assertion. "That wasn't your only lie. A few weeks ago you disappeared, but you weren't with Raven or Meredith as you claimed. How do you explain that?"

"I visited a Gypsy fortune-teller at a fair. I hoped to discover if there was a way to break the curse. I couldn't divulge my purpose to you, Lucian, don't you see? I couldn't admit loving you, even to myself." Her voice caught on a sob. "I was too afraid I would cause your death."

"But you're not afraid now?"

"Yes, I'm afraid! But it's too late. I can't help my feelings for you."

He remained silent, his eyes dark and distrustful. "And did your Gypsy know of a remedy?" he asked finally.

"She said . . . I would have to be willing to give my life for you."

His mouth curled. "I can't imagine that happening."

Brynn looked away, misery choking her. Lucian didn't believe her, didn't trust a word she said. Nor could she blame him. She had never done anything to deserve his trust. She had only fought with him and lied to him and tried to drug him. . . .

Bleak despair washed over her. She felt tears streaming down her face, tears that Lucian evidently noticed.

"Weeping won't sway me, Brynn."

"I know," she whispered, fiercely wiping them away.

He hesitated a moment before saying in a deadened voice, "What of the babe? Why did you lie about that?"

Her gaze flew to his.

"You didn't think I would find out, did you?" Lucian's eyes were icy and lethal. "Why would you conceal such a revelation from me, Brynn? Because you intended to leave me? You meant to deprive me of my child without even letting me know of his existence?"

She remained mute, unable to refute his accusation.

He ground his teeth, as if striving for control, but for an instant she saw the despair in his blazing, searching eyes. "I waited for you to tell me, Brynn. I hoped . . . You know how much I wanted a son." There was a rawness in the quiet words that tore at her heart.

Brynn hung her head. Perhaps she had been wrong to withhold the news of her pregnancy from Lucian; she had robbed him of the joy of finding out from her, of sharing in her great discovery. And yet . . . "I didn't dare tell you."

"Why not, damn you?"

She lifted a pleading gaze to him. "Because I was afraid for your *life*! Once you discovered that I'd conceived, I knew you would never let me go. But I couldn't stay with you any longer without falling in love with you. Without bringing the curse down on your head."

Lucian stared at his beautiful wife, trying to read the truth in her emerald eyes. Had she really wanted to protect him from that damned curse, or was she merely trying to save her own skin?

His mouth twisted sardonically. "Well, I doubt you would have kept the secret much longer now that your complicity has been revealed."

She bit her quivering lip. "What do you mean?"

"Surely you're aware of the advantage in divulging your condition? Breeding is the rare circumstance that can keep a female traitor from the hangman's noose. Indeed, perhaps that's why you seemed eager to conceive my child—as surety against having to pay so severely for your crime."

Her chin came up, while her eyes flashed. "That is a despicable insinuation. I wouldn't want to conceive a child just to escape punishment, even if I were guilty. I am *not* a traitor, Lucian, whether you believe me or not. And I *don't* want you to die. Even if I didn't love you, I would still want you safe. That's all I've ever wanted. To keep you safe."

Lucian remained grimly silent. He desperately wanted to believe her profession of love, but he couldn't allow himself. He had played the fool with Brynn once too often.

As if understanding his struggle, she rose and went to him, stopping a mere foot away. He could feel her warmth, her devastating allure, even dressed as she was in male clothing.

Determinedly Lucian clenched his hands at his sides as he fought for control. He wanted to shake Brynn, to dredge the truth from her. He wanted to strip away the deception between them, the dark secrets, the lies. He wanted to pull her into his arms. . . .

Damn her to hell. She stood looking up at him in the dim lamplight, her eyes shimmering pools of green. She seemed utterly sincere. Was she guilty of treason, or was she only trying to protect her brother?

"I cannot prove my innocence, Lucian," she said softly. "But I swear on our child's life, I am telling you the truth."

A surge of anger shot through him at her callous oath. Brynn was manipulating his sympathies, using his greatest vulnerability against him. It would serve her right if he arrested her and turned her over to the British government—

Silently Lucian cursed himself. He couldn't send Brynn to prison, even if she was a traitor. God knew, he didn't want anything or anyone to hurt her. She was his wife. The woman he loved. Even now his desire for her burned hotter than ever. It was a hungering ache that never left him.

Guilty or not, he couldn't act against her. Even if it meant having to sacrifice his own honor, he couldn't allow her to suffer the punishment for treason.

Lucian squeezed his eyes shut, blocking out the sight of her exquisite face. He would risk anything to protect the beautiful deceiver who owned his heart.

Still . . . he had to consider his duty. He had to prevent her further betrayal. And he had to keep her safe. He could think of one possible way. . . .

Hardening his heart, Lucian made himself meet her gaze. "You've caused enough damage, Brynn, but I don't mean to give you any further opportunity. As soon as I deal with your brother, I plan to take you to Wales."

"Wales?"

"To the Wycliff castle there, where you'll remain until my child is born. It will serve to separate you from your brother. Meanwhile, you may consider yourself under house arrest."

"Arrest?" Her eyes widened with alarm.

"Yes. This house is surrounded, Brynn. If you attempt to leave, you'll be arrested. Your brother, as well. You won't succeed in your conspiracy."

"Lucian, please—"

"I've heard enough."

He started to turn away, but Brynn grasped his arm, detaining him. "What do you intend to do?"

"Prevent your brother from delivering the gold to our country's enemies."

A look of fear crossed her face. "You can't involve yourself, Lucian."

"Can't I?"

"You'll be killed. Please, I beg you. . . ."

Lucian gritted his teeth. She wasn't as concerned for his life as for her brother's, he well knew. He could understand why Brynn wanted to protect Sir Grayson—because she was fiercely loyal to her family—but it galled him just the same that she would choose a traitor over him. But no amount of pleading would keep him from apprehending her brother.

Brynn evidently sensed his determination, for she took a deep, shaky breath. "Very well, then. I will take you to Grayson."

Lucian gave her a sharp glance. Her tears were under control now, and her expression was emotionless, without a show of any feeling whatsoever. "What are you saying?"

"You don't know where to look for him. I can show you."

"I don't need your help. I told you, if he attempts to leave, he'll be arrested. He won't get far."

"He won't be seen leaving the house, Lucian. You may search all you want, but you won't find him."

Lucian hesitated, wondering if this was yet another of Brynn's silken lies.

"I will lead you to him. And the gold. I believe I know where he's hidden it."

His eyes narrowed. "Tell me."

"No." Brynn shook her head. "I won't let you go alone, Lucian."

He took a menacing step toward her, but she held her ground. "I am going with you."

"Do you think me a complete gull? You expect me to follow you blindly into a trap you've plotted with your brother?"

A look of pain crossed her face. "I haven't plotted any trap."

"You aren't going anywhere, Brynn. You are still my wife, and carrying my child. Traitor or not, I don't want you endangered."

"I don't want you endangered, either. In any case, my brother would never harm me."

"But his cohorts would. He's right about the smuggling ring being vicious. They won't think twice about wrapping that fiery hair of yours around your throat and strangling you with it."

"I know. Why do you think I wanted a pistol?"

When that gave him pause, she pressed her argument. "What do you think I was planning, Lucian? I intended to stop Grayson myself, so you wouldn't have to. I know you don't believe me, but it's true."

Irate that she would continue her brash falsehoods, Lucian raised both hands to cup them around her throat in a velvet grip.

She gazed back at him mutely, anguish in her eyes.

With another savage oath, Lucian let his hands fall away. "Wait here," he demanded.

"Lucian . . ."

Rejecting her plea out of hand, he left Brynn in the study, shutting and locking the door behind him. Striding swiftly along the corridor to the front entrance, he let himself out and descended into the darkness.

Philip Barton appeared out of the night. "My lord?"

"What have you seen of Sir Grayson? Has he made an appearance this evening?"

"No, he hasn't left the house."

At least not by any of the conventional portals, Lucian concluded. He could order the house searched, but he suspected Brynn was being truthful for once; Sir Grayson wouldn't be found. There had to be a hidden passage within the house, Lucian realized. He might find it eventually, but his efforts could prove too late.

Philip seemed able to read his mind. "I have men patrolling the beach, as you ordered."

"They still could slip past with the gold," Lucian said grimly.

"What do you wish me to do?"

What indeed? Lucian wondered. If Brynn was telling the truth, she could lead him to her brother and the gold.

And what then? Would she then spring her trap?

Did he really have a choice, though? He couldn't risk letting the gold fall into French hands. He would have to accept Brynn's terms, despite the danger.

"Have your men maintain their posts," Lucian said, turning on his heel. The price of trusting his wife might be his own life, but he had no better option.

Chapter Twenty-one

Lucian allowed Brynn to go first with the lamp while he carried his own pistol at the ready. He wasn't surprised when she led him through the now-dark kitchens to the wine cellars below, nor when she slipped behind a wall of casks and bent low to open a short oaken door.

"This leads to the coast?" he asked.

"Yes. There are several caves beneath the house, connected by tunnels. The entrance from the shore is hidden in a crevice in the cliff wall."

"Convenient for your family," Lucian remarked sardonically.

Brynn shot him a glance but didn't respond.

When she disappeared through the opening, Lucian followed. A narrow flight of steps hewn into the rock descended into the darkness.

Neither of them spoke as they moved downward. Brynn's lamp cast flickering shadows over the rock, which was streaked with red and green and purple. When they reached the bottom step, the underground passage flattened out, but Lucian had to stoop to keep from striking his head.

Eventually the tunnel opened into a small cavern

where he could stand up straight. This natural hideaway would be ideal for storing a cache of contraband, he knew. The Cornish coast was honeycombed with coves and ravines where a smuggler's ketch could slip in undetected, but getting the trafficked goods to and from the beach presented a greater challenge. The usual goods would be bulky— bolts of silk, velvet, and lace, casks of wine, kegs of brandy, perhaps tea, all smuggled into the country to avoid the high taxes imposed by the British government because of the interminable war.

The floor of the cavern was wet and treacherously slick, Lucian saw, the rock worn smooth over the centuries by a trickling stream coming from deep underground. When Brynn slipped once, he reached out instinctively to steady her. She flinched at that casual contact, and Lucian drew his hand back abruptly, feeling burned himself.

She moved on through the cave into another man-made passageway cut through the rock. He glanced around carefully, marking his way, before following her. Soon he could hear the distant sound of the sea as it surged against the base of the cliffs.

Shortly the tunnel spilled into another cavern, this one already dimly illuminated by a lantern. Urgently Lucian put a hand on Brynn's shoulder, silently detaining her. Some fifteen feet away, her brother Grayson was pacing the floor—rather nervously, Lucian saw.

Stepping past Brynn into the cavern, Lucian called out Sir Grayson's name. The man spun around, reaching for the pistol in his belt. He froze when he saw the weapon aimed at his heart.

Lucian gestured with the barrel of his gun. "I suggest you put it down . . . slowly."

For a moment Grayson's hand clenched around the grip, but then he did as he was bid, carefully withdrawing his pistol and setting it on the rocky ground.

Then he flung his sister a despairing look. "You led him here, didn't you? Are you pleased with yourself, Brynn, betraying your own flesh and blood?"

The pain on her face was visible, Lucian saw with a glance over his shoulder.

"I didn't betray you," she said hoarsely. "Lucian found us out somehow. But I was coming to find you, in any case. There may be another way out, Gray. One that doesn't involve committing treason."

Grayson clenched his fists, his fury evident. "Damn you, I told you, there is no other way."

"What's this?" Lucian interjected sardonically. "Dissension among thieves? I should think, Sir Grayson, you would show your sister more gratitude. You could never have stolen my seal ring without her help."

Grayson's wrathful focus shifted, and he glared at Lucian. "Brynn had nothing whatever to do with my appropriating your ring. I took it from your study over her adamant objections, and then tricked her into keeping silent."

"Then used it to help our country's enemies steal a scheduled shipment of gold."

His gaze lowered. "Apparently so. I'm not proud of that. But you cannot blame Brynn. She played no part in it."

Lucian raised a skeptical eyebrow, unsurprised that Grayson had come so readily to her defense. "You expect me to believe you? A traitor?"

"Believe what you choose, my lord. But I am solely responsible. Brynn hasn't been involved until tonight when I demanded that she drug you."

Lucian's mouth curled. "And drugging me is supposed to absolve her?"

"She did it to save your hide, to keep you safe from Caliban's men. You're the one who should be grateful, Wycliff."

A strange sense of relief filled Lucian to hear Brynn's claim repeated. Perhaps, just possibly, she wasn't guilty of treason after all.

"I intend to deal with my wife later," Lucian replied. "For now, you're my chief concern. I'll thank you to return to the house with me."

Grayson's shoulders slumped. "No," he said quietly.

"It will only go harder for you if you resist."

He offered a bitter smile. "How can anything go harder than hanging? No, I'm afraid you will have to kill me, my lord. I would sooner die from a bullet than be executed for treason."

Brynn gasped, but her brother nodded toward Lucian's weapon. "Go ahead and fire. I don't intend to let you arrest me."

She stepped forward, the lamp she carried sending shadows jumping around the cavern. "No, Lucian, you *can't*. I tell you, Grayson didn't mean to commit treason. He didn't know what he was doing. He was only trying to pay his debts, to protect his family. Please . . . Gray, *tell* him. . . ."

"Brynn, I want you to leave," Lucian ordered.

"No, I can't let you shoot him—"

"Brynn," Grayson said gently, "being shot is a far better way to die. It would spare you the shame of my hanging, as well as keep you safe. If I'm dead, Caliban and his ilk will no longer be a threat to you and Theo."

Lucian hesitated, feeling a grudging respect for the man he should hold only in contempt. Grayson was prepared to die, that was certain. The shame in his eyes, the misery, the quiet resignation all shouted his resolve.

That hopeless look was all too familiar, Lucian reflected with a grimace. He'd seen that same despair on the face of his friend Giles. The friend he had *killed*.

Flinching, Lucian steeled himself against the anguishing memory, yet for an instant he was in another time—confronting Giles for his treason, being forced to end his life. For months afterward, Lucian remembered, he'd cursed the unfairness of it. Caliban was to blame for ruining countless men, men who were basically good and honorable. The bastard had ruined Sir Grayson the same way—with threats and extortion—Lucian had no doubt.

His gaze fell to the pistol in his hand. Could he repeat the past? Could he instigate Sir Grayson's death? It would be tantamount to murder to try to apprehend the man just now, for like Giles, Grayson wouldn't allow himself to be taken alive.

Brynn must have had the same thought, for she moved between them, tears sparkling in her eyes.

"You can't kill him, Lucian. Please . . . please, I beg you. . . ."

"Brynn, stay out of this," her brother commanded.

She bit back a sob, a despairing sound that tore at Lucian's heart. Hardening his resolve, he returned his gaze to Grayson. "Where do you have the gold secreted?"

Grayson nodded toward the back of the cave. "Beneath a shallow pool of water. You should take it. There's no longer any point in my trying to keep possession of it."

"I presume you're waiting for your French contact to arrive?"

"Yes. A man named Jack. He was to meet me before the tide fell too low. He should have been here by now."

"Perhaps he's having difficulty eluding my patrols," Lucian remarked. "I have men posted at various intervals along the coast."

"I suspect he would have seen your patrols, but Jack is quite resourceful. He would have contrived a diversion so he could slip in to fetch the gold." Grayson looked pointedly at the pistol. "You had best get on with it, so you can take Brynn away from here. Jack has threatened more than once to kill her. Every moment you delay only endangers her."

Lucian felt a muscle flex in his jaw. "You're suggesting I shoot you in cold blood?"

"If you would rather not, I can perform the task myself—that is, if you would trust me with a weapon. I give you my word of honor I will see to it." His mouth twisted in a bitter smile. "My word

once meant something. Before this, I was an honorable man."

Grayson was deadly serious, Lucian knew; he
meant to take his own life.

"Or perhaps," Grayson added, "all you need do
is wait. Jack will be more than eager to put a period
to my existence when I can't deliver the gold. You
could leave me a weapon. I promise you I would attempt to take him with me."

"You would be willing to turn on your cohort?"

"More than willing. Jack isn't my cohort. He's
the bastard who threatened to kill my family. . . ."
Grayson's features contorted in a grimace. "Why
do you think I gave in to their demands? Nothing
else could have induced me to commit treason. But I
doubt you could understand such weakness, Wycliff. You have never cared for anyone as much as
your honor. You would have been stronger, had you
found yourself in my place."

Would I have been stronger? Lucian wondered to
himself. *I would have fought back, certainly. I
would have mobilized all the private resources at
my disposal, all the government forces at my command.* But Grayson had few resources and fewer
government contacts. And still there would have
been a risk to Brynn. . . .

Lucian shook his head, knowing he was lying
to himself. He would have sacrificed his honor
for Brynn's sake. He would have done anything to
save her.

Was he really so much better than her brother?

Just then Brynn took another step toward Lucian. She didn't utter a sound, but the plea in her

green eyes was wrenchingly eloquent. She might hate him if he killed her brother.

"Your sister is right," Lucian said slowly, thinking hard. "There may be another way. For her sake, I might consider making you an offer."

"An offer?"

Lucian glanced at Brynn. She had pressed a hand to her mouth, as if not daring to hope. "I want Caliban, Sir Grayson. But I would need your help in exposing him."

The hope that had flared in Grayson's eyes was quickly extinguished. "I would be more than happy to help, but I'm afraid I would be of no use to you. I've never seen Caliban."

"But you've seen his confederates. You know his methods."

"That won't solve my dilemma—the threat to my family. I would rather die than see my sister or my brothers harmed. You can't protect them from Caliban, my lord. At least if I'm dead, my family will be safe."

"Your death could be arranged. . . ." Lucian replied, his mind working furiously.

"*No!*" Brynn exclaimed in horror.

Lucian turned his attention to her, prepared to offer an explanation, but he caught the faint scrape of boot soles on rock. His glance flew at once to the far end of the cavern.

A figure moved out of the shadows into the open—a man dressed in black, holding two pistols cocked and aimed. One was directed at Grayson, the other at Brynn.

"You severely disappoint me, Sir Grayson," the

newcomer declared with the barest trace of a French accent. "I thought we had a bargain."

Grayson's features took on a sneer. "Jack. I have no compunction about reneging on a bargain with the likes of you."

"Jacques, please. Jack is so . . . English." The Frenchman turned to Lucian. "Lord Wycliff." The softly spoken name held a wealth of satisfaction.

"Do I know you?" Lucian remarked, cursing himself for his inexcusable negligence in allowing the Frenchman to slip in undetected.

"No, but I know you." The cold, black eyes moved over him. "Lord Caliban has recently put a large price on your head. You have proved to be too painful a thorn in his side."

"Obviously not painful enough." Lucian flashed a cynical smile. "So your spineless employer is in the business of assassination as well as treason?"

"Lord Caliban is hardly spineless."

"Yet he sends his lackeys to do his vile work."

"I intend to kill you and collect the reward, if that is what you mean. And claim the gold as well." Jack waved one of his pistols at Brynn. "Is this your lovely lady?"

Mentally Lucian voiced a violent oath, his mind searching frantically as he tried to conceal his desperation. He wouldn't survive this encounter, he suspected, but he could perhaps bargain for Brynn's safety.

He was clearly at a disadvantage, though. He and Jack had their pistols trained on each other, but Brynn stood closer to the Frenchman, partially in the way. If he moved too quickly, Lucian knew, he risked her being shot. And Jack was growing impatient.

"You will oblige me by putting down your weapon," the Frenchman ordered.

Keeping his features a cool mask, Lucian shook his head. "And relinquish my only asset? No, *monsieur,* I prefer the current odds. With your two pistols to my one, you cannot hit all three of us."

"But I can certainly shoot Lady Wycliff. She will be the first, and then I will take great pleasure in dispatching you."

"Let her go, and I will consider disarming."

Lucian stepped forward slowly, making himself a bigger target, but the Frenchman barked out a sharp command. "That is far enough!"

Halting, Lucian balanced on the balls of his feet, preparing to spring and pull Brynn behind him.

"I told you to put down your pistol," Jack repeated.

"Let my wife go free, and I will."

Jack's mouth curled in a sneer. "Do you think me a fool?"

Lucian started to reply when, from the corner of his eye, he saw Grayson stooping, evidently intent on picking up his discarded weapon.

Smoothly, with scarcely a blink, Jack shifted his focus and fired one pistol directly at Grayson, who abruptly clutched his side in pain. The explosion reverberated with a hollow ring all around the cave, mingling with Brynn's scream of horror as Grayson crumpled to the ground. Lucian's heart jolted in his chest.

Everything afterward seemed to move with infinite slowness. . . . The Frenchman swerved his aim back to Lucian and got off a second shot just as Brynn lunged at the traitor.

Lucian's heart ceased beating entirely as she leapt into the path of the bullet, shielding him with her own body while throwing her lamp at the Frenchman with all her might. The lamp shattered in midair a scarce instant before she pitched face-forward on the ground, whether from tripping or being shot, Lucian couldn't tell.

Terror exploded inside him, along with a blinding rage. Rashly he raised his pistol and fired, but the Frenchman dodged and the shot went wide, careening off the rock wall, splintering and sending dusty fragments flying.

In motion before the blast's echo had faded, Lucian gave a roar of pure animal fury and dove across the cave. He hurled himself at the Frenchman, aiming for the thighs, his full weight behind his assault.

Jack reeled backward under the bone-jarring impact of being tackled to the cold rock floor, his useless weapons clattering to the ground.

Taking advantage of his opponent's momentary daze, Lucian pushed himself up to a straddling position and landed a blow with his fist, determined to pummel the Frenchman into a bloody pulp. He released another brutally powerful punch to the jaw, then another, showing no mercy despite the man's cries of pain.

When Jack raised his hands in an effort to defend himself against the ferocious onslaught, Lucian glanced fleetingly over his shoulder, desperately seeking Brynn, needing to know the worst. He saw her struggling to rise from the ground and felt a fierce surge of relief, knowing she couldn't be too terribly injured.

His distraction proved costly, however. The Frenchman's fist struck his temple, pain blinding him for a precious second as the skin above his eye split.

Cursing, Lucian dodged his opponent's next blows and tried to clear his vision of the blood dripping from his wound. An instant later he was choking as Jack's clawing fingers caught him by the throat. He let fly another hard jab and rolled to the side, forcing the Frenchman to loosen his grip.

Behind him, Brynn staggered to her knees, trying to clear her dazed senses. She was winded from having tripped, and her arm stung like fire from a gunshot wound. But the bullet had missed Lucian, that was all that mattered. Her relief was so profound, she felt weak—a relief that was short-lived.

She saw Lucian fighting, while Gray lay on his back, his hands groping his side, his face ashen. She bit back a sob. Grayson was alive at least, while Lucian needed help.

Her frantic gaze landed on her brother's pistol, which lay several yards from her. Jolting herself from her paralysis, she climbed to her feet and stumbled over to the weapon, catching it up to hold the grip in both hands.

She couldn't shoot, though, without fear of hitting Lucian, who was locked in mortal combat. When she heard a groan at her feet, she spared a brief glance for her brother.

"I never knew . . . being shot . . . would hurt so much," he gasped.

His voice was almost drowned out by the grunts of the combatants, but it was Lucian's sharp curse that sent cold horror spiraling down to Brynn's belly. The two men were wrestling side by side now, but the Frenchman had a knife!

The blade flashed as he raised his arm and stabbed downward. With another curse, Lucian jerked backward, then reached up to grasp his opponent's wrist with both hands.

Brynn watched, her breath frozen in her throat as the Frenchman jerked his arm free. Drawing back, he struck again, flailing with the dagger.

She moved forward, helplessly aiming her pistol, but just then, Lucian rolled free. Panting for breath, the Frenchman leapt up and made a dash for the entrance to the tunnel. Climbing wearily to his feet, Lucian sprinted after him.

Brynn started to follow but threw a desperate glance over her shoulder at her wounded brother.

"Go . . . I'll be all right. . . ." Gray rasped. "Try to save him."

She lunged for the tunnel where the two men had disappeared. Her legs shaking, her pulse pounding, she plunged into the darkness.

She was blind for a moment, but when she heard the distant echo of footsteps, she pressed on sightlessly, using the tunnel wall as a guide.

She was breathless by the time she came to the tunnel's end, her chest aching with fear. She could detect a faint hint of light, but she had to round a sharp corner and move past a crevice in the rock wall before stumbling out onto the shingle beach.

The dark night was thick with a brewing storm, the ghostly clouds above silvered by a hint of moonlight and swept along by a chill salt breeze. Frantic, Brynn glanced down the shoreline each way, seeing nothing but outcroppings of rock, hearing nothing over the sound of the waves and her own ragged breaths.

Struggling to drag air into her lungs, she looked back over her shoulder, her gaze climbing upward along the cliff face. Her heart jolted when she saw two black shapes overhead; the Frenchman was racing up the cliff walk, Lucian hard on his heels. She could almost hear the harsh sound of their panting.

A moment later, Lucian caught his prey. With a staggering lunge, he tumbled Jack to the rough path.

Both men were on their feet in an instant. Rather than continuing to flee, though, Jack suddenly spun and swung his deadly blade. Lucian stumbled backward and slipped, nearly losing his footing on the narrow track. Brynn barely stifled a scream as he pressed against the cliff wall to regain his balance.

Her heart in her throat, she clutched the pistol in her shaking grasp, trying to aim at the Frenchman. Did she dare shoot? They were so close to each other. . . .

She had no choice, for Jack attacked again, his knife held high as he charged Lucian. Praying, Brynn squeezed the trigger.

The gunshot exploded in her ears. An instant later she heard a cry from one of the men. Then Jack crashed into Lucian, who couldn't brace for the impact.

For one endless moment, the two combatants stood locked together on the brink of the precipice. Then, with agonizing slowness, they hurtled over the ledge.

Her heart no longer beating, Brynn watched in helpless terror as they tumbled together in a death grip onto the rocky shore below.

Chapter Twenty-two

The nightmare was real, Lucian thought, dazed. Brynn stood over him in the darkness, her fiery hair spilling around her shoulders, her hands slick with his blood. . . .

Was he dying? The dull ache in his head—in his entire body—made him think so.

He squeezed his eyes shut, but when he opened them again, Brynn was still there, kneeling beside him, weeping, gently cradling his face with searching fingers. She seemed distraught as she pleaded hoarsely with him, "Lucian, please . . . please . . . you can't die. . . . Dear God, please . . ."

Her lips moved over his face in frantic despair, as if she truly cared whether he lived or died. As if she truly loved him. . . .

His heart wrenched with hope. Wincing, Lucian stiffly turned his head. The Frenchman lay on his back, eyes wide, his neck twisted at an unnatural angle.

Realization struck Lucian, slicing through his churning thoughts. His nightmare had not come true. He wasn't dying. He had lived when his enemy had not.

At his brief movement, he heard Brynn inhale

sharply, her sobs arrested as she stared down at him. In the dimness, he could see her eyes alight with stark fear, with hope, could see the glitter of tears streaking her cheeks.

"Lucian?" she uttered, her voice raw and trembling.

He raised his hand to brush a tendril of wildly cascading hair from her face. She had lost her seaman's cap, and her tresses shimmered like dark flame in the faint moonlight.

"I'm alive. . . ." he whispered.

She gave another sob, a strangled sound of pure joy, while her fingers clutched reflexively at his shirt. "I d-didn't shoot you?"

"No, your shot hit Jack. . . ." Reacting with primal instinct, Lucian pulled her into his arms, capturing her mouth in a hard caress, needing to feel her warm body pressed against him, needing to share the exhilaration of being alive.

For an instant Brynn froze in startlement at his sudden passion, but then she returned his kiss fervently, with the same desperation. She seemed to be laughing and crying at the same time, relief and gladness profoundly evident in her response.

He held her closer, drinking of her mouth, his arms tightening around her fiercely—until he heard her gasp of pain. His fingers had grasped the upper part of her left arm.

Drawing back, Lucian probed her arm in the darkness, feeling the rent in her jacket. The fabric was wet with blood, he realized, suddenly chilled.

"You're *wounded*," he said, his tone accusing.

Brynn glanced down at her arm, almost in surprise. "I suppose I am."

His jaw clenched as he remembered what had happened in the cave: Brynn leaping in front of the bullet that was meant for him, deflecting the shot with her lantern just enough to save his life. His heart turned over. Dear God, she had come so close to dying for his sake. . . .

Another realization struck him at the same moment. In his dark dreams, the blood on Brynn's hands was *his*, not hers. But this outcome was different; she was the one wounded. She hadn't sought to kill him as he'd seen in his nightmare. Instead she had saved his life a second time when she'd shot his enemy and kept him from being gutted by Jack's knife.

Gratitude shuddered through Lucian, mingled with dread at what might have happened to her. He had been so wrong about Brynn.

"It is only a flesh wound," she murmured at his grim silence, but he wasn't reassured.

"Are you certain?" he demanded. "You're not hurt elsewhere?" He reached out to press his hand against her abdomen. "The babe?"

Her hand covered his protectively. "I don't think it was harmed."

His frantic thoughts eased a degree.

"You're bleeding as well," she said, still concerned. When she touched the split flesh above his eye, Lucian winced. "Where else are you hurt?"

Gingerly he tested his arms and legs. He seemed to be in one piece. "I'm only battered." He pushed himself up, stifling a groan at the protest of his bruised body.

Brynn shuddered. "Oh, Lucian, I thought . . . I thought the curse had come true, that I had killed you."

He had shared her same dark thoughts. "The curse didn't come true, Brynn."

"Can you stand?" She glanced at the dead Frenchman and shuddered again. "We should summon a doctor for you and—" She drew a sharp breath, as if remembering. "Grayson . . . he was badly wounded, Lucian. I need to see to him."

Before he could reply, they heard the sounds of footsteps on the cliff walk. That would be Philip Barton and his men, Lucian knew.

He mentally voiced an oath. He wanted to be alone with Brynn, for they had a great deal to say to each other. But now they would have no further chance for intimacy for some time. Not when the smugglers must still be dealt with and Grayson's fate determined.

Grimacing, Lucian set Brynn carefully away and climbed determinedly to his feet.

The next hours were a blur for Brynn. The immediate peril was over, but the future was far from certain—both hers and Gray's.

The moment his men arrived, Lucian called for a doctor to see to her and her brother, but then he seemed to withdraw from her, as if he'd recalled her crimes now that the danger had passed.

Worried for Gray, Brynn was allowed to return to the cave—but under escort. Her heart sank at the implication of Lucian's orders: she wasn't to be trusted alone with her brother. She wondered if she was still under house arrest.

She left Lucian quietly conferring with his collaborator, Philip Barton. Brynn suspected he was dispatching men to intercept the crew of French smugglers and to dispose of Jack's body, as well as retrieve the stolen gold. Lucian glanced back at her only once before she disappeared through the crevice in the rock wall, urgently seeking her brother.

Grayson lay where she had left him, looking pale and in pain but still conscious. She knelt beside him and opened his jacket to find his shirt soaked in blood. Biting back fear, she tore the cambric away to expose the raw flesh. The wound was on the right side of his chest, just below his armpit. Grayson grimaced in pain as she gently probed.

"The ball passed through," she murmured in relief, "but I think the rib may be broken." She touched his forehead, feeling for fever. "Does it hurt badly?"

"Like the very devil." His eyes searched her face. "What of Wycliff?"

"He's alive, Gray," she replied with a shudder. "Jack isn't."

"Good," Gray said with grim satisfaction.

She glanced around her despairingly. "You cannot stay here. We must get you to bed."

The leader of her guard detail spoke up behind her. "Forgive me, my lady, but I am under orders. I am to make Sir Grayson as comfortable as possible, but he cannot leave the caves. A doctor will be here shortly to tend him, and you as well."

Brynn stiffened at the callousness of keeping her brother incarcerated here. "Surely it would do no harm to take him to his rooms, even if he is a prisoner. He is in no condition to try to escape."

Oddly, the guard looked puzzled. "Sir Grayson is not a prisoner, my lady. Lord Wycliff merely does not wish him to be seen by your household servants."

"Brynn," Gray murmured, "it's all right. I would rather not move much just now."

She hesitated, realizing the futility of arguing. Gray was too wounded to walk, certainly to climb stairs. It would be painful even being carried through the tunnels, and she could not manage the task alone.

"If you won't allow him to be moved," Brynn said tersely to the guard, "would you be so kind as to fetch him some blankets? A cold rock floor is no place for a wounded man."

"Yes, certainly, my lady," he replied, his tone deferential. "It is being seen to."

She took off her coat and covered Grayson with it. Then she waited anxiously while the promise of blankets was made good.

A doctor came shortly as well—or at least a man with a medical bag. Brynn had never seen him before, which meant he wasn't from the district. She could only conjecture that Lucian had anticipated the danger of the operation and brought his own surgeon.

The man tended Gray's injuries, confirming that the bullet hadn't lodged in his chest or pierced a lung, but that a rib was shattered. With Brynn holding the lamp, the doctor grimly searched for splinters, then liberally doused the raw flesh with basilicum powder and bandaged the ribs.

"You are a very fortunate man," the doctor pronounced, "but the wound is quite serious with the bone so fragmented. You may take some months to heal." He drew up the blankets over his patient, who was clenching his teeth in obvious discomfort. "I regret I can give you only a taste of laudanum for the pain," the doctor added. "Lord Wycliff wishes you to be alert when he speaks to you."

Brynn felt a cold knot re-form in her stomach. She was greatly relieved to hear her brother's prognosis, but Gray still faced charges of treason. And while she was infinitely grateful that Lucian was unharmed, her own betrayal had perhaps created an insurmountable obstacle between them.

The doctor bandaged her arm, which was beginning to throb, then took his leave. Brynn sat quietly beside her brother and watched as the strongboxes of gold were retrieved from the pool and carried away.

The men who performed the task scarcely gave her a glance. If they were taken aback by events or by seeing Lord Wycliff's countess dressed in breeches, they politely pretended not to show it. Not that Brynn could summon the energy to be concerned. After the terrible tension of the past few days, she felt drained, despondent, filled with dread at the punishment her brother would be dealt.

Her nerves were raw again by the time Lucian finally came.

The cut over his eyes had been cleaned of blood, she saw, but his features looked drawn and weary.

He met her gaze only briefly before glancing down at her brother. "I believe we have some important matters left to settle, Sir Grayson."

"Yes," he said hoarsely.

"Are you still anxious for me to put a period to your existence, as you were a short while ago?"

Gray's mouth twisted with dark humor. "No . . . Lying here, I've had time to reconsider. I really don't want to die."

Brynn reached out to grasp her brother's hand, whether giving or seeking comfort she wasn't certain.

"Am I under arrest?" Gray asked.

"Of a sort."

"Then you mean to send me to prison?"

"No." Lucian gazed at him steadily. "Not as long as you honor your pledge to help expose Caliban. He still remains unknown and at large, and despite this night's work, our prospects of capturing him have suffered. With Jack dead, we are back to where we started. His crew has been apprehended and will be interrogated, of course, but I doubt they know anything about their leader. You are still the closest link we have to Caliban."

"I told you, I will help in any way possible. But I cannot endanger my family any further."

"I agree," Lucian replied tersely. "Which is why you will have to disappear for a time."

"Disappear?"

"Go into hiding. It is the only way to ensure your sister and brothers' safety. As you said, if you are dead, Caliban will no longer have the leverage to blackmail you. So you will be presumed dead. We will put out the story that you were drowned at sea, that your body was never recovered."

"Will anyone believe it?"

"I don't see why not. I mean to say that you were

in my employ all along. You have been working for the British government, Sir Grayson, trying to get close to the smugglers and win their confidence." Lucian paused. "There is no proof otherwise."

"You would do that for me?" Gray asked, his tone hoarse.

Lucian shot Brynn an enigmatic glance. "Yes. You were only aiding me in my duty, attempting to keep my wife safe. If you cannot be found, Caliban will no longer threaten her or your brothers. Once we catch him, you can return to the world. It may be some months, however. Caliban has proven damnably elusive. But you can use the interval to recover. The doctor tells me you will be bedridden for a time."

Brynn let out the breath she had been holding. *Grayson was not going to prison.* She felt tears fill her eyes as she squeezed his hand.

When Gray remained silent, deep in thought, she spoke up. "What do we tell our brothers . . . Theo? They will be devastated to think Grayson dead."

"If their acting skills are good enough, you can tell them the truth. Their grief must be convincing enough to fool Caliban, though."

"Theo will consider it a lark," Gray asserted. "And I'm certain we can count on the others to keep up the pretense."

"At least the presumption of your drowning avoids one problem," Lucian expounded. "If there is no body, there will be no immediate question of your heir assuming your title and holdings, so there will be no legal mess to sort out when you return to life."

"Where will Grayson go?" Brynn asked.

"I thought Scotland. I have property in the Highlands where he will be safe. One of my ships is anchored at Falmouth and can convey him there." His gaze focused again on Gray. "My colleague, Philip Barton, will accompany you. You can use the journey to tell him everything you know about Caliban. If you agree to the plan, I will have a stretcher brought in to carry you to the ship."

"Now?" Brynn repeated. "So soon?"

"Tonight?" Gray asked.

"It will be best if you disappear immediately," Lucian answered. "The subterfuge may become too difficult to sustain otherwise. If your servants see you wounded, it will be harder to make credible your sudden disappearance at sea."

Brynn suddenly comprehended. "That was why you didn't want Gray moved from the caves."

"Yes," Lucian replied. "Then you agree to my plan, Sir Grayson?"

Gray looked at Brynn, who nodded, unable to speak for the tears in her throat. Lucian had given her brother a reprieve. She could not have imagined he would be so generous. She returned Lucian's gaze fervently.

"*Thank you,*" she uttered, her heart filled with gratitude.

Gray echoed her sentiment. "Yes, I thank you, my lord. I know I don't deserve such leniency. As for your plan, I will do whatever you think best."

Lucian seemed to brush off his thanks with a hard stare. "You should have come to me first. I trust I needn't warn you of the consequences if you ever dare involve your sister in treason again?"

Gray's mouth curled in a harsh smile. "No, I need no warning."

"Very well then . . . I expect you will want a few moments to say farewell. I have some matters to tie up, so I will leave you two alone." His glance went to Brynn, but she couldn't read his expression. "We still have a great deal to discuss."

"Yes," she murmured.

"Perhaps you will await me in your rooms. I will join you there when I can."

"Very well."

Brynn bit her trembling lower lip as she watched him leave, not knowing how to interpret Lucian's sudden coolness.

Realizing her brother was watching her, though, she forced herself to wipe her eyes. "I can scarcely credit Lucian is letting you go free," she remarked, trying to summon a smile.

"It is solely for your sake, Brynn. I think he must care for you a great deal."

She bit her lip, unable to let herself hope. "We should have gone to Lucian from the start, I see that now. It might have spared us a great deal of terror. Perhaps if you had told me earlier what you were facing . . ."

"I'm sorry for what I put you through," Gray said quietly.

"I know, dearest." Bending, she embraced him carefully, mindful of his injury. "But if you ever *dare* become involved in something so dangerous again and try to shoulder the burden all yourself, I swear I truly will shoot you myself."

*   *   *

A short while later she stood at the window of her bedchamber, waiting for her husband to come . . . for her fate to be decided.

Her farewell to Gray had been bittersweet, filled with both relief and sadness. She'd watched as her brother was carried away on a stretcher, knowing how fortunate he was to be given a second chance.

Would she be given the same chance?

Brynn shivered as she stared out at the night. The storm had apparently passed them by, leaving a few clouds of mist scudding across the dark sky. The faint moonlight painted the ocean silver, transforming it into a cold, flickering mirror.

She felt just as cold; she felt empty, aching. She wouldn't blame Lucian in the least if he hated her for what she had done.

Trying not to think about it, Brynn busied herself stoking the fire. She froze when she heard the door to her bedchamber open and then slowly shut. Hardly daring to breathe, she turned to face Lucian.

He stood just inside the room, his features eclipsed by shadow, much as he had looked earlier in the evening when she'd attempted to drug him.

Was that only hours ago?

He was the first to speak. "How is your arm?"

"It throbs a little, but it's nothing, really. Merely a flesh wound."

His eyes narrowed as he stepped into the light. "I don't consider a bullet wound 'nothing.' That was a damned foolish thing to do, Brynn, lunging in front of me."

"You're welcome," she retorted, stung to defiance by his criticism.

His voice was unnervingly quiet when he replied. "You could have been killed."

She couldn't tell whether that prospect would have saddened him or not. "Would it have mattered to you?"

"Certainly it would have mattered." There was a moment's pause before he added, "You are carrying my child, did you consider that?"

Brynn's hand went to her abdomen in dismay. "No, I didn't stop to think."

He moved toward her, his gaze piercing as it bored relentlessly into her. "You didn't realize you were endangering our child?"

"Not at that moment. All I thought about was that Jack meant to shoot you and that I had to stop him."

Lucian halted a short distance from her. She could see the tightness in his face, could sense the thrumming tension coiled in his hard, elegant body.

She regarded him in mute wretchedness. He cared deeply about their child, she knew, but did he care about her in the least? Perhaps he couldn't forgive her for her crimes after all.

"I'm sorry," she said finally, miserably.

To her shock, Lucian reached up to touch her cheek. "No, I am the one who should be sorry. For doubting you. You saved my life, Brynn." Her breath caught as his thumb brushed the corner of her mouth. "You terrified me," he whispered. "I thought I would die of fear when you stepped in front of that bullet."

She returned his searching gaze, unable to speak for the hope filling her.

"My dream was wrong, wasn't it?" Lucian murmured. "In my nightmare, you are standing over me as I lie dying. You want me dead. But you couldn't want my death if you were willing to give your life for me."

"That dream is terribly wrong." Brynn felt tears spring to her eyes. "Your death is the last thing I would ever want." She gazed up at him earnestly. "I know I betrayed you, Lucian, but I only wanted to keep you safe. Even if you can never forgive me . . . I did it for you."

"I know that now, love. I regret I ever distrusted you. I should have listened to my heart, not my head."

She gazed at him with longing. "Your heart?"

Taking her hand, he pressed her palm to his chest. "I love you, Brynn. I have for a long time, even though I refused to acknowledge it."

For a long moment she simply stared. Then blindly she walked into his arms. Burying her face in his shoulder, she gave a sob. "I thought you hated me. . . ."

"No, I could never hate you." His arms wrapped around her, holding her close. "Even when I thought the worst . . . Ah, don't cry, Brynn." He could feel love and despair pulse through her body, feel her trembling.

"I fought against loving you," he murmured. "I tried to convince myself that what I felt was merely an obsession. But I should have realized the truth much sooner."

She shuddered. "The thought of you hating me tore me apart."

He drew back, gazing down at her, seeing her

lashes spiky with tears. Her hair in the firelight shimmered like molten embers. Gently he touched her face. "You arouse any number of feelings in me, siren. You make me burn with passion or fear or fury, but never hate."

She gave a shaky laugh. "Certainly fury. I've given you ample reason to be furious with me."

"Even so, I've loved you almost from the first time I saw you."

Slowly Brynn shook her head. "It was only the curse."

"No," he said gravely. "Perhaps a spell could make me want you, desire you, but it couldn't make me love you. I love you, Brynn, not because of any Gypsy spell or your physical allure, but because of the woman you are. You make me feel complete. You fill the part of my soul that was missing."

"Oh, Lucian . . ."

He took a deep breath, seeking courage. "Brynn, I know ours was to be a marriage of convenience, that you wanted us to live apart after our child is born, but I hope to God you will reconsider. I want to be your husband, Brynn. Loved, honored, cherished for all the world to see."

Her expression softened. "You *are* loved, Lucian. I told you the truth earlier tonight. I love you. I was afraid to admit it only because of the curse. I hope you believe me."

"How can I not believe you after tonight?" Lucian asked, his voice suddenly husky. "You proved your love more than adequately, throwing yourself in front of a bullet meant for me. . . ." He shuddered with soul-deep terror, realizing how close he had come to losing Brynn. He had wealth, titles, all the privileges money and rank could buy, but they were all worthless if he lost the one thing that mattered most. And he knew Brynn felt something similar if she had been willing to sacrifice herself for him.

His brows drew together as he recalled something she had said earlier. "What was it the Gypsy at the fair told you? That you must be willing to give your life for me?"

"That I had to love you enough, yes."

"If her prophecy is true, then the curse should be broken."

Her eyes widened. "Perhaps it is," she said in wonder.

Lucian held her gaze. "So you don't intend to leave me?"

"No. I never wanted us to live separate lives. I only thought I must to protect you."

"The best way to protect me is to stay with me. I might as well cut out my heart if you leave me."

"I won't ever leave you, Lucian. I can't live without you. I know that now."

The soft light in her eyes reflected her quiet smile, catching his heart and sending it thudding after his racing pulse.

He drew her into his arms once more, pressing his lips against her hair, his relief overwhelming. Only now was he realizing how desperately he needed her love, how rare and precious that love was.

Brynn stood in the warmth of his embrace, cherishing the feel of his hard body against hers. She could feel her fear easing. Perhaps the curse had indeed been broken because she had risked her life for him. If so, then she was free to love Lucian with all her heart.

"I love you so much," she murmured, repeating her own declaration of love.

That made him raise his head. His voice was gentle, as were his eyes. "I'm not certain I know why. I've never given you any reason to love me."

"That isn't true. What you did for Theo was reason enough. And now Grayson . . . I thank you from the bottom of my heart, Lucian. Can you ever forgive me for what I did?"

"Only if you can forgive me." His soft laughter was self-mocking. "What an arrogant bastard I was. . . . Arrogant, selfish, thinking only of myself, my own needs. I thought I could easily charm you into doing my bidding. I forced you to conceive a child because that was what *I* wanted. . . . You deserved more, Brynn. I would say that you have far more to forgive than I do."

"But still . . ."

He pressed his fingers to her lips. "No more regrets about the past. We have only the future ahead of us."

His arms encircled her once more, and she reciprocated, relishing his embrace. For a long moment they simply held each other, until Lucian broke the silence with a quiet question.

"Brynn, will you come away with me?"

"Come away with you? Where?"

"I thought the castle in Wales, the one I gave you as a belated wedding gift."

Pulling back, Brynn glanced up at him, trying not to leap to conclusions. "Why?" she asked, feigning lightness. "You want to incarcerate me there to keep me from committing treason again?"

"Not in the least. You said I don't know you well, and it's true. But I want that chance to know you, Brynn, and for you to know me. We need time to explore each other, time for love and trust to build. If we were to go away together, we could have that time. It could be a new start for our marriage."

"But what of your duty? You have yet to apprehend Caliban."

"I've come to realize you're far more important to me than apprehending traitors. There will likely be a lull in his treachery in any case. We dealt a blow to his ring tonight, and he will have to reorganize. I'm not proposing we live there forever, merely visit for a few weeks."

"I should like that," she said softly. "A new beginning."

The smoldering look in his eyes made her breath catch.

He bent his head to kiss her, to seal their pledge. Fire flowed between them as their lips met, fire and want and need.

Lucian felt himself tremble with it. Fierce desire burned through him, desire that had nothing to do with any curse.

They *would* make a new beginning, Lucian vowed solemnly. Yet this time he would earn Brynn's love. He would prove himself worthy of her. And he wouldn't rest till he had wholly won the enchantress who had enslaved his heart and soul.

Epilogue

Gwyndar, Wales, October 1813

A half smile playing on his lips, Lucian watched his countess cavort in the sun-warmed tidal pool. They had arrived in Wales two weeks ago at the castle that had been his wedding gift to her.

Gwyndar was a place of strange enchantment, with its crystalline caves and secret coves and cascading waterfalls, but until now Lucian had never appreciated the beauty. By some quirk of nature and ocean currents, the climate of this northern stretch of Welsh coast was as temperate as southern England; newborn lambs and rare butterflies thrived here. And despite the lateness of the year, this was a particularly glorious afternoon, drenched with sunshine, caressed by the mildest of sea breezes.

He and Brynn had discovered the sandy cove during their first exploration of the castle environs. Although the tidal pool was heated by the sun's rays, it still wasn't warm enough for Lucian to brave the water, yet Brynn seemed to relish the chill. She was part sea siren, he was convinced.

She was his heart. She had insinuated herself so

deeply into his soul that he could no longer fathom living without her.

The past weeks had been a new beginning for them, just as he'd hoped. Since nearly losing each other, their time together seemed infinitely more precious. They had spent the magical hours here becoming true lovers, exploring each other's thoughts, sharing secrets and hot sultry kisses, making love wherever and whenever they could, falling deeper in love. . . .

Lucian marveled at the depth of his feelings for Brynn. He had never expected to be overwhelmed by the power of love, so shaken by passion. He had never imagined finding anyone who set his heart afire, a temptress who met his passion with her own and left him gasping. A soul mate who completed him.

"You should join me, Lucian," Brynn called teasingly, interrupting his thoughts.

His mouth curled. He had stripped down to his breeches, but that was far enough for his taste. "I'm not mad enough to swim in that icy water. Your gooseflesh must be the size of mountains."

"You will have to warm me, then."

Across the stretch of sand, he met the brilliant sparkle of her emerald eyes and felt lust and love surge through him. "Come here, siren, and I will."

She emerged from the water, her flaming hair cascading wildly around her naked breasts, seawater foaming around her calves. Lucian's breath faltered at the beguiling sight.

His gaze sweeping every tempting curve of her body, he rose and went to her. His very hands burned with the need to touch her.

His arms slipped about her waist, catching her close, crushing her soft breasts against his bare chest. "This reminds me of the first time I saw you. I thought you were a fantasy. . . ." His voice grew husky as he stared down into her eyes that were translucent pools of green. "You still are. I dream of you like this now . . . fiery, vibrant, sensual . . . *mine*."

Her soft smile held an erotic allure. "I am no fantasy, Lucian," she responded, reaching up to slip her arms around his neck. "I am flesh and blood—and just at this moment I am about to turn into an icicle. Didn't you promise to warm me? You are gravely neglecting your obligations."

He flashed her a wicked grin. "Consider me duly chastened, my love."

Lifting her in his arms, he carried her to the stretch of sand that held their blankets and laid her down, then tenderly dried her sun-kissed skin. When he sat back on his heels to look at her, Brynn shivered. The heat of his gaze set her blood on fire, leaving her breasts tingling for want of his caress, her secret hollows throbbing.

He bent to kiss her lightly, his tongue playing upon her lips, warming her as his hands drifted over her body. His palms felt like flames against her chilled skin, his fingers shaping the sensitive mounds of her breasts, her peaked nipples. . . .

She drew a slow breath as his searing lips joined his hands, sliding down her throat to her bosom, sending tremors of delight rippling through her. Her limbs felt suddenly languid, weak with longing. The sand was warm at her back as his mouth poised over one taut, swollen bud. Her fingers clenched in the blanket when finally he dipped to tease it with his tongue.

He didn't stop there. With exquisite sensitivity, his flaming tongue swirled over her breasts in a deliberate attack on her senses. Brynn twisted her head restlessly, fighting back a moan.

Lucian gave a murmur of satisfaction deep in his own throat. "Your nipples taste salty. I wonder what the rest of you tastes like."

Dazed by the erotic warmth in his voice, she made no protest when hands moved slowly down her bare flanks to her ankles, then back up again along her shivering inner thighs, where he paused. He was watching her, contemplating her with a wicked half smile, his persistent gaze branding her like a blaze.

Her skin felt suddenly hot and flushed, along with her nerves, when she realized his intent. Parting her thighs, Lucian lowered his head to kiss the petals of her woman's flesh.

"You are scandalous," she accused, although breathlessly anticipating his caresses.

"And whose fault is that? You would tempt the devil, siren."

Quite deliberately, he draped her legs over his shoulders and bent to pleasure her. Wet white heat scalded her as he suckled the bud of her desire. His long, clever tongue lapped at her, delving, tasting, ravishing her, ruthlessly driving her to the edge until she was panting and flushed with blazing heat.

She clutched his thick, dark hair, craving release. Yet he didn't allow her fulfillment. Instead he left her writhing on the brink of climax, shuddering with agonized need.

"Lucian . . ." she warned and pleaded at the same time.

He drew back, the wicked satisfaction in his eyes replaced by a deeper smoldering light. "I would be happy to oblige, my lady."

He shed his breeches quickly and with a lithe, athletic motion joined her on the blanket, lowering himself to cover her body with his, easing between her spread thighs.

Brynn arched against him hungrily. She loved the feel of him against her, the smooth, hard planes and ridges, the heat, the way his magnificent arousal pulsed and throbbed. The rigid rod felt huge and hot as she fully absorbed its swollen length. She gave a whimper of bliss as he thrust home, shuddering at the incredible sensation of being filled with him.

"I love feeling you so deep inside me," she murmured, her voice suddenly hoarse. "I love you, Lucian. . . ."

His gaze locked with hers. "And I love you, Brynn," he said, low and hushed. "You are my life."

"As you are mine," she echoed, a promise.

That was all the encouragement necessary to shatter his pretense of sanguinity. His gentleness fraying, he surged inside her, impaling her with his thick, pulsing shaft. Yet Brynn welcomed his fever joyfully. Her legs locking around his hips, she clung to him, meeting him stroke for stroke, measure for measure. In only a moment their joining turned frenzied, the rhythm building to sudden wildness.

Brynn held on tightly as bliss burst upon them in an explosion of convulsive pleasure, her cries mingling with his harsh groans. Lucian poured himself into her welcoming body before finally collapsing upon her, shaking with the force of their fierce mating.

They lay locked together, the delicious sweetness slowly ebbing with the frenzied echo of their heartbeats. When the turbulence stilled, Lucian eased his weight to his side and drew the blankets over their still-entwined limbs.

Limp and sated, Brynn nuzzled her cheek in the curve of his shoulder, her fingers splaying over his smooth-muscled chest.

"Warm enough now?" he asked, stroking her hair weakly.

"Yes." Brynn's breath escaped in a soft sigh. Lucian made her feel so cherished. She knew it was not the Gypsy's curse driving his attraction, either. She could see the love in his eyes each time he looked at her, could feel it in every beat of his heart.

She felt his hand move to her lower abdomen to gently caress the place where their child lay quietly growing inside her, and she smiled. Her cup of happiness could not be much fuller. She would bear her husband a child. Grayson was safe in Scotland, and they had received word that his injury was healing. Theo was being covertly protected by two full-time bodyguards, while he and her other brothers were willingly keeping up the pretense of Gray's disappearance. . . .

The thought of that still-unresolved issue drew Brynn's brows into a troubled frown. She never wanted this bliss to end, yet she knew that she and Lucian would have to return to London soon. Raven's wedding was to be held shortly, for one thing. And Caliban was still at large, no doubt planning how to wreak further evil.

Brynn suspected Lucian would soon become restless to fulfill his duty; with her newly attuned instincts, she sensed that his failure to apprehend the traitor was already gnawing at his conscience. Yet she was reluctant for Lucian to face the threat again.

"I almost wish we didn't have to return to London," she murmured quietly. "I don't like to think of the danger to you, or how Caliban wants you dead."

He seemed to hesitate. "I intend to take precautions—for both of us. You may not care for it, love, but I plan to have you guarded day and night. I'm not about to lose something so precious to me."

"I couldn't bear to lose you, either, Lucian."

Easing away from her, he lay on his side. Surprisingly there was a hint of laughter in his sapphire eyes. "I am the one who should be wary of returning. Doubtless I'll have to fight to keep your beaux away from you, but I'm damned if I want to share you."

She couldn't help but smile at the jealous edge in his voice. "If the curse has ended, then I should no longer have to suffer their unwanted attentions."

Lucian's mouth curved wryly. "I don't imagine you will ever be free from male attention, love. Certainly not mine. I expect to fawn over you till the day I die."

Brynn's smile faded as she remembered how close he had come to dying. "I beg you, don't say that."

His own expression remained light. "Never fear. I plan to live a very, very long time and beget countless sons and daughters on you."

Her eyebrow rose. "Countless? And do I have any say in the matter, my arrogant lord?"

"I might consider allowing you an opinion if you're extremely well-behaved and properly subservient for the next forty or fifty years."

With a soft laugh, Brynn wrapped her arms around her husband's neck. "I believe you have the wrong bride if you want subservience."

Suddenly sober, Lucian shook his head, gazing deeply into her eyes. "No, love, I have the perfect bride. You're my destiny, Brynn. I think I knew it the first moment we met. We were fated to be together. You're my fate, and I am yours."

Her own gaze softened, as did her heart. "I can think of no more wonderful fortune."

His fingers rose to touch her lips. "For so long I thought there was something missing in myself. I know what it was now. You. I just hadn't met you yet. You fill the hunger in my soul."

Tears filling her eyes, she searched his beautiful features, his face so beloved it hurt her to look at him. "I love you so much, Lucian," she answered, feeling the same magical completion that he did.

Lying back, he drew her close and pressed her head down on his shoulder. With a contented sigh Brynn shut her eyes, feeling her limbs grow warm and languid. She slept.

The sand was warm beneath her feet as she watched her family frolic in the surf, her heart so full she thought it might burst. They were playing a game of tag, a young boy with dark hair and blue eyes like Lucian's, two beautiful little girls, both with vivid red hair like her own. As if of one mind, the children suddenly turned on their father and gleefully pelted him with seawater. With a ferocious mock growl, Lucian went on the attack, catching a daughter under each arm and making them squeal with laughter as he stalked after his son. . . .

Brynn came awake abruptly, an incredible sense of serenity filling her. She lifted her head to stare down at Lucian, wondering if he had shared the same dream.

He stirred awake more slowly, but when he opened his eyes, she could see comprehension and joy in the blue depths.

His gaze locked with hers for an intense moment.

"A son," she murmured.

"And two daughters," he added, his voice rough with awe.

"Do you think that dream really was our future?"

Slowly Lucian smiled. "God, I hope so. I intend to do my damnedest to make it come true."

When she smiled in return, Lucian's gaze dropped to her mouth, his blue eyes darkening with sensual fire. "I can't promise to know the future, Brynn," he whispered, his mouth moving closer. "I can only promise to cherish you for all eternity."

"That is more than enough, my love." Her heart overflowing, Brynn lifted her face to his and gave herself up to his passionate kiss.

Read on for a sneak peek at

Ecstacy

the next breathtaking historical romance from
Nicole Jordan

Coming Fall 2002

London, November 1813

"Doubtless you have a good reason for summoning me from my fencing match," Kell Lasseter remarked mildly as he reached the second floor of his gaming house.

His beautiful hostess, Emma Walsh, awaited him at the head of the stairs. "A most urgent reason," she replied in obvious agitation. "Your brother . . ."

Kell felt a prick of alarm, his familiar protective feelings suddenly roused. "What's amiss? Has Sean been hurt?"

"No, not hurt. But he brought a lady here, Kell, and I fear he means her harm. He has a whip, and he's bound her to the bed."

Kell's dark eyebrows snapped together, a different kind of alarm coursing through him. His charming rogue of a younger brother could be wild at times, even dangerous when driven to it—although he'd never known Sean to behave with violence toward a woman.

"Our reputation . . ." Emma shuddered in horror. "If he rapes her . . ."

Emma was as desirous of protecting the club's renown as he was, Kell knew, but she would doubtless feel sympathy for any vulnerable female because of her own harsh past.

"You must stop him, Kell. Miss Kendrick is well known in society, and she has powerful connections."

At the notorious name, he felt himself stiffen. Miss Raven Kendrick was the darling of the ton, and for a time last summer, she had turned his brother's life into a living hell—delivering him to the unspeakable brutality of the British navy.

Kell clenched his jaw, striving not to leap to conclusions. "Where are they?"

"In your bedchamber."

Swiftly he strode down the corridor to the bedchamber he normally used when staying overnight at his club. The Golden Fleece was an elegant gaming hell, but the gambling took place on the ground floor below, while this floor held only private rooms.

The door to his bedchamber was locked, he discovered. Kell rapped sharply, uttering one terse word. *"Sean."*

When there was no reply, he spun on his heel and made his way to the adjacent study, then crossed to a second door that connected with his bedchamber. Finding this one unlocked, Kell entered and came up short, taking stock.

On the bed, a disheveled woman lay on her side, her bound hands stretched overhead and tied to the headboard. She wasn't quite naked, but her fine cambric shift was hiked up above her knees, exposing long slender legs, while her ebony hair flowed in wild disarray over her bare shoulders.

Kell felt his heart give an unsteady jolt. So this was Miss Raven Kendrick. The dazzling debutante who commanded the homage of nobles. Their paths had never directly crossed before, probably because he actively shunned her ilk and her elevated social circles. Unlike his brother, who'd earnestly aspired to join her elite ranks.

Her eyes were closed, and she didn't stir, yet she was clearly a damsel in distress.

Kell's first mad impulse was to rescue her from her plight, but he fought down his natural instincts. He had to remember who she was. A deadly temptress with a heart of ice. One who lured impressionable young men to their doom simply for sport. She deserved to be punished in some fashion for the misery and suffering she'd caused his brother— although this was perhaps too harsh a penance.

Kell's gaze shifted to his brother. Sean sat slumped in a wing chair near the hearth, cradling a whiskey bottle in one hand, a riding whip in the other. Three long scratches scored the left side of his face.

Involuntarily Kell reached up to touch his own cheek and the wicked scar there. But his scar was an old one and no longer painful, unlike the ones his brother bore, both visible and hidden.

Outwardly, though, they were much alike, with jet black hair and athletic builds, although Sean was slighter and not quite as tall, and his eyes were shamrock green, not nearly black like Kell's.

Sean glanced up now, his green eyes bloodshot, as if he was deep in his cups.

"Would you care to explain why you've barricaded

yourself in my bedchamber like this?" Kell said finally, stepping inside and closing the door.

Sean waved his bottle toward the quiescent beauty on the bed. "Thish is my revenge," he muttered, slurring his words. "I abducted her. Ruined her noble marriagsh. Her curshed duke won't have her now."

"And the whip?" Kell asked.

"Mean to flog her like I was flogged. A whip, not a cat-o'-nine-tails. Won't hurt as much, morsh the pity." Sean made a scoffing sound deep in his throat. "Devil is . . . couldn't do it shober. . . . Needed courage . . ." He held up the bottle.

Strangely, Kell felt a measure of relief that his brother couldn't cold-bloodedly carry out his planned vengeance but needed to work himself into a drunken stupor. Sean was a charming, reckless rogue with the devil's own tongue, but while he could be volatile and hot-tempered at times—no doubt a product of his half-Irish blood—his tantrums blew over as quickly as summer storms. Unlike Kell, whose cold hatreds, once earned, remained intense forever.

In this case, however, Sean's bitterness was entirely justified. Last June, the treacherous Miss Kendrick had sent her groom to thrash him for daring to aspire to her hand. Left unconscious on the London streets, Sean had been taken up by an impressment gang and forced to serve in the Royal Navy for four brutal months, an experience that had left livid scars on his back.

Kell couldn't think of that time without dread and guilt. When his brother had suddenly disappeared, he'd searched frantically and finally rescued Sean from the inhumaneness of the British navy. Yet Kell had once more been tormented by self-blame because he hadn't prevented Sean's suffering or shielded the brother he'd vowed to protect.

Tears suddenly filled Sean's green eyes before he lowered his head. "I *loved* her, Kell. Why'd ssshe have to do that? Taunted and teashed me, then spurned me to wed her cursed duke an' dishposed of me like so much offal. Heartless bish."

Kell himself was filled with anger at the vicious seductress who'd so callously orchestrated his brother's impressment. Even so, flogging her now was overly severe.

Crossing to his brother, Kell reached for the whip. "You don't really want to beat her, Sean."

When he took the whip away, Sean immediately protested. "Yes, I do. . . . Sheesh my hostage. Gonna hurt her th' way ssshe hurt me."

Kell tossed the whip on the adjacent table and noted the other weapons his brother had staged there—a pistol and a lethal-looking knife. Sean had obviously come prepared for every eventuality.

Just then the woman on the bed stirred, giving a low moan. Taking up the knife, Kell went to her. Her face was flushed and feverish, but he crushed his feelings of sympathy and carefully sliced away her bonds, freeing her hands.

For an instant she opened her eyes, looking up at him with a vacant stare. Kell froze in reaction. Long, sooty black lashes rimmed incredible blue eyes, making him suddenly understand the bewitching effect she'd had on his brother.

From the huge size of her pupils, though, she'd

clearly been drugged. Her lashes lowered and fluttered against ivory skin. Then rolling over with a weak groan, she pressed her face into the pillow.

Deliberately he drew the corner of the counterpane over her, as much to shield her near nakedness from his sight as to ensure her warmth.

"What did you give her, Sean?" he asked over his shoulder.

" 'phrodisac. Made her drink it. Thash when she scratched me."

"Not cantharides?" Kell said sharply. "Did you give her Spanish fly?"

"No . . . not that. Shomething Oriental. S'posed to work as well. Got it from Madame Fouchet."

Kell felt another twinge of relief. Madame Fouchet was the proprietor of a high-class brothel Sean frequented. She would have knowledge of aphrodisiacs and appropriate doses. More crucially, she would have shunned Spanish fly, which reportedly could be deadly. Still, it would likely be many hours before this drug wore off. . . .

Kell ran a hand impatiently through his hair, wondering what to do about this damnable situation.

"Why an aphrodisiac?" he asked absently. "Why not simply a sleeping potion if you wanted to render her unable to fight you?"

"To make her want me." Sean flashed a sad, watery smile. "Like she once did. She wanted me, Kell. Sheee was so hot . . . couldn't get enough of me."

With that, Sean struggled to his feet and moved toward the bed, determination etching his features. "Gonna use her body the way she did mine. . . ."

Kell stepped in his path. Sean blinked at him, then frowned. "You mean to stop me?"

"You can't go about ravishing young ladies, no matter how reprehensible they are."

"But sheesh no lady," Sean replied plaintively. "She looks innocent enough, but she gave me her body. An' doan' forget, she's Englissh."

The reminder was like twisting a knife inside Kell. Miss Kendrick had reportedly turned down his brother's proposal of marriage not only because Sean was untitled, but because he was half Irish.

Kell felt his jaw clench. Undoubtedly the haughty temptress had the same callous contempt for those beneath her social standing that the disdainful English Lasseters had had for his Irish mother. The same contempt that had led to his mother's death and that still made him seethe.

He glanced over his shoulder, torn between his brother's rightful desire for justice and his own reflexive urge to protect the helpless beauty in his bed.

He shook his head. How could he possibly feel sympathy for a femme fatale who'd so viciously left a trail of broken hearts across half of England? Especially when he'd sworn years ago never to let anyone hurt his brother again?

Yet, still . . . in stopping Sean now, wouldn't he be protecting him? Sean had evidently planned to seduce and abandon the beautiful Jezebel, but there would be hell to pay as a result.

"You don't honestly want to see her tortured," Kell asserted in a low voice.

"Yesh, I do!"

"What of the club? Do you want my reputation destroyed by a violent assault on a reputed lady?"

Grimacing, Sean brought his bottle to his lips. "Doan' care," he muttered.

Kell narrowed his gaze, belatedly wondering why Sean had brought Miss Kendrick here instead of to his own lodgings. Perhaps deep inside he'd wanted to be prevented from carrying out his planned vengeance. Or perhaps he'd purposely involved Kell in his machinations, bent on another sort of revenge. . . .

Feeling a familiar ache at his brother's festering resentment, Kell put a hand on his arm. "You should go home, Sean. You won't find any further satisfaction by hurting her. Miss Kendrick's reputation is thoroughly ruined now. Adequate enough revenge, wouldn't you say?"

With a snarl, Sean shook off the restraining hand. "No! Not enough."

Kell gave his brother a steady, intent stare. "Sean," he said in a quiet, warning voice.

The younger man ducked his head, suddenly looking as if he might cry. After another glance at the helpless woman on the bed, however, he nodded drunkenly.

Kell led his brother to the main bedchamber door and unlocked it, glad to find Emma waiting anxiously in the corridor.

"Have someone see that he gets safely home," Kell murmured.

"Yes, of course," Emma said, putting a supporting arm around Sean's waist and urging him toward the far staircase.

After watching them go, Kell shut the door softly,

but he took a deep breath before turning to face his dilemma. What in hell's name was he to do with the suffering, senseless woman in his bed?

Most certainly he couldn't return her to her family in this condition. Indeed, for her own safety, he would have to keep a close eye on her. If the aphrodisiac she'd been given was even half as powerful as cantharides, she would be driven by sheer lust. And if left on her own, she might assault any man she encountered. . . .

No. Better to let her sleep off the drug and return her to her family in the morning.

Kell frowned. Raven Kendrick had thrown off the cover and was thrashing her bare legs feverishly, twisting her head from side to side on the pillow. Steeling himself, he approached the bed.

She had turned onto her back, and her gossamer chemise did little to hide her sweet, firm breasts with their rose-hued nipples or the dark thatch of curls between her thighs. But it was the glorious raven tresses framing her heart-shaped face that held him momentarily spellbound—

Suddenly she reached out, her fingers clutching his arm with surprising strength as she gazed up at him, her eyes wide and unfocused. Kell found himself staring into deep pools of blue, fringed by heavy lashes.

He cursed, damning the sudden quickening in his loins.

Yet, as if comforted by the sight of him, she abruptly stilled and let her eyes close. "My pirate," she whispered. The faint smile that wreathed her delicate lips held incredible sensuality. . . .

Hell and damnation. It was nearly impossible for him not to soften toward his beautiful, unwanted hostage. But he had to harden his heart if he had any chance of making it through the night unscathed.

Extricating his arm from her astonishingly strong grasp, he went to the washstand to make certain the pitcher and basin held enough water to cool her fevered body. He'd seen the effects of a similar drug before, at a debauched revelry during his wilder days. She would eventually become as hot as a volcano, simmering with sexual need, threatening to explode at any moment. And if he had the least measure of compassion, he would have to give her surcease, would have to help ease her pain. . . .

He glanced at the windows where a gray winter light still shone, grimly noting that it was late afternoon. Crossing to the fireplace, he stirred the embers and added a scoop of coal to counter the growing chill. He would have Emma bring up supper later.

At the bureau, Kell poured himself a generous glass of whiskey from a crystal decanter. Then, gritting his teeth, he sank into the chair to wait, knowing it would doubtless be a long night.